"Are You Watching, Adolph Rupp?"

DAN DOYLE

STADIA PUBLISHERS
P.O. BOX 1677
KINGSTON, RI 02881-1677
401-792-5460

Library of Congress Cataloging-in-Publication Data

Doyle, Jr., Daniel E., 1949-
Are You Watching, Adolph Rupp?

I. Title.
PS3554.O9743A83 1989   813¹.54   88-62238
ISBN 0-929938-00-3

First printing 1989
Second printing 1989

Printed and bound in the United States of America

FOREWORD

Dan Doyle has written an accurate and comprehensive account of one of the most serious problems facing our sports oriented society. While drugs and crime dominate our headlines on a daily basis, there is another insidious and morally destructive force at work. Amateur sports are wreaking havoc on the values of many of our top student athletes—the sports heroes of tomorrow.

Unfortunately, the problem does not get the attention it deserves, given its potential for long-term harm. Blue-chip teen athletes tend to be corrupted at a very impressionable age. And they are the idols and role models for younger children.

Doyle documents well how the financial rewards for a successful college athletic program increase in the form of TV revenues, alumni contributions and gate receipts. Along with this largess, reckless abuse and violations—as well as outright cheating—increase commensurately.

And as the "pot of gold" grows larger, the pressure to keep up, to succeed, mushrooms. Doyle shows how it can start with acquiescence at the very top, with the college president or trustees. Then it works its sinister way down, until most everyone in the program is compromised to some degree.

Are You Watching, Adolph Rupp? touches every base. It is fast-paced, no-nonsense, dynamic. Because it's done in fictional form, the element of excitement and suspense is constantly present, yet it reveals the real story. The apologists responsible for "policing" the system will tell you Doyle is an alarmist; that he exaggerates a problem they are dealing with effectively. The rebuttal is simple: it is impossible to cope objectively with the evils of a system that you happen to be part of. That's why politicians created the "special prosecutors."

Doyle uses a prototype school to build his scenario, so the reader is left to decide how widespread this evil happens to be. Whether you agree or disagree with the premise, you will definitely be entertained and enlightened by *Are You Watching, Adolph Rupp?*.

Robert J. "Bob" Cousy

PREFACE

Are You Watching, Adolph Rupp? is the most thought provoking book on sport since James Michener's *Sport in America*. Although presented as fiction, Dan Doyle's novel is about the "real world" of Division I revenue producing sport. Doyle's experiences as athlete, coach, administrator and sports promoter, combined with his advanced graduate study in international sport, gives him the insight to write this eye opening book.

Dan Doyle may very well do for the development of honesty and values in collegiate sport, what Ben Johnson did for insuring that future Olympics will be drug free.

In an interesting and most pleasing to read manner, Doyle tells a story about what happens when the love of money, success, fame, and fortune grow uncontrolled. When the leaders of sport are more concerned with ratings, polls, fund raising, and using athletes, the honesty of sport is lost. Rather than developing positive character and mental, emotional, and physical well-being, sport becomes a mechanism which spreads personal decay and mental and emotional disease. Instead of teaching athletes to develop to their fullest human potential, the sport experience teaches athletes to use artificial aids, take short cuts and find ways to beat the rules to gain an unfair advantage. The true meaning of the contest is lost and the opportunity for healthy development is given away.

Are You Watching, Adolph Rupp? is destined to be required reading for all future coaches, sport scientists, sport journalists, and athletic administrators, as well as parents of young athletes. It is these individuals and the fans who will shape the future direction of sport.

Doyle builds a realistic and touching example which shows that being number one and being honest, sensitive, caring, and compassionate are not mutually exclusive. Coaches who are good guys and look out for the best interests of their players do come out on top.

Perhaps the most important aspect of Doyle's book is that rather than serving as a book of despair, it is a book about hope for the future. It is made clear that sport is not the problem. The athletes are not the problem. Weak leaders lacking in character are the problem and in the future they must choose to continue to be the problem or the solution.

Dr. Robert Rotella
Director: Sport Psychology
Curry School of Education
University of Virginia

To Kathy, Danny, Matt, the "Winged Monkey," Meg, Carrie *and* Julia.

Chapter 1

Jackie McHale saw his Uncle Bill only at Christmas time, but even in those early childhood days he knew that others in the family treated his favorite uncle with special respect. Bill McHale was the first college graduate from a long line of McHales who had emigrated from Athy, Ireland, in the 1860's. On this Christmas, seven-year-old Jackie knew that his uncle would be staying longer because the school from which he graduated was playing some kind of basketball game.

The whole thing seemed a puzzle to Jackie; the basketball game was all Jackie's uncle and his father, Frank, had talked about over Christmas dinner and well into the next day. On December 27, as this frequent and by now frenzied discussion continued, Uncle Bill approached young Jackie.

"Jackie, how would you like to come with your dad and me to the game at the Garden?"

Jackie McHale's eyes lit up. He knew nothing about the game or a place called the Garden. He knew only that basketball was played with this large round ball that he would often see the big boys tossing about at St. John's Parish Hall.

It was the first time that Jackie had gone out in the evening with his dad and Uncle Bill. The three of them left the two bedroom tenement on 79th Street in Brooklyn at 5:30 and walked to Spiro's Deli.

"We always come here first to pick up some dill pickles, Jackie. It's good luck," his father smiled.

From there they walked two more blocks to the subway station. The station was darkened by the night. As Jackie approached the stairway which led down to the subway, he noticed that the pace of all those surrounding him, including his uncle and father, quickened. Some of the ugliest men he had ever seen were watching him, daring him to look at them.

"Next one leaves in three minutes," barked a man in a uniform standing atop a platform. The pace of the crowd picked up even more and Jackie's heart began to pound. The subway clattered into the station, lurching to an abrupt stop. At once, everyone seemed to rush through the open doors together.

On the subway, nestled close to his father and uncle, Jackie felt safe again. The ride, while only several minutes long, was so exciting. Everyone seemed to talk only of this game. Jackie had never seen people so happy.

Moments later, the three got off the subway. Blending in with the huge crowd, young Jackie clasped his right hand tight around his father's and his left around Uncle Bill's. As they walked up the stairway and out onto 34th Street, a wonderful aroma permeated the air, the blend of peanuts and hot dogs filling Jackie's nostrils and bringing an elation he had never known. The three walked four blocks and around a corner, where Uncle Bill stopped and pointed.

"There it is, Jackie."

Jackie had to crane his neck as he looked up at this mass of bricks with a neon sign atop which beckoned him: *Madison Square Garden.*

Jackie's eyes grew wider as the mass of human flesh stood one behind the other, waiting for a man with an MSG cap to take each ticket, rip it in half and pass the half ticket back. Finally, after what felt like an eternity, they passed by the man. Uncle Bill let Jackie hand the man with the cap the three tickets.

"He looks like another Bob Cousy," the ticket man smiled at Frank.

"Not a chance," Frank countered; "he's Dick McGuire."

After they received their tickets, they continued to walk up more steps. At every ten or fifteen steps, they were stopped by someone who would look at their tickets and point in one direction or another. When they reached what seemed to be the very top floor of the building, Uncle Bill said to Frank, "Why don't you and Jackie get some hot dogs while I find my friend."

"Make sure you don't blow your Christmas bonus," laughed Jackie's dad.

Jackie McHale had never tasted a better hot dog. When he had finished and Uncle Bill returned, the three then walked around the corner where another man with a hat stopped them, looked at their tickets and said, "Right up the stairs, gentlemen."

They walked up six more steps. Jackie McHale stopped and gasped. It was as if all of New York City sat in front of him. He had never seen so many people in one place.

Hanging down from the ceiling but still high above the court was a massive, rectangular scoreboard. Jackie could read the words "Home" and "Away." Just above the words, there was some sort of unusual clock.

The aroma in the air was slightly different from that outside, but every bit as enticing; the scent of hot dogs and peanuts was now accompanied by a sweet smell of cigar tobacco. As Jackie peered out, he could see an almost cloud-like pall of smoke wafting up into the rafters.

Far below was a long wooden court, where girls in costumes waved streamers of purple and white. Organ music was playing and just as the three settled into their seats, the crowd started to roar. Jackie's father and uncle began to clap their hands.

At the far end of the building a very tall man with blond hair, followed by eleven shorter men, all with dark purple uniforms, ran onto the floor.

Moments later, at the other end of the building, and with considerably less noise, an even taller black man and his group of white clad teammates followed suit. Jackie McHale could sense that he was about to see something special and his heart began to pound again. The purple team, from his Uncle Bill's school, was the good team, the team to root for, his father and uncle had told him. He knew that the other team was from very far away, from California, and a place called San Francisco.

As the game began, a man behind him, whose voice seemed very loud to Jackie, said to his two sons, "Tommy'll show the nigger." Hearing this, Frank McHale put his arm around his son, who had never heard this word before, yet somehow found it chilling.

"That's not a word we use in our house, Jackie," he frowned. "I'll talk to you about that later."

The rest of the night was sheer magic. Uncle Bill and Frank cheered for the purple team; Jackie McHale cheered for both teams. While others on the court were skilled and graceful, it was the tall blond player and the taller black player that Jackie noticed most. They stood apart from the other eight on the floor.

The tall blond player had a shot which excited the crowd, one that travelled in an almost straight line toward the basket. The taller black player from San Francisco took no such shot. In fact, when the game had ended, Jackie could barely remember him shooting at all. Perhaps it was because of this that he seemed so special to Jackie, so powerful, a giant fly swatter intent on forcing back every shot taken by the purple team. He was able to make everyone on the wooden floor respond to him, as if he controlled their thoughts and actions.

At the end of the game, the tall blond and taller black player met at the middle of the wooden floor and shook hands. The crowd roared. The white team had won the game. Young Jackie noticed that as the game ended, some people, including his Uncle Bill, passed money back and forth to each other. Those who received the money appeared happy, their faces creased with smiles, their arms moving rapidly, their voices raised in excitement.

Jackie then noticed one man, who had been giving his money away, turn and walk in his direction. The man shook his head slightly and then put it down, his chin tucked almost into his chest. As he walked by, Jackie looked up at his face, which was ghostly pale. Jackie had never seen a person look so sad.

Uncle Bill was more disappointed than was Jackie's father about the team in white winning. By the subway ride home, though, both had forgotten about the winners and losers and were more intent on talking about the tall black man.

"Tommy's good, but the big guy is better."

"How can you say better?" responded Bill McHale. "Look how much better Tommy can shoot. Isn't shooting the whole game?"

3

"Look who won," said Jackie's dad.

They laughed as they spoke, but Jackie sensed something special, a warmth between the two that grew out of the game. While he could not describe this bonding, he could feel it, not only with his father and uncle, but with others on the subway.

As they exited the station, young boys were hawking the evening edition. "Dons Crush Crusaders!" the sports headline rang out. Young Jackie could not believe the speed with which the results had been delivered. *I was there,* he marveled to himself.

When the three arrived home, Jackie's mother was waiting up.

"Now you put your pj's on, Jackie McHale. It's way past your bedtime," she smiled. Moments later, as Jackie snuggled under his covers, his mother walked into his room.

"Did you have a good time, son?" she asked somewhat ruefully, aware of the new passage in both of their lives.

"I had the best time of my whole life, Mum," he responded.

As she bent down to kiss his cheek, Jackie saw a curious sadness in his mother's eyes.

Dazed from the wonder of what he had experienced, Jackie almost failed to notice the brand new basketball on his bed. In the years to come, there would be countless differing emotions resulting from his love of this game. On frequent occasions, when experiencing the enormous range of those feelings, he would think back to that first magical introduction at Madison Square Garden, on December 27, 1955.

Chapter 2

Jackie McHale entered State University of New York in 1966. College, up until that point, had been more of a dream than a reality. He had grown up in the streets of Brooklyn and had known at an early age that athletics would offer him the best chance of escape. A college scholarship would be the ticket.

By seventeen, Jackie had a physical presence more associated with a man in his middle 20's. He was 6'2", with a wiry but firm upper body and muscular thighs which allowed him to run forever. His hair, while naturally curly, was cut in a close-cropped fashion. His face was ruggedly handsome. But it was his eyes, china blue, which anyone first noticed upon meeting him. They were friendly but firm. Even as a teenager, Jackie McHale had no difficulty establishing eye contact with whomever he encountered.

From the day he received his treasured first basketball, seldom did the McHale third floor tenement in Brooklyn not resound with the bounce of that ball. At times, Jackie's mother wondered how the McDermotts, one floor below, could stand all the noise and never once complain.

For Jackie, the game became his life, consuming virtually every minute of time not spent in school, at meals, or at church on Sunday. In the winter, it was the St. John's Parish Hall with hoops at both ends. The place was cold and damp, for everyone in the parish knew that the only time Father O'Brien would turn on the heat was for the Friday night bingo game. Jackie would spend hours there alone, as the thud of the dribble and the swish of the ball rippling through the nets echoed throughout the dimly lit hall.

"Jackie, you're twenty minutes late for dinner," Father O'Brien would shout in his thick Irish brogue.

Thud...Thud... "Father, just a few more shots." Thud ... thud..., the ball slamming the cracked wood below.

On Saturdays, Jackie would arrive at the Parish Hall at 9 a.m. with his lunch in a brown paper bag, stay until 4 p.m. and then go home and soak in the hot bath his mother had waiting.

In the spring, summer and fall, Jackie virtually camped out at the Graylag Playground, his favorite haunt, three blocks from home. He would ride his bike there each day, bumping along the cobblestone streets, with one hand on the wheel and the other clutching his ball. Fastened to the handlebars of his bike was an extra net, given to him by his Uncle Bill as a birthday present. The net came in handy, as the Graylag Playground twine was sometimes torn and tattered. When he arrived at the playground, his first chore was to walk about the court and pick up the broken glass left by the neighborhood gang that had been carousing there the previous night.

This cracked piece of pavement was Jackie's paradise. When alone, Jackie would play games with himself, 1-on-0, the Graylag Playground now transformed into Madison Square Garden, with a throng of 20,000 cheering wildly.

In the beginning, when actual games were played, he would mostly sit and watch the older boys choose up sides. But as he grew older, bigger and stronger, he would be chosen for the games. As time went on, he was often the first chosen. Be it a balmy, spring afternoon with enough players for 5-on-5 full court, or a sizzling summer day when Jackie would be working on his moves alone, he could always be found at Graylag.

Although he lived in Knicks territory, Jackie became a Boston Celtics fan, not only because of his early kinship with Heinsohn and Russell, but also because of the magical sleight of hand of his favorite, Bob Cousy. It soon became obvious to Jackie McHale that while he was nothing more than an ordinary student, he had been endowed with other gifts, physical gifts. He was quick and agile, the best in his neighborhood in every sport he tried.

Basketball was the sport in New York for any kid with a dream like Jackie. By his senior year, he had become an All-City guard at St. John's High School. The attention that any young star received in his own neighborhood was magnified far beyond St. John's parish. College coaches from throughout the East came to scout Jackie McHale and to try to woo him to their universities.

Uncle Bill tried hard to get his school to recruit Jackie, but when word came back that Holy Cross had decided on another guard from New Jersey, the family turned to an old friend of Jackie's dad, who served as a trustee of the State University.

"Frank, I'm going to arrange for Red Mihalik to meet with you and Jackie and I'd like to come along," the friend said.

Red Mihalik was a legend in New York City. By the time his car had stopped at the curb alongside the McHale tenement, word of his visit had swept through the neighborhood.

The meeting was held in the McHale kitchen. The mere presence of Mihalik caused Jackie to feel greater anxiety than he had ever experienced in any game. Red Mihalik was the coach every city kid wanted to play for.

"Frank, Coach Mihalik has seen Jackie play," said the friend. "I want him to tell you in his own words what he has in mind."

"Mr. McHale, we think your boy can help us," said the famous coach, "but all that we're promising is a good education. Whatever he gets on the basketball court, he'll have to earn."

As he spoke to Frank McHale, he appeared to ignore Jackie's presence in the room.

"My boy has been taught to earn everything he gets," replied Frank firmly. "His mother and I would like to see him go to State."

Before Jackie had any say, it was decided. He would enroll at State University on a full basketball scholarship. Little did he know at that time that State would become such a part of his life. In fact, it would be his life.

As a Brooklyn kid who thought the basketball world ended at the Williamsburg Bridge, Jackie went to State assuming he would be as dominating a player at the college level as he had been in high school. He soon found out that there were players quicker, faster and stronger than he. Few, however, had his desire or court instincts.

A father-son kind of relationship developed with Red Mihalik. "Jack, you're my eyes and mind on the floor," Mihalik would often say. "Your job is to run the team, to keep the other four guys happy."

Jack achieved a starting position in his junior year and was named co-captain as a senior. While never a star, he performed well in his four years at State. He majored in physical education and graduated on time, in May of 1970.

When graduation approached, Mihalik asked McHale if he would be interested in becoming an assistant coach.

"Jack, I want someone who'll work twenty-four hours a day, someone who knows our system. Most importantly, someone who will be loyal. It's your job if you want it." McHale thought he would be lucky to land a high school position. When Red's offer came, it was a gift from heaven, or at least from the basketball gods.

Jack's primary role as assistant was to serve as chief recruiter. It seemed so funny now, so different from the way it was back then. The recruiting budget was $3,500 and scouting was limited to the New York and New Jersey area. But all the players any major college program could need were within those geographic boundaries. Jack worked hard at recruiting, earning every bit of his $7,100 salary. Moreover, he was good at it, very good.

"I believe in our university and I believe in Coach Mihalik," he liked to tell a recruit. "In the past ten years, every one of our players has graduated. Two are now doctors, three are lawyers, there's a stockbroker, a teacher. . . they're all part of the State family." Then, leaning forward with conviction, his eyes directly aimed into those of the recruit, McHale would say, "We want you to be part of our family."

From the very beginning, he loved coaching but the changes that would occur during his eighteen years in the profession would be dramatic. When Jack had started as an assistant, summers were devoted to such diversions as golf, the beach and an occasional foray to Five Star Basketball Camp, an operation which was just starting in Honesdale, Pennsylvania, and would soon become a must stop for all college recruiters looking for serious players.

In the earlier days, the basketball office shared a secretary with football, baseball and soccer. During his first four or five years in coaching, there was no discussion about the profits accruing to the school. Later, it would seem to Jack that profits, television contracts, and exposure were the only things that the administration cared about. But that was later.

Jack's elevation to head coach had come under unusual and tragic circumstances. He was playing racquetball with Red Mihalik. At the time, Red was in his late fifties. Although he had complained of some dizziness once or twice before, he passed it off to the pressures of the early season. During the racquetball game, Red suffered a stroke. He died that night at St. Francis Hospital.

Red Mihalik had been an institution at State; Jack had been his boy. When Athletic Director Andy Farrell faced the problem of selecting a new coach, he decided that Jack would be named as interim coach and that a Search Committee would be formed. Farrell intended for McHale, who was only twenty-five years old, to serve out the season. State would then conduct a national search and bring in a big-name coach, who would then be told to retain Jack as an assistant.

Neither Farrell, nor anyone else connected with the State athletic department, realized that while McHale was young, he had a great depth of knowledge of the game. He was ready. The team, 4-3 at Red's death and struggling, came together, won fifteen straight and advanced to the NCAA regional finals before losing to Frank McGuire's South Carolina Gamecocks.

"I blew it," McHale had said to his wife Sally following that game. "I was in awe of the guy. From now on, in any game I coach, whether it's McGuire, Wooden, Rupp or Smith, I'm their equal. That's the way it's got to be."

The Search Committee had little choice but to name Jack head coach. During the first eight years under McHale's tutelage, the team reached as many post-season tournaments. McHale was regarded as one of the brightest young coaches in basketball, a rising star in a profession that was still not clearly defined. His clubs were well prepared, they executed precisely and were always referred to as among the smartest teams in the East.

In 1978, with the NCAA looking more favorably on conference winners for Division I tournament berths, a group of athletic directors and coaches formed the Big East Conference. State would have been a shoo-in with its tradition and metropolitan New York location. Moreover, the Big East creators quite appropriately chose schools that had good basketball programs and that were also situated in areas with mass television appeal.

Farrell, nearing the end of his tenure as athletic director, was a football man, and not held in much favor with the "New England basketball crowd," as he put it. He felt that State's program could stand on its own. McHale, however, saw the future for what it was and pleaded with Farrell to enter the Big East.

"Andy, this league will gobble up everyone who's not a part of it. We have to move and we have to move quickly," McHale implored.

"There are a lot of variables, Jack. Some of them make me uncomfortable. I'm just not certain," Farrell responded.

In one of his last acts at State, Farrell decided against the Big East in favor of an independent schedule. The decision would spell nothing but trouble for Jack McHale's future and his basketball program.

In 1980, the Big East began its quick climb toward becoming one of the leading conferences in the country. UMass, Holy Cross, URI, Rutgers and, perhaps, most notably, State, were literally swallowed up by this new monster. The Greater Metropolitan area players, who in years past would have given anything to play for Jack McHale, no longer even looked at State as among their final four or five choices.

Scheduling became a nightmare and television, in the East once limited to Channel 12 in Providence and Channel 27 in Worcester, had become omnipresent. This omnipresence, unfortunately, did not include State, whose only arrangement was with Madison Square Garden Cable, a far cry from the contracts the Big East had signed with CBS and ESPN.

As the Big East Express rolled on, State's program, once one of the most respected in the Northeast, became mired in mediocrity. McHale, accustomed to producing twenty-game winners in the 70's, saw his team slip to .500 records from '82-'84, and then suffer two consecutive losing seasons, finishing 13-14 in '85-'86 and 12-16 in '86-'87.

In 1977, when State reached its fifth consecutive NCAA tournament, McHale had been rewarded with a five-year contract, almost unheard of in college basketball. The norm for Eastern coaches had been two or three years. McHale's deal in '77 was, by coaching salary standards at that time, outstanding. The contract included a base salary of $42,000, which then made him the highest paid coach in the East. In addition, there were a number of perquisites, including a sneaker contract which called for a base of $6,000 in '77, with fifteen percent increases each year.

Jack also had the only television show among his peers—a five year deal with a local cable outlet—which brought him $10,000 a year. By far the most attractive aspect of his contract, however, was one which, at the time, only Charles "Lefty" Driesell of Maryland had been able to negotiate: a rollover clause. At the end of each year, McHale would re-sign, extending his contract for still another year.

For his part, McHale showed great loyalty to the school. He turned down a number of offers, including a package from an Atlantic Coast Conference school in 1980 that would have placed him well on his way to millionaire status at an early age. The recruiting school's officials were incredulous.

"You mean to tell me that you ain't gonna' accept our offer?" asked the unsuccessful booster club head, in his best Southern drawl.

"You just don't understand," replied McHale. "State has been my life. It's done more for me than I can every repay. I'm staying."

Once he spoke those words and hung up the phone, Jack wondered if he had made the right choice. He was then thirty-three years old, with a wife and two young children. But McHale's roots were in New York and his loyalty was to State. He had no other choice.

In 1980 Andy Farrell resigned as athletic director. Recognizing that its once revered program would face some difficult years, State conducted an exhaustive search for a successor. It was apparent even then that a mistake had been made in not entering the Big East. That decision, coupled with the increasing role of television in all college sports, made State's administration seek, for the first time, not an ex-football coach, but a marketing man. Their decision was reached in the person of Steve Ellovitch.

Ellovitch's background included a law degree from Cornell and an MBA from NYU. He was thirty-four, bright, articulate and extremely aggressive. His job was to package State so that it would become a nationally known college athletic program. McHale had played an active role on the selection committee.

When the candidates were reduced to three, McHale had become increasingly uncomfortable with Ellovitch as the final choice. Clearly, Ellovitch had credentials and vision, but Jack was concerned with his abrasive style. He realized that of the eleven-person selection committee, only he would end up working with the new athletic director.

"Jack, we're all concerned that you're not high on Ellovitch," the Search Committee Chairman said to McHale at the conclusion of a committee meeting.

"You know my feelings," McHale shrugged. "It's not just his style, it's something else about him. I guess I've always had this thing about people who can't look you in the eye."

However, the committee decided clearly in Ellovitch's favor, as the vote (supposedly confidential) wound up 7-4. McHale voted in the minority.

Almost immediately upon Ellovitch's arrival, there was friction between he and McHale. McHale often wondered if it was due to the fact that his vote was made public by a well-intentioned student reporter.

McHale did his best in those transition years. He had kept the team at .500 until 1984, despite losing recruits on a regular basis to the Big East and other powerful conferences, all of them armed with national television exposure and superior facilities. However, Ellovitch possessed aspirations far beyond those of serving merely as a college athletic director. He was dissatisfied with State's lack of progress, and, at least in McHale's judgment, refused to grasp the inordinate difficulty of maintaining an athletic program on an independent level, particularly with all the hype surrounding the Big East.

Nevertheless, in 1987, Ellovitch informed McHale that the rollover was no longer in effect; that he had one year to turn the program around or

State would buy out the remainder of his contract. Jack McHale was now in a position that all coaches recognize can come one day.

He had to win...immediately.

Chapter 3

Steve Ellovitch had done all the right things. Up until the time he assumed the athletic director's position at State in 1980, he had viewed his career as tantamount to Rodin sculpting a masterpiece. A foundation had been crafted for what he knew would be a meteoric rise to the top of the sports world.

It had not always been easy for Ellovitch. While intelligent and well-spoken, those two traits did not happily coexist with his growing up on the lower east side of Manhattan. He was short and rather frail, his gaunt features offset by a protruding nose and razor thin lips. He had darting dark brown eyes. His hunched gait made him walk as if accompanied by some unknown burden. Being one of the only Jewish boys in his neighborhood, he had borne the brunt of many insults in grade school. His acerbic manner did not improve the situation; when problems arose, he became testy and insolent.

Ellovitch studied hard in school. While unable to make any of the sports teams, he always was affiliated with them as the manager, statistician, or scorekeeper. His grades were good-good enough, in fact, to win him a National Merit Scholarship to Brown University in Providence.

At Brown, his confidence grew. He became manager of the basketball team. His physical limitations were no longer an issue and, as he matured, he found his peers in college to be far more understanding of his good points, most notably his organizational skills.

Ellovitch flourished at Brown, emerging from his shell and the deep inferiority complex he had developed as a youngster. His grades, as always, were excellent. He even made friends and became an integral part of the athletic program, computerizing the statistics for every Brown team. While physically unable to compete, he studied and understood the many nuances of sports. He determined during his college days that while he would pursue a law degree and an MBA, his goal was to become a major figure in the world of sports.

After graduating from Brown, Ellovitch entered Cornell Law School where he made the *Law Review* and graduated with honors. He grasped any chance he had to learn more about the sports business. He made personal appointments with sports agents and made visits to Bowie Kuhn's office on several different occasions, finally achieving a short meeting with the then-commissioner of baseball. He accomplished the same with Commissioner Larry O'Brien of basketball and Commissioner Pete Rozelle of football. Ellovitch attended seminars, read books and learned everything there was to learn about the business of sports—and those in positions of influence who might someday assist him.

After Cornell, Ellovitch's next step toward attaining his goal was a Master's in Business from New York University. He knew he needed to have the business acumen as well as the legal background to run a major sports team. At the age of twenty-seven, armed with superb academic credentials and serious ambition, he received his first job as Assistant Athletic Director at Cornell. Ellovitch worked hard and developed a number of marketing programs which won him praise from colleagues throughout the country.

In 1974 he was offered a job as associate producer of NBC Sports. Ellovitch spent six productive years there, helping to shore up the programming department and, in particular, NBC's production of college basketball. He was involved in contract negotiations with all the major conferences and developed a reputation not only as a bright and able administrator, but also as a tough negotiator.

In 1980, the State University athletic director's position opened. Ellovitch had always admired people who saw a situation not for what it was, but for what it could become. Despite the fact that the Big East had jumped off to an impressive start, Ellovitch viewed the State job as one that would provide him with the background and exposure he needed in his quest to serve as the head of a major sports franchise. His application certainly possessed no basis in allegiance to State or to student-athletes.

Steve Ellovitch arrived at the job knowing that the most prominent member of the athletic community, Jack McHale, had not supported his candidacy. McHale brought to the surface many of the old insecurities deeply entrenched within Ellovitch. McHale was the prototype of the kid who had made fun of Ellovitch in his grammar and high school days—the skilled jock who looked down his nose at the weakling bookworm.

McHale, 6'2", and good looking, walked erect and confident, greeting anyone he met with a firm handshake and direct eye contact. Ellovitch, 5'8" and bespectacled, with his button-down oxford shirt and tie knotted tightly around the neck, always seemed to be looking around and about, as if someone were stalking him. He resented the differences between McHale and himself. Moreover, he resented the fact that McHale had not backed him. How could he not have recognized that Ellovitch was far and away the best candidate? Ellovitch determined at the outset that one of his major goals would be to become bigger than Jack McHale. It was the only way.

The early '80's were not good times for State's athletic program. Despite Ellovitch's ideas and work ethic, progress was slower than he had imagined. First, the Big East was simply too large an obstacle. Second, Ellovitch's efforts to put the football program back on firm footing were slowed, at least in Ellovitch's judgment, by a coach who did not have the imagination or foresight needed to make State a national football power.

The fact that football had not progressed was not nearly as galling to Ellovitch as the stalled basketball program. While McHale had done wondrous things in the '70's, it appeared to Ellovitch that he was not the person who could take State over this most difficult hump in the 80's. Ellovitch felt that McHale's early success was principally due to the foundation laid years previously by Red Mihalik, not to mention the lack of real competition for players.

In Ellovitch's mind, college athletics had displayed an inordinate lack of imagination for the previous two decades; so it was not surprising that someone with mediocre ability (which was how he categorized McHale) could fare so well. Now, with the coaches' pay scales dramatically increased, a new breed of mentor, more diverse in background and more creative, would, in Ellovitch's mind, displace the Jack McHale's. State's flagging basketball fortunes, coupled with Ellovitch's resentment of McHale, made confrontation an aim in Ellovitch's mind.

Ellovitch's primary goal was to gain greater control of the basketball program. To do otherwise might cause the one phenomenon Ellovitch had never experienced—being fired. It was a phenomenon which he feared; one which he determined never to encounter.

In order to avoid personal disaster, Ellovitch worked hard to overcome the considerable loyalties McHale had accumulated over an extended career as a player and a coach. He had to do it in a way that would not be construed as undermining McHale, but instead as serving the good of the program. Most importantly, Ellovitch had to do it in a way that would cast no aspersions on him.

The first step would be a difficult one: to wrest control of the schedule from McHale. Scheduling had become a more difficult task since the inception of the Big East. Opponents, who in years past had plenty of open dates, were now locked into conference games.

As the coach and commentator Al McGuire had once said, "scheduling is seventy percent of a college basketball season's success or failure." In 1984, after a considerable tug of war between Ellovitch and McHale, Ellovitch was able to assume control of the schedule through an athletic department reorganization scheme.

Ellovitch's next plan called for an immediate and dramatic upgrading of the schedule, which had been comprised principally of long-standing Eastern opponents with few intersectional games. Improving the schedule would accomplish a number of things. It would allow Ellovitch, in his self-imposed role as a recruiter, to dangle high level opponents in front of prospective recruits and provide greater opportunity for television contracts. While he had gained considerable expertise in his earlier stint at NBC, Ellovitch had been able to do little in the way of television packaging because of State's mediocre records and its regional scheduling. A big-time schedule would change this.

Still, he needed McHale's agreement. Ellovitch had already informed McHale that his job was tenuous at best. He knew McHale, knew that at his very core he breathed the fires of competitive zeal. Ellovitch would put it in such a way that McHale would have no choice but to accept.

"Jack, you've been complaining about the facility and about your recruiting budget. With this new schedule and the larger guarantees, plus possible television revenue, I'm going to increase your budget slightly. It'll be assumed, however, that with a tougher schedule and increased budget will come increased expectations."

As Ellovitch spoke, he rose from his chair, leaning forward from his desk, trying to look down at McHale. McHale sat erect, looking directly into Ellovitch's shifting eyes.

"I assume the same expectations will hold true for you, Steve," the coach responded. "Scheduling is a big part of the success of a basketball program."

McHale then slowly rose to his feet, his large and muscular frame almost towering over Ellovitch. "I'll consider what you said and get back to you."

McHale did as Ellovitch expected he would. He accepted the challenge head-on and made his commitment known to the media. If State won, both McHale and Ellovitch would profit. Should they lose, it would be McHale's head.

With a big time schedule, Steve Ellovitch would now be more firmly entrenched in the network of decision-makers at the intercollegiate college level. He had climbed another step. Now it was a matter of finding the right players and convincing them to attend State.

Chapter 4

Power: it was the only thing that Robert Steincross cared about, the only shrine at which he worshipped. Steincross had not grown close to State through any educational or social background. He graduated bachelor of hard knocks, of the black-and-blue variety. Despite his lack of formal education, and an upbringing that should have resulted in a life of failure, Robert Steincross overcame adversity and enormous odds to become one of New York's wealthiest citizens. He had achieved his wealth principally in two areas: car dealerships and a flourishing construction business which was now one of New York's top ten.

Steincross' allegiance to State was born more out of practicality than any loyalty or affection for the institution. Although he was a member of State's Board of Directors, he found most people at the university to be boorish and felt he had very little in common with them. However, it was important for a person of Steincross' financial position to align himself with institutions of high repute. Yes, Robert Steincross, much to his personal bemusement, had become something of a patron of the arts, a benefactor, a philanthropist. It helped his business and increased his sphere of influence. This was what mattered.

Steincross not only lacked formal education, he also lacked formal athletic background. While only 5'7", he had broad shoulders connected to muscular arms. His jet black hair was slicked back to accentuate a face which seemed most comfortable when adorned with a snarl. He had been a boxer as a kid, once advancing to the quarterfinals of the New York Golden Gloves as a middleweight. Like most children in his neighborhood, he had wanted to participate in team sports, and was jealous of those who could. Unfortunately, he had a family upbringing that did not allow for it.

The name Steincross was not even his. His father, Robert Lombardo, was a numbers man for the mob in the Bronx. One day he left home when young Robert was thirteen and never returned. Six months later, his body was discovered in the East River.

A few months after his father's death, Robert came home from school several hours earlier than normal, having been dismissed for what seemed to be a bad case of the flu. As he entered through the rear parlor, his mother's bedroom door was ajar. He could hear sounds and knew immediately she was with a man. What he heard her say made his flu-ridden body tremble with anger.

"I'm glad he's dead," said the mother to her lover, "and I think because of him I've never been able to love my son. I have no feeling for him, nothing"

Two weeks later, Robert left home. At fifteen he was caught with a group of other young thugs robbing a gas station. He was sent to a detention home for four months and released the day before his sixteenth birthday. When he went to apply for a social security number, he changed his name from Lombardo to Steincross, with the aid of an inattentive federal employee. He had chosen the name from a newspaper article he was reading while waiting in line. One month later, he moved out of the Bronx, found a job as a used car salesman, and never again played the part of Robert Lombardo.

Steincross' rise had been not atypical of the American dream. He used whatever means available to him in his car sales techniques. "Hey boss, you know that old broad who was in yesterday?" he would crow. "Well, I switched stickers, ended up selling her a car at $300 more than face value. She never knew the difference."

The boss, who came from a similar background, took a liking to young Steincross and soon promoted him to an assistant sales manager. By the age of twenty-three, Steincross had garnered enough capital to buy into the business. Four years later, he bought his own car dealership. At thirty-six, he owned seven dealerships and had founded a construction company.

Steincross was nineteen when he married the office assistant at his first place of employment. They had four children, all girls. Like many successful men, his family became secondary to his pursuit of power and wealth. He finally divorced his wife. Animosity ran high, to the extent that in twelve years he had neither seen nor spoken to her or his four daughters. He did not really care.

The State athletic program had become a source of interest to Steincross. His one true passion had always been a love of sport. His support of the athletic program brought him new friends, people of influence. Besides, it provided him with something else which he had come to enjoy, the semi-celebrity status accorded the program's chief patron.

Like most others, Steincross had grown increasingly disenchanted with the lack of success in the athletic department. His dislike for Steve Ellovitch was well known throughout State's athletic community. Steincross felt he was a self-centered know-it-all, grasping for headlines to advance his own career.

"He's nothing more than a smart ass," Steincross would say to anyone who cared to listen. "I don't trust the guy." Steincross also realized that his position as one of State's major financial backers, coupled with the drifting of the athletic program, might enable him to exercise more clout in the decision-making process. Several years earlier, he had formed the State Athletic Advisory Council. While relatively powerless, it was comprised of people whose financial support of the institution had been earmarked specifically for its athletic program. The Advisory Council provided these benefactors with a sounding board; a chance at least to have their opinions heard by Ellovitch and President Edward Pendelton. Steincross had grown increasingly irritated with the lack of influence the Advisory Council exerted on the State athletic program. He wanted more control.

Booster clubs had become prevalent in college athletics. President Pendelton had always taken a dim view of such activities. He felt that authority might eventually rest erroneously with a strong, well-backed booster club than with the people State had hired to run the program.

Steincross fought long and hard to change this attitude. It was his public argument that State needed more funds and, in particular, a new facility. It was toward this end that he called attorney Richard Shoppels, one of the brightest tax lawyers in New York. Steincross had an idea which, if implemented, would place him in control of State's athletic fortunes. With the athletic program on the wane, people were dissatisfied. This was his chance to move.

Chapter 5

*K*illarney, *County Kerry, Ireland*
It was not a place you would expect to find a blue chip college basketball prospect. To be sure, if you were looking for a hurler, Irish footballer, or perhaps a camogie player, Killarney could hold its own with any of the twenty-six counties that made up the Republic of Ireland. But basketball, until the late 1970's, had been a game seen only through visits from American servicemen or perhaps through a brief film clip of an NBA championship game shown on RTE, the Irish television network.

That all changed in 1979, with new leadership in the Dublin-based Irish Basketball Association. Dan Quinn, all of 5'5" and a Dublin school-teacher, became President of the IBBA. Quinn and his colleagues on the IBBA executive board realized that if the game were to take on meaning in Ireland, a relationship with the United States had to be established. In June of 1980, Quinn made a trip to the United States, hoping to meet with some American coaches. Among those coaches he encountered was Jack McHale.

The meeting happened quite by accident. Upon arrival at JFK, Quinn told the customs officer that he was visiting the States as a representative of Irish basketball and hoped to form an alliance with American coaches. The customs officer had grown up in the same parish as Jack McHale and had gone to elementary school with the State coach. He suggested that Quinn contact McHale. He then went one step further, ushering Quinn into his office and placing the call to McHale himself. McHale was delighted to hear from an old friend from Brooklyn and even more pleased when he learned of Quinn's plans to upgrade basketball in Ireland.

Cormack McDonough was ten years old when this historic (by Irish basketball standards) trip took place. He lived in the Agadoe section of Killarney with his parents and seven brothers and sisters. His father, Michael, had been one of the greatest Irish footballers in Kerry history and had played for three All-Ireland champions. "Mickey Mac" was still a legendary figure in County Kerry and, indeed, throughout Ireland. Like so many of his contemporaries, Michael had lost his dream of wealth and prosperity many years before. He now drifted from job to job, supporting his family from the dole and spending a majority of his days and evenings at O'Reilly's Pub on Main Street in Killarney.

Young Cormack, even at an early age, had his father's instincts on the football field. He was the tallest boy in his grade at St. Peter's Grammar School, standing a full head above the rest of his classmates. He had long beanpole-like legs and a slender upper body. His shock of curly red hair covered a freckled face set off by piercing brown eyes. He was by far the best athlete in his class, mastering virtually any sport he tried. The most striking of his physical traits were his hands. Even at age eleven, upon his first encounter with a basketball, he could grip it, actually palm it as if it were a softball.

In June, 1981, McHale and a National Basketball Association coach paid a visit to Killarney as part of a ten-day clinic tour sponsored by the Irish Basketball Association. Their purpose was to introduce basketball into the rural sections of Ireland. Young Cormack had no knowledge and, in fact, no interest in the game. But the chance to meet Americans was always a thrill for any young Kerryman. When he heard that the two American coaches would be at St. Peter's Parish Hall, he ventured there, more out of curiosity than anything else.

Cormack was hooked immediately. The NBA coach put on a dazzling display; McHale, more low key, but every bit as eloquent, talked of American ties with Ireland. He also spoke about the great potential which basketball offered any Irishman who loved sport and who hoped to travel to the United States some day. As McHale spoke, he could not help but notice a gangly young lad in the back of the hall, whose eyes and ears seemed fixed on his every movement and word.

The game itself fascinated young Cormack even more than the speeches. As was customary with most international clinics, the NBA coach and McHale had brought along ten top-flight United States players, two of whom played for McHale at State. As the NBA coach and McHale spoke, the players demonstrated jump shots, spin moves, between-the-leg dribbles, and finally a tremendous display of full-court basketball. Cormack was mesmerized. After the clinic McHale, seeing young McDonough, threw the ball to him. He grasped it easily in one massive hand and tossed it back to the American coach.

"Have you ever played the game, son?" asked McHale.

The young Irishman looked down at the floor and quietly said, "No, sir, but I'd like to try it."

"I'll meet you here tomorrow morning at 9 a.m.," said McHale.

"I'll be here, sir," McDonough smiled as he ran from the gym.

For three hours the following morning, McHale, aided by two young American players, worked with Cormack on the fundamentals of the game. From that day on, young McDonough forgot about succeeding his father as a member of the County Kerry Irish football team in the All-Ireland classic. Basketball would be his game.

Just after his fourteenth birthday, word came from Dublin that the Irish

Basketball Association would be awarding three scholarships to the States and an invitation to a camp called Five Star in Honesdale, Pennsylvania. Cormack knew nothing of the camp and had lost touch with McHale, but he dreamed of seeing the United States. He applied to Quinn and, with great pressure from the Kerry Basketball Board (one of the twenty-six formed throughout Ireland), he was selected.

In June, he and two other youngsters, all three dressed in their best Sunday suits, boarded Aer Lingus Flight 301 from Shannon Airport and arrived in New York six-and-a-half long hours later. A camp counselor met them at the airport. They boarded a van and then traveled four more hours to the Honesdale camp site.

The trip proved unforgettable. The beauty of the homes, the people dressed as if going to heaven, the brand new cars: it all seemed so exciting to a fourteen-year-old boy who, up until that time, had never journeyed more than ten miles outside his home town.

Five Star was the premier basketball camp in the country. It was originally conceived to bring together the best high school players in the East. As the camp grew, so, too, did the geographic distribution of the campers, first on a national and then an international scale. Five Star was a haven for college recruiters. It was also a proving ground for any player who hoped to get out of the inner city of New York, or in this case, even the hills of Killarney.

The camp was rooted in the philosophy of securing the best players at all four grades of high school. Seniors were to comprise roughly sixty percent of the camp, juniors twenty-five percent, sophomores ten percent, and freshmen five percent.

Cormack had never played against such rugged competition. While only fourteen, he had already grown to 6'3", with a physique that reminded Kerrymen of his legendary father. Although outclassed in most of the games, his pleasant disposition and his raw athletic talent caught the fancy of the coaches. By the end of the week, Cormack had achieved minor celebrity status, earning the nickname "Louie White Legs": the young Irishman new to the game, with a brogue as thick as Irish stew. While by no means a polished player, he clearly showed promise.

Also at the camp, but with a vastly different background from young McDonough, was a gangly fourteen-year-old named Marvin Lewis. The 6'1" Lewis had come to Five Star under far different circumstances than McDonough's.

Lewis had been born in Mobile, Alabama, but at the age of two, his mother decided the South was no place to rear her nine children. She had a cousin in Worcester, Massachusetts who had moved there some ten years earlier and who always spoke well of the city in her letters to Marvin's mother. Worcester possessed a very small percentage of blacks, but racism, at least as Mrs. Lewis had grown accustomed to it in the South, did not exist in

Worcester; so said the cousin. When she could scrape together enough money in 1971, Cornelia Lewis journeyed to the local bus station and bought ten tickets—one way.

In Worcester, Cornelia was able to find steady work. She found dignity and comfort for her children. Marvin was her second youngest and the last boy. His father, a truck driver who sped through Mobile twice a month, had not been seen since the day Cornelia told him she was pregnant again.

From his early childhood, Marvin had been a natural, with his tall, angular body and unusually long arms. In the first grade at Canterbury Street School on Olympic Day, he won three track events, while competing against students from the second and third grade.

Worcester, only forty miles west of Boston, had been a basketball town since the mid-40's. Holy Cross College, under the tutelage of Hall of Fame Coach Doggie Julian and featuring such greats as Bob Cousy, had won the NCAA championship in 1947. A tiny Jesuit College of only 2,000 students, Holy Cross left an indelible mark on the basketball world. Basketball was the sport in a city referred to as the hub of Massachusetts.

This trend continued throughout the 1950's with the success of the Celtics. It helped that Cousy and another Celtics star, Tom Heinsohn, also a Holy Cross graduate, resided in Worcester and made the forty-mile trek to Boston each day. In 1958, with the help of Cousy and others, a summer league called the "Chi Rho" was formed. It would lure thousands of youngsters off the streets throughout the years. Marvin Lewis was among them.

In the sixth grade Lewis once scored 43 points in a basketball game. At Chandler Junior High School he led his team to the city-wide championship, scoring 36 points and hauling down 17 rebounds in the finals. When Five Star scouts queried throughout New England as for the best prospects, the word from Central Massachusetts came back loud and clear: Marvin Lewis was a blue chipper. The day after his junior high graduation, an invitation personally signed by the camp's owner arrived. Marvin had been offered a full scholarship to attend the Five Star Basketball Camp.

Chapter 6

The absurdity of the situation often struck Jack McHale. At Five Star Camp, fourteen-year-old kids were brought in to perform before a horde of coaches. In most cases, these kids had never played in front of more than fifty or one hundred people at a junior high game. Their expressions of hope belied a lack of awareness of how systematic the evaluation of their skills had become; their physical attributes generally far exceeded their emotional make-up. Yet they were expected, in a brief period of time, to show the coaches their potential.

At the same time, coaches did not like precociousness in the young players. "Yes sir" and "No sir" were all they looked for. If a kid questioned a coach's judgment, or looked at an official in a less than respectful way, within a few hours at Five Star Camp, as at others around the country, word of the kid's "bad attitude" would spread. Fortunately for Marvin Lewis and Cormack McDonough, their week at Five Star as freshmen was spent playing basketball and avoiding any confrontation that might negatively label them. Both kept very low profiles off court and, thus, departed camp in high esteem.

McDonough returned to Killarney, County Kerry, and immediately made the Irish Junior National Team, which consisted of players seventeen and under. By gaining a spot on the Junior National Team, McDonough was assured the best possible competition offered in Ireland, plus relatively frequent travel to Europe. A good portion of the Irish Basketball Association's budget went toward funding the team's trips.

At age fifteen, Cormack, now 6'4" and seemingly getting better with each passing day, competed with the Junior Nationals in a tournament in Reykjavik, Iceland. He was the leading scorer. At sixteen, he was 6'5" and clearly the team's best player.

Recruiting had now become an international project for most colleges. Word of Cormack's feats on the European circuit quickly got back to the United States via the FIBA International Basketball newsletter, to which virtually every coach in the United States subscribed. Because of his success at Five Star, Cormack was invited each year thereafter, an important factor in his continued development.

By his senior year, Cormack, now a wiry 6'7" and 190 pounds, made the All-Star Team for the second straight summer at Five Star. He was also the one-on-one champion, and was voted outstanding camper—the title given to a player the "amateur psychologists" had felt best displayed solid basketball talent and all-around attitude. Cormack had elevated himself to *Five Star* status, which meant that he had major Division I star potential. Anything below a four rating targeted a youngster for Division II and III schools. Two years earlier, perhaps Cormack might have been headed in that direction. But how quickly things had changed. . . .

Meanwhile, by his sophomore year, Marvin Lewis had grown to 6'4" and 180 pounds. He added two more inches in his junior year, and by his senior year at Five Star Camp, Lewis had blossomed to 6'8", 210 pounds: a legitimate Division I center.

When the two players arrived in Honesdale for the summer preceding their senior year, as Division I prospects, both had already been deluged with letters, telegrams, birthday cards, floral arrangements sent to their mothers and all of the other tactics employed by virtually every Division I school in the country. Lewis and McDonough found the process exciting, the attention still refreshing. They enjoyed the compliments and what they both perceived to be genuine interest in their accomplishments.

* * * * * * *

Blue-chip high school athletes often had overseers—people whose responsibility was to marshal the youngster through the recruitment maze. Whether a coach, parent or friend, the overseer served as a protector of sorts, restricting the deluge of phone calls and visitations which could otherwise consume a young athlete. These same overseers often found the whole recruiting process to be exciting and even fun. How often did a Dean Smith or a Bob Knight call with words of praise and encouragement? Those were intoxicating moments indeed.

In the cases of Marvin Lewis and Cormack McDonough, their fathers wound up playing the prized role of guardians to their sons' personal basketball kingdoms. That Thomas Mahon would grow into this role was initially unsettling and puzzling, at least from Marvin's perspective. His mother had warned him of Mahon's habitual irresponsibility, of his disregard for family and friends. But when Mahon travelled to Worcester and reappeared in Marvin's life, those warnings were doomed to fall on deaf ears.

Word had filtered down to Thomas Mahon in Alabama that his son was considered a recruiting plum. His lackadaisical, meaningless existence suddenly assumed focus. He made his way to Worcester for the start of Marvin's junior year. In fact, as soon as he found a cheap motel, he threw his belongings down and hastened to the gym for one of Marvin's games. He watched with satisfaction as his rediscovered pride and joy pumped in 22 points and hauled down 15 rebounds while blocking three shots.

As soon as the final buzzer sounded, Mahon practically leapfrogged his way through the stands in order to meet Marvin on the floor. When the crowd of teammates and admirers that had gathered around young Lewis finally subsided, Mahon walked purposefully toward his son, almost block-ing his path to the locker room.

He stared at Marvin for a few seconds, as a smile slowly ridged his face. "Nice game...son," he said. "Isn't it about time your father saw you play?"

Marvin stood there, dumbfounded. Suddenly, all had grown silent around him. "You're Thomas Mahon?" he asked in a barely audible tone.

"Well, I'd rather you call me Dad, or Pop," Mahon smiled back.

"Dad? . . . Pop? Now? Here? Where did you come from?" Marvin angrily stammered.

"I don't blame you for wonderin' where I've been. But I'm here now."

With that Mahon held out his hand to young Marvin. Young Lewis tensed, his reaction a combination of shock, confusion and anger. He tried to speak but was so overwrought with emotion that he quickly turned and ran from the gym. As he arrived home that evening, his mother could see that her youngest son was distraught.

"Why is he showing up now?" he yelled to no one in particular. He then closed his bedroom door. For twenty-four hours he remained in his room. "Where the hell have you been for my first 16 years?" he asked, as if Mahon were present to answer his questions, to salve his psychological wounds.

With much prodding from his mother, Marvin was finally able to return to school the following morning. Later that day, as practice ended, he walked from the gym out into the crisp evening air. There by the curb stood his father.

"Marvin...son, you have to hear me out...there's a lot you don't know. C'mon now, get into the warm car and I'll drive you home!"

Lewis at first turned away, but with gentle persuasion, Mahon coaxed his son into the car.

On the ride home, Mahon spoke of his love for Marvin, how difficult his own life had been, and that he was now here ..."to right things with you, son."

Marvin sat in his seat, numb. As the car pulled up to the Lewis flat, Mahon said almost sheepishly, "See you at the next game, son."

Mahon indeed attended Marvin's next game, and every one thereafter. Whether it was an in-season game or a post-season tournament contest, from Worcester to Honesdale, Thomas Mahon followed his son to every port of call. Marvin, unaccustomed to such attention, grew to appreciate his father's interest, even though he sometimes wondered, "Why all of a sudden?" When this question came to mind, he quickly dismissed it. Thomas was his father; he loved Marvin, and this was Mahon's way of paying him back for the sixteen missed years in his life.

While Marvin remained close to his mother, Cornelia could do little about the intensifying relationship between father and son. She knew Thomas, knew about his many scrapes with the law and about his host of illegitimate children. She knew that Thomas had no interest in work, that before his new-found affection for his son he had cared about nothing and no one but himself.

Meanwhile, Marvin's high school coach was overwhelmed by the recruiting process. He had been coaching at Worcester East for sixteen years. The best players he ever had ended up at Assumption, Bentley and Merrimack, all Division II basketball programs. None of those schools had the recruiting approach of the Marylands, UCLAs, North Carolinas, and Louisvilles, all of which were now knocking—hard—on Marvin's door.

Customarily, the recruiters first gravitated toward the high school coach. But when the recruiting rush hit, at the end of Marvin's junior year, the coach and his family had embarked on a summer camping trip to Canada. Thus, there was no set format for the recruitment of Marvin Lewis and no screening process. The school, specifically the athletic director, along with the Lewis home, were bombarded with phone calls. Chaos reigned. All this confusion played into the selfish hands of Thomas Mahon.

Two years earlier, when he had first heard of his son's potential, Mahon had done some checking. Several other acquaintances had sons recruited by Southern football powers. He knew that in many cases the schools were not at all reluctant to "take care" of the parent or whoever else assumed the role of overseer.

To be sure, Mahon's trek to Worcester had not been out of filial affection alone. He had heard of the fine cars, the women, the cash and the travel that came with the deliverance of a blue chip player. Times had been rough. He had not been able to hold a steady job and besides, he had no real reason to stay in Mobile.

In truth, Mahon did derive some pleasure spending time with his son. The boy could really play and Mahon enjoyed the attention of being the proud father at his son's games. What he enjoyed even more, however, was that Marvin, after a lengthy discussion with his father, decided that all schools would recruit him through Thomas Mahon.

* * * * *

The recruiting of Cormack McDonough, meanwhile, assumed the proportions of international intrigue. While the Irish Basketball Association had grown tremendously, Irish basketball had never possessed a recruitable commodity for Division I basketball in America—until Cormack. By the mid 1980's, recruitment of international players had become almost as sophisticated as recruitment of domestic players. If a foreign player was identified as a blue chipper, then a whole network of contacts could be utilized.

In order to secure foreign talent, a college might implore its representative in Congress to contact the embassy in the particular country where that player lived, or, perhaps, that school might initiate contact through graduates working in multi-national firms. American executives in Italy, Spain or Ireland were always happy to lend their assistance.

There were other recruiting methods as well. If a school knew of a great prospect, arrangements could easily be made for its coach to travel to the country and provide clinics in the spring or summer. The NCAA still had difficulty monitoring overseas recruiting. Knowing this, coaches were eager not only to visit a country, but also to make certain that one or more "bumps" occurred. With all of the new NCAA legislation involving cutbacks on home visits and personal contact, the bump—a not-so-accidental collision with a prospect on the street or in a gymnasium—became more and more common.

While Marvin Lewis' high school coach was unable to provide much structure in the recruitment of his star, the president of the Irish Basketball Association quickly recognized that a set of criteria must be developed for the recruitment of Cormack McDonough. He sought advice from many of the more than forty United States "Irish Advisory Coaches." They emphasized the importance of identifying someone to handle the recruitment, someone who would have young Cormack's best interests at heart.

While the IBBA president was armed with the proper information, the problem remained that Killarney was more than four hours from Dublin and the system of communication in Ireland was still circa 1920. Cormack, in fact, did not even have a phone. The president had to rely on phone contact through the Killarney Basketball Club president, himself a busy accountant, along with and through someone else whose involvement in the process had only begun in recent weeks—Michael McDonough. The president always knew where to find "Mickey Mac," at O'Reilly's Pub, anytime from noon on. If he could not reach the Club president, he was forced to call Michael with news on Cormack's recruiting.

It had been many years and many dreams since "Mickey Mac" had led Kerry to the All-Ireland Championships. As the star of the Kerry Footballers, the favors had abounded during his career. He had held a job with the Great Southern Hotel as a "greeter." He was, after all, charming and had become something of a fixture during his twelve year playing career for Kerry. The best parts of his job were the flexible hours and reasonably good pay. Mickey Mac also had unlimited use of the bar.

When his career ended, Mickey faced the sad quandary that many star athletes have to face: the transition from the athletic field to the real world of responsibility. It had been a difficult change for Michael McDonough. He soon found that he was expected to arrive at work on time and to perform duties other than sitting in the bar and greeting customers and friends.

Mickey Mac had always been told by his coaches and friends that if you were a success in football, surely you would be a success later in life. He now knew that the two did not necessarily correlate. Irish football had been easy. He loved it and possessed the physical tools to excel. The rest of his life, however, was far different. He had never been highly motivated nor had he needed to be. At first, he became a social drinker, then a morning drinker and then a full-blown drunkard. He was let go by the Great Southern after one particularly embarrassing scene when he passed out in the lounge at a dinner party. That was in 1980, and things had continued to worsen for the once great "Mickey Mac."

A new opportunity, however, had arisen. At first to his chagrin, but now more to his curiosity, his son had become a great basketball player. Initially, the elder McDonough dismissed the game as nothing more than a male version of rounders, which had been popular with Irish women in the parochial schools when he was growing up. The IBBA president's frequent calls convinced him otherwise. He recognized that his boy was quite special. He also saw that there might be a role for him to play in Cormack's future in America.

Chapter 7

Recruiting—the life blood of a successful intercollegiate program— used to be fun and uncomplicated for Jack McHale. State had been a school that any Metropolitan New York kid would always place among his top three or four choices. In the early 70's, when McHale was an assistant to Red Mihalik, and then during the early stages of his own head coaching career, recruiting merely meant identifying five or six scholastic stars in Greater New York during their junior year, establishing a relationship with them, and then setting up a visit in the fall of their senior year. In McHale's first ten years as assistant and as head coach at State, he signed one out of every two prospects State sought in earnest.

One of the first changes forced on McHale with the advent of the Big East had been an alteration of his recruiting geography, from local terrain to regional and then to national—all in the space of five years.

By 1985, McHale's local yield had dropped to ten percent. He had increased the number of recruits he pursued from six to ten, but signed only one, a 6'2" guard from Queens, who was seventh on McHale's overall list, and only his second choice at point guard. It was now necessary to recruit on a regional basis, focusing on Philadelphia, Washington, D.C., Boston, Connecticut, New Jersey and Upstate New York.

The first problem McHale encountered was to convince Steve Ellovitch to increase his recruiting budget further. The administration at State had grown accustomed not only to winning basketball, but also to paltry recruiting expenditures. As McHale emphasized to Ellovitch, the emerging changes in college basketball had necessitated altering the recruiting strategy.

"Look, it's not only our program but Holy Cross, Rutgers, UMass, Rhode Island—all of us are in the same boat. The Big East is killing us. The only way we can get out of the hole is to increase our budget," said McHale firmly.

Ellovitch, fidgeting in his seat, looked out the window as he spoke. "I've heard all this before, Jack, and, in fact, it was for this reason that I authorized a small increase last year. A lot of people around here think that before we go any further, we should see some results."

"What people are you referring to?" McHale flared back, forcing Ellovitch to turn and look at him directly. McHale then pushed further.

"We were as competitive as any team in the East before that Conference.

And in case you've forgotten, I'll remind you that I tried as hard as I could to convince your predecessor to get us in. We're in a tough situation and the only way we can dig ourselves out is to increase our recruiting budget. There's no other choice."

Ellovitch paused, looked briefly at McHale, then looked away and said, "All right, I'll go along with it...but we better see some results. Soon."

McHale set out to establish links with high school coaches in the targeted communities. In most good high school programs, the head coach develops long-time ties with certain colleges. It would not be easy for McHale to break into this tradition. The first step took place when McHale decided to spend one week in each city and to visit as many high school head coaches as he could, especially those with winning programs. His sojourn proved to be educational, if not productive. He realized how badly State's basketball fortunes had fallen in the eyes of high school coaches. All they seemed to talk about was the Big East.

McHale's two assistants, Mike Lambert and Brian McCray, spent virtually all their time on the road. Lambert, black and a former star at Rutgers, had been with McHale since 1979. McCray, white, joined the staff in 1981 and had previously played sixth man on some of McHale's better teams in the mid-70's. Lambert primarily recruited black players, while McCray concentrated on white players. This sort of "ethnic consideration" was a common recruiting ploy in college basketball.

By 1987, McHale realized that the regional approach could not work; few, if any, four- or five-star players from the Northeast were showing remote interest in State. State would have to expand to a national recruiting effort. Again, he had to confront Ellovitch. Again, Ellovitch resisted. He did so as a challenge to McHale. After all, athletic directors were schooled to take a hard line with coaches, who understood precious little about the bottom line.

McHale had to employ methods which were in many ways repulsive to him, including the use of alumni and friends, to exert pressure on Ellovitch. One of those associates was Robert Steincross. McHale knew Steincross loathed Ellovitch and would do anything he could to undermine the Athletic Director. At McHale's request, Steincross called the President. Two days later, the new recruiting budget was approved.

The national program meant many more hours on the road for McHale and his staff. It meant travelling to areas they had never visited and where they had precious few contacts. McHale knew he had no choice. He was willing to do anything within reason to attract the freshman class that would save his job.

From April through June, just prior to the time that they could make their first direct contact with prospects, McHale, Lambert and McCray spent ten to twelve hours a day researching a list of the one-hundred top prospects which they had culled from various scouting services. They whittled the list down to a dozen players and then began to formulate a recruiting game plan. Two names appeared at the top of the list: Cormack McDonough and Marvin Lewis. Little did McHale realize that they would serve as the focal point of a pitched battle with Steve Ellovitch.

Chapter 8

Ted Patterson had just completed a successful season. It was the culmination of sixteen years of hard work from his beginnings at the junior high school level to his position now as one of the top college basketball officials in the United States. The climb had not been easy, but in the last few days, conversations with the chiefs of officials from major conferences throughout the nation confirmed that Patterson had enjoyed a banner year. His ratings, submitted by the coaches whose games he had worked, were outstanding. Not only that, but he had a good Big East tournament and was selected to work in the NCAA first round competition and regional finals.

A so-so athlete, Patterson always had a zest for basketball unlike any kid in his neighborhood. He grew up in New Haven, Connecticut, and the best he had ever done as a player was to become a member of the junior varsity team at the famed Wilbur Cross High School. He sat on the bench as a JV player, and then as a manager of the high school varsity, watching Cross win three consecutive State titles. In high school he was a stocky 5'8" and 165 pounds. He lacked any of the physical prerequisites necessary to become even a marginal player in the game he loved.

Upon graduation from Wilbur Cross, Patterson, possessing modest grades but an excellent work ethic, matriculated at Central Connecticut State University. Knowing it would be hopeless, but wanting in the worst way to give it one last shot, he tried out for the junior varsity team at Central. He was promptly and unceremoniously cut after the first intra-squad scrimmage of the season. Yet that scrimmage, quite by accident, provided Patterson with a new sense of direction.

As the scrimmage ended and Patterson plodded off the floor, the assistant coach at Central beckoned to him.

"Teddy, there is simply no way you're going to be a college basketball player. Yet in all my years of coaching, I don't think I've ever seen a kid who has such an obvious love for the game as you. I was talking to Billy Esposito, the referee, before the scrimmage. Billy was asking me if there were any kids at Central who might be interested in taking the official's exam. There's a course involved and it costs $25. According to Billy, if you go through the course and pass the exam, they'll put you right into some high school

JV games where you can pick up $25 or $30 a game. Why don't you think about it and get back to me?"

Patterson's response was immediate. "If you could arrange for a meeting with Mr. Esposito, I'd like to find out more about it."

Bill Esposito had been in officiating for twenty years. It consumed a sizeable part of his life and offered him much pride. But now in his early fifties, he was no longer able to get up and down the court as he once had as one of the top college officials in the East. He still worked high school games, but his primary interest was instructing young officials. He continually kept on the look-out for good prospects; he sought young men who had not necessarily excelled in basketball, but who had accumulated a knowledge of and feel for the game.

The Central coach then contacted Esposito and told him about young Patterson. "Billy, the kid doesn't have a lick of ability, but what an interest in the game! I told him I'd talk to you and left it to him. Without a blink, he said he'd be interested in meeting you."

The following Tuesday, Esposito came over to the Central gymnasium where he met Patterson for the first time. Immediately the two developed a chemistry. Esposito saw a lot of himself in Patterson: the young kid who loved sports, who could not make the team, yet who was dying to be part of it all. The two talked at length about the importance of good referees and the fact that officiating was a great way to stay involved with the sport. From that day on, Ted Patterson, while pursuing other vocations, would always think of himself first and foremost as an official.

Patterson took Esposito's course and finished first in the class. In Esposito's sixteen years of teaching the course, Teddy Patterson was the first person ever to score a perfect 100 on the final exam. He soaked up every bit of information on rules, regulations and technique. Esposito even found himself often staying thirty or forty minutes after class with Patterson, answering his questions and discussing different game possibilities and rule interpretations.

In the beginning, Patterson was not quite comfortable on the court. While he had played in enough pickup and CYO games to have a good sense of the floor and the movement of the game, he lacked the presence or confidence in his early career to control the game the way the best ones did. What he did have, however, was a booster in Bill Esposito. In Patterson's first year as a JV official—he was still only a freshman at Central Connecticut—Esposito came to almost every one of his games and would critique Patterson's performance.

"Teddy, you need to have more command," Esposito implored. "You're in control and you have to let everyone in the damned gymnasium know it. There's probably no official in the United States of America who knows the rules better than you, and you've only been at it for a few months. But when you are out on that court, you, not the coach, not the players, and sure as hell not the fans, are the one running the show. As soon as you can get that down, you're going to be one hell of a good referee."

Esposito had been greatly respected within the officiating ranks, but upon retiring, his sphere of influence was limited to the central Connecticut region and the high school level. Because of this, he urged Patterson, "to meet as many college officials as you can. As important as ability is, contacts are of equal importance. It's no different from anything else in life. College officiating is like a club; if you'll spend the time to get to know the key members, someday you'll become one of 'em."

After two years as a JV official, and with his confidence and skill increasing, Patterson moved up to the high school ranks at the age of twenty-one. Four years later, with continued support from Esposito, he found himself working Connecticut state tournaments, including the championship game in 1978—which pitted his old school, Wilbur Cross, against local New Haven rival Hillhouse.

Patterson continued to hone his skills, taking every opportunity to attend clinics. In the summer of 1978, he spent six weeks on the road (despite the fact that he had a wife and two young sons) and attended officiating schools nationwide. In 1978-79, after another outstanding high school season brought him ratings at the highest level, Ted Patterson received his first big break. A supervisor of officials in the ECAC called him in June to say, "Teddy, we're going to let you work some Division III games."

Patterson never forgot the feeling of that phone call. He was elated, and the first person he called to share in the victory was Bill Esposito. "You're on your way, Teddy," Esposito exulted, and indeed Patterson was. By 1982 he had moved from Division III to Division II, even working some low-level Division I games. But the litmus test of success for an official was to work in one of the major conferences. Finally, in 1983, after eleven years of hard work and continued improvement, Ted Patterson became an official in the Big East, as well as the Atlantic Ten and Ivy League.

While reaching this level was not easy, staying there was even harder. Patterson quickly discovered how difficult coaches could be. At the high school and small college levels, coaches were under a certain amount of pressure to win, but not overwhelmingly so. Working Big East and Atlantic Ten games offered a whole different atmosphere. Here, Patterson encountered coaches making six-figure salaries; coaches whose income depended solely on winning games. Most had achieved their positions through a wealth of expertise. Among other things, these coaches were particularly skilled in baiting officials.

That first year of Big East officiating, with noisy capacity crowds and frantic coaches pacing the sidelines, reminded Patterson of Doberman Pinschers attacking their prey. He almost found himself swept out before his college career had begun.

One night at the Carrier Dome in Syracuse, in front of 32,000 people,

Patterson flat out blew a call at the end of the game which cost Syracuse a victory against Boston College. He barely made it out of the Dome alive.

In situations such as this, where one or two bad calls down the stretch had a clear impact on the outcome of the game, the official in question could expect some serious repercussions. This was the case after the Syracuse-Boston College game. Letters from the coaching staff, administrators and fans poured into the Big East office, all asking for Patterson's scalp.

Several other incidents, while not as pronounced as this one, also took place. At the end of his first year, Patterson sweated from March until June, waiting to hear whether he would be invited back. Much of his discomfort stemmed from the fact that if an official was not asked back to a major conference after his first year, it might take several more years of almost flawless effort on a lower level to return. Indeed, once kicked out, many guys never got back up.

Part of the reason was that officials were now well paid. Whereas Patterson would receive $25 to $30 for working high school JV games in the mid-70's, he was now paid $350, plus all travel expenses, for Big East games. Over a period of four months, Ted Patterson could pick up between $20,000 and $25,000 of added income. For those fortunate enough to get into the post season tournaments, the money was even better. Only the strong survived in big-time college officiating. In June, the call finally came telling Patterson that he would be asked back, but that significant improvement would be expected.

As he entered his second year in the Big Time, the word on Patterson around the major college circuit was, "You can get to him." Coaches felt Patterson was a guy they could intimidate.

During the summer preceding this second year, Patterson had viewed the films of every single game he had worked in the previous season. At his side for every minute of the film viewing was Esposito, whose critiques, while sometimes harsh, were always constructive and fatherly.

"Teddy, the big thing you have to establish right at the outset of next season is that you are not going to take any of their crap. The first time Boeheim or Thompson gets in your face, you have to hit them up and hit them up quick with a technical foul. You may find that in the early season you'll be calling technicals in the first four or five minutes of each game. Believe me, if you do it and do it with authority, you'll have their respect, which is all an official can hope for."

Patterson took heed of Esposito's advice. In 1984, in the same Carrier Dome where he had experienced his lowest moment as an official, Patterson worked the Georgetown-Syracuse game, calling technicals on both Thompson and Boeheim in the first half. He then worked to the utmost of his professional abilities. As the Big East Color commentator noted, "You can always tell a good official when you don't even notice he's out there. That's exactly what Patterson is doing tonight."

Patterson sped through that year and the next, improving all the while. By 1987 he was granted the highest honor a college official could receive: he was asked to work the NCAA tournament up through the regional finals. Ted Patterson had made it as a college basketball referee. If only his personal life could run so smoothly. . . .

Chapter 9

L ike most coaches, paperwork was not Jack McHale's long suit. And so Steve Ellovitch, to goad McHale further, implemented a policy in which the coach, because of the . . ."concern of the administration regarding the basketball program," was required to file weekly typewritten reports to Ellovitch on the progress of off-season recruiting. Ellovitch knew this would irritate McHale, while providing him with the information necessary to implement his own recruitment plan.

Ellovitch had made it clear to McHale that he, the athletic director, would be playing a role in the year's recruiting. In most Division I programs, particularly in institutions with varsity football, the athletic director stayed almost completely out of recruiting. In general, the only role the AD played would be to greet prospective recruits during their visit and perhaps make a phone call as decision time neared.

When Ellovitch told him of his plan to become involved, McHale became furious. So furious, in fact, that he contemplated going to the President. He knew, however, that his own situation was tenuous and that it was not the right time for a showdown with his Athletic Director.

Meanwhile, the long hours McHale and his staff had put in began to pay dividends. Of the twelve blue-chip prospects, McHale ended up with ten home visits. He then convinced the extraordinary number of six to visit State's campus. Two of them were Marvin Lewis and Cormack McDonough. Since the inception of the Big East, State had not been able to entice more than two of the top one hundred to visit in a given year. To attract six was a significant accomplishment.

With the six recruits planning September and October visits, McHale knew that his best chance for signing two or three of these blue-chippers was to pursue the early signing date set forth by the NCAA. In 1984 the NCAA had decreed that a mid-November signing date would be honored by all NCAA institutions, and that from mid-November until mid-March of a prospect's senior year, no recruiting could occur. Schools thus geared their recruiting to sign as many players as possible before November 15.

McHale also knew that if State could get a blue-chip player to visit in the fall, and should that player be interested in an early signing, then some of the major programs (like Kentucky or North Carolina) would be precluded from putting on a late recruiting push. Cutting down the time element from six months to forty-five days could lend considerable advantage to a smaller program such as State's.

A great deal of strategy was employed in deciding what would be the appropriate weekend for recruits to visit. In the case of Lewis and McDonough, the staff decided that since both players knew each other from Five Star and seemed to be friends, it would be advantageous to bring them to State together.

The NCAA, in allowing a player to visit, also allowed for at least one parent to come along on an expenses-paid basis. From McHale's reports, Ellovitch knew that Thomas Mahon and Michael McDonough would be accompanying their sons to the State campus. He instructed McHale that part of the weekend visit by both players would include the opportunity for Ellovitch to greet both parents separately. In the meantime, there were other foundations to be laid—in the form of steel and concrete.

Chapter 10

R obert Steincross had not set an easy task before his attorney, Richard Shoppels. The need for a new arena at State University had long been apparent. A presidential task force reported that State could not be competitive with other institutions without a modern, all-purpose facility. It took two-and-a-half years to conclude what had been painfully obvious even to the most casual of State followers.

In 1986, upon completion of the task force report, State, through its Development Office, attempted to implement a $12.4 million campaign to raise funds for the new athletic center. The campaign would include a $3 million grant from the state legislature's educational fund, with the additional $9.4 million to be raised from outside sources. The State University Campaign Committee, headed by the Vice President of Development, felt that a legislative grant was a crucial first step in executing the fund-raising program. After considerable lobbying by the Department of Public Relations, and by the Chief Lobbyist for the University, the grant proposal passed through the appropriate legislative bodies. Ultimately, it was placed on the 1987 ballot, as part of the general state referenda.

Lobbyists for State University, including President Pendelton, spent considerable time and money working toward a victory for Referendum 902. State even produced a 60-second television commercial, featuring Pendelton and Athletic Director Steve Ellovitch, to sway the voters.

Despite the expenditure of resources, the referendum was voted down—a crushing blow to the President and his staff; one that would paralyze the entire project. Robert Steincross, always ready to seize an opportunity, recognized that one had arrived. Armed with the knowledge that the State campaign had made a very important tactical error by trying to secure New York State money before securing private money—a point not lost on the electorate of New York—Steincross arranged to meet with Richard Shoppels.

Shoppels had represented Steincross during his economic rise to power. The attorney was often uncomfortable with the type of work his client requested. The law mattered little to Steincross, he simply wished to manipulate it to suit his own needs. Shoppels was acknowledged as one of the premier tax lawyers in New York. His advice had saved Steincross millions of dollars over the past decade, and he was paid a considerable sum for his services.

Steincross did not hesitate to mention this during a meeting with Shoppels to discuss the formation of a tax-exempt foundation. The foundation would be separate and distinct from the University and would receive federal and state exemptions, thus freeing it from all property taxes. The purpose of this foundation: to raise funds for a multi-purpose sports facility that would be located approximately five hundred yards from State's campus.

Before meeting with Shoppels, Steincross had met with President Pendelton to discuss the legislative defeat and the options now available for constructing a sports' facility. Pendelton was under considerable pressure, for it was he who had advocated the policy of securing state money first before turning to the private sector. Steincross knew that the President, concerned about his own position, was eager to arrive at a solution that would placate his Board of Directors and the public.

Clearly, one of the reasons that State's athletic fortunes had fallen on hard times was the lack of a suitable facility. Jack McHale, ever the loyal soldier, had privately bemoaned the situation to Ellovitch, but had never gone public. It was obvious, however, that the antiquated gymnasium in which State played simply did not match up to the Carrier Dome in Syracuse, the Dean Smith Dome in North Carolina or other facilities throughout the country. Blue chip athletes were not impressed by playing before crowds of 3,400.

Steincross' approach, as always, was bluntly direct. He told Pendelton that as a member of the Board he was displeased with the strategy employed by the University. He laid the blame squarely on the President's shoulders and further pointed out that a fund raising campaign initiated by State would, in all likelihood, fail. Thus, he had devised his own plan.

Pendleton, groping for any viable solution, did not necessarily agree with Steincross regarding the inability of State to lead a fund raising campaign. The Vice President for Development had sent Pendelton a report which indicated that such an approach could still be successful, provided State could find leadership from the corporate community of New York. When briefed on the Vice President's report, Steincross told Pendelton that such leadership was nonexistent and would remain that way for several more years, due to the bad taste left by the failed referendum.

Steincross told Pendelton that he was prepared to form his tax-exempt foundation, and that for a nominal sum the University could lease the planned facility. Steincross had already commissioned an architect to design the building, which carried a $13.5 million price tag and would seat 13,000 for basketball, while housing virtually every other indoor sport.

Steincross made it clear, however, that the administration of this facility would rest with its own Board of Directors, of which Steincross would be Chairman. The University, while offered a seat on the Board, would have no say in policy. Steincross also insisted that all concession revenue would go to one of his own subsidiaries, his payback for setting up the entire project. Finally, as Chairman, he would exercise final approval of all building contracts.

The President, still reeling from defeat, saw the picture clearly. He knew that the revenue generated from the concessions would be by far the most significant financial benefit of the new facility. And he knew that Steincross, while not involving his own construction company directly, could curry favor with those builders chosen. He further recognized that Steincross, due to his position on the University's Board, was able to wield power in the State educational hierarchy.

With the construction of this facility, Steincross could now gain almost complete control over State's athletic fortunes, perhaps even to the extent of having major input into the hiring and firing of various staff members. But without that facility, Pendelton himself might be looking for a new job. He offered Steincross his full support.

Shoppels' job next focused on the creation of a partnership between the University and the foundation. The Charter he developed stated that a Board separate from the University would operate the facility and that the University would sign a ninety-nine-year lease for one dollar per year, plus all costs related to the operation of the facility. In addition, it further stated that a separate entity would retain all concession rights.

Shoppels presented the document to Steincross, who immediately called a United States Senator. Steincross had been one of the Senator's staunchest supporters, and they had become friends. The Senator provided Steincross with a name at the Internal Revenue Service and suggested that the letter of application include a blind copy to the Senator. The Senator indicated that he would do all he could to see it through.

As Shoppels pointed out to Steincross, it normally would take as little as four months, and in some cases as much as a year or two, for a foundation to receive tax-exempt status from the Internal Revenue Service. Three weeks after Shoppels sent the application to the Internal Revenue Service, word came back that the "Athletic Achievement Foundation" had been granted such status.

Steincross' next step was to retain the services of a seasoned fund-raiser. While $13.5 million did not seem insurmountable, he needed to raise it quickly, and with as few pitfalls as possible. After interviewing several candidates, he settled on Robert O'Connell. O'Connell previously had served as Director of Development for Williams College. He had left Williams after successfully heading up its $50 million library campaign to venture out on his own as a private consultant. One of the more favorable recommendations received by Steincross on O'Connell was that "he actually enjoys asking people for money."

This fund-raising campaign possessed a unique feature. Not only would O'Connell be able to solicit private foundations and individual donors, but he could also approach a large corporation which, rather than donating money earmarked for tax deductible purposes, could draw from its advertising budget and thus become the "major corporate sponsor" of the building.

He would pursue a company, which, in return for its generous gift, would receive significant publicity and acclaim.

O'Connell studied Fortune 500 companies whose major corporate offices were housed in New York. He then identified six possible target companies whose earnings and advertising campaigns would qualify them to become the major donor of a facility to which their name would be affixed forever. The one which stood well above the other five was the Gunderson Brewing Company.

Chapter 11

State's recruiting came down to three players. One was Billy Powers, a 6'1" point guard from All Hallows High School in New York. Jack McHale had known Powers since he first attended McHale's camp at the age of ten. Powers' dad, Bobby Powers, also grew up in Brooklyn, not too far from McHale. They were acquaintances in high school and became friends later on. McHale liked both Powers very much.

Scouting services had rated Billy Powers a solid 4-star on a scale of five, but McHale felt that in the right system he could become as valuable a point guard as any in the high school senior crop. McHale also recognized that in order to compete with some of the teams that Ellovitch had placed on future schedules, he would need a point guard of Powers' skill. Powers was what McHale referred to as a "gamer"—a kid who loved to play, who understood how to play, and was at his best in clutch situations. McHale coveted him and felt that his chances were at least fifty-fifty, based on early reports.

The other two players McHale sought were Cormack McDonough and Marvin Lewis. After a great deal of discussion with his assistants and even with Ellovitch, McHale felt that the best strategy was to bring in all three prospects on the same weekend. It might be the most important weekend of his coaching career.

Both McDonough and Lewis continued to remain at the top of most scouting lists. McDonough's ability was a bit more difficult to evaluate because the only opportunity McHale had to see him against any kind of reasonable competition occurred at Five Star. Still, McHale had found that the established scouts were extremely adept at judging talent. Indeed, the scouting system for evaluating high school seniors had become, on the whole, very reliable over the last fifteen years. If five stars were affixed to the player's name, it was likely that he would become an outstanding competitor at the Division I college level.

McHale placed Brian McCray in charge of Cormack's visit to State, while Mike Lambert would handle Marvin Lewis' visit. McHale himself would oversee Powers' visit because of his relationship with Powers' father. A graduate assistant would aid all three coaches in the nuts-and-bolts aspects of each visit, but particularly McHale, because of the Head Coach's obligation to the other two recruits.

In many schools, it was common to have the team's best player host a recruit. McHale, while not necessarily excluding his team's best players, had abandoned that theory several years before. Often, the best players recognized that a new recruit might steal some of their thunder. In two particular cases in the early '80's, McHale felt that key recruits were lost because those top players had not done their jobs well on the weekend visitations.

"The most important thing we're looking for here," McHale reiterated to his assistants, "is loyalty. We can't afford to have any of these kids stay with someone who won't be totally loyal to the program."

The three State players chosen were briefed in McHale's office for thirty minutes on the importance of the weekend. One was a regular; the other two were subs. McHale was confident that all three would speak well of the program, the coaching staff and the school. While the player-hosts did not fully understand the magnitude of the weekend's visitations, they assured McHale that they were prepared to get the job done.

The next step was to plan the weekend to the minute. McHale had to take into consideration Ellovitch's new role in the recruiting. While at first somewhat uncomfortable with it, he recognized that the athletic director was a good salesman and reluctantly admitted to his assistants that Ellovitch could probably help.

The weekend activities had to portray State as a quality program which did everything in a first class way. When Cormack McDonough arrived at JFK with his father, McHale had a limousine waiting. The same was true when Marvin Lewis and Thomas Mahon landed at LaGuardia. McHale even sent a limo to East 52nd Street in Brooklyn to pick up Billy Powers and his father. When Bobby Powers arrived on campus, he sought out McHale, saying the last time a car like that appeared in the neighborhood was for a funeral.

"I'm not ready to go to my grave," Powers laughed.

The NCAA allowed recruits to stay on campus for a period of forty-eight hours. Anything beyond that would be a violation. McHale's strategy was to have the players arrive on campus Friday afternoon. Their first activity was to attend a class. He was careful to choose a class that would interest the recruits. He also chose professors with a good sense of humor; ones who were sympathetic to State's athletic fortunes. McHale always asked the professors to spend a few moments with the players after the class.

McHale, through a contact with a State alumnus now serving as the Governor's chief of staff, had managed to get the Governor, down from Albany for the day, to see the three athletes in his New York City office. With classes completed, and a limousine waiting outside, the three players were ushered into downtown New York for the meeting. While McHale could not expect the Governor to speak with any degree of authority on State's athletic fortunes, the mere fact that such a prominent figure would take time to visit with three high school basketball players was sure to leave a positive impression.

Lewis, McDonough, and Powers had come to know each other through the Five Star camp. They liked and respected each other, particularly their unique basketball abilities. The major pitch of the weekend was that these three players could come in together and turn State's basketball fortunes around. While McHale knew it might not happen as quickly as the three perceived, it was nonetheless crucial that the players establish a rapport with each other while he stressed their potential as saviors.

After the Governor's visit, the players were escorted back to campus to meet with the faculty advisor for student athletes. The advisor had been hired because a number of State athletes were falling well below NCAA academic standards, thus jeopardizing their eligibility. She had been effective in providing the proper tutorial assistance to players. McHale felt that she would give a positive impression of the tutorial program. This was particularly important to Lewis who, while putting forth reasonable effort in the classroom, had struggled through his junior year and was in some danger of not complying with the newly-created Proposition 48, which set minimum academic entrance standards for those wishing to play intercollegiate athletics.

McHale then arranged for a visit to President Pendelton's home. The President was hosting a reception for prominent alumni, which he customarily did on big football weekends. In attendance at the reception was Robert Steincross. McHale's feelings toward Steincross were mixed. He recognized that Steincross was becoming an increasing power in State's athletic fortunes, and he knew of Steincross' plan to build the arena. Still, he had a certain uneasiness about Steincross. But McHale knew that with Steincross at the reception, it was almost mandatory that the players meet him.

Steincross could not have performed better. He sat the three players down, told them of his own difficult background and how much State meant to him. He then assured them that by the beginning of their sophomore years they would be part of an opening night celebration of a brand new arena.

"Fella's, you can go to the bank with that," said Steincross. The recruits were clearly impressed; so, too, was McHale.

The President then offered a few brief offhanded remarks to the players. McHale knew that athletic recruiting ranked with professional wrestling on his list of distasteful things.

After the reception, the three were brought to McHale's office, where they met with the player hosts. From seven o'clock that evening until breakfast the next morning, the three recruits were entrusted to the hosts. Willie Nelson was on campus for a concert as part of the homecoming festivities and then there would be fraternity parties. McHale, with deep conviction, implored all six of the young men to have fun, but to "keep your noses clean." Although he laughed when he said it, he had heard plenty of horror stories about recruits and their one night stands with coeds on other college campuses—some prearranged by the coaching staff.

With the three players now accounted for until Saturday morning breakfast, McHale and his assistants turned their attention to the fathers. McHale had found that most parents were interested in finding out about him not just as a coach, but as a person. He decided to invite the parents to dinner at the McHale home.

McHale's wife Sally, long accustomed to these recruiting weekends, was as proficient a hostess as she was a homemaker. She prepared roast rack of lamb and potatoes au gratin. The evening's conversation centered around State's basketball fortunes and McHale's hopes for the future. In McHale's mind, however, the real point was to assure the parents that Jack McHale was a good person, a decent family man, and somebody who would look after their sons as if they were one of his own.

McHale had always enjoyed Bobby Powers' company. While he was able to establish a rapport with Michael McDonough (due to their Irish linkages), he still felt somewhat uncomfortable with McDonough and particularly uncomfortable with Thomas Mahon. Mahon continuously looked at his watch all night. Finally, after the guests had returned to McHale's living room for coffee and apple strudel, Mahon, fidgeting in his seat, said, "I'm a bit tired. With all that's planned tomorrow, I'd best get some sleep."

After the fathers departed, McHale continued to feel uneasy about McDonough and Mahon. He did not doubt their interest in State, but he found both of them to be abounding in character flaws. In essence, what it came down to was this: McHale really did not like either one and found it a bit distasteful to have to recruit them in order to sign their sons.

* * * * * *

Brian McCray had asked one of the player hosts to call him at 1 a.m. with a report on the evening. He wanted to make sure that the players had gotten into the concert and that they had arrived back at the dorms at a reasonable hour. By establishing different check points with the three player hosts, McCray hoped they would clearly understand the importance of the weekend. After learning that all had gone well, McCray phoned McHale.

McHale and his staff agreed that the first item on Saturday morning's agenda would be a lavish breakfast for the prospects at the McHales' home. Part of the research for the weekend visitation included what the players liked to eat, so the breakfast included Irish bacon burned to a crisp, scones, sausage, omelettes, blueberry pancakes and freshly squeezed orange juice.

After breakfast, Brian McCray and Mike Lambert took the players on a tour of the campus. In their pre-visit strategy session, the staff had agreed to spend as little time in the old field house and as much time as possible showing them the architectural renderings of Steincross' dream building. The recruits were then brought to State's basketball film library where they looked at footage of some of State's past great victories. It became obvious to all that the film presentation, prepared by Lambert, was top heavy with footage of the successful '70's, with limited scenes from the struggle-filled '80's.

Lambert said, "We figure that when we bring recruits here in 1991, the footage will be primarily of you guys." He laughed, but there was a serious edge to his voice.

McHale then met each player for thirty minutes. This would not be the final pitch, for that would come Sunday morning. Instead it was merely an opportunity for McHale to emphasize that he viewed each one as an "impact player," someone who could come in and play right away as a freshman.

In McHale's career as a head coach, he had never actually promised a player a starting position. In the past, with prime recruits, he would simply tell them, "If you're as good as we think you are, you'll get considerable time right away." He knew, however, that this tack would not be good enough for such a prized trio. In all cases, they were being promised starting positions. McHale had heard, in fact, that two Big East schools, both hot on Lewis' trail, had guaranteed his position as a starting center, despite the fact that their current centers were sophomores. How these schools would live up to this promise was, in McHale's mind, another matter. With much prompting from his two assistants, McHale reluctantly decided that he would do what he previously felt to be unethical. He told the three recruits that he expected them to be in the starting lineup, should they choose State. McHale also discussed the recruits' academic interests, their hopes for the future, as well as his own hopes for State's basketball program.

After the meetings, the staff took the three recruits to lunch, at three separate places, for more individual discussion. They agreed to meet later at the "Will Call Window" and pick up tickets for the football game which was scheduled that afternoon. That State won a thrilling come-from-behind victory certainly helped.

After the game, the strategy called for the recruits going off again with the three player hosts who had arranged for dates for each of them. McHale made it clear, however, that the tactics used at other schools, such as sexual alliances, were not to be included as part of the evening's festivities.

"If anything happens," said McHale to his three players during the pre-visit discussion, "let the recruits initiate it."

Sunday morning brought the final and most important part of the recruiting weekend. In order to comply with the NCAA rules, the recruits had to be off campus by noon, so another elaborate brunch was planned. Research revealed that both Billy Powers and Cormack McDonough attended mass every Sunday, so McHale picked them up at 8:30 a.m. and brought them to the 9:00 mass at St. Joseph's Chapel, on campus. He had also arranged for Monsignor Sullivan to say hello to the players right after the mass and to encourage them to attend State. Since Lewis did not go to church, the subject was not brought up.

After church and brunch, the plan called for McHale to sit down with each player and his father. Here he would make his final pitch.

Before doing this, McHale felt no different from the way he did before a big game. These meetings would be crucial to his future, so his stomach was churning. The first to enter his office were Billy and Bobby Powers, as well as Marian Powers, who had joined father and son for the Sunday morning brunch. After fifteen minutes of discussion, McHale could see that the Powers family had made up their minds.

The discussion concluded with Bobby Powers saying, "Jack, I've always had nothing but respect for you. If you feel my boy can help your program, we're ready to sign on the dotted line."

McHale could not hide his exuberance. He jumped up, shook hands with all three, and exclaimed, "This is one great day for State basketball."

Powers' decision was important, and not just because of McHale's belief that Billy Powers would be an outstanding point guard in college. Indeed, he had intentionally scheduled the Powers family first, hoping to get a commitment from them and then being able to tell the other two families that Billy Powers had decided on State.

When Marvin Lewis and Thomas Mahon came into his office, McHale began the conversation by saying that Billy Powers had committed.

"Marvin, I think you know what he could mean to your career with his passing ability," McHale pointed out.

From there the discussion proceeded to the other aspects of State's program, and then to a reiteration of McHale's intent of giving Marvin a starting position at center. During the meeting McHale felt continual uneasiness about Thomas Mahon. It was clear the boy was leaning heavily on his father for final judgment.

At the conclusion of the discussion, Mahon looked at McHale and said, "I've been very impressed with what I've seen and I think you have a real good shot at my boy. I'll tell you what I'm going to do. Call me tomorrow night. We'll give you our final decision."

McHale was pleased when he heard this. He knew that Mahon had had at least one more visit planned for the following weekend at LSU. When Mahon told him that the decision would be made tomorrow evening, he knew that State was now in the youngster's final two or three choices.

Michael McDonough, his eyes reddened from early morning quaffing, walked into the office with his son. McHale again began by pointing out that Billy Powers had committed. The conversation went back and forth for about ten minutes. McHale could see that Cormack, like Marvin Lewis, was relying on his father's judgment. He could also see in Michael's statements and body language that State was clearly in the hunt.

At the conclusion of the conversation, Michael McDonough looked at his son, then at McHale, and said, "Mr. McHale, we'll call you tomorrow evening from Killarney."

Chapter 12

"Ego Management." Robert O'Connell had had the inscription etched on Connemara Marble he had bought several years earlier. He often laughed about it, but it was the key to his business. O'Connell was a craftsman, no different from a master builder or an artisan. His task was to build fund-raising campaigns, while managing colossal egos.

The most critical (and sizeable) ego that O'Connell had to bring into the campaign fold belonged to William Riley, President and CEO of Gunderson Brewery. Riley's rise in the Gunderson Brewing Company had been nothing short of spectacular. As a junior marketing executive in his late twenties, Riley recognized the importance of hooking up with a mentor in order to get on the company's fast track. In 1967 he put his wheels in motion.

Riley's boss, John Spiro, seven years his elder, was clearly earmarked for big things at Gunderson. Riley took a look around the company and saw that the senior executives for the most part had one of two factors in their favor: either they were direct descendants of Bradford Gunderson or, early on in their careers, they had identified with someone on whose coattails they would ride to success. Riley similarly decided to identify with someone who would recognize his abilities, someone he could follow to the top of the Gunderson Brewing Company. He had made the right choice in John Spiro.

From his first position as junior marketing executive, Bill Riley rose through the ranks. In a span of ten years he received four promotions, not unusual for someone designated as a member of the company's fast track. Those on the fast track recognized that such promotions were plentiful. So too, however, were resignations in the event of failure.

By the age of thirty-seven, Riley had been promoted to Vice President in charge of Marketing, a critical position in the company. The difference among most of the better-selling beers was not all that significant in terms of quality, and so the advertising campaigns of the companies became crucial to success. As Vice President in charge of Marketing, Riley had the responsibility of overseeing a $160 million budget.

The Gunderson Brewing Company had fallen on lean times, and a number of changes had been made in the higher echelons of the company. Not only was Riley's promotion to Vice President a recognition of his talent, but it was also a stepping stone which could lead to the presidency of the company. Such potential success, however, depended upon a marketing strategy that would reverse the fortunes of the giant brewery. For the first time in its 110-year history, Gunderson's share of the market in the ten major cities had fallen below fifty percent.

At the Board of Directors' meeting during which Riley was promoted to Executive Vice President, it was made clear to all by Chairman of the Board, Bradford Gunderson III, that the company's misfortune over the last several years had to be reversed to avoid massive lay-offs and a plant closing. The company had long prided itself on its commitment to its workers. In fact, many sons and daughters of employees dating all the way back to Bradford Gunderson I had worked at the brewery and advanced to executive level positions. Gunderson warned that all of this would have to change unless a turnaround occurred.

Riley's ascension to Vice President had not been without its pitfalls. His almost uncontrollable ambition to reach the highest level of the company had sometimes caused him to alienate even those closest to him. This happened with John Spiro once Riley's aggressive pursuit placed him on several important company planning committees, to the exclusion of his old ally. Riley looked upon this as part of the business. It bothered him somewhat, yet he recognized that Spiro had similar ambitions to serve as company President. The odds were strong that the two would lock horns at some point.

When appointed Vice President, Riley immediately called a meeting of the advertising executives, including the senior representatives of the Plunkett Advertising Agency. He told the ad agency that changes were going to be made, and that unless a fifty percent share was achieved in at least five of the ten major markets in the coming six months, their twenty-six-year relationship with the brewery would be terminated. As Riley saw it, the Plunkett Advertising Agency had become too set in its ways and lacked aggressiveness. He was about to change all that.

For starters, Gunderson would become more heavily involved with the sports market and explore new areas which, in Riley's judgment, attracted a typical beer drinker. The strategy became known as "Riley's Revolution," and showed immediate results. In 1977, a fifty percent share was once again achieved in seven major markets. By 1980, the Gunderson Brewery, staving off the challenge of the foreign imports, had again regained its pre-eminence in the beer industry. This fact was not lost on the Board of Directors when the Gunderson President and Chief Executive Officer suffered a critical heart attack. At an emergency meeting, the Board voted that the President would be given a one year "leave of absence" and that William Riley would be promoted to President of the Company—at the age of forty-two. This exceeded even Riley's expectations.

When Robert O'Connell told Robert Steincross that the Gunderson Brewing Company was the most logical prospect to make a major gift for a sports' facility, Steincross agreed to arrange a luncheon meeting with William Riley.

But he did so with that rarest of emotions—trepidation. The William Rileys of the world actually intimidated Steincross, with his hardscrabble upbringing and unpolished ways. Yes, he was wealthy, but he lacked the corporate panache of Riley...his millions seemed dirtier.

Nonetheless, he picked up the phone and dialed Riley's office. It would be his first attempt at fusing two different worlds.

Chapter 13

Steve Ellovitch was always one to do his homework. When Jack McHale presented him with his final three prospects, Ellovitch swung into action. But his research assumed a different direction from McHale's.

After considerable study on each of the final three prospects, Ellovitch decided that his two most realistic candidates would be Cormack McDonough and Marvin Lewis. This attention was not due to any character deficiencies in the two young men; in fact, it had nothing to do with them. However, it had everything to do with their star-crossed overseers.

Ellovitch knew that both men would play a role in the decision of their two sons. Thomas Mahon and Michael McDonough were of poor character and limited financial means. Thanks to a local credit bureau, Ellovitch was able to piece together virtually every aspect of the financial wherewithal of Mahon. According to his IRS returns and other information garnered by a credit check, he had been unemployed for four years and lacked any income other than his monthly unemployment check. He was a gambler, a drinker, a womanizer.

Maybe Marvin Lewis did not realize it, but Ellovitch knew that the real reason Mahon had migrated to Worcester was to take advantage of his son's athletic prowess. Mahon was never one to conceal his feelings. He had made it known on more than one occasion (after a bit too much to drink at Gilrein's on Main Street in Worcester) that when Marvin was ready to sign, his own ship would come to port as well.

Michael McDonough was similar to Mahon in many ways. Since the conclusion of his legendary football career, McDonough's life had gone steadily downhill. He was now nothing more than the town drunk in Killarney. Ellovitch had checked him out thoroughly through various contacts in Ireland. He knew that McDonough had little or no money and that, while rejecting his son's interest in basketball at the outset, he had all of a sudden come around. McDonough's sudden interest in his son and American basketball were no different from Mahon's motive for moving from Alabama to Worcester.

Ellovitch made it clear to McHale that he wanted the opportunity to meet the two players upon their arrival for the recruiting visit. From all that he could gather, neither player had any understanding of big time college sports or of the money it generated. His reports indicated that both were quite naive, that basketball was the focal point of their lives, and that neither would be interested in any financial gain. They simply wanted to play Division I basketball and someday have the opportunity to land a spot on an NBA roster. Ellovitch needed to determine the accuracy of these assumptions, and exactly how much influence the fathers would have on their sons' decisions.

While a student at Cornell Law School, Ellovitch became skilled at cross-examination. He put this talent to good use in his separate meetings with McDonough and Lewis. Ellovitch asked each player carefully, but directly, how much influence his father would have in lodging a final decision on State. Marvin and Cormack both responded that parental influence would be significant. This was all Ellovitch needed to hear.

Since Ellovitch had Michael McDonough and Thomas Mahon only for a weekend, he wanted to make sure that he left an impression strong enough to gain their commitment. He knew other schools paid off parents and players. While he was not aware of any school in particular making such overtures to the two fathers, he did not want to take any chances. When McDonough arrived at his suite at the Grand Hyatt Hotel he found an iced-down six pack of Guinness Stout. And when Mahon arrived at his suite at the same hotel, he not only found a bottle of Dom Perignon, but some additional entertainment in the form of a high-priced call girl. Again, it all came down to research.

While Ellovitch did not feel it appropriate to convey to either player or parent that Jack McHale stood on shaky ground, he nonetheless wanted all of them to know that he ultimately was in control. The plush hotel suites and other gifts would be signs of Ellovitch's position of strength.

Ellovitch arranged to meet first with Thomas Mahon on Saturday, in the Athletic Director's office. He made sure that no one was in the outer suite when Mahon arrived. There was no mistaking that he was Marvin Lewis' father, his tall angular body causing him to stoop below the entranceway into Ellovitch's office. A cigarette dangled from his mouth, his hair was in a Chuck Berry-like pomp, and his smile revealed the gleam of a shiny gold tooth.

The conversation began with the usual civilities. Ellovitch complimented Mahon on the wonderful job he had done in rearing his son and told him how much State would like to acquire the services of Marvin Lewis.

The small talk concluded, Ellovitch proceeded with caution. He first told Mahon his own views of rearing children: how difficult it was to educate them, and the tremendous cost involved. Mahon seized every opportunity to agree with Ellovitch. To Ellovitch, it almost seemed comical. Yet Mahon, while uneducated, was no fool. It became apparent after fifteen minutes of conversation that both men knew the reason they were together. So Ellovitch came right to the point.

"Thomas, I want your son to come to State. I recognize how much you've done for him and how much he relies on your judgment. I also know that times have been hard for you. I'm prepared to offer you a little assistance along the way. It would come in the form of $15,000 per year for four years. In addition, I have a good friend who owns a very fine car dealership; I'd be happy to provide you with a car."

When Ellovitch made his offer for $15,000 per year plus car, he did not expect Mahon to accept it immediately.

"Mr. Ellovitch, I really appreciate your understanding of my situation. Times have been hard and despite my difficulties with Cornelia, I've been a good father. Maybe I haven't been as good as I'd hoped to be, but still good. It's real important for me to stay close to Marvin in these times. You're a generous man, but my concern is, what with inflation and all, how's a fellow like me going to get by on $15,000 a year?"

Ellovitch nearly laughed inside. He knew what he was dealing with and allowed Mahon to continue.

"Surely, with a big fine school like this and what with Marvin's importance to the program, the University will be making quite a lot of money in the next four years. What would you say to a bit more, something along the lines of $20,000 the first year, $25,000 the second, $30,000 the third, and $40,000 in Marvin's senior year?"

The Athletic Director quickly organized his thoughts. Before he could offer his response, Mahon jumped in, knowing he had the upper hand. "Of course, should Marvin lead the team into a tournament, maybe a little bit of a bonus wouldn't be all that bad an idea."

Ellovitch knew that Mahon was street smart, but he did not expect him to have an understanding of escalating income and bonuses. Thinking back to his legal training, he realized that from a standpoint of negotiation, Mahon not only held a stronger position, but also knew that he did.

"All right, Thomas, this is what we'll do," Ellovitch countered. "We'll provide you $20,000 the first year, $22,000 the second, $25,000 the third, and $30,000 in Marvin's senior year. If in any of those four years we advance to an NCAA Tournament, we'll agree on a $3,000 bonus per game. Is that satisfactory?"

"Now, we're getting a lot closer, Mr. Ellovitch." Ellovitch smiled at the use of the term "Mr." Mahon then continued, "But I was wonderin'. It'll be real important for me to keep an eye out for Marvin. As you know, he's a young boy, somewhat immature. I want to make sure I can be at all the games.

"That can be arranged," said Ellovitch.

Mahon smiled. "In addition, while I'm at the games, I sure would appreciate some companionship, you know what I mean?"

Ellovitch paused. "Thomas, we'll go along with your terms, including some companionship, but there are a couple of things I want to make clear. First, we'll be dealing in cash only. As a result, I don't even want you to open up a bank account. Nothing can be traceable. If at any time I find out that you've opened a bank account, or that you've in any way leaked that you're being given this money, all bets are off."

Mahon said, "That's fine with me. You've got my word."

"One last thing," said Ellovitch. "The money will not start until Marvin sets foot on campus in September."

"Understood," said Mahon.

Ellovitch felt that Michael McDonough would be a far different challenge. His research for the meeting covered not only "Mickey Mac" but also the Irish in general. He learned that in matters of money, they trusted no one. One American lawyer, who represented a multi-national firm which had built a plant in Ireland, told Ellovitch, "They are absolutely the hardest people to make a financial deal with. You'll think you have a deal and all of a sudden, they'll back out. It's because they've never had any money that they find the whole notion of money to be very intimidating. Be prepared for some tough sledding if you plan to do business with an Irishman." Ellovitch did not forget those words as he prepared to meet with McDonough.

Later that Saturday afternoon, McDonough entered Ellovitch's office. He was a large man, particularly by Irish standards—6'4", carrying a paunch with his slouched gait. But there was no mistaking that he had once been a great athlete. Times had changed, however, and his appearance looked almost slovenly. As they shook hands, Ellovitch could not help but notice McDonough's red nose and glazed eyes.

Ellovitch began. "This is your first time in the States, Michael. How are you enjoying it?"

"I must say that your area is a wee bit like Killarney, what with all the trees. Quite beautiful, in fact." Ellovitch had the keen sense that McDonough knew exactly why they were meeting. He immediately started on a line of conversation that would lead directly to his point.

"Michael, I understand that unemployment in Killarney has almost reached sixty percent. My God, how do you make it?"

"Well, Mr. Ellovitch, the dole has become the only way. We in Ireland have not been as fortunate as you Americans in our business practices. As a result, a fellow like me, always anxious to make an honest pound, has had to put my dignity in my pocket and take the monthly check that comes from Dublin."

"It must be hard for a man of your pride," Ellovitch replied.

"It's been more than hard, Mr. Ellovitch. The only pride I can take has been the wonderful development of my son, Cormack. By the way, I want you to know how delighted I am that he is looking at your fine school."

"Michael, your son would be of great value to us. I know times are hard in Ireland. Given these factors, I'm able to offer you some money each year to tide you over. No doubt in four years Cormack will be an NBA player, and perhaps then, should times be right for you, you could pay me back."

Ellovitch did this intentionally. While he knew it was not necessary to couch the payoff in terms of a loan to Thomas Mahon (and while it was still an NCAA violation anyway), Ellovitch understood the Irish mentality. He felt that this might be an easier way to get to McDonough.

"In other words," said McDonough, "it would be sort of a loan, something that, should my boy become what you call an NBA player and make a lot of shillings, we would then repay you."

"That's exactly right, Michael. Of course, nothing would be in writing and it would be imperative that nothing be said to anyone about this arrangement. Unfortunately, people who govern athletics are not always sensitive to the hard economic times that some parents must face. We look at this in the form of a loan. When you get yourself straight, we can discuss the payback."

Both parties knew there would never be a payback. McDonough, as Mahon had done before him, seized the opportunity to say, "A fellow would need more than a few shillings to get by in Killarney now. What would you be proposin'?"

"Well," answered Ellovitch, "how would it sound if we came up with about 13,000 pounds the first year, and a gradual increase in each of the next three." Ellovitch knew that the value of the pound had changed dramatically in the last year and that an American dollar did not go nearly as far. He felt it would be better to deal in pounds. He also felt that in the unlikely event Mahon and McDonough ever talked, the amounts they received had better be close. Thus, Ellovitch was prepared to offer McDonough essentially the same package as Mahon.

"Let me think on it a bit," said McDonough, "and perhaps I can get back to you."

Ellovitch was prepared for this response; it was typical of the Irish and their way of doing business. "That would put me in a very difficult position, Michael," Ellovitch immediately responded. "There is a certain individual who will be providing this loan. Naturally, he doesn't want his name revealed. As you may understand, we're looking at several other fine prospects and I wouldn't want to put you in the quandary of not having any funds available, should you delay too long in the decision."

"I understand," said McDonough. "I'll tell you what. Let me sleep on it and I'll call you tomorrow." Ellovitch and McDonough then negotiated the exact amount. They agreed that McDonough would receive 13,000£, 15,000£, 17,000£ and 20,000£ from Cormack's freshman through senior year, as well as a bonus similar to Mahon's. The only thing that Ellovitch did not offer was a car. Making arrangements for a car in Killarney would be difficult. Few people drove cars in that part of Ireland. It would attract attention, something which Ellovitch wanted to avoid.

Ellovitch made it clear to McDonough that no money would be forthcoming until young Cormack actually enrolled at State in September. He concluded his meeting with McDonough by asking, "How much influence will you have?"

"My boy will do what I say," McDonough answered.

At 8 a.m. the next morning, Michael McDonough called Ellovitch at home and said, "Mr. Ellovitch, you've got a deal."

Chapter 14

A good fund raiser always placed himself in a deferential position to those for whom he worked. Robert O'Connell, for instance, would call his campaign chairman "Mister," whether he thought of him as a Mister or not.

He had been in the business for twenty-five years, and he knew several irrefutable facts. First, in any campaign, the cause mattered not so much as the person asking. O'Connell had seen many instances of well-meaning people, fostering good causes, who got nowhere. On the other hand, he himself had been involved in a number of successful campaigns for charities that were merely an extension of the chairman's or committee's ego.

It was crucial to have people involved who could provide large gifts. To achieve this end, O'Connell had devised a system he felt was foolproof, a system based principally on the leadership and commitment of at least one extremely wealthy and powerful person.

O'Connell's experience further told him that before an institution or foundation could make a final decision to launch a capital campaign, it first had to evaluate the chances of success, based on comprehensive planning, not guess work. For that reason, O'Connell requested that all of his clients undertake a capital campaign planning study. The study was something he had developed over the years, something that other competitors and top fund-raising companies had copied almost verbatim.

O'Connell first insisted that the client, in this case Robert Steincross and his Athletic Achievement Foundation, produce what O'Connell referred to as a summary statement of the case. This was designed to educate potential givers as to the importance of the campaign. The statement included the history and rationale for the campaign. O'Connell wanted the summary statement to be brief but powerful, to demonstrate in compelling terms why a potential giver should cast in his lot with this charity instead of another.

O'Connell next prepared a table of needs with Steincross' assistance. This table broke down each part of the campaign (in this case a particular portion of the building) and affixed an amount to each portion for giving purposes. With Steincross' input, O'Connell established that in order for the actual building to be named in someone's honor, a gift of $4.5 million was required. Lesser amounts would offer a donor name recognition in various parts of the building, ranging from the basketball court to the lavatories;

the sum of these gifts totalled the $13.5 million necessary to build the facility.

The people who could make or break a campaign naturally were those in positions of wealth, and generally those who operated at the highest corporate levels. Not only did they have the personal means, but also the access to company money. It was not at all uncommon for a CEO or President to have at his or her discretion large sums of money for gift-giving, as long as it was in the best interests of the company.

O'Connell carefully reviewed this entire strategy with Steincross. While referring to him as "Mr. Steincross," O'Connell made it clear that he, too, was a professional and knew exactly how to achieve Steincross' goal. O'Connell also made it clear to Steincross that one of the critical aspects of the campaign was for Steincross "to deliver Bill Riley."

O'Connell liked Riley as a prospect for three reasons. He had enormous personal wealth; he had become known as an advocate of sports through the brewery's sports sponsorships, and Riley's position at Gunderson afforded O'Connell the opportunity for getting some of Gunderson's foundation money that was earmarked for gift-giving, particularly in the New York State area.

A luncheon was arranged at a private club where both Steincross and Riley had memberships. O'Connell was ready. The strategy called for Steincross to open up the discussion. Handling his lines well, he offered the usual amenities and then spoke of the importance of an athletic facility for the University and the state.

O'Connell then took over. He pointed out to Riley the unique advantages of this particular program: company name recognition, goodwill and sizeable profits from the exclusive rights to sell beer.

After twenty-five years in the business, O'Connell could easily read the response of a potential giver. Riley had concentrated on his every word, and his facial expressions conveyed more than a casual interest. O'Connell had learned much about Gunderson. He knew that Riley personally oversaw more than $150 million a year in sports marketing sponsorships and that the construction of a building would fall into this category. In addition, he was aware that Riley, through the Gunderson foundation, had access to discretionary giving in excess of $500,000 per year.

Finally, O'Connell understood that whoever had the exclusive rights to sell beer in the facility, even though it would be done through Steincross' new company, stood to make a considerable sum of money. He made it known to Riley that there was a special gift category available, should Riley and Gunderson Brewing be predisposed to the major donation of $4.5 million. In addition, O'Connell pointed out the importance of a major gift-giver also taking a leadership position on the campaign steering committee. Clearly, the $4.5 million was crucial; however, an additional $9 million had to be raised.

"Let me be frank," said O'Connell forcefully. "As much as we need Gunderson's gift, we need your own network of connections. We can't succeed without your personal influence."

Riley had received fund raising pitches before, but never quite as slick as that being presented by O'Connell. After listening to both Steincross and O'Connell, he said, "Let's get to the bottom line. For $4.5 million, regardless of which sources we tap, the building will be named in honor of the company. In addition, we would have the exclusive on beer and you would want me to serve as chairman of the campaign committee. I assume that as chairman it would be my responsibility, with some help from Bob Steincross, to put together a group of other people to come up with the other $9 million?"

O'Connell looked him straight in the eye. "That is exactly correct, Mr. Riley."

Riley leaned back, took a puff on his cigar imported from Cuba, looked first at O'Connell and then at Steincross. "OK," he said, "we're in."

Chapter 15

The signings of Cormack McDonough, Marvin Lewis and Billy Powers sent shock waves through college basketball. Recruiting had evolved into an exacting science. One statistical trend showed that 5-star players tended to choose from the ACC, Big East, Big Ten, Pac Ten, Big Eight, and perhaps one or two other conferences. In some cases, they might select a major independent, such as a Notre Dame or a DePaul. In other cases, they might choose a school close to home. But never (or at least hardly ever) did they choose a school such as State University for no apparent rhyme or reason.

True, Billy Powers' dad was close to Jack McHale, but Lewis and McDonough were a different, more puzzling story. Still, State had always run a clean program, and Jack McHale had a reputation for integrity. While people expressed surprise, no one pointed any fingers. Most observers, particularly those in the coaching fraternity who liked McHale—and they were legion—chalked it up to a job well done by the staff and the fact that a new facility had advanced beyond the rumor stage.

While McHale was basking in his momentary joy, both Brian McCray and Mike Lambert felt a similar sense of fulfillment and relief. After all, recruiting was the primary gauge for measuring the performance of assistant coaches.

McCray and Lambert had come to State with aspirations of becoming head coaches at the Division I college level. Both understood the system. First they had to gain an apprenticeship as an assistant. Such apprenticeship did not come merely for the asking; assistant coaching jobs at Division I colleges were at a premium. When State's basketball fortunes peaked in the '70's, the assistant's slot was considered a plum job. In fact, Jack McHale had sent two other assistants on to head coaching jobs. He possessed many contacts in the business. Under his guidance, an aggressive assistant could advance.

In order to become an assistant coach, candidates needed at least one of two requisites. Either they had to have been Division I stars, or they had to have established a close relationship with a Division I coach who would act as their mentor. Brian McCray, while not a Division I star, had a solid career at State. As a slender, 6'1" sixth man on some of McHale's better teams, McCray acted like a coach on the floor. Based on his understanding of the game and his close relationship with McHale, State followers assumed that McCray would go on to a coaching career. To no one's surprise, McHale hired him as his full-time assistant in 1981.

As a player at State, McCray believed in Jack McHale and his system. Like many others, Brian McCray had no inkling of the impact the Big East would exert on State's fortunes. When that impact hit full force, McCray quickly realized that assistant coaches in losing programs had little opportunity for advancement, and often wound up searching for new jobs. He also saw a great many assistant coaches, now in their mid-thirties, who had traveled from job to job still chasing a dream. Suddenly, they reached a stage where they would apply for any head job that opened, be it a high-level Division I or a low-level Division III.

The "HAVE RESUME, WILL TRAVEL" syndrome was, McCray recognized, the most unsettling part of his profession. After working at State for six years, and being part of two straight losing seasons, he knew that unless things turned around, he either would have to break with McHale and find another school, or leave coaching completely. He would not spend his adult life traveling across the country as a coaching vagabond.

McCray also disliked the constant travel his job entailed. At first, the opportunity to get on a plane with State's credit card, stay in a nice hotel and talk basketball with families was alluring. But it began to wear thin on McCray. He had wed immediately after college. Now the father of two young sons, McCray knew that his marriage was deteriorating. He laid the blame principally on his travel schedule, which put him on the road for virtually six months of the year. It was not unusual for McCray to spend four or five consecutive days away, return home for one night, then hit the road again. If State had been winning, this would have been bearable. But the facts that State was losing, that his career seemed headed nowhere, and that his marriage was failing caused McCray to think long and hard about his future.

McCray did have other options. He had made a good name for himself as a player and established several contacts in the business community through the State Booster Club and alumni organizations. He could even try high school coaching, but that did not especially appeal to him. McCray's position was simple: if the team did not start to reverse its fortunes, he would have to leave the coaching profession. He also knew that once he left, it would be virtually impossible to return.

State's other assistant came from a vastly different background. At the age of seventeen, some called Mike Lambert the best high school basketball player in the country. He had grown up on the streets of New York and had matured, physically, at a very young age. He was leaps and bounds ahead of the players he competed against in high school. In Harlem, Bedford Sty, the Rucker League and all the other places where the "City Game" was played, Mike Lambert became a high school legend. When he graduated from Alexander Hamilton High School in 1974, he was selected player of the year in New York City and named to nearly every high school All American team. He was a blue chipper, one of the most heavily recruited players in the country.

After a recruiting war involving virtually every Division I school, Lambert chose Rutgers. He viewed it as a program on the move, a place where he would easily fit in. The problem that he would face, however, was that he had peaked too early.

Lambert was a 6'4" forward in high school, extremely strong, quick and blessed with a good shooting touch. Three years later as a junior at Rutgers, he found himself confronted with opponents who, while 6'4" in high school and not in possession of Lambert's physical tools, now had grown to 6'7", with the strength to match Lambert's. Mike Lambert, meanwhile, was still the same height, the same size. No matter how hard he tried to adjust his game, he was an inside player. He simply could not make the transition to guard.

While Lambert had a reasonably good career at Rutgers, it was not as fulfilling as he had hoped, or as others had predicted. He led the team in scoring for each of his last three seasons, was named All East, and even carried his team into the final sixteen in the 1978 NCAA tournament. Still, when it came time for the June NBA draft, Mike Lambert, one of the premier high school players in the country only four years earlier, was the 163rd player selected. It had been a shattering experience.

One of the worst things that can happen to a young person is to achieve success early and never fulfill the promise others hold for him. Mike Lambert, once the main man in New York City, had seen players pass by him, while his own promise faded. It was not due to a lack of effort on his part. At age sixteen he had been blessed with the body of a twenty-five year-old; he simply had no more magic, no more improvement to generate from within himself.

Of the many incidents that Lambert had endured because of his perceived lack of accomplishment, one painfully stood out. During the summer prior to his senior year at Rutgers, he was asked by a YMCA Director in a local town to spend a morning working with children on basketball fundamentals. Lambert always looked forward to this type of activity. He enjoyed kids and especially enjoyed the opportunity to teach them the game he loved. On this particular day, seven youngsters from the Y.M.C.A. Youth Program joined him at the gymnasium. At the conclusion of the program, one of the boys, a fourteen-year-old, approached him and said, "I remembered your name as soon as the "Y" Director said you were coming over. Our youth coach always uses you as an example."

"Oh yeah?" replied Lambert quizzically.

"Yeah, he says you're someone we shouldn't be like, someone who could've been great but never worked hard enough."

Lambert never forgot those words.

Then there were the basketball cynics, particularly several writers from New York City, who had been hard on Lambert during his college career. They looked only at the fact that he had been a great high school player who, for some inexplicable reason, had never developed. Some members of the coaching fraternity took the same position as those ignorant writers. Those who were closer, however, saw that Lambert had given it his best shot. He had simply been victimized by an unusually early maturation process.

He was cut by the Phoenix Suns after the first week of rookie camp. His future unsure, he went to see Jack McHale, whom he had known since his high school days. Knowing that good black assistants were crucial cogs in any Division I machine, McHale looked deeper into Lambert's career. When State's black assistant took a head coaching job at a Division II school in the South, McHale decided to take a gamble and bring in Lambert. Although Lambert was young, he was an extremely attractive man, well-spoken and gifted with a radiant smile. McHale figured that Lambert had never gotten a chance to reach the level to which he had aspired as a player, and that he would be hungry to show the world his true mettle.

When Lambert arrived at State, he immediately found himself caught in the whirlwind of two successive NCAA teams. Like McCray, and everyone else connected with State basketball, he had no idea how devastating the Big East would prove to the program. When the team started losing, Lambert sensed that as difficult as it was for a black assistant to become a head coach under any circumstances, it would be next to impossible in a losing program.

Mike Lambert had done his best during his early years as an assistant. His disheartening experience as a college athlete now seemed to be repeating itself in his career as a coach. At times the frustration seemed more than he could handle, and it clearly affected his work habits. McHale even expressed concern. He talked to Lambert at length, but with Ellovitch's new insistence on a constant evaluation of State's basketball staff, McHale had to submit several reports during the year. While guarded as much as possible by McHale, Lambert's decreased work level had been reflected either directly or indirectly in some of McHale's written comments to Ellovitch.

Lambert had never married. His entire focal point in his early twenties had been to recruit hard and learn as much about the game as he possibly could. It was one thing for Brian McCray to see his career evaporate, but for Mike Lambert it was quite another. In no way would his options be comparable.

However, the role that he had played in the signing of the players, particularly Marvin Lewis, represented a fresh start, a recharging of his emotional battery. For the first time in seven or eight years, Lambert began to feel good about himself again. But would it last? Would one more cruel rejection by the sport he loved lead him to succumb to temptation that would taint his life forever?

Chapter 16

Robert O'Connell was delighted but not surprised with the decision of Gunderson and William Riley. He knew that the Gunderson Brewing Company had not made a donation so much as it had made an investment. "Cause marketing," to use corporate terminology, simply made good business sense.

O'Connell was also pleased, because he could now negotiate a significant fee with Robert Steincross. After all, he had been the one to point out the importance of involving Riley and Gunderson Brewing in the campaign. O'Connell had an inkling that his instincts would prove fortuitous and thus held off negotiating an actual contract for himself. He and Steincross had simply agreed that O'Connell would be paid a fee of $10,000 to do an "initial study," after which an actual contract would be negotiated.

Immediately after the meeting with Riley, O'Connell asked Steincross if they could meet briefly in the coffee shop downstairs. He knew Steincross was on a high. O'Connell opened the conversation by summing up the state of the campaign.

"Mr. Steincross, we're now past our initial stage. As we discussed, should the first stage be successful, as it obviously has, the understanding was that I would be retained on a long-term basis. I have drawn up some preliminary calculations on the length of the campaign and the various costs. I thought it might be appropriate for you to look them over."

Steincross, while exultant over the results, was no fool. He did not appreciate the fact that O'Connell wanted to discuss the specifics of a long-term financial relationship only ten minutes after the Riley meeting. But he also realized that O'Connell had done his job. He had identified Riley as the best candidate, and Riley had just forked over $4.5 million.

Steincross looked at the contract. He recalled from his earlier conversations with O'Connell that to perform a campaign such as this the compensation would generally fall into the $150,000 to $175,000 category. He noted that the price had increased; that O'Connell's estimates were for a campaign fee of $400,000. Before he had a chance to react, O'Connell struck first.

"As you know, we need to raise over $13 million. My fee of $400,000 plus expenses is really quite paltry when you consider the goal. In fact, Mr. Steincross, it comes to roughly three percent, which is well within the standards of our association's recommendations."

Steincross nearly laughed. He was aware that the Fund Raisers Association had set forth strict guidelines which opposed the taking of a percentage. Steincross had said to O'Connell in their first meeting that he would almost prefer a percentage because it was a fair indicator of success. He also recognized that by refusing the percentage, it locked the fund raisers into high hourly fees. Doing some quick calculation in his own mind, he estimated that O'Connell would be receiving roughly $1,000 an hour for this campaign. Still, Steincross was a businessman and he knew he had gotten the best in O'Connell.

"OK, Bob, you've got it. How do we proceed from here?"

O'Connell explained that the next step was to organize a steering committee whose function would be to provide some additional seed money to the campaign and, more importantly, to provide names of potential donors.

"Mr. Steincross, it's crucial that you and Mr. Riley meet within the next week or two while we have the momentum in our favor. The purpose of your meeting will be to go over as many names of individuals and companies as possible, all of whom would have the capacity to eventually make a minimum donation of $100,000. In addition, you would want to immediately select ten members to serve on our steering committee who would know of other people who might make six-figure contributions. It's extremely important that their relationship be such that they could ask, with our assistance of course, for the gift. In addition, we would want them to be able to provide an immediate $40,000 gift as part of our seed funding."

"How much, Bob?" Steincross asked warily.

"$40,000, Mr. Steincross."

Steincross recognized that what O'Connell was essentially doing was locking in his own fee of $400,000, assuming that ten people would be secured for the steering committee.

Steincross agreed to get back in touch with Riley immediately, set a meeting, identify the ten members of the Steering Committee, and start to cull lists of people who they knew personally, people who would be able to provide total funding for the building.

* * * * * *

William Riley had not become the CEO of Gunderson Brewery due to any lack of foresight. When the call came from Bob Steincross to set up a meeting, Riley asked Steincross about the nature of the meeting. After he was told it had to do with the multi-purpose sports facility, Riley immediately ordered his staff, including Senior Marketing Executive John Meyers, to assess the deal. He knew that Steincross would be coming to ask for a major contribution for State's proposed arena. He wanted to be prepared.

"John," asked Riley, "If we put the money up, we obviously expect to have exclusive rights for our beer in the facility. So how much would it mean to us on a yearly basis? Secondly, should we provide a lead gift and have our name affixed to the building? What would that be worth to us? Lastly, what about the signage? I know, for example, that we're paying $500,000 a year for our signage at Shea Stadium."

"That's correct, Mr. Riley. The high costs for signage would be $500,000 to $600,000 for the major league sports arenas. At some of the Division I colleges, we pay approximately $80,000 a year."

"That's fine. Let's check that out as well and see exactly what the deal is worth to us. I need this information before Friday."

Meyers gave Riley the raw data he needed. Twenty-four hours before his meeting with Steincross and O'Connell, Riley could see that the deal would be worth plenty to Gunderson. Exclusive rights to beer sales, even with a concessionaire in the middle, would mean approximately $800,000 per year. The Gunderson marketing experts, utilizing a formula which focused on the number of media and visual impressions per year, estimated that the name association from the building was worth anywhere from $3.5 to $4 million. The signage within the building could be worth as much as $300,000 to $400,000 because the arena would attract a number of major events other than just college sports. Riley knew that he was looking at a deal which would not only bring direct revenue, but also some very attractive indirect advertising as well. He would be prepared to go up to a $7.5 million sponsorship. When Steincross and O'Connell had discussed the $4.5 million figure, Riley smiled to himself. Gunderson was getting a steal.

After Steincross and O'Connell left, Riley had called down to Meyers and said, "John, we've gotten the deal for $4.5 million. Let's take ninety percent from advertising and the other ten percent from my discretionary fund over a three year period. Let's make darn sure, however, that I have a little bit left in the discretionary fund. I've got some of these other charities that I have to support, particularly some of my wife's programs." They both laughed.

* * * * * *

Steincross and Riley immediately assembled their group of ten Steering Committee members. They knew that a letter co-signed by both of them would be sure to bring the people to a meeting.

The meeting was called in early December, allowing each person the normal three week-notice accorded chief executives, as long as the invitation came from a peer. The meeting took place in Riley's board room. Caviar, shrimp and other assorted hors d'oeuvres were served, along with several of the Gunderson product lines. When the meeting started, Riley immediately assumed command.

"Gentlemen, we're here to discuss a project important to our state and to our State University. As you all know, we are in dire need of a new athletic facility. Gunderson Brewery believes in this concept and has decided to provide a lead gift of $4.5 million." As Riley had expected, the statement immediately drew the attention of everyone in the room. Riley continued: "This is Bob Steincross' baby and we are pleased to be a part of it. Bob has secured the services of Robert O'Connell. Mr. O'Connell will fill you in on how we hope to proceed."

In his silky smooth manner, O'Connell described the role of the Steering Committee. He neatly slid in the fact that each Steering Committee member would be asked to make a seed gift of $40,000.

"More importantly," he stressed, "your role will be to provide us with entrees to people who can make gifts at the minimum of six figures."

"Why the hell do we have to go through all of this nonsense?" stated the CEO of a major cosmetics company. "With our contacts, we should be able to just make the phone calls and get the money."

O'Connell had expected this. He knew that anytime people of this ilk came together, there was bound to be someone who would perceive the job as easier than it actually was. In anticipation of this, he had told Steincross that it would be his responsibility to address such questions.

"I think I can speak to that," said Steincross. "Certainly all of us have a lot of friends in high places who have the capacity to make these kinds of gifts. However, it has been my experience, and I believe the experience of Bill,"—Riley nodded—"that we need a certain discipline for this campaign. This is why we've hired Robert O'Connell. The methods he uses are time tested. They have proven successful. My feeling is that we've hired an expert. Let's go with his advice." Riley nodded again and so did the Chairman of the Board of Discovery Aluminum, a close friend and supporter of Riley.

As was normally the case in this atmosphere, when two or three leaders gestured in accord, everyone else fell into line. O'Connell breathed a sigh of relief. Though not overly concerned, he knew that one or two people could foul up an entire campaign by thinking they knew more than they actually did.

After O'Connell completed his discussion of the role of the Steering Committee, Riley immediately spoke.

"Well, gentlemen, what do you think? Is everyone in?"

As Riley, Steincross and O'Connell all knew, it would be impossible for anyone to refuse. They all depended on each other for business and favors. When Bill Riley and Bob Steincross asked for something, the other ten people in the room knew that they had little choice but to say yes.

"When and where do we send the checks?" asked Joe Kett of Merrill Lynch.

O'Connell again took the floor and went through the payment procedure as well as the all-important task of providing names. "We would like the names no later than January 10th. Can we all agree on that, and call our next meeting for January 14th? At that time, we'll all review each other's names and pull together what we feel are the top prospects. I will then go see each of them and hopefully ascertain their interest and commitment."

Everyone agreed that this would be the right course. Steincross, Riley and O'Connell all felt that the meeting had gone splendidly. How long this harmony would prevail was entirely another question.

Chapter 17

The recruitment of McDonough, Lewis and Powers had different effects on the people connected with State's basketball fortunes. The current players at State expressed happiness, although several knew their playing time would be cut. Mike Lambert and Brian McCray, both given a lion's share of the credit by Jack McHale, felt relieved. Steve Ellovitch meanwhile had a different, more subdued reaction; this puzzled McHale, but the coach was too preoccupied to give it much thought.

For Jack McHale, the signings accomplished one very important thing. They extended his coaching tenure at State for at least one additional year. McHale recognized that as soon as the three star scholastic players committed, the State followers were ready to switch their focus from the past to the future. Since McHale and his staff were responsible for signing the three players, public opinion held that they be given the opportunity to coach the blue chippers. While McHale recognized that 1988-1989 might end up being a murderous season, with great expectations brought on by the three recruits, at least he now had the opportunity to collect his thoughts. . . and prepare.

McHale had placed himself under great stress for the past seven years, since his last twenty-win season. From the time he had been a sophomore in college, he had thought of nothing else but a coaching career. As practice started for the current campaign, he found himself reconsidering coaching as a profession and his own role within that profession.

When McHale had decided to become a coach, circumstances and conditions were far different. As a player at State, he had grown extremely fond of Red Mihalik and recognized, as did all of Red's players, the wonderful influence Red exerted on the lives of the athletes who came under his tutelage. McHale had seen coaching as a way to stay in the game he loved. He also viewed it as a perfect vehicle to work with and help young people. It seemed the ideal way to spend his life.

Under Mihalik, State's program was a winner. He recruited good kids. While all were not Rhodes scholars, they did reasonably well in the classroom, they graduated and for the most part, went on to successful careers. Much credit accrued to Mihalik. His role in shaping the values and directions of his players was acknowledged by all familiar with the State program. It was not difficult to see why McHale gravitated toward coaching. He never thought much of money. Coaching offered a satisfaction which transcended material considerations.

When Red Mihalik coached at State, his recruiting was done pretty much from his office. There were no elaborate publications on State's basketball fortunes. There were no recruiting strategies set forth at the beginning of each year. Five-Star camp was in its infancy. Players were not called and recalled on the telephone every other night just to say hello.

When McHale started his career and encountered success, changes in the profession were on the horizon. Yet his strong start had not compelled him to reflect on these changes, or on his motives for entering the field in the first place. Because of his early achievement he was, at a young age, properly rewarded both in material gain and in the prestige that accompanied any successful coach in a Division I program.

On the surface, Jack McHale was tough. But the losing, the constant grind of recruiting and the shifting goals of the program, which seemed based more on monetary gain than on any advancement of values, had now become more and more apparent to him. While others gloated over the commitment of the three players, McHale found himself in a state of quiet reflection. What price renewed success?

Having survived many hard campaigns as a head coach, McHale could now look at his schedule and his team, and realistically gauge its potential. His 1987-1988 team was by no means laden with talent. With the euphoria over the three recruits and the deflection of pressure from this season to next, he knew that his team was good enough to play close to .500 basketball. This would avert a disastrous season and allow the State faithful to look forward to 1988-1989.

The 1987-1988 team finished 13-15. Yet the season seemed almost comical at times. The media paid more attention to the game-by-game progress of the recruits still in high school than to State's performance. When Marvin Lewis scored 52 points against Worcester Vocational School, his feat became a headline in the student newspaper. When Cormack McDonough led the Irish Junior National Team to a European 19-and-under championship in Reykjavik, Iceland, the *New York Post* carried a picture of McDonough receiving the most valuable player award trophy with the heading, "The Future Looks Bright."

Even the perquisites, which had been on the decline in McHale's recent years, once again picked up. During the great seasons, McHale had little difficulty making an arrangement with a local auto dealer for the loan of a top-of-the-line car. In the past several years, he found himself driving a Chevy Citation, and that only at the insistent pleas of State's Promotions Director to one of the local dealers. After the signings, McHale received three calls from local auto dealers, all offering expensive, elegant cars in return for advertising in the program. They expressed no interest in the 1987-1988 brochure, but wanted to make certain that the use of the car would result in significant advertising in 1988-1989 advertising campaign. Naturally, they, too, wanted to barter season tickets as part of the deal.

In the late 1970's, McHale generally found himself with three or four speaking engagements a week at the conclusion of each season. In 1986, from March through June, he had only a total of four speaking engagements. Now requests for his speaking increased dramatically.

Other circumstances changed as well. State was now sought by the premier holiday tournaments, ranging from the Great Alaskan Shootout to the Aloha Classic in Hawaii. One tournament, a new one, offered a unique twist. Normally when teams traveled to tournaments, particularly the more prestigious ones, custom held that each receive a significant guarantee to participate, thus covering air fare and hotel costs, while leaving a profit for the school's athletic program. McHale received one query which not only included the customary guarantees to the team and school, but also a special request for McHale to appear as one of the featured speakers at the tournament's luncheon. The speaking fee: $5,000.

McHale had been concerned that one of the future scandals of college basketball would revolve around the sneaker contract dealings of coaches. He himself had been with a particular company for several years. The deal was quite standard. The coach would sign a contract with a sneaker company and receive a fee. In return, he would guarantee that his players wear the sneakers. McHale's fee had been $15,000 per year. Big name coaches received upwards of $100,000 a year for similar contracts. In return, they had to make certain that their players wore the company's sneakers.

McHale often wondered aloud: what would happen if one or two of the players decided not to wear the sneakers? Despite these misgivings, McHale took the money. After his prize recruits committed, he found that he was now being courted by a number of sneaker companies, one of which made a high offer of $40,000 and a guaranteed three-year contract.

Those close to McHale assumed that he would be ecstatic over his change of fortunes. One coaching rival of his said, "Jack, you'll be back where you belong in the profession." McHale's multitude of coaching acquaintances seemed to share that attitude.

Of course, such opinions suggested the fragility of the profession. As much as they professed to love their jobs, and to the extent they felt there was little else they could do professionally, coaches walked a psychological tightrope. For them, the future meant months, not decades. It was not uncommon for coaches to uproot their families every two or three years in search of money, respect and, ironically enough, stability.

McHale felt himself further entrenched in this mercenary world. He found himself questioning the ethics of his profession as he sought to place coaching in a larger context.

He had been a reasonably good student in school, but knowing that coaching would be his profession, he chose not to pay significant attention to his books. In his twenties and early thirties he was the shining star among his classmates, making good money and receiving many accolades for his work. Any time McHale would get together with old schoolmates, the subject of conversation centered not on what they were doing, but on how he and his team were doing.

As he reached his fortieth birthday, he noticed that many of these former classmates were now secure in their own professions, and in many ways had passed McHale. Those interning for small law firms in their twenties were now at the partnership level in their late thirties. While their income and prestige steadily grew, McHale looked at himself and recognized that if he did not produce a successful season soon, he would have to seek new employment. Quite possibly, it would be in a completely new field, one in which he would have to start at the very beginning.

McHale never thought much about power or the power structure. But as he met with old friends and viewed their successes, he also had more opportunity for reflection. He recognized how minuscule was the role of the college coach. Classmates who had looked up to McHale were now making two or three times the money and, more importantly, were in positions of decision-making and influence that would only increase in the years to come.

McHale recalled a player he had spent some time recruiting in the late '70's. The boy was a nice and bright young man, 6'9", with extremely limited skills. However, he was white (McHale knew this was still an important factor with many coaches), a good student and one of the few available big-man prospects in the East that year. For that reason McHale, along with roughly two-hundred other coaches, pursued the young man through normal recruiting procedures. Little did McHale and others know at the time that the boy's mother was an aspiring writer. Several months after the boy enrolled at a university, a major story appeared in *Sports Illustrated*, written by the boy's mother, about the recruiting travails of her son. She portrayed coaching in a most uncomplimentary fashion.

At the time, McHale had little regard for this mother, feeling that she had taken advantage of her son's situation and placed him in an embarrassing position. When the article was printed, he recalled how angry the coaches in question were and how hypocritically they felt the mother had behaved; she had accepted their goodwill and guidance, then performed a hack job on the profession. While McHale had little respect for her or her article, he did recall her saying that coaches were "Willy Lomans in pin-striped suits and tasseled loafers, carrying their briefcases from recruit to recruit, trying to make the sale." McHale found himself thinking about this more and more, and realized that he even agreed with some of the points of the story.

Unlike many of his contemporaries, McHale had been able to manage a stable, supportive home life. He attributed this to his wife. The couple had married the year McHale graduated from State. Sally McHale was a bright, exciting and loving wife whose top priority in a world of changing feminist views was her family. McHale was thankful for this. While he loved his wife and two children dearly, and looked forward to being with them at the end of the day, he was not one who could leave his profession at the office. Had it not been for Sally's strength and wisdom in rearing the kids, he realized that his home life might have been as disastrous as many of his colleagues'.

As the 1987-1988 season wound down, and McHale commenced with recruiting strategies and preparation for 1988-1989, he experienced a sensation that had been previously alien to him. Jack McHale was afraid.

Chapter 18

State's recruiting coup represented a mixed triumph for Steve Ellovitch. The fans, media, alumni and even the President himself all had exhibited great enthusiasm. Yet Ellovitch found himself uncomfortable with the entire scenario. The promised pay-offs to Michael McDonough and Thomas Mahon had placed him in a vulnerable position. His career rested upon the whims of two unstable men. He found himself having more and more difficulty than he had anticipated in coping with the notion of possible exposure.

The persistent praise McHale and his staff received for the successful signings of the three blue chippers also bothered Ellovitch. He had not envisioned the groundswell of support for McHale once the signings became public, and recognized that getting rid of the coach might not be as easy as he had thought. The media and alumni had already made it apparent that the current season possessed little or no meaning. There was a common awareness that it might take a year or two for the recruits to reach full bloom.

Ellovitch thus faced two challenges. First, he had to cover his own tracks; second, he had to continue advancing to his next goal, professional sports management. He needed to encounter success—soon.

Ellovitch had intentionally left several games open for the '88-'89 season, figuring that his plan of buying off two or three blue chippers would prove successful. He left early season contest dates open, hoping to schedule powerhouses in December, since their league play normally started in January.

In the past, the best Ellovitch could have hoped for against the likes of an Indiana, North Carolina or Notre Dame was to get an away game with a large guarantee. Given all of the hoopla of the new recruits, Ellovitch now found that State had become a very marketable team. When he contacted schools in the ACC, Big Ten and Pac Ten, he discovered they were amenable to playing home-and-home. In fact, when an opposing athletic director indicated interest in a home-and-home and even offered to play the first game at State, Ellovitch quickly acknowledged that he did not mind playing a few tough games early on the road. Ellovitch said he was speaking for Coach McHale, and that it would be perfectly acceptable to play home-and-home with the first game being on enemy turf.

One of the concessions Ellovitch had made when he took over the scheduling from McHale was to allow Mike Lambert to assist him. Ellovitch agreed to this because he knew that Lambert would pose no threat to his control of the schedule. It also seemed to appease McHale; it would have seemed suspicious to refuse. While angry about Ellovitch's scheduling takeover, McHale felt that if at least one of his assistants were a part of the process, he would still retain some say.

Ellovitch had little regard for Lambert. He thought of him as a loser, someone who had been endowed with great physical gifts and had never reached his potential. He found it difficult to look at someone like Lambert and not feel a certain degree of contempt.

Another result of the recruiting coup that Ellovitch turned to his advantage was the fact that both Madison Square Garden and the Meadowlands were now expressing interest in State's games. Ellovitch believed he could pacify Lambert by allowing him to meet with both buildings' management teams to discuss possible dates. Thus, Ellovitch could continue creating the schedule while keeping Lambert busy.

Ellovitch finally put together an '88-'89 slate that included fifteen away games and twelve home games. Seven out of the first nine games would be on the road, a murderous task for even a veteran team.

Ellovitch explained to Lambert that this schedule was extremely confidential information until an agreement with one of the two buildings was finalized. Then, and only then, would the information be made public. Ellovitch did not bother to elaborate any further. The less said the better.

During the scheduling process, Ellovitch also opened a new and important door, not only for State's basketball program but, indeed, for his own career: television. The three recruits, combined with the attractive opponents Ellovitch had been able to place on the 1988-89 schedule, afforded him the opportunity to pursue three separate revenue- producing television contracts: local cable for virtually all of State's home games, ESPN for four home games, and last, but by no means least, an arrangement with NBC for a February home game with Nevada-Las Vegas.

Keeping busy with the schedule for '88-'89 allowed Ellovitch to fight off the nagging doubts of his earlier activities. He had understood the full implications of his actions prior to making the financial offer to both Mahon and McDonough. What he had not realized was the effect it would have on him. He found it difficult to sleep, governed as he was by his obsessions. Ellovitch attempted to rationalize his behavior by often reminding himself that if he had not acted this way, State would continue to wallow in mediocrity and that he would never be able to reach his personal goals. But would he cover his tracks?

Ellovitch first had to determine how he would sift the money from the Athletic Department to pay off McDonough and Mahon. This would be relatively simple. State's Athletic Department was audited once a year by a member of the University's business office, whom Ellovitch regarded as little more than "a lightweight." Since State operated mostly on a cash basis, via gate receipts and sale of concessions at games, Ellovitch devised a simple plan that involved the pilfering of small sums of money from each home football and basketball game. He would divert money both from ticket sales and concessions.

State's ticket manager had been with the University for more than thirty years. He was, in Ellovitch's judgment, lax in his work habits. Ellovitch decided that for each home football and basketball game he would have an additional three-hundred tickets printed, all bearing the same ticket numbers of those already in stock. At the conclusion of each home game, before the ticket manager filed his final game report, Ellovitch would simply add the new tickets, replacing those already sold. He would then be in a position to withdraw the equivalent of three-hundred reserve tickets, totalling the sum of $3,000 per game. Another $300-$400 per game could be siphoned from concessions, due to the sloppy handling of inventory by undergraduates, eager to get to their post-game parties.

Although Ellovitch felt this was a satisfactory financial plan, he remained concerned about Mahon and McDonough doing the unpredictable. Ellovitch had little trust for either one. Several things could go wrong. McDonough caused particular concern because of his heavy drinking and loquaciousness in those times of great imbibing. Mahon was also unpredictable. Ellovitch, in one nightmare, envisioned Mahon getting into a fight after one of the State home games and having a wad of cash fall out of his pocket onto the street. Ellovitch decided that before turning over the money to the two, he would have a long and serious discussion with them about the importance of discretion. While he had covered it briefly during his final recruiting pitch, he recognized that in his haste to close the deal with both men, he had neglected to properly emphasize this topic.

Ellovitch also had to protect his administrative turf. He was upset that Robert Steincross and President Pendleton planned the athletic facility without consulting him. He knew that Steincross had little regard for him. He felt, too, that Steincross was anti-Semitic. He also was aware that should this building come to fruition, Steincross' power within the Athletic Department would increase dramatically. Ellovitch realized that this, as well as McHale's resurrected popularity, made it all the more important for him to establish career options.

Of course, Ellovitch had been planning this next course for some time. More influential contacts were all he needed. So he turned his attention to the rental of either Madison Square Garden or the Meadowlands, now that State's bargaining position had strengthened appreciably. He also had his television contacts. He would use these strengths not so much to get State the best rental or TV deal, but to further the career of Steve Ellovitch.

Chapter 19

A s Robert O'Connell had expected, each of the ten Steering Committee members forwarded their "seed money" within seven days of the meeting. Since one of the pieces of O'Connell's large puzzle involved the solicitation of a major gift from one of New York's financial institutions, O'Connell, Riley, and Steincross huddled to discuss which institution would be most likely to make that large donation. O'Connell pointed out to Riley and Steincross that it would be advantageous for the campaign to open an account at the bank which would be the likely candidate for the major gift. O'Connell then prevailed upon Riley and Gunderson to provide $500,000 of their $4.5 million gift immediately for this reason.

He explained to Riley that if he were able to go to that bank which they had chosen as the top prospect with $500,000 from Gunderson, plus the $400,000 seed money provided by each of the ten Steering Committee Members, then a $900,000 deposit would surely gain the attention of the bank's board. Furthermore, O'Connell would be able to offer the bank the opportunity of holding the account on a long-term basis. Given the fact that it could swell well into the millions, even despite periodic payments to O'Connell, architects, contractors and the like, the chosen bank could not walk away from this deal.

The three power-brokers realized that the State Bank of New York was the obvious candidate for the major gift. For starters, State Bank had several Gunderson accounts and Steincross had done some of his banking there. In addition, of the ten Steering Committee members, four had accounts at State Bank. There already was a strong financial connection.

Since a major role of the Steering Committee was to provide names of people of affluence (and influence) who might have interest in making substantial gifts to the building fund, O'Connell visited each member individually and discussed possible candidates. He had extensive experience in these types of "interviews." The first thing he always conveyed to the respondent was that whatever names were discussed would be completely confidential. Each time a name was given, O'Connell would ask a number of questions, the first one being whether this individual was capable of a seven figure gift; if not, a six figure gift. Short of that, a five figure gift would be acceptable. He found that people at the highest corporate levels had an excellent grasp of their contemporaries' personal finances and interests, as well as their personal and corporate giving capabilities. Thus, before the January 14 meeting, O'Connell met with each of the ten members and culled a list of more than one hundred candidates. From this point, the committee would ferret out the top thirty-five to fifty prospects.

Meanwhile, Steincross generally had been pleased with the development of the campaign. He was on the verge of achieving a power coup within the university ranks, and to this end, while keeping President Pendelton informed, he did little else to make him feel part of the overall program.

Despite the fact that the campaign and Steincross' business were both doing extremely well, Steincross' life was by no means a happy one. He found that even with his achievements, he was never satisfied. While this trait had helped him during his rise, he thought that at this point in his life, with success and financial stability intact, he should be able to relax, to enjoy life more. Such was not the case. With each triumph he grew all the more obsessed with seeking a new victory. And he had another problem of late. His gambling, which at one point was a pleasurable avocation, had gotten out of hand. At a Leonard-Hagler fight in Las Vegas, for instance, Steincross wagered and lost $500,000 on Hagler—the largest single bet on the books in Vegas for the fight.

While the campaign was progressing as planned, Steincross found himself increasingly concerned with Riley. Steincross now viewed Riley as little more than a self-righteous phony who had been fortunate enough to latch on to the right person in the course of his elevation to power at Gunderson. Steincross found Riley's holier-than-thou attitude often aggravating.

He also felt that Riley looked down on him. While he himself was attempting to latch onto charities and projects which would enhance his reputation and business contacts, he recognized that Riley had written the book on this subject, that he did things only for his own glorification or that of Gunderson Brewery. While Steincross would be the last person in the world to accuse others of hypocrisy, he nevertheless ascribed this trait to Riley.

O'Connell persistently rode herd on the Steering Committee. When he called the meeting of January 14, his list of donor prospects read like a Who's Who in New York. More important than that was the fact that each member of the Steering Committee had direct contact with every person on the list. Again and again, O'Connell repeated his litany to the Committee: "The cause matters less than the person who asks."

At the January 14 meeting, each person was asked to rank his top three to five potential givers for a committee total of thirty-five to fifty names. At the conclusion of the meeting, O'Connell asked each committee member to make contact with the persons he had named and to set up a meeting with O'Connell. He assumed that of the thirty-five to fifty, a small percentage would decline the meeting, thus bringing the number down to the twenty-five he felt was needed. He would then solicit each individual, armed with an introduction from one of his peers.

The final "interviews" would take three months. The Committee and O'Connell had agreed that on April 15 they would gather again, for practical as well as symbolic reasons. At that time, O'Connell would provide his report and offer his assessment of the campaign's potential.

The Committee promptly entered the Board Room of Gunderson Brewery three months later at 9 a.m. on April 15. After welcoming the Committee, Riley turned the meeting over to O'Connell, much to the annoyance of Steincross, who had hoped to make some introductory remarks. Steincross was beginning to realize that Riley, armed with his lead gift, was attempting to wrest control of the project from him.

It took O'Connell approximately fifteen minutes to describe the interviews he had conducted. "Gentlemen," he concluded, "it would appear from the list of respondents, all personal friends of various individuals in this room, that this campaign has the capacity to raise $25 million." Even Riley gasped.

In tackling this project, O'Connell knew it had the ingredients of success. He had no idea, however, of its magnitude. His candidates had responded in an even more favorable fashion than he had anticipated. Everyone he solicited, it seemed, wanted to follow Gunderson's lead gift and join the team.

Joe Kett of Merrill Lynch summed up the mood of the committee by calling out, "When do we go into the damn ground?" That brought nods of approval and chuckles from around the table.

Steincross, finally seizing the floor, stood up and said, "Gentlemen, this has obviously been a big success. We owe a debt of gratitude to Bill Riley and certainly to Bob O'Connell for their efforts. Also, indeed, to all of you in this room. Let's build the building!"

In eight short months, Steincross, Riley and O'Connell had crafted a successful fund-raising scheme which it had taken the University several years to attempt and fail. The original plan calling for a $13.5 million facility was discarded. Riley, the Gunderson Chief Executive now assuming more and more control, met again with an architect and instructed him to redesign the facility as an $18 million multi-purpose sports arena. The remaining $7 million would be held in escrow and used for administration and maintenance of the building.

On paper, Riley, O'Connell and Steincross shared a major triumph. Steincross, however, felt increasingly uncomfortable with this power triangle. The chip on his shoulder was once again growing heavy.

Chapter 20

When Ted Patterson was a senior at Central Connecticut he met Joan Hart. A year later they married. Both were education majors and Ted set his sights on becoming a guidance counselor someday. With Joan substitute teaching, Ted pursued a master's at Central Connecticut in guidance while working as a full-time science teacher in the Hartford school system. Two years later, with his new degree in hand, Patterson was promoted to guidance counselor. With Joan now home raising the kids and Ted's officiating career on the rise, those early years were happy times. The couple bought a home in Newington, on the outskirts of Hartford. Ted's salary as a guidance counselor and his supplemental income from officiating provided enough for a comfortable life style for his family.

In 1980, with their oldest son Todd ready for school, the Pattersons began thinking about the opportunities they wanted for their two boys. Not happy with the public school system in their town, they sent Todd to a Catholic elementary school. This added an extra expense of $1,200 a year and for the first time compelled Ted Patterson to think about new job opportunities.

In 1982, Patterson and his wife were looking at the Sunday *Hartford Courant* and noticed an ad which read, "Franchise Opportunity, own your own travel agency." They called the toll-free number in New York City.

It was one of the largest travel agencies in the country, one that was now franchising on a nationwide basis. The cost per franchise was $10,000 and the deal was simple. The buyer would purchase the franchise and the well-known "Creamer Travel" name.

Ted and Joan Patterson had been able to save some money and had invested it in a small apartment in Hartford. They calculated their net worth at $120,000. The Creamer people, in marketing their franchises, wanted a minimum net worth of $75,000 plus the $10,000 in cash, as well as a line of credit of $25,000 in order to open an office. There were other parameters set forth by Creamer, which included at least two people working full-time on the business, an office with a toll-free number, and participation in the three-month training program that would certify them as travel agents.

After some long, hard thinking and a very big gulp, Ted and Joan Patterson decided to invest the $10,000 and open the agency. It would mean major changes in their lives. Ted resigned his secure position as guidance counselor. Joan, with both children in school, would leave home and work alongside Ted, thus meeting one of the most important criteria in the franchising deal.

If things went reasonably well, they could be netting an income of approximately $50,000 within two to three years. In addition, the agency would give Ted more opportunity for travel in his expanding role as a college basketball official. He was now his own boss, and with the reduced travel costs afforded travel agents, Ted would have greater flexibility and thus more income from officiating, It all seemed to make sense.

The Creamer President was candid in telling the Pattersons that it might take them a year or two to start earning decent money. "One of the keys to success will be an aggressive pursuit of corporate accounts in the Greater Hartford area," he told them. "This should present some real opportunities, with all the insurance companies, but it will be up to the two of you to make your pitch and get the business."

The Pattersons decided from the outset to run a first class operation. They invested heavily in state-of-the-art equipment, including a computerized line, recommended by Creamer, that linked them into every major airline in the United States. They had quick and easy access to all travel schedules of all airlines and were able to fully service their customers. While things went slowly at first, the business soon began to grow. Their first year, 1983, had been moderately successful and while the Pattersons showed a net profit of approximately $21,000, the agency had blossomed to the point where their bank felt comfortable continuing to finance the operation through 1984. And 1984 showed continued growth, as Ted and Joan acquired more and more accounts with the Hartford corporate sector.

By December of 1985, Ted and Joan Patterson decided that the 1986 season would be spent concentrating their efforts more on the foreign market. As Ted pointed out, "We stand to almost double our gross dollars by getting involved in some of these overseas travel programs. With the dollar rate being what it is in Europe, we'd be crazy not to take advantage of it."

In January 1986, the Patterson Agency invested in several overseas charter opportunities. This was a simple matter. The agency would put up a certain amount of money to buy in with several other agencies in chartering flights to Europe. This group of agencies would, in effect, own the flights. They would market the flights in-house and also work side deals with other travel agents around the country. By doing this, they were obviously exposing themselves to the possibility of loss; in order for this venture to be profitable, the planes had to be approximately eighty percent of capacity. However, the Pattersons learned that for the last three years every charter of this type had been full. Not only that, it appeared the dollar would be even stronger in Europe in the summer of '86.

At the time they made this decision, the Pattersons thought nothing of the trouble then brewing abroad, particularly in Europe and the Middle

East. In late February of 1986, three people were killed in a terrorist bombing at the Rome airport. Two weeks later another terrorist attack killed five Americans at the DeGaulle Airport in Paris. At the time of these killings, the Patterson's charter venture was proceeding smoothly, with almost sixty percent of capacity sold and four months remaining.

As more terrorist bombings ensued, a panic came over American travelers. The *New York Times*, *USA Today*, *Time* and *Newsweek* all ran headline stories talking about the perils of travel. By mid-April of 1986, more than half of Patterson's charter customers had cancelled their flights, with virtually no new bookings coming in. By May, it was apparent to the Pattersons that they were facing a major loss and perhaps full cancellation of the charter program. In June, at a meeting in New York, the partner travel agencies all agreed that they could no longer run the program, now that the flights were barely ten percent full. The other four agencies, while far better established than the Pattersons, were facing a difficult financial loss. For the Pattersons, the loss would be devastating.

Ted Patterson had all he could do to keep his mind on basketball. His day-to-day routine included calling the bank to make sure that no checks had bounced, calling the airlines to see if credit could be reestablished and then trying desperately to find new banks that would finance his business after a $150,000 loss due to the defunct charter program.

At the end of the '86-'87 basketball season—by far Patterson's best—he met with his lawyer and his accountant. The meeting followed increasingly tense times with his wife and months of negotiations with his creditors. Joan, loyal to her husband but ill-equipped to handle such financial burdens, was reduced to tears almost every day at the office.

When she and Ted had started the business, Joan served as the bookkeeper, secretary, receptionist and jack-of-all-trades, tasks she handled with efficiency. As the financial losses increased, the pressure had an almost numbing effect on her. She could not perform her functions at work, had difficulty sleeping and was taking out her frustrations on Ted and the boys.

In April of 1987, Patterson met again with his lawyer and accountant; they told him what he already knew was obvious: "Ted, you'll have to file for Chapter 11. You are bankrupt."

Chapter 21

The signings of Lewis, McDonough and Powers renewed Mike Lambert's dream of becoming a Division I head coach.

Still, Lambert was a realist. When he had entered coaching in 1979, black head coaches were still few and far between in Division I. But he saw a shift in the balance of power. As black athletes became more and more prevalent in the 1960's and 1970's, white head coaches recognized that an aggressive black assistant was a key component in recruiting. George Raveling was the forerunner of the successful black assistant. Raveling, with Jack Kraft at Villanova and then Lefty Driesell at Maryland, had performed wonders as a hard working, aggressive recruiter who would beat the bushes nationally for the best players. By the late 1970's, virtually every Division I program had at least one black assistant.

Since Lambert's roots as an athlete and coach were in the New York and New Jersey area, he hoped to remain in the East. Lambert had been keeping his eyes focused on New Jersey State University, which went Division I in 1981. In making that commitment, the administration had also committed significant dollars. The school not only hired a head coach and two full-time assistants, but their budget for recruiting was almost equal to that of some Big East teams. In addition, in order to promote the program, they had retained a public relations firm. It was not uncommon to see a glitzy New Jersey State ad campaign on television pitching season tickets. Included in the marketing plan were frequent rental of the Meadowlands Arena and the addition of concert acts to perform after the games in order to sell more tickets. The entire idea worked beautifully, except for one problem. After six years, the team was still not winning. So it was no surprise to Lambert when word leaked in late February that the head coach and his staff were being fired.

The job at New Jersey State was one which Lambert had privately coveted for some time. It was on his turf. It was a program that clearly possessed national aspirations, and one that would no doubt recognize the worth of an aggressive young black head coach who could tap into the considerable market of talent in New York and New Jersey. Also, this new job would give Lambert a chance to put behind him for good the unfair reputation he had acquired in his career at Rutgers.

The pursuit of a head coaching position at the Division I level involved a myriad of factors which needed merging into one overall game plan. As the famed coach Al McGuire had said (and demonstrated), one such factor was the acquisition of a "Rabbi." McGuire's career, first at Belmont Abbey in North Carolina and then at Marquette, was helped considerably by the influence of his former college coach, Frank McGuire. "Coaching pedigree" had become an oft-used expression, but it took on real meaning when examining many of the successful Division I coaches throughout the country. As Al McGuire often pointed out, "If you don't have a Rabbi, or at least a great reputation as a former player, forget it."

The examples were endless. Dean Smith of North Carolina was a substitute on a national championship team at Kansas under the legendary Phog Allen. It was Allen who helped him get his start as an assistant coach at North Carolina under Frank McGuire. Indiana's Bobby Knight had been sixth man on a national championship team at Ohio State under Fred Taylor. Bobby Cremins of Georgia Tech was another Frank McGuire protégé. Denny Crum had been both a player and an assistant under John Wooden of UCLA. The list went on and on. In Lambert's own back yard, it had been Red Mihalik who had helped Jack McHale become a head coach at the age of twenty-six. Lambert's Rabbi was McHale.

New Jersey State University had formed a Search Committee. Lambert tried to find out as much as he possibly could about the job and, indeed, the school. He called the New Jersey State Admissions Office for a catalogue. He then called as many people he knew who had any kind of relationship with Jersey State to ask about the school, the program and, most importantly, about the President and the Athletic Director. He researched the backgrounds of the people on the Search Committee and found that only one was black. He accurately concluded that the job would come down to a decision by the President and, to a lesser extent, by the Athletic Director.

Lambert's competition would include virtually every Division I assistant drawn from successful teams around the United States. This would mean that the coaches' mentor program would be in full swing. Bobby Knight could have a candidate; if not his own assistant, then someone close to him. The same would be true of Dean Smith, John Thompson and the other heavyweights of college coaching. Lambert knew that McHale did not exercise such clout in the eyes of either the public or college administrators. But with the proximity of State University of New York to New Jersey State U, McHale's solid reputation among his contemporaries, and the stir created by the recruitment of the three blue chippers, Lambert felt that McHale's influence would be helpful. He sought McHale's advice.

"Realistically, Mike, I think you've got a shot. A lot of people will be pushing for this job and when that's the case just about anything can happen. My influence may not be as strong as a Knight's or a Smith's, but on the other hand, I don't think I'll hurt you," McHale said.

Lambert had always liked this about McHale. No matter what the situation, he found McHale to be straightforward and realistic about his own role.

"We need to work on getting someone close to the school, hopefully someone of influence, maybe a big donor or member of the Board of Trustees, to back you. That, along with our recruiting victory will probably get you an interview. After that, it'll be pretty much up to you."

Satisfied with McHale's assessment, Lambert immediately sought someone of influence connected with State. He found that person almost immediately. Robert Gilmartin was a highly successful lawyer and senior partner of Gilmartin, Bowers and Smith in Newark, New Jersey. He also was a heavy donor to New Jersey State and a member of their Board. Most importantly, however, Bob Gilmartin's son, Scott, had been manager of the Rutgers team during Lambert's college career. Lambert had a good relationship with Scott Gilmartin. He always found Scott to be empathetic with his plight as a player. He soon called his college friend.

"Scotty, about this New Jersey State job; it's one that I want to go for. I think that I might have a shot at it. Do you think your Dad might help me?"

"Mike, I honestly don't know what his position is about the job, but I can certainly ask."

Two days later, the young Gilmartin got back to Lambert. "Mike, my Dad will see you. He's not making any promises, but he's willing to talk it over."

Lambert quickly set up an appointment with Bob Gilmartin. In preparation, he refined his résumé and sought the input of others. One person whose help he knew he had to solicit, however distasteful, was Steve Ellovitch. Surprisingly, he found Ellovitch quite receptive to the idea. As with everything else Ellovitch did, Lambert felt that he had ulterior motives. Lambert knew that Ellovitch had no respect for him and perhaps saw this as a way to get him out of the program. In any event, Ellovitch indicated that he would write a strong recommendation to the New Jersey State Athletic Director. When Lambert received the blind carbon copy, he was pleased and quite surprised with the strength of Ellovitch's support.

Lambert met with Gilmartin on March 16. Gilmartin's office was located in a high-rise complex in Newark. Lavishly decorated, it spoke to his considerable success as one of New Jersey's leading attorneys. As a college athlete, Lambert had known Gilmartin slightly, and only as Scott's father. He had seemed pleasant enough during their brief encounters years earlier. Researching before the interview, Lambert discovered that the senior Gilmartin had done a great deal for State, not only as a contributor and member of its Board, but also as a legal representative, performing some of State's work *pro bono*. For this, Gilmartin could no doubt cull favors from the University when needed.

"Mike, it's been a long time although I've certainly followed your career with interest," said Gilmartin, then coming right to the point.

"Let's talk about this job. How can I help?"

Lambert explained that his work as a recruiter and his close observation of McHale's system had primed him for a top job in Division I. Gilmartin asked pointed questions, many of which were related to State's lack of success in recent years. Lambert was ready with good responses, alluding primarily to the steamrolling effect of the Big East.

Gilmartin was satisfied with Lambert's answers. "I'll be happy to call the President and recommend that the Committee talk with you about the position," he said at the end of the meeting.

Lambert left elated. Five days later, he received a phone call from the New Jersey State Athletic Director.

"Mike, we've looked at a host of candidates and are now at a point of interviewing the ones we feel are the cream of the crop. I'm happy to inform you that we'd like to have you come in for an interview with our search committee on Saturday, March 28."

This would be Lambert's first real shot at a head position. He had applied for others in the past, but had never even come close to getting an interview. He wanted to make certain that he left nothing to chance. He conducted even more research on each of the members of the committee and also, with McHale, studied a "worst case scenario."

"Coach, what would be the toughest questions they could ask me?"

McHale responded by touching on areas such as State's decline and Lambert's lack of head coaching experience. He delicately broached another issue: the fact that Lambert never achieved the stardom predicted for him as a player.

"Mike, it's an issue they may raise and you're going to have to be prepared to deal with it."

"I'll deal with it," said Lambert as he tensed in his chair.

The interview took place in the President's board room, and although the President was not present, Lambert had not expected him to be at this initial meeting. Lambert felt prepared and relaxed.

The Athletic Director broke the ice by asking Lambert, "Mike, perhaps you could share with the committee why you feel qualified for this job."

Lambert's response led to a series of other questions. The interview lasted about an hour and forty-five minutes. When it was over, the Athletic Director walked Lambert to his car.

"We're glad you came in, Mike, and appreciated the way you handled the questions. We'll get back to you."

Lambert felt good about the interview. He had answered the questions directly and effectively; his reading of body language told him that most of the committee members were comfortable with his responses. Only the Athletic Director concerned him. There seemed to be something there that Lambert could not quite identify. Then again, perhaps he was misreading the signals.

One week later, while attending the NCAA Final Four, Lambert received a message to call the New Jersey State Athletic Director immediately.

Lambert felt his stomach churn. He knew that the Athletic Director's call would tell him either that he had advanced to the final choices, or that he had been eliminated from consideration. With some trepidation, he made the call.

"Hi, this is Mike Lambert. I'm out at the Final Four and I understand you've been trying to reach me."

"Thanks for calling back, Mike. The committee met with ten candidates and we now have it down to three. You're one of the final three. We'd like to get together with you next weekend."

"Name the time and place and I'll be there."

At the Final Four, coaches spoke of little else other than jobs and recruiting. No more than fifteen minutes after Lambert had hung up, everyone he met knew he was a finalist at New Jersey State.

Lambert found out that his two competitors were a long-time assistant to Bobby Knight and a highly successful Division II coach. Both were formidable opponents, both white.

It was one of Lambert's admitted difficulties that he overreacted to situations, becoming too high after a success and too low after a failure. He kept telling himself that this would not be the case with the New Jersey job, that just to get to the final three was an accomplishment. In his heart, however, he wanted it more than he had wanted anything else in his life. This was not only his chance to become a Division I head coach but, moreover, it was his chance to prove to many people the stuff of which Mike Lambert was really made.

The final interview would consist first of another question-and- answer session with the search committee, then a conversation with the President. Lambert again rehearsed with Jack McHale.

The interview lasted approximately two-and-a-half hours. All of the members of the committee seemed pleasant, although the Athletic Director's questions were more pointed than the others and directed not only to Lambert's lack of experience as a head coach, but also to his willingness to "pay the price." Lambert knew exactly what the Athletic Director was alluding to, but he felt that he handled himself effectively. After the interview, he was ushered into the President's office. The President first spoke with Lambert in general terms, but then made the importance of this position quite clear.

"Mike, what we are looking for is a leader. A guy that can come in here, get this turned around, and do it in such a way that will reflect positively on our institution."

Lambert responded to the point by making known his commitment to young people and education, as well as his burning desire to succeed as a head coach.

"I've had ups and downs like everyone else, but I've always hung in there. This is a job that I've always felt was perfect for me. If I'm fortunate enough to get it, I won't let you down," Lambert said, staring directly into the President's eyes.

Mike Lambert left the President's office feeling he had done all he could.

The waiting game was the most excruciating part of the pursuit of a college coaching job. The Athletic Director had told Lambert that the committee wanted to make its decision promptly, as precious recruiting days were being lost. The call would come no later than Wednesday. Lambert got little sleep in the following days. He made a number of phone calls to find out if anyone had heard any news, or if any last-minute strategies should be employed. McHale gave what Lambert felt to be the best advice: "You've done about all you can. Anything more now might be overkill."

The call from the Athletic Director finally came. Ten seconds into the conversation, Lambert knew the result. The Athletic Director started by saying how difficult it was to hire someone in this situation. Lambert could feel his heart sink down to his stomach. As the conversation went on, the Athletic Director made it clear that the Division II coach had gotten the job, but that Lambert had comported himself well, "despite a few minor problems." Lambert could not resist asking what those problems were.

"Mike, to be honest with you, you certainly have come a long way. But there is a lingering doubt that you're not the kind of guy who can perform up to his abilities."

Lambert had been forever dogged by this perception, but to hear it spoken in such direct terms was a crushing blow. He had labored long and hard to overcome such opinions, and the people closest to him recognized that it was an unfair label affixed by those who neither knew nor cared much about him. Lambert left his office without saying a word to anyone and went to his apartment.

He did not show up at the office on Thursday or Friday and had great difficulty sleeping. McHale tried to reach him, but all he got was Lambert's phone recording. Lambert felt as low as he had ever remembered, even lower than the depths he experienced at Rutgers when he read in the paper that he was a guy with big-time ability and small-time motivation.

Lambert desperately needed to reverse his flagging fortunes. He thought of George DiOrgio, a fraternity brother of his at Rutgers who had gone on to become one of the leading rock promoters in the United States. His territory was principally New York and New Jersey. DiOrgio, a person Lambert thought would do practically anything in order to succeed, had recently offered a temptation to Lambert that the assistant coach had been resisting. But at the age of twenty-nine, Mike Lambert had a net worth of about $5,000, no wife, no family and $500 in the bank. He felt his resistance fading.

Out of despair more than anything else, Lambert picked up the phone. "George, about that conversation we had—I'm ready to sit down."

Chapter 22

Jack McHale's freshest challenge was to keep a close eye on his prize recruits. In college basketball, once a blue chip recruit had been signed, the operative term became "baby-sitting." The role of a head coach and his staff had evolved into one of keeping a watchful eye over the recruit without becoming burdensome to the recruit or his family. Although the NCAA letter of intent bound a player to a school, not all Division I schools would abide by the letter. Even those which did had been known from time to time to try to sway a young man's decision. McHale and his staff had to make certain that the three prize recruits were both content and insulated from outside temptation. If any inkling of an illegal offer from another school came to the fore, State would be ready to react by confronting the offending institution and reporting it to the NCAA.

McHale assigned Mike Lambert to baby-sit Marvin Lewis and Brian McCray to do the same with Cormack McDonough and Billy Powers. It was the job of Lambert and McCray to attend as many of the recruits' games as possible, and to stay in touch (via phone) with them, their parents, as well as their coach.

"Kids have a tendency to question their decision," McHale emphasized to his two assistants. "We constantly have to reinforce the fact that their decision to come to State was the right one. Don't lose contact with them for more than a day at a time. Let them know that we want them as badly now as we did when they agreed to come."

All three players had outstanding senior years. Lewis led his team to its second consecutive state championship, defeating Cambridge Rindge and Latin in the finals at the Centrum in Worcester before 13,000 people. Lewis scored 36 points and hauled down 21 rebounds in the final game, typical of his play all year.

Powers, his confidence buoyed by the attention he had received for signing along with Lewis and McDonough, got better with each game. His team advanced to the semi-finals of the New York City tournament, and while beaten in a close game by Archbishop Molloy, Powers played one of the outstanding games in his high school career, scoring 28 points and dishing out 17 assists. The college recruiters who had once labeled him as a 3-star now recognized how well he would mesh with the other blue-chippers coming to State. Those same recruiters were now calling Powers a 4+.

Cormack McDonough did not play for a school team. As was customary in Ireland and most European countries, he performed for his club team, GlenEagle of Killarney. McDonough was not only the youngest player on GlenEagle, but also the youngest player in all of Ireland in Division I basketball. The Division I league in Ireland consisted of ten teams, including two teams from Northern Ireland. Each team was allowed two American players. This was the norm throughout Europe. Playing for Division I GlenEagle provided Cormack with the toughest daily competition available, thus softening the major concern other coaches held for him.

The club system in Ireland was like that in all of Europe. The club solicited the best players from a certain area of the country and typically featured a Division I team, with lower level teams for the younger players. The faster a player matured, the quicker his opportunity to advance to the Division I level. McDonough was clearly an exception, however, in making the team at the age of seventeen. In Ireland, and indeed throughout Europe, a player would usually not advance to a Division I team until at least the age of nineteen or twenty.

McDonough performed well for GlenEagle. He led the team in scoring and finished second in rebounds and third in assists. Most importantly, his body started to mature. Since the European game was very physical, it became obvious that his increased strength (one of his father's major athletic gifts) stood him in good stead for the nightly pounding he received. GlenEagle reached the final four of Ireland, losing to Annadale of Belfast, 107-104 in the semi-finals. McDonough scored 36 points in that game. He gained acclaim in Ireland and throughout Europe. As for U.S. college basketball, he was labeled a "can't miss" prospect.

Both Lambert and McCray were on the phone almost daily with the three recruits. Lambert attended eighteen of Marvin Lewis' twenty-one games, McCray attended seventeen of Powers' games and flew to Ireland for the final four competition to watch McDonough. At the conclusion of the season, Powers was selected to play in a number of all-star games which McCray attended. Lewis, because of his growing reputation and outstanding season, was asked to play in the McDonald's Classic at the Capitol Center in Landover, Maryland.

The McDonald's Classic featured a game between an all-star team drawn from across the nation and an all-star team from the Washington, D.C. area. Lewis was selected as one of the top twelve players throughout the United States, a tremendous honor and one which clearly placed him among the elite high school players in the country.

Played in April, the game was always a sellout at D.C.'s Capitol Center. Since 1986 it had been shown on ABC's Wide World of Sports. McHale knew that if ever there was a time in which Lewis might be tempted by opposing coaches, it would be during the Classic. The NCAA, because of past problems with high school all-star games, and with the unethical recruiting practices used by schools during these games, had placed strong restrictions on the post-season play. Players were now allowed to compete in only two such games at the end of the senior season.

Another source of anxiety to McHale was Thomas Mahon. The more McHale saw of him, the more concerned he became about the impact Mahon exerted on his son's life. He resolved to keep an eye on Mahon during the Classic and to be particularly watchful of any contacts the father might have with other schools.

McHale and his staff landed in Washington on Wednesday afternoon, at approximately the same time the flights of the athletes arrived. While NCAA regulations prohibited State from transporting Lewis from the airport to the hotel, McHale made arrangements to greet Lewis at the airport and take a taxi that would follow the team bus to the hotel. From that point on to the end of the Classic, McHale and his staff charted out an assignment sheet which assured coverage of Lewis morning, noon and night. Thankfully, practices went off smoothly for Marvin Lewis. At no time did any of the coaches see any bumps or illegal inducements.

On many occasions, coaches would attend an all-star game with great hope for a prize recruit. Then, ten minutes into the game, the coach would realize that the recruit was not all he had been touted to be. At summer camps, and particularly during a high school season, it was often difficult to accurately gauge a recruit's true talent. Defense was sometimes lax; also, zones were employed, thus negating the opportunity to carefully observe a player's one-on-one offensive abilities. In addition, an outstanding player seldom encountered competition that was even remotely close to what he would experience in college.

Because of this, McHale and his staff watched Lewis with a keen eye during the practices, and particularly during the game. Playing against the nation's cream, Lewis did not disappoint them. In the practices he was the most dominating player for the USA All-Stars. During the game, he scored 21 points and grabbed 16 rebounds in only twenty-two minutes of play. Team USA defeated Washington, D.C., 96-92 and Marvin Lewis was named MVP. State University, mired in mediocrity for the past six years, had recruited the most valuable player of the McDonald's Classic! Who would have thought it? A few months ago, perhaps not even Jack McHale.

McHale did have difficulty shadowing Thomas Mahon. While McHale could not say, "Thomas, I'm here to keep an eye on you," he did want Mahon to recognize that this was a time in which temptation would be at its peak. For hours at a time McHale had absolutely no idea where Mahon was, or, most importantly, whose company he kept. It seemed as if Mahon were hiding something. Still, the practices and games had gone well. There was no obvious reason to be concerned.

At the conclusion of the Irish basketball season, Cormack McDonough was selected to play for an all-European side in a post-season tournament in Prague, Czechoslovakia. The competition would pit the All-European 19-and-Under's team against the Soviet National 19-and-Under team and two 19-and-Under All-Star teams from Czechoslovakia, Team Sparta of Prague and Zilina representing Slovakia. McHale, upon learning that Cormack McDonough had made the team, initially did not feel it necessary to send McCray to the tournament. McCray had recently returned from his trip to Ireland and told McHale, "He's solid, Coach. There's no way we're going to lose him."

McHale, however, recalled other bizarre incidents. Perhaps during the tournament, a representative of another European team, in Italy or Spain, might approach Cormack McDonough and try to make a deal for his services. As McHale said to McCray, "Brian, if Real Madrid, or Torino of Italy approaches the kid and waves $50,000 in front of him, you never know what he might do. As expensive as it is, I think you'd better go to Prague."

McCray had not realized the difficulty of fulfilling McHale's order. While he had a passport, the trip to Prague also required a visa and an explanation to the Czech Embassy as to why the visa was needed. After countless calls to the Embassy and some last minute assistance from one of New York's Senators, McCray received both the passport and a lesson in Eastern bloc bureaucracy.

McCray's flight, connecting through Dusseldorf Airport in West Germany, took ten hours. When he arrived at the Ruzyn International Airport in Prague, the Czech Basketball Federation President was waiting with a sign bearing McCray's name and a picture of a basketball.

"Mr. McCray, we are pleased you are here. It is not often that we have American basketball people visit our country. I hope your appetite for discussion is a large one," he said.

From the airport, the Czech Basketball President proceeded down Lenin Boulevard to a bridge passing over the Vltava River and onto the Inter Continental Hotel. During the ride, he apprised McCray of the growth of basketball in Czechoslovakia and reflected on the small but strong ties with the USA.

"In 1972 your great star, Bob Cousy, visited us. It was just at the end of his tenure as coach at Boston College. He spent two weeks here showing us a great deal about the Celtics' fast break and also about a double stack offense that he used at Boston College. You will still find that offense being quite prominent in this tournament, as well as a number of other things Cousy taught us.

"Since his departure in 1972, we have not had that many coaches come. But please be assured that any time one is in our country, that our coaches and players will, how do you say, 'pick your brains.'" McCray and his host both laughed.

The accommodations at the Inter Continental Hotel were better than

McCray had expected. His trip to Ireland had been his first abroad; Czechoslovakia was far different. It was, as he wrote in a postcard to his wife, "like being in the seventeenth or eighteenth century. The people seem content but not overly happy."

After he had rested, McCray walked alone for about an hour on the streets of Prague, first through Parisian Street, then straight to Wenceslas Square. The first thing he noticed in the Square was a big red star atop the administration building. On the flight over he had done a bit of reading on Czechoslovakia and learned that in 1968 Soviet tanks had driven up the street on which he now stood, in violent response to Czechoslavia's new attempt at liberation. From the Square, he headed back to the Inter Continental Hotel, stopping at a roadside stand to purchase a klobasa, the Czech version of an American hot dog.

While McCray found Prague interesting and its people friendly (they smiled at him, saying in broken English, "American, American."), he was there on business. When he returned from his walk, he immediately went about locating Cormack McDonough.

As was the case in many Eastern bloc countries, playing arenas were often adjacent to dormitory-style living quarters for the athletes. The tournament, dubbed the "Prague Junior Festival," was played at the Motol Sport "bubble" facility in Southwest Prague. The Czech Basketball President, who could not have been more hospitable, picked up McCray at the hotel at 4:30 p.m. and drove him to the facility. When they arrived, McCray excused himself from the President, explaining that he would like to say hello to McDonough and make certain that things were going well for the young Irishman.

"No problem, Brian. I have read enough of American basketball to know how important recruiting is."

McCray circled the arena and came upon the dormitory. He was pointed in the direction of the third floor where the European Juniors were staying. As he approached one of the rooms, he overheard the familiar voice of Cormack McDonough. He knocked on the open door. Cormack wheeled around and smiled from ear to ear.

"Coach, am I glad to see you. As they say, this might be a nice place to visit but . . . ."

The room was old and small, but clean and comfortable. McDonough told McCray how scary the entire situation had been. "I've been to other European countries to play, but never to an Eastern bloc country. When we got off the plane and I saw the soldiers standing at the platform with guns, my knees quivered. It took us an hour to get through customs. But once we cleared customs and met the basketball people, things seemed to get right."

McCray certainly agreed with him. "Cormack, I find that wherever I go, people united by a common interest—in our case basketball—are able to communicate."

McCray immediately sensed that McDonough was still firm in his commitment to State and flattered that McCray would come all the way to Prague to watch him play. And play he did. The Soviet Junior team featured the best 19-and-under players in all of the Soviet Union. While the two Czech teams were weaker, both possessed several skilled players, thus providing a good test for Cormack. He responded to the challenge. The tournament was a round robin format. The European Juniors handily defeated team Zilina in the first round and they went on to defeat Sparta, setting up a meeting with the Russians in the finals. The Russians measured 6'10", 6'10" and 6'9" across the forward line. They played the standard type of international basketball, very rigid and controlled and they executed flawlessly.

It was an interesting game, one which showed Brian McCray in no uncertain terms how good McDonough would be. He not only played with great skill, but also exuded confidence. It was truly a thrill to view this blossoming player. In the finals, McDonough scored 38 points, had 21 rebounds and 12 assists. When McCray was finally able to get a call through from his Inter Continental Hotel room to Jack McHale, he literally gushed with enthusiasm.

"Coach, the kid was terrific, by far the best player on the court, and that includes the Russian team. We've got ourselves a real comer. Without question he's committed to us."

This pleased McHale, of course. Schools with even higher profiles and greater success than his had lost recruits after they originally committed. With State's star threesome, it looked as if things were going to be fine. Clearly, there would be a lot of work to do, especially in terms of building up their bodies and preparing them for the grind of Division I basketball. There was no doubt, however, that the three players were as good as advertised. In fact, it was obvious now to McHale that they might even be better—not that he was about to tell anyone.

Chapter 23

Steve Ellovitch received Jack McHale's reports, in accordance with his earlier mandate for constant communication on recruiting. He was pleased to see how well the recruits had played in the post-season all-star games. Still, he found himself agitated. The worrying was in no way lessened when he received a phone call from Thomas Mahon.

"Mr. Ellovitch, I've just come from the McDonald's Classic. I imagine you heard how well my boy did."

"I did hear, Thomas," said Ellovitch sternly. "By the way, I told you if we had to talk, to call me at my home."

"Well, Mr. Ellovitch, I do remember you saying that, but the more I've been thinking, the more I think we may have to sit down and talk a bit more."

Ellovitch could feel the blood rising to his head. He knew exactly where Mahon was headed. It was clear from his lifestyle that Mahon could be influenced. Obviously, one or more teams had waved money in his face in Washington, D.C. His call to Ellovitch was an attempt to try and up the ante.

"Thomas, the terms we discussed were agreed upon by both sides. I don't know what else we have to talk about."

"Well, Mr. Ellovitch," Mahon said, becoming a bit testy, "there's an old saying, 'No deal is final until the ink dries.' My son showed that he is probably the top player in the United States. I think we may have a bit of renegotiating to do. You know where to reach me. I wouldn't wait too long."

Mahon abruptly hung up the phone. The call did not surprise Ellovitch, but he was extremely concerned by the tone of Mahon's voice. Mahon obviously understood the value of his son to other college basketball programs. He was prepared to do whatever it took to get as much money as he could for Marvin's services. Steve Ellovitch had been worrying for good reason.

Chapter 24

"I'd like to speak with Bill Riley."

"May I ask who's calling?" the receptionist asked.

"This is Bob Steincross."

"Mr. Steincross...could you hold for a moment?" Steincross sat with the phone against his ear. He felt himself become increasingly tense and angry. Two minutes later, Riley's personal secretary came on the line. "Mr. Steincross, I'm awfully sorry. Mr. Riley is in conference and he'll have to get back to you."

"This is the third time I've called in the last two weeks. Would you tell Mr. Riley that I want to hear from him today?"

Since that Steering Committee meeting when the group finalized its fundraising goals for State's facility, Steincross had developed real enmity for Riley. He had suspected before the meeting that Riley, in making the lead gift and in assisting with the securing of other funds, was taking a more visible role in the building project. Those suspicions were hardened when Riley took control of the meeting and paid Steincross only scant attention. After Robert O'Connell had reported his $25 million goal to the Board, Steincross had approached Riley on the way out.

"Bill, I think we ought to get together."

Riley looked back at Steincross and said offhandedly, "Oh, certainly Bob. Just call my secretary and she can set something up." Riley then immediately turned away from Steincross and headed to the elevator, leaving Steincross standing at the doorway alone.

Since becoming a man of wealth and influence in his late twenties, Steincross' dealings with corporate heads like Riley had been primarily social. Steincross had observed Riley in a number of situations and recognized his callous disregard for anyone whom he perceived as an underling. Yet, prior to the building campaign, Steincross had felt that Riley thought of him as a peer. Riley's recent conduct, however, left Steincross humiliated and angry.

Riley, meanwhile, always made certain that he was perceived by any who met him as a captain of industry. His lifestyle reflected it. He and his wife, Kara, their twin daughters, their son Sean and a nanny lived in a co-op on Fifth Avenue replete with marble floors, fireplaced bedrooms, oak mouldings, and a garden terrace with a panoramic view of the City and Central Park. Their country home, a thirteen bedroom estate located on twenty-six acres in Brewster, New York, served as the Riley's place of refuge on weekends. Kara Riley, in the words of a close family friend, "had literally been dragged through life by her husband." Basically a shy and retiring person, she constantly grappled with the role into which she had been thrust, that of the wife of one America's most powerful businessmen.

Bill Riley was hardly a devoted family man, and he rarely spoke of his daughters. But he exhibited an almost overbearing affection for his son. Sean Riley was, by any standard, nothing more than an ordinary kid. He was a C student at the Westchester Country Day School and an average athlete. But his father refused to see the boy's mediocrity. In any conversation with Bill Riley, the subject of his son was almost sure to come up, along with the glowing reports. "Despite the fact that I'm his father," Riley would chortle, "he's a great kid in all respects, respectful of others, a terrific athlete."

Riley was obsessed with his son becoming something that, in all probability, he had neither the wish nor the ability to become. One particular aberration of Riley's was thinking of his son as an outstanding basketball player. Sean Riley was 5'11", 155 pounds, and had been a slow, sixth man on the Westchester Country Day School team. That was before senior Riley, in a private meeting with the Headmaster, had the head coach removed and a new coach brought in who would "understand the game better and also understand Sean's capabilities more." This was the case in virtually every facet of Sean's life. If Sean did not find success in a particular project, Bill Riley would step in and use his influence, money, or both, to make things right.

Aside from this obsessive devotion to his son, Riley maintained a superficially loving relationship with his wife and two daughters. While his corporate upbringing demanded that he maintain the facade of a strong family bond, in reality, he had fallen out of love with his wife many years before. He found her boring and burdensome. As for his two daughters, they reminded him too much of his wife to generate any degree of affection. He thus sought refuge in his work, his discreet philandering, his son and in his so-called philanthropy.

Bill Riley's principal interests in philanthropy were based on his own self-promotion and the promotion of his company. He recognized that corporate causes were always self-serving, that few companies gave out of sheer benevolence. This was the case in any of Riley's ventures, State's facility included.

Associates had privately expressed concern over Riley's ego, now becoming less and less in control. "Bill has all the money and power. His next move in life is to become a celebrity," those who knew him said, in one form or another. True enough, Riley remembered reading an article on the late actor John Houseman, who achieved celebrity status in the final years of his life. "I had money and other niceties," Riley recalled Houseman writing, "But being a celebrity is something quite unique. A celebrity is pampered, treated differently, looked upon differently."

Indeed, Riley had as much power and wealth as virtually any corporate officer in America. However, he was not as famous as he wished. Recently he sent this memo to the Gunderson public relations firm:

> I think it would be a good idea, as in the case of Lee Iacocca, to get a person connected with the company more in line with our advertising campaign. I do not think Brad Gunderson would be comfortable with it. Although I've no real interest in seeing myself on television all the time, I would like you to gear up our next campaign using me as the focal point.

* * * * * *

Steincross had seen something of himself in Riley: an aggressive, all-consuming person who sought as much power, wealth and (in Riley's case) fame as he could garner. He realized that Riley's wealth far exceeded his and, more importantly, so did his power. Riley's position as the head of a corporation with more than 25,000 employees placed him on a different level from Steincross.

One week after Steincross placed his third call to Riley's secretary, he received a call from a Dan O'Leary of Gunderson Brewery. Steincross knew O'Leary. As with many companies, the Chief Executive Officer designated a younger subordinate to serve as his "Administrative Assistant," a glorified lackey. O'Leary played this role at Gunderson; he was twenty-nine years old and not terribly bright, but in awe of Riley. Steincross was all the more angry when he picked up the phone and heard O'Leary's voice rather than Riley's.

"Bob, things have been very busy over here at the Brewery. I know you've been trying to get hold of Bill. I'm calling to let you know that he will be able to see you right after Wednesday's press conference."

"What press conference are you talking about?"

"Gee, Bob, I thought you knew. We're holding the press conference to announce the building campaign next Wednesday at 10 a.m. at the Waldorf."

"What the hell do you mean you're holding the press conference next Wednesday? Why wasn't I informed of this?"

"Bob, my marching orders are simply to call and let you know that Bill will meet with you next Wednesday right after the press conference in the Gunderson suite."

"Take your goddamn marching orders and stuff them," Steincross screamed into the phone.

He was livid. To him, O'Leary was an arrogant know-nothing whose relatively small influence stemmed from Riley having taken him under his wing. It was a known fact that Riley hired O'Leary, a former collegiate basketball star, not only to serve as his aide but also to tutor his son.

After O'Leary's call, Steincross immediately had his secretary get State University's President Pendelton on the line. "What the hell is going on with this press conference?" he screeched at Pendelton.

"Bob, it seems as if Bill Riley has decided that next Wednesday is the date we are going to make this announcement. I honestly thought you'd been notified."

"Like hell I'd been notified. This was done deliberately by Riley. In case you've forgotten, this whole concept was mine. You know damn well what my role has been. After this press conference, I want you in on the meeting with Riley."

"I'm not sure that would be possible, Bob. Maybe after you've cooled down a bit, we can discuss this further."

As Steincross hung up the phone, the message became all the more obvious: Riley and Gunderson Brewery, not Bob Steincross, now controlled the building campaign.

Steincross had undertaken this project to establish as much hold as he could over the athletic program of State University. But he had another, more pragmatic reason. In constructing the legal document, Steincross had instructed his attorney to set up a new corporation under New York State Statute. As part of the overall agreement, Steincross told his lawyer to effect a contract between this corporation, whose sole stockholder would be Robert Steincross, and the "Athletic Achievement Foundation." The agreement was designed to provide this corporation with exclusive concession rights to the building. While Gunderson would have the right to sell their product, the product could be sold only through the concessionaire.

Significant revenue would be secured by anyone who controlled the concessions of this arena. Steincross' net worth had taken a beating as of late, not due to any lack of success of his various enterprises, but instead to his increasing appetite for gambling.

Until recently, Steincross had been able to keep this problem under check and relatively quiet. Gambling debts were getting out of hand, however. He not only had to tighten the reins on his habit, but also replenish the loss in his net worth. Owning the concession rights to State's facility would go a long way toward solving these dilemmas.

The press conference that following Wednesday was typically Gunderson. The public relations firm which had served Gunderson for so many years had designed it to highlight Gunderson's participation in the project. As Steincross walked into the Grand Ballroom at the Waldorf, it seemed as if all he could see were the banners carrying the Gunderson name.

"Mr. Steincross, we're so pleased you could join us," said a young lady bearing the name tag of the PR firm. "You will be seated right in the front row along with the other committee members."

Steincross glared at her. "Do you mean I will not be on the dais?"

"Mr. Steincross, all I know is that I was told that you were to sit in the front row with other Steering Committee members." At this point, Steincross' eyes met those of Riley, who was standing on the other side of the Ballroom. Steincross immediately walked toward him, but Riley turned away from Steincross and proceeded to the dais. He ordered one of his aides who would serve as Master of Ceremonies to get the meeting underway.

If there had been any room left for additional hostility in Robert Steincross, it was quickly filled in the next fifteen minutes. While each member of the Steering Committee was introduced, almost all of the credit for this "...wonderful and important undertaking..." was bestowed on Gunderson and principally upon its chief executive, William Riley. Riley was the last to speak. As always, he read from a prepared text. Citing "Gunderson's commitment to youth and athletics," Riley said, "...this is indeed a great day for our company, for State University, and for the State of New York."

Riley concluded his speech by saying, "Lastly, I'd like to give my thanks to Bill Farragher and the Farragher Concessions Company. As you may know, Bill and his fine company have a long association with Gunderson. They will be making a $750,000 donation to the Building Fund." Steincross could not believe his ears.

As the press conference broke up, Steincross stormed over to Dan O'Leary and said, "I'll be in the suite waiting for him." Twenty minutes later Riley arrived. Steincross lunged out of the chair. "What the hell is going on?" he screamed. "Who are you to introduce some concessionaire that I didn't even know about?" Steincross was clearly out of control. "You know damn well that the concessions are my deal. It's part of the original agreement."

President Pendelton had accompanied Riley into the suite. Riley turned to him and said, "Dr. Pendelton, do you know about this agreement?"

Pendelton, not willing to have his eyes meet Steincross, looked down and said, "No, Bill, I do not."

Steincross lunged toward Riley, his face red with fury. He was intercepted by the Chief of Security of Gunderson Brewery.

Riley now glowered at Steincross, "This project is the project of Gunderson Brewery. It's our company that's putting in a great deal of the money. It's our company that got other people to put their money up. If you have any role in this, it will be the role we choose for you or no role at all. And, by the way, if you think our company or the State University will be embarrassed by some gambling crazy lunatic, you've got another thing coming."

Steincross shot back a glare at Riley that was almost chilling. Even Riley, toughened to difficult situations, was taken aback.

"You'll regret this, Riley. Believe me, you'll regret this," Steincross hissed, as the security officer shoved him out the door.

In Room 1212, immediately adjacent to William Riley's executive suite,

New York Star reporter John Massey scribbled his notes furiously. "Holy shit!" Massey said to himself.

Chapter 25

At first Steve Ellovitch declined to meet with Thomas Mahon, but as his wariness increased, he decided to adhere to Mahon's mandate. Ellovitch knew that while he was not in a position of strength, he still had cut a deal with Mahon. Marvin Lewis had committed to State in a well-publicized decision. He knew Mahon was smart enough to recognize that a change would cause suspicion. He intended to make this clear to Mahon; his position was not as weak as it seemed.

"Thomas, this is Steve Ellovitch. I've thought over our conversation and decided to meet with you. But I'm not certain how much can be accomplished." Mahon, who had been drinking, seemed a bit dazed.

"Well, Mr. Ellovitch, I want only the best for my son. Let's get together and talk this matter out." They agreed to meet the following weekend at a restaurant approximately twenty miles away from the State campus, a bistro which would attract little attention.

Ellovitch now knew that Mahon had a firm grasp of the financial implications of a big-time basketball program. In traveling to the meeting, he tried to prepare himself for Mahon's demands.

Although their meeting had been set for 6:30, Ellovitch decided to take advantage of the fact that Mahon was not at peak performance after a couple of drinks. So he showed up at 7 p.m., figuring that Mahon would not be thinking clearly.

"It's so nice to see you," Mahon said. "I can't tell you how I appreciate an important man like yourself taking time to meet me." Mahon spoke again of the great pride he took both in Marvin's accomplishments and the renewal of their family ties.

Finally, Ellovitch leaned forward and said, "Thomas, let's get to the point of the meeting. You and I had a deal. This is a highly difficult situation for me to begin with. It's not that easy to get money for these kinds of things."

Mahon, who appeared disoriented during the early stage of the conversation, all of a sudden became clear-eyed and lucid. "Mr. Ellovitch, when we spoke in November, my son was not considered to be the best senior high school player in all of the USA. He is considered that now, and you and I both know that that means a lot of interest on the part of other colleges."

"That may be true," Ellovitch countered, "but you and I also know that if Marvin were to have a change of heart, that a lot of questions would be asked."

"Questions will be asked no matter what my son does," Mahon fired back. "I want the best for him. I've always wanted the best for me and my family."

Ellovitch could stand it no more. "Let's cut the family crap, Thomas. You know damn well the family has nothing to do with it."

In taking this aggressive tack, Ellovitch knew he was at risk, but he also knew that he could not over the next four years be placed in the untenable position of having Thomas Mahon call him to ask for an increase in the financial arrangement every time Marvin scored 30 points.

"All right," Mahon replied, "if you want to be direct, then I'll be direct too. We had agreed on a number for each year, along with a percentage for NCAA appearances. The new number, if you want my son, is $150,000, paid in equal installments over four years."

"Are you crazy?" an incredulous Ellovitch asked. "There is no way that I can get that kind of money, and you know it."

"Mr. Ellovitch, I'm only talking about a sum of money that's been waved in my face by more than one of your competitors. Either you come up with it, or my son goes elsewhere."

Ellovitch was taken aback by the numbers as well as Mahon's steely-eyed resolve. There was no room for negotiation. He also knew that losing Marvin Lewis, after all of the hoopla of his McDonald's play, would be disastrous for State's athletic program and his own career.

"What's to assure me that if we do agree on this number that you won't come back to me next year asking for more?"

"You have my word, Mr. Ellovitch."

"Your word is worth shit," Ellovitch snarled. "But you're exactly right. I probably don't have much of a choice. Let me tell you something, though. I'm going to go with this number and I'm also going to spend as much time as I can thinking. . .thinking that if you should come back to me asking for more, how I can screw you in no uncertain terms."

"At least we know where we both stand," replied Mahon. "When do I get my first check?"

"First, I told you last fall that you won't get a check; it will be cash; secondly, you'll get it the day your son shows up on campus as a registered freshman. Is that it, Thomas?"

"That's it, Mr. Ellovitch. Again, I want to thank —"

"Thomas, save the b.s. for someone else. You and I both know what we are. You'll have your money. Don't come back for any more."

As Ellovitch walked to his car he felt his knees weaken. He had gotten himself into a situation which could only worsen. Yet there was no escaping. On the drive back to State, two questions plagued him. How was he going to sift that kind of money out of the athletic coffers? And how would he make certain that no similar renegotiation took place with Michael McDonough?

Chapter 26

With the anticipated surge of interest in State's basketball program, the existing 3,400 seat arena could in no way handle the school's immediate aspirations. Yet the new facility would not be ready until at least the junior year of the incoming star recruits. So Steve Ellovitch initiated contact with both Madison Square Garden and the Meadowlands as possible sites for a good number of State's home games for the next two seasons.

The two arenas had both made public commitments to bring back college basketball to the New York area. While the Big East had helped, it was really only St. John's that drew large crowds in greater New York City. In the '40's and '50's, the Garden had been the focal point of college basketball. Management in both arenas wanted to revive those "Golden Days." When they learned that Jack McHale had several prize recruits matriculating, their interest in State intensified.

Ellovitch's deal with Thomas Mahon compelled him to proceed at an almost frantic rate to complete the scheduling. After all, Ellovitch needed commitments from big time opponents to meet the illegal payoffs to his avaricious patriarchs.

Ellovitch also believed that State was now in a position to consider hosting its own Christmas tournament. Particularly in recent years, State had found itself traveling at Christmas to places far away, such as Hawaii or Florida, seeking warm locations and the best guarantees possible. In order to host a Christmas tournament, a school had to offer high guarantees and a quality arena. Ellovitch realized that State now met both of those requirements and, most importantly, could solicit corporate sponsorship for the tournament.

Ellovitch knew that Robert Steincross had initiated a relationship with Gunderson Brewery which would lead to the construction of the building. Thus, Gunderson might be the ideal candidate to sponsor a big-time Christmas tournament in 1990. With this in mind, Ellovitch called Steincross and got his usual curt response: "If you want to talk with Gunderson, that's up to you. Just don't do anything that would get in the way of our building." The best Ellovitch could do was extract the name of the Director of Sports Promotions for Gunderson. He called the Director at Gunderson and arranged a meeting.

"We sponsor a host of events, Steve," the Director said. "The motto of our department is that we'll look at anything that'll sell beer. I know you've got some good recruits coming in and I also know that Bill Riley has taken a real interest in this Building Fund. What are you thinking of?"

"We'd like to start the tournament for Christmas '90, playing either at the Garden or Meadowlands, then move it to the new facility when it's ready," said Ellovitch. "I think I can bring in three top level teams. We'll need a corporate sponsor, though, to cover the guarantees, which should run approximately $30,000 per team."

"What about gate receipts?" replied the Director. "Wouldn't this income offset expenses?"

"It would," said Ellovitch, "but frankly we feel we're in a position, with the type of players we have coming in, to elicit this kind of sponsorship for a big time Christmas tournament, particularly with two years of preparation. We would keep the gate receipts. You would have sponsor recognition on the entire event."

Ellovitch continued, "We'd also like to have you look at next year's home game package with a view toward some television buys. I'm setting up a TV network for State games. We'll need the support of a major sponsor like Gunderson to do this."

"To be honest with you, Steve, we've never laid out this kind of money for a college basketball tournament. On the other hand, the New York market is an important one to us. I'll pass the TV idea on to our Director of Communications. Also, let me talk over the tournament with my staff and we'll get back to you."

"I appreciate it, but I would also appreciate hearing from you within the next couple of weeks as we've got a couple of other companies interested," Ellovitch answered.

Ellovitch was lying. He had contacted no other companies. But Gunderson Brewery represented his best chance. So he followed the common strategy of asking for the moon. If he did not get it, there were always other businesses to tap.

Two weeks later, Ellovitch received a call from the Director of Promotions. "We've looked at both proposals," he said. "The TV buys are set and as long as you can get the three teams you said, we're in on the tournament as well."

Ellovitch was delighted. It was the first good thing that had happened to him in weeks. He immediately picked up the phone and called the Athletic Directors of UCLA, Brigham Young and Oklahoma.

"I've just talked with the people at Gunderson," he told them. "They've agreed to sponsor us and we're in a position to provide the kind of guarantees we spoke of. Are you in?" All three schools, knowing the importance of playing in the New York Metropolitan area, readily agreed to enter the tournament.

Ellovitch spent the remainder of the spring finalizing the schedule, which he announced at a mid-May press conference. Of the twenty-seven games set for 1988-89, fifteen would be on the road, twelve at home. The schedule included the likes of Michigan State, Notre Dame, Nevada Las Vegas and some tough early season games on the road.

Meanwhile Mike Lambert, despite his assignment to work with Ellovitch on scheduling, had played a minimal role in the negotiations. Still depressed over his failure to get the New Jersey State job, he became increasingly disenchanted with his current position at State. Yet, he remained loyal to McHale and kept him posted as the schedule evolved.

"Coach," he warned McHale, "this guy is digging a hole for us and you better do something about it."

"Mike, I don't know what I can do," McHale replied. "If we can get through next year, we should be a real good team by '90." But in his own mind, McHale knew that Ellovitch had committed too much too fast.

Lambert continued to battle himself. Four weeks prior to the public presentation of State's schedule, he received a copy of it from Ellovitch with the tentative dates for the Garden and Meadowlands penciled in. Lambert knew that Ellovitch had still not made any final arrangements with either building, hoping to play one off the other in his negotiations. Lambert also knew that Ellovitch had committed to opponents who, because of their conference affiliations, would have little flexibility in the movement of dates. Lambert suspected that this could be a critical mistake.

Chapter 27

A t first, the notion of code names like Slater and Hondo seemed right out of a grade B movie. But the more the idea evolved, the more they realized they must, at all costs, keep their names completely confidential.

If they could pull it off, they stood to make a small fortune. Before reaching any final decision on a definite plan, they had to do their homework. They looked into every sport where large dollars were wagered, and ended up focusing on three: boxing, basketball and football. They eliminated boxing because of its shadowy past and many investigations by state commissions. Football was ruled out because its complexities would undercut their intentions. No, basketball was the most logical choice.

Having decided on basketball, they proceeded to their research phase. They studied the game inside and out, looked at films, read books, delved into the history of the sport; in short, they became experts. The key was to decide which piece of the puzzle best suited their goal. The first and most obvious area: the players. But they decided against that.

They remembered vividly the tales that included gamblers who had lost almost as much as they had made. The scandals in the '50's and '60's typically involved a player who was supposed to dump the game. Too often, he was either unable to do it, or was pulled out of the game by his coach for poor play. This same scenario had occurred in the early '80's at Boston College. Large bets were laid on BC games, but the players were not able to pull it off, and so the gamblers ended up losing. Some even wound up in prison.

Coaches represented the next possibility, since few if any meaningful attempts had been made to lure them. But it all came down to money. Had they broached this idea in the '50's or '60's, a coach might well have been their target. In those days coaches were making paltry sums. Now, any respected Division I coach earned well into six figures. To risk it all, dumping a few games for dollars, did not make sense.

The last option: referees. This appeared to be practical for several reasons. Referees exerted enormous control over the outcome of games. Also, at no time in the history of the game had a referee been suspected of foul play. This was not to suggest that it never happened, but in their research they could not find even so much as a rumor of a referee intentionally dumping a game. Finally, referees came from all walks of life and all socio-economic backgrounds. As a rule of thumb, they needed the income.

When they chose basketball, they also chose their code nicknames, Slater and Hondo. Slater was for Slater Martin, a tough little guard of the Minneapolis Lakers and St. Louis Hawks in the '40's and '50's; Hondo was for John Havlicek, the Boston Celtic great of the '60's and '70's. Both made a pact that in any discussion related to their scam, the only names to be used were their code names.

When they decided to study referees, Hondo handled the research. He first contacted the ECAC Conference Headquarters in Hyannis, Massachusetts. He had been tipped off that the ECAC offices had the names and addresses of every college basketball official on the East Coast. He expected some resistance when calling to ask for the list; he had his excuse ready.

"Sir, normally we do not give the list out," replied the receptionist, who sounded like a summer intern.

"Well," replied Hondo, "I'm doing post-graduate study at Boston College on college athletics. Part of my study involves basketball officials. The list would be a great help."

"Oh, you're at Boston College?" responded the receptionist. "I go there too. I'm a junior in political science."

"Political science?" he responded, "I hear it's a terrific program. Isn't Dr. Jenka the head of the Department?"

"In fact she is," responded the receptionist, now a good deal more accommodating.

"Actually, my work is in the MBA program."

"Oh, I hear that's really a tough program."

"Yeah, it is. You would think they'd at least give us a little time off in the summer," Hondo laughed.

"Well, since you're a BC person, I guess I'll help you out," she said.

Hondo was not surprised at her response. He had made it his practice to be prepared. The information about her being a BC student had been obtained by his calling the previous week and asking the secretary of the executive director if they had a summer intern program. The secretary responded without hesitation and went on to tell Hondo about the two students and how they were chosen. He waited five days, called back and received the response he had hoped for.

"I'll send it along today. Where would you like it to go?" the intern said.

Hondo gave her a fake name and a post office box in Chestnut Hill, Massachusetts, where he had paid $10 for six month use of the post office box.

Once the list arrived, the next step would be simple. Slater, a successful businessman, was able to run a credit check on the 146 names. Because of the sophistication of his computer equipment, he was even able to run the check despite the fact that he did not have social security numbers. The names and their addresses were fed into the computer, which had the capability of scanning social security numbers. The credit check was available in a matter of twenty-four hours.

The game plan they set was simple but brilliant. They would identify one referee in dire financial straits. They would make a deal with him. The program would start in December. Normally, a referee would handle three games a week; they would ask him to dump only one game a week. In December they would make certain that the games were non-league and not televised, thus guaranteeing minimal interest and exposure. They would bet small sums of money.

They did this for two reasons. First, to make sure that the referee would be able to control the outcome; secondly, since December betting traditionally proved much smaller than January, February and March, when league and tournament games were played, they did not want to draw special attention with large wagering in December.

By January, they would know whether or not the referee could handle the assignment. If he proved he could, they would gradually increase the size of their bets, laying them off in different betting houses throughout the country in nominal sums. The total, however, would be significant. Again, they would limit their bets to one game a week in January.

They knew it was imperative that neither the coaches nor the supervisor of officials begin to question the referee. It was not unusual for a referee to have one bad game in every three or four. They felt if they could get a high-level official, he could cover his tracks in those odd games in which they did not employ him. By February, they would increase their bets still more, but the big payoff would be March, during the post-season tournaments and NCAA's. As long as all went well, they calculated that even if they lost one out of every three games, they would still end up with a profit in excess of a million dollars. This included payment to the official of $5,000 a game. Now all they needed was the right person.

The computer, with absolute efficiency, spit out eleven of the 146 names as persons with poor credit ratings. Once the eleven names were secured, Slater's job was to run a check on them as to their officiating ability and the likelihood of their working important games, including the all-important NCAA tournament. It would provide Slater and Hondo with the opportunity to lay large wagers that would be untraceable, since betting on college basketball games increased tenfold throughout the country once the NCAA tournament rolled around. No one would ever suspect anything.

Slater narrowed the list to three candidates. He then presented it to Hondo, who fed more data into the computer and discussed each name in greater detail with Slater.

In the end, there was only one obvious choice: Ted Patterson.

Chapter 28

As a teenager, Mike Lambert had looked into the crystal ball of life and saw a professional basketball career and large dollar signs. Now, at age twenty-eight, all of those dreams had evaporated. He began to realize that his emotional devastation stemmed in large part from trying to please others, trying to live up to their unrealistic expectations. The time had come for Lambert to act in his own best interests.

Lambert never liked Steve Ellovitch, who was the self-centered prototype of avarice and ambition. Lambert knew that Ellovitch's strong recommendation to New Jersey State was probably based more on Ellovitch's wish to get rid of him than on any loyalty or belief in Lambert's abilities. He also knew (and he told Jack McHale of this) that Ellovitch's scheduling owed more to self-promotion than the welfare of the basketball program. That McHale did not respond more aggressively to those concerns was disturbing to Lambert. But that was McHale, ever the company man.

Lambert surmised that Ellovitch had made one crucial mistake in planning the schedule. Ellovitch was dealing primarily with teams which belonged to conferences. They had little flexibility in scheduling outside games. Ellovitch had made certain commitments (in writing) to these teams without getting a final commitment on dates from the Garden or Meadowlands. Both arenas were aggressively pursuing State's schedule. However, Ellovitch, gloating in his newly-found power, admitted to Lambert that he had decided to play one off the other.

"What we'll do is get the teams lined up and then go to the Garden and the Meadowlands, present the schedule, and cut the best deal for State. With the way the Knicks and Nets are drawing, and the demise of the NIT, both arenas are chomping at the bit to get us." Ellovitch was brash in saying this, but he was also correct. State was hot property.

* * * * * *

George DiOrgio had known Mike Lambert since the two were undergraduate students at Rutgers. DiOrgio was not an athlete, but he always harbored a great love of college basketball. His profession was music. As a college student he had achieved considerable success in managing two bands. This led him into the promotion business. At the age of twenty-three, he began promoting rock concerts in various Eastern cities. By the age of twenty-six, he was considered one of the leading rock promoters in the country.

DiOrgio was based in New York City. He had not achieved so much so quickly by being meek. The rock concert promotion business was often an unsavory, cut-throat enterprise. The established promoters, to ensure continued success, had to stake out their own territories and zealously protect them. This included developing close ties with arenas in those territories. These links in turn necessitated cooperation from both the administrators of the arenas as well as the unions who, in large part, controlled the operation of the arenas. When a promoter found any encroachment on his territory, he had to react as aggressively as possible.

While having no legal basis, and usually in complete defiance of anti-trust laws, promoters challenged each other on this issue of territorial violation. If the raiding competitor sought to promote an event on foreign turf, the incumbent promoter would often resort to other more extreme measures, such as using his clout with the building administrators or unions to stop the aspiring promoter. DiOrgio was no stranger to this type of activity.

Big-time promoters had the ability to curry favors with people in high places. DiOrgio promoted some of the biggest concerts in the East. Big concerts brought sell-outs. DiOrgio, as part of his agreement with the building, always held anywhere from 150 to 200 of the best tickets for his top concerts for private sale. Unlike other promoters, DiOrgio never became involved with the scalping business. But he made good use of those prime tickets, making them available to union leaders, politicians and city officials, corporate heads and even the arena administrators who, due to the guidelines set forth by the town fathers, often had less access to tickets than the promoter.

DiOrgio also excelled at creating a relationship with the bands and their agents. Again, he felt no reluctance to offer favors. He spoke the musicians' language and possessed the willingness to become subservient to every whim of the rock stars. If a star wanted a limo with caviar and Dom Perignon in the back seat upon arrival at the airport, DiOrgio provided it. If a licentious diversion was requested, he provided it as well.

Rock stars and agents needed a promoter they could depend on in each arena, if for no other reason than to reduce the amount of time spent on the things they found distasteful, such as hotel arrangements, airport pickups and negotiating arena deals. DiOrgio was more than willing to take care of this business. By mastering such activities, he had become the principal rock n' roll promoter in New York and New Jersey. His fee per concert was generally about fifteen percent of gross, or an average of $30,000.

As a New York native, DiOrgio had grown up a fan of State University. Like other fans, he suffered through the losing seasons and reacted with enthusiasm at the commitments to State of Cormack McDonough, Marvin Lewis and Billy Powers.

While an undergraduate at Rutgers, DiOrgio had made it a point to attend virtually all the home games. He liked Lambert and empathized with his plight. He knew how deeply Lambert had been hurt by the "unfulfilled potential" label placed on him. When Lambert became an assistant to Jack McHale, DiOrgio contacted him for reasons of business potential as well as friendship. During Lambert's tenure as assistant at State, he often called DiOrgio for tickets to concerts. DiOrgio happily obliged, and in the process the two became even closer than during their college days.

When news of the three prize recruits was announced, DiOrgio phoned Lambert and invited him to lunch at the 21 Club in New York. This was DiOrgio's normal *modus operandi*. He dined at the best clubs and always travelled first class. It was something that Lambert admired about him. When they met for lunch, the conversation centered mostly around State's basketball fortunes and how happy DiOrgio had been to learn of the signings of the blue chippers.

Toward the end of the luncheon, DiOrgio leaned forward in his chair, looked Lambert in the eye and said, "Mike, you know there might be a way for both of us to make a bit of money on what is sure to be a lot of success for State basketball with the great talent coming in."

Lambert looked at DiOrgio quizzically. In all the time he had known DiOrgio, it was DiOrgio who did Lambert the favors, never asking for anything in return, save a couple of complimentary tickets to State games, which, as everyone knew, were not exactly at a premium.

"What exactly do you mean, George?" asked Lambert.

DiOrgio explained that his areas of New York and New Jersey included extensive business dealings with both Madison Square Garden and the Meadowlands. He knew both arenas were making a concerted effort to package State's home games.

"This is not something I'm guessing on, Mike," DiOrgio said. "I've talked to insiders from both places."

Lambert still had no idea where DiOrgio was going, but DiOrgio quickly made his point known. "Mike, I know that you have a part in the scheduling. What I'm saying, and obviously it can't be repeated to anyone, is that knowledge of who State will be playing and when the games will be played could be extremely valuable information."

"How do you mean?" asked Lambert, becoming uncomfortable with the direction of the conversation. DiOrgio explained that what he wanted from Lambert was advance notice of who State was playing. He would then go to the arenas and put "holds" on the various dates, telling the arenas that he planned to book major concerts. If DiOrgio's guess proved to be accurate—that Ellovitch would make agreements with the teams before finalizing the dates with the two arenas—then Ellovitch would have to come to

DiOrgio for the dates. In order to get the dates, DiOrgio would present Ellovitch two options: first, a buy-out in which State would have to pay DiOrgio a certain amount of money to release the dates, or second, a co-promotion venture in which DiOrgio would be part of the promotion of the games.

"It's done all the time in the business, Mike, particularly on closed circuit fights. People will scurry around like mad men, trying to find out the dates of big fights or concerts so they can put holds on the arenas."

"How can they possibly get away with it?" replied Lambert.

"It's easy," said DiOrgio. "I give both the Garden and the Meadowlands several million dollars of gross business each year. I have a lot of chits in both places. If I go to the Garden tomorrow and put holds on a couple of dates with deposits and if Steve Ellovitch, who has never even rented the Garden, comes in the next day, sure the Garden wants State's games but they also won't want to mess with me. What they'll tell Ellovitch is that they want the games, but that he'll have to make a deal with George DiOrgio."

Lambert could hardly believe his ears. "Isn't that blackmail or something illegal?" Lambert queried.

"Maybe so, but it's done all the time. What I'm saying is if you'll provide me this information before Ellovitch goes to the two arenas, I'll make it worth your while."

Like everyone else, Lambert had done some things in his life that he would like to take back. But he had never done anything that he considered to be blatantly unethical, particularly when it came to the State basketball program. As he left the luncheon he told DiOrgio that he would think it over and get back to him.

Lambert had given nothing but blood to State, as he had done to Rutgers and any other project he had undertaken. But at the age of twenty-eight, he had a career of little promise, virtually no money in the bank, and his only other net asset was his car, for which he still had two years of loan payments. So he called George DiOrgio and said, "I'm ready to sit down."

DiOrgio seized the opportunity immediately and had his limo take him to Lambert's apartment. The two met for a couple of hours. DiOrgio explained exactly how the deal would work.

"The first thing that's important is that Ellovitch not go to the two arenas to book dates. From what you've told me about Ellovitch, he feels that he is in a position to play one off the other."

"That's right," replied Lambert.

"Fine. Your role—and this is where you have to be very careful—is to continue to gently encourage the playing off of one against the other whenever possible, but not to make it so obvious that Ellovitch knows what you're doing."

"I don't know how well I can do that. To be honest, I don't think that Ellovitch listens to me at all."

"OK, if that's the case, then just lay back and let's hope he makes the deals with the Indianas, Notre Dames and North Carolinas, feeling that he can then go to the arenas and get the best deal based on the strength of the schedule."

Sure enough, DiOrgio's reading of Ellovitch was correct. Upon getting the confidential listing of the 1988-1989 opponents, Lambert called DiOrgio and said, "George, I've got the schedule and to my knowledge Ellovitch hasn't done anything firm about dates with either the Garden or the Meadowlands."

DiOrgio met with Lambert and got the schedule. He then immediately went to both arenas and booked the dates of the proposed home games. In almost all cases, Ellovitch had booked games against teams who would have little flexibility in the date.

"In effect, George, Ellovitch knows that he's lucky to get these teams. There's no way that if he calls a Villanova or Nevada Las Vegas back and asks for a change of date, that they'll be able to do it. I can't believe how stupid he is," said Lambert.

"It's not all that unusual in the business, Mike," replied DiOrgio. "Ellovitch is the kind of guy who has high aspirations for himself. All of a sudden, he's now placed in a position of perceived power and he wants to milk it all the way. He's reacting to the power and forgetting about common sense."

DiOrgio had no difficulty booking the dates. And both the Garden and Meadowlands indicated to him that they were dealing with Ellovitch.

"Has he reserved any dates?" DiOrgio asked. The answer in both cases was "No." To which he responded, "Well, I give you a lot of business every year and these are important dates to me. Do you want them or not?" DiOrgio knew the question was rhetorical.

Both Lambert and DiOrgio agreed to complete secrecy. Meetings would take place in either of their two apartments or in out-of-the-way restaurants. Phone calls would be made away from the office.

"What about the fact that you and I have talked a lot in the past. Don't you think someone will know it?" Lambert wondered.

"I doubt it. I guarantee you that in my office we've done stuff like this before and it certainly won't leak out from our end," DiOrgio answered.

* * * * * *

Upon completion of the scheduling, Steve Ellovitch arranged meetings with both arenas. The Garden meeting would take place at 10 a.m., the Meadowlands at 3 p.m. This would give Ellovitch plenty of time to meet at the Garden, go over the dates and get across the George Washington Bridge before the traffic rush and meet with the Meadowlands' officials.

His meeting at the Garden took place with the Director of Promotions and Amateur Athletic Events. "I think you're going to be pretty excited when you see the teams we've scheduled," said Ellovitch.

He put the list in front of the Director, who surveyed it and said, "Wow! Steve, you're bringing in the heavyweights. Are you sure the team will be ready for this schedule?"

"I'm not worried at all. I imagine you've heard how well Lewis played in the McDonald's Classic."

"Yeah, I sure did hear. What the heck, you and McHale are the professionals; I'm just a fan. Let's pull out the date book and see how we stand."

The Director went into the other room and came back with the master date book for the Garden. "Let's start with the December games. H'mm, holds have been put on those dates by George DiOrgio, the rock promoter. Let's look at some of the other dates."

As the Director went down the list one by one, Ellovitch got more of a sinking feeling in his stomach. "Nope, DiOrgio has that date, too," the Director repeated.

"Who the hell is this DiOrgio guy anyway?" said Ellovitch.

"He's probably the biggest rock promoter in the country. As you know, Steve, you're looking for choice dates here and DiOrgio, no doubt, has a couple of big concert projects in mind. You may have to make a deal with him."

"Like hell I'll make a deal with him. I'll just go across to the Meadowlands and make my deal."

"Look, we certainly don't want that," said the Director. "We want the games as much as you want to have them here, but you have to understand, George DiOrgio is a power. We depend on him for a lot of dates. Steve, we can ill-afford to get on DiOrgio's shit list."

"Exactly what does this mean?" asked Ellovitch. The Director said that Ellovitch would have to contact DiOrgio, talk about the dates and see if DiOrgio would agree to release them.

"Knowing DiOrgio, there's no way he'll release without getting something in return. What he'll probably be looking for is a buy out or some kind of a joint venture," the Garden Director advised Ellovitch.

"How the hell can he do this kind of thing?" Ellovitch's face was now red with anger.

"Very simple. Like I said, he's a big promoter. He came in here last week and put deposits on each of these dates. We are legally bound to him unless you can work something out."

Ellovitch left the building feeling stunned. Fortunately, he had another option. Four hours later he learned that DiOrgio had done the exact same thing with the Meadowlands. "Do you think he had some advance notice of this?" Ellovitch asked the Booking Director of the Meadowlands.

"He might have," replied the Director. "It's hard to tell. DiOrgio books a lot of dates in here. I'll admit that it does look kind of fishy that he came in only a week before you. Whatever the case may be, he has you over a barrel."

Ellovitch went back to his office and decided to sleep on the situation before contacting DiOrgio. At 9 a.m. the next morning, Ellovitch called DiOrgio's office and left a message for the promoter, who had not yet arrived. Two hours later, the call was returned.

"This is George DiOrgio. What can I do for you, Mr. Ellovitch?"

"Well, I was at both Madison Square Garden and the Meadowlands yesterday to book some dates for our basketball team for next year. It seems as if you've got all the dates."

"What dates are you talking about?"

DiOrgio, of course, knew exactly what dates he was talking about, but nonetheless Ellovitch read them to the promoter.

"Oh, yeah, well as I'm sure you know, those are prime dates, particularly the Friday night and Saturday night dates. I'm planning some big concerts during that time period."

"Would you mind telling me what concerts?" said Ellovitch testily.

"Yeah, as a matter of fact I would mind," replied DiOrgio. "Look, you called me and I returned your call. I'm in the rock promotion business and I have every right to book an arena. But I don't like the tone of your voice or the direction of this phone call, so if you'll excuse me . . . ."

"Wait!" yelled Ellovitch into the phone. "You and I both know that State is going to need dates at one of those two arenas. You also know that we wield a considerable amount of influence in this area."

"So do I," replied DiOrgio.

Ellovitch felt himself getting backed further into a corner. "I'd like to get together with you," he said, "to see if we could work something out."

"That's fine with me," replied DiOrgio. "You name the place and the time and I'll be there."

Chapter 29

Jack McHale felt himself riding an off-season emotional roller coaster. Traditionally, late spring and summer had been a time of diversion for him. While Nevada-Las Vegas' Jerry Tarkanian had once said, "Good coaches don't have time for golf," golf and jogging had, in fact, always been a big part of McHale's relaxation. But not now. When not attending to business, McHale would often find his mind wandering; he constantly asked himself difficult questions, all of which related to his coaching career, his relationship with his family and his overall direction in life.

If he were to be fired from State, McHale knew that he could find another coaching job. In his profession there were twenty-five or thirty elite coaches, people like Bobby Knight, Dean Smith and Jim Valvano—guys who, if dismissed, would be sure to hook on to another head coaching job. While certainly not in this category, McHale felt that he was only a step below. This group consisted of fifty or so coaches, all of whom had good reputations and, in the event they lost their jobs, would be strong candidates for another head coaching position, possibly at a lower-level Division I school. They might even reemerge as a top assistant in big time Division I, or perhaps as an assistant in the pros.

McHale realized that he feared not only being fired, but also *not* being fired. He continued to reflect about coaching as a lifelong career. What concerned him most was that he was trained to do virtually nothing else. And with a six-figure income level, thanks to his summer camp, it was highly unlikely that he could find an equally lucrative career outside basketball.

Even more profound for McHale was the distinct realization that coaches, at least at his level, were not really educators. He had been drawn to coaching because he had believed he could make a difference in those lives he would touch. But now, his true role had been clearly defined by the constant theme of Steve Ellovitch's missives: *Win. . .everything else is secondary.*

Jack McHale knew that 1988-89 would be one of the most significant seasons of his life. A great year would translate into a contract extension. Anything else would mean crisis, in one form or another.

Chapter 30

John Massey had been a reporter for the *New York Star*, New York's second-leading tabloid, for eleven years. His first assignment had been as a sports writer. He was later assigned to business. As sports grew more into a business, Massey's recent assignments concerned the business of sport. He was good at it; like any practiced reporter, he had a sixth sense for a scoop.

At the press conference to announce the Gunderson Brewery gift to the Building Fund, most of the media focused their attention on William Riley and others who spoke. Massey knew that whatever was said from the dais would also be repeated in the press release passed out by the Gunderson public relations firm. He long ago learned that the story behind the story was generally far more compelling. Because of this, Massey would focus his attention on people connected with an event, not necessarily the principals.

He had heard that Robert Steincross conceived the idea. He knew Steincross was a tough, hard-boiled, self-made millionaire, who did not quite seem to fit with the William Rileys of the world.

When Steincross entered the press conference, Massey was standing at the other side of the hall. He immediately noticed, however, that Steincross had become angry with the female representative of the public relations firm. He caught Steincross' and Riley's eyes clashing and Riley's quick pirouette to the dais. From that point on, Massey focused his attention on Steincross. He overheard Steincross demanding to meet Riley. Massey sensed there might be a story in the meeting.

Massey knew that Gunderson was sure to have a suite somewhere in the hotel to conduct business privately before and after the press conference. He also knew that hotels did not commonly provide the room number of a guest. Not wishing to risk the loss of his story, Massey decided to follow Steincross up to the suite. This was easily accomplished, since Steincross did not know Massey. It was simply a matter of Massey's getting on the same elevator as Steincross and getting off at the same floor. Since the hotel had only two suites on each floor, all Massey had to do was observe which direction Steincross turned upon exiting the elevator and record the room number. Massey went in the opposite direction and immediately took a stairway down one flight. He got back on the elevator and proceeded to the front desk.

"I'm John Massey and I need a room. I would like one on the 12th floor. Do you have anything adjacent to room 1213?" Before the young attendant could ask Massey for the reason he wished such a specific location, Massey continued. "You see we're having a meeting in Mr. Riley's suite, which is room number 1213. It would be much more convenient for me to be next door."

"You're right, Mr. Massey. Mr. Riley is in that suite and fortunately we have the room adjacent to it open." Massey then presented his credit card and proceeded to register for the room.

"Do you need any help with your bags?" asked the attendant. Massey looked back over his shoulder. "I don't have any bags."

The layout of room 1212 was exactly as Massey had hoped. The room had a double door which led into Riley's suite. One door could be opened from Massey's room. When Massey opened the door on his side he could hear Steincross loudly conversing on the phone with his office staff. Massey then positioned his chair next to the door, pulled out his tape recorder and prepared his note book. Five minutes later, Riley came into the suite with President Pendelton and several representatives of Gunderson. Massey, scribbling his notes furiously, heard the entire conversation. He waited until all parties had left and immediately proceeded downstairs and back to his office at the *Star*.

"Look," Massey said to his editor, "I think I've got a hell of a story."

Massey then went on to research the background of the building campaign. He discovered that Steincross had conceived the entire project and that it was Steincross who went to the President after that ill-fated referendum. Massey checked with the Internal Revenue Service and found that Steincross' attorney, Richard Shoppels, had put together the tax-exempt application. Further checking by Massey found that Shoppels, on the same day that he had made application for a tax-exempt foundation, had also filed for another corporation with the State of New York, this one entitled, "R.S. Concessions."

The entire picture was becoming quite clear. Steincross had crafted the deal not out of benevolence, but (among other things) out of greed for the important concessions rights. And it was Steincross who recruited Riley. As was typical with Gunderson operatives, after they had come on board and invested money, they decided that they would take over the operation. Massey suspected that Riley then went to Farragher and told him that a large contribution would help Riley get Steincross out of the concession deal and put Farragher in, thus creating a more direct line between Gunderson and the concessionaire.

Massey's hunch was not too far from the truth. Riley and his Gunderson cohorts had not only cut a shrewd deal by putting up the seed money, but then also stood to earn considerable revenue through the concessions themselves. Although Gunderson had an exclusive on the sale of beer under

Steincross, they would be dealing with someone they could trust in Farragher; someone whose experience in the concession business would likely result in higher profits for Gunderson. When Riley found out about Steincross' gambling problems, he had the moral excuse to unseat Steincross. More importantly, Gunderson attorneys uncovered an inexcusable error made by Richard Shoppels in drafting the legal agreement binding Steincross as concessionaire. The by-laws provided that two-thirds majority of the board members had to vote on all contracts and that *any voting member had six months to rescind his or her vote.*

Riley immediately sought out President Pendelton. He told him of Steincross' inexperience as a concessionaire and of his gambling habits that could embarrass the entire project now and in the future. When Pendelton was made aware that the Board could legally remove Steincross, he quickly agreed to the coup.

A three-person action team from the Building Fund Board was formed, comprised of President Pendelton, Riley, and Joe Kett of Merrill Lynch, a generous contributor to the project and a close ally of Riley's. They agreed that they would rescind their votes, thus sending the concessions contract back to the Board. With most of the members of the Board having been recruited by Riley, he knew Farragher would be awarded the contract.

Riley predicted that Steincross' reaction likely would be to pull out of the deal. He also predicted that Steincross would attempt to cause problems, but he was used to these types of situations. Riley, Kett and Pendelton agreed to call another Board meeting following the hotel confrontation for the purpose of awarding contracts for the construction and architectural design of the building, as well as the concessions.

When informed of the meeting, Steincross felt it best, in light of the violent disagreement he had with Riley and the President, not to attend. Instead, he instructed Shoppels to appear on his behalf. Riley took control of the meeting at the outset. The first topic on the agenda was the concessions contract.

"As you know," Riley began, "one of the more important aspects of the building, in terms of future revenue, is the concessions. Joe Kett, President Pendelton and I have looked at the situation. It is our recommendation that Bill Farragher and his company be given the contract." Riley went on to list a number of reasons, carefully avoiding the fact that Farragher and Gunderson Brewery had a long and close association. When he concluded, he looked around the room for any reaction. Shoppels immediately raised his hand.

"Mr. Chairman, I am here representing Robert Steincross. As you may or may not be aware, the Foundation was originally incorporated before the entire Board was formed. At that time, the Foundation entered into an agreement with the R.S. Corporation for concessions. I pass around the table for your review the document. You will note at the time there were only five members on the Board and the five voted their approval". Riley looked at the document. He smiled.

"It certainly looks like a solid legal document," Riley said to Shoppels. "However, the bylaws clearly state that a voting member has six months to rescind his or her vote on matters such as this. In light of the fact that the Farragher Company appears to be a viable alternative, I wonder if any of the members might want to reconsider." Shoppels' face immediately grew flush. He knew instantly that he had made a critical error; one that in all likelihood would cost Steincross the concessions.

"I have given it some thought," stated Pendelton. "In light of the points that Bill has raised, I think that I would feel more comfortable with the Farragher Company. Because of this, I've decided to rescind my vote." Kett followed suit.

Riley took the matter up again. "My understanding of the situation is that it's now up to a Board member to introduce a new resolution." Kett did so, and Riley then asked the Board for a show of hands. The vote was eleven to one. Shoppels, representing Steincross, was the sole dissenter.

Steincross' reaction to Shoppels' phone call was predictable. "You're a stupid son of a bitch," Steincross raged. "Send me a bill for your services. I never want to see you again."

John Massey, meanwhile, had left several messages with Steincross. Steincross was generally uncomfortable when dealing with the media, so he chose not to return any of the reporter's calls. Finally, Massey called again and left not only another message, but his reason for calling. Steincross, after giving the matter some thought, decided to return Massey's call.

"Mr. Steincross, I've been doing a good deal of research on the building program and have uncovered a couple of areas of concern. I'd like to have a chance to talk with you about it."

"Exactly what areas of concern are you referring to?" Steincross shot back.

Massey asked Steincross a series of questions. Initially, Steincross was not responsive. As it became more evident, however, that Massey knew the exact sequence of events which had transpired, Steincross agreed to talk, but off the record.

Massey continued to research his story and made regular contact with Gunderson, although he was never able to get Riley on the phone. Ten days later he submitted his final draft of the State expose. While not a story that would have anyone indicted, it was a certain front page blockbluster; one that would bring considerable embarrassment to Gunderson, Riley and President Pendelton.

Massey went home to his apartment on East 32nd Street and popped open a Gunderson Ale. "What the hell, I might as well support the company," he laughed. Five minutes later his phone rang. It was his editor.

"John, we're going to kill the story".

Chapter 31

Steve Ellovitch had no choice. George DiOrgio had blocked every avenue. He had put holds on Madison Square Garden and the Meadowlands for all the dates Ellovitch desperately needed for games to which he was already committed. Nor would DiOrgio surrender those dates. His promotion company provided the most business to both arenas.

DiOrgio and Ellovitch conducted a series of meetings to reach an agreement, one that would allow State to make money despite DiOrgio's involvement and still satisfy Ellovitch's superior, the Vice President of Financial Affairs. Ellovitch, at best, had a strained relationship with the Vice President, a man who recognized Ellovitch's aptitude, but did not care for him either at a professional or personal level. Ellovitch knew that the Vice President was not one of his major backers in the University. And he realized that he had made a tactical mistake in committing to games with high guarantee dollars but without definite arena agreements. Clearly, the strain of the payoffs was affecting Ellovitch's judgment in other areas. He knew that in order to cover his blunder, he would have to cover DiOrgio, as well, by making him a partner in one way or another.

In meeting with DiOrgio, Ellovitch explained his dilemma. "OK, you've got me by the balls, but what you have to know is that there are other complications. I report to a vice president who doesn't know whether a basketball is blown up or stuffed. He's a bottom line guy. I'm going to have to give him a damn good reason why we're cutting you into the deal. The reason that you were smart enough to put holds on the arenas won't be good enough."

DiOrgio, in his own curious way, was fair: once you agreed to do business with him, he would work to help you.

"Steve, I understand the predicament you're in. What you have to understand is that I'm a professional promoter, and I have to protect myself. One of the ways that guys like me can protect ourselves is to put holds on dates, when we know that there are other promoters, athletic departments or whatever, who are looking at those arenas."

"How the hell did you know about the dates?" asked Ellovitch.

"It really doesn't matter. What does matter is that you and I have to strike a deal that will save your ass with the Vice President and still be fair to all sides. Let me make some suggestions."

At this point, DiOrgio described what he thought would be an equitable solution.

"First of all, because of the amount of shows I bring in to both arenas, I get a discount. By working with me, the discount will save you roughly $7,500 a night on the basic rent. By the way, please feel free to check with the arenas if you question what I'm telling you."

Ellovitch nodded and DiOrgio continued. "In addition, I can save you a lot of headaches with the unions. It's tough to put a dollar amount on it, but let's say that State's game against Princeton looks like it's not going to do more than 10,000 people. If you were walking off the street and renting the arena, I'll guarantee you that the unions would insist on a full crew. What that essentially means is that your labor and security costs that night would be in the vicinity of $20,000. You and I both know that college basketball is not the type of event to attract a crowd that's likely to cause serious problems. My relationship with the unions and the police is good, good enough so that I can go to them and say that we're not going to do quite as well this particular night at the gate as we'd hoped. They'll agree to back off a bit on the security and other arena charges. So on top of the $7,500 I can save you, I would estimate that I'd save you another $3,000 per game on labor and security."

Despite his dislike of DiOrgio, and his greater dislike of being beaten to the punch, Ellovitch acknowledged in his own mind that DiOrgio was providing accurate, if not compelling reasons to include him.

"As I see it, we have two options. One, you can buy me out, and to buy me out I would want $7,000 per game. In other words, if you're playing the twelve games you had talked about, you'd have to write me a check for $84,000. I have another suggestion, however, which might make sense for both you and me."

DiOrgio offered a scenario in which he would become the co-promoter of the games; on the games that had the least chance of selling out, DiOrgio would bring in a popular group to perform a concert immediately following the game.

"As you probably know, this is being done quite successfully by the University of Hartford at the Hartford Civic Center. Your case is a little bit different in that you have a superior team, but let's face it, there will be some nights, particularly with the games we talked about, where you won't come close to a sellout. I can bring in acts for a reasonable cost. Since we've already paid the basic rent for the building, our only increased overhead will be the additional hourly wages that we'll have to pay the arena staff. This goes back to my relationship with the unions. They'll be fair with me on this since they're already getting a night's work. I'm going to put some numbers on paper for you, including what I'd want for my fee, and some projections on what we should realistically gross. As you'll see, by having me involved, it won't cost you an extra penny."

Ellovitch knew he was getting a fast education in the world of big-time promotion. He also knew that he could use this knowledge in his future pursuits. What he had suspected, DiOrgio made clear as they departed.

"You might not have appreciated my methods initially. But having me involved is not at all to your detriment. By doing it my way, you can get your Vice President to go along with it and not lift an eyebrow. One thing I want to make clear, however, is that as long as State intends to play in one of these two arenas, I'm involved." Ellovitch looked at him, shrugged and walked away. He knew that DiOrgio was a co-promoter to stay.

This second option that DiOrgio had presented to Ellovitch involved the promoter receiving a fee of $10,000 per game for twelve games plus a twenty percent cut of all profits. This included DiOrgio setting up the concerts, utilizing his considerable weight for negotiating the rental deals with the arena and working closely with the unions to limit the overhead. Ellovitch argued to the Vice President that working with DiOrgio would mean that the university would avoid any potential problems with unions and management and, in all likelihood, State would probably end up making even more money, while considerably reducing the risk of loss or embarrassment—despite DiOrgio's hefty fee. To Ellovitch's surprise, the Vice President went along with the entire proposal.

One question, however, kept gnawing at Ellovitch: how had DiOrgio found out about the dates?

Mike Lambert stayed in touch with DiOrgio on a regular basis. DiOrgio kept Lambert posted on the progress of his talks with Ellovitch. Lambert knew DiOrgio well enough to assume that he would be able to make a deal. When DiOrgio told him about the $10,000 fee (he left out the twenty percent cut on profit), Lambert was surprised. He never dreamed that the deal would be as much as $10,000 per game.

When the two met to discuss their arrangement, DiOrgio decided to use the first principal of negotiation: put the ball in the opposition's court for a first offer.

"Mike, if it wasn't for you, I wouldn't have gotten this deal. In terms of your own compensation, what do you think is fair?"

Lambert had never been confronted with a situation like this. He didn't know whether to ask for $500 a game or $5,000 a game. He knew that DiOrgio was, in his own way, a decent person. He also realized that to some extent DiOrgio now held Lambert's future in his hands. If word ever leaked out that Lambert had provided DiOrgio with the dates, Lambert felt that any chance he had for a head coaching job would be gone forever.

Lambert gulped. "Since you're getting $10,000, how about if I get a $1,000?" he asked meekly.

"Mike, if you think that's fair, I'll go along with it." DiOrgio smiled. He was ready to go up to $2,500 a game for the information that Lambert had provided.

Lambert constantly kept his mind on the arrangement with DiOrgio. He had never done anything that was blatantly dishonest, anything that would jeopardize his career. He found himself nervous and irritable. He feared that other people, Jack McHale in particular, might suspect something. He would cover up as best he could. But it was agony.

Chapter 32

John Connelly had always gone by the book. He had been State's Athletic Business Manager for twenty-six years. He knew from the outset of his career that he would never advance beyond his job as Business Manager, but still he took great pride in his work. He was a member of the board of the National Association of Athletic Business Managers, attended all the meetings and, at the last session, was elected Vice President. In all his years, he had missed three days of work, when his sister passed away. He did not like Steve Ellovitch, who treated him with a lack of respect, something that his predecessor Andy Farrell had never done.

One of the talents Connelly did have, with a mere glance at the crowd, was the ability to estimate within twenty-five to fifty people the number of fans at a football or basketball game. He had developed this uncanny skill over a period of years. Knowing the exact number of seats in each section of the football and basketball venues, he could scan those sections, paying particular attention to the number of empty seats. Then, through quick calculation, he would arrive at his estimate.

He first suspected wrongdoing at the beginning of the '87-'88 basketball season. His suspicion grew as the season went on, but nothing seemed to make sense. At each game, Connelly would look at the crowd and see more people than the ticket proceeds would reflect at the end of the night. For awhile, he thought his special ability might have been fading, until he attended the National Association Conference. One of the topics of discussion centered on an episode at another university. While not a story that would make the front pages of the New York Times, the ticket manager at this university knew that something was not right in the count each night. He found that one of the student assistants had devised a scheme—simple, but quite effective—of printing the same color tickets, using the same numbering system and replacing the used tickets at the end of each night with the newly printed tickets. Thus, the student was able to sift off $500 to $1,000 a game.

The ticket manager of this university decided to purchase a coded marker seen only through an infra red lamp. The manager would mark the top and bottom of each ticket. At the end of the night he would retrieve the tickets, putting the "sold" tickets under the lamp. It was obvious that these tickets had not been used, and that others had. It was simply a matter of time before he was able to catch the student with help from the campus police.

Connelly decided that he would try the same thing. In the last two home basketball games, he implemented this plan. Both games confirmed that someone was taking the Athletic Department for a rather substantial ride, in the vicinity of $3,000 per contest. Connelly determined he would conduct further investigations during the upcoming football season, in hopes that the culprit had not graduated or left school.

Chapter 33

State was no different from most colleges and universities. The freshmen appeared on campus first, with the upperclassmen following several days later. Jack McHale and his staff were ready for the arrival of their three blue chippers.

One of the most critical times in an athlete's college career is his first several weeks on campus. McHale found that his players, like most other freshmen, were overwhelmed by their initial weeks of college life. They had come from backgrounds where they had been the main focus of attention. Now they had to blend into a new environment and new basketball program. For the first time, they would be away from home for an extended period. They would make new friends, have new freedoms, face new difficulties.

This was a time in which McHale and his staff had always excelled. McHale's edict that all staff remain on campus the first two weeks of the fall semester helped to ensure that the freshmen experienced a smooth transition. When the two week indoctrination ended, McHale made certain that at least one staff member was always available in the office. This was not the case in most other Division I programs, where early September would bring a flurry of recruiting activity.

The first decision that McHale had to make was assigning his prize recruits to roommates. While a player would spend time with other teammates, it was to his roommate that he would feel the closest bond. A roommate could be a great asset or a great liability. McHale and his staff spent hours discussing the best possible matches.

Cormack McDonough and Marvin Lewis had known each other for four years and had become friends. While Irish-Americans had never been known for their advanced thinking in race relations, at no time since McHale had known McDonough had the Irishman expressed resentment because of a person's color. The same was true of Lewis. The two just got along well. McHale, with agreement from Lambert and McCray, decided that Lewis and McDonough would room together.

As for Billy Powers, Jr., he had been friendly with a young man named John O'Brien throughout high school. O'Brien was a starter on Powers' high school team. Because of his close friendship with Powers, O'Brien opted to attend State as a walk-on. Powers asked Jack McHale if he could room with O'Brien. McHale talked it over with Bobby Powers, and came to the conclusion that at least for their first year, the two would be matched. O'Brien seemed like a good enough kid. In all likelihood, McHale would keep him as the thirteenth man on the team. He didn't see any problem with the combination.

Like most other large universities, State had recently appointed a new full-time Athletic Academic Coordinator, Dr. Jane Kirkwood. In the past, McHale had done most of the academic counseling himself. He was a bit wary of the new coordinator. She arrived with impeccable credentials and an extremely large ego. The adversarial positions she took with other coaches annoyed McHale. He was proud of his graduation record, one of the best in the country. But other sports programs at State had not fared as well, and McHale found her condescending attitude distasteful. Despite this, he resolved to work with her. When Lewis, McDonough and Powers arrived on campus, he scheduled meetings for the three recruits with the Coordinator.

Her role would be to provide the three players with a direction for major course concentration. All three had decided they would start out in the School of Liberal Arts. Powers and McDonough both indicated their desire to major in English. Lewis had expressed an interest in History. The Coordinator had been told, not only by McHale but also by Ellovitch and others connected with the Department, that these three athletes had to stay eligible. By now, she was familiar with their high school transcripts.

Lewis, in spite of a poor educational background as a youngster, had made steady progress. Despite the intense traveling for the All-Star competitions in the spring, he had finished his senior year in strong fashion. In addition, his SAT scores had improved to 940 (480 in English and 460 in Math). He certainly seemed equipped to handle the work at State with proper effort.

Both Powers and McDonough had been excellent students in high school. Powers had scored 1060 on the SAT's and had graduated in the top ten percent of his class. McDonough, too, had fared well, graduating with honors in the rigid Irish system. All three players were ready for a full college curriculum and the Coordinator said as much to McHale.

"That may be true, but these kids are going to be under enormous pressure," McHale responded. "I've taken a lot of pride in our graduation record. One of the things we implemented here, long before it was popular, is a very specific academic plan for our players. When we recruited the players, we promised them that they would have five years to graduate with a full scholarship and that any courses they took in the summer would be paid for. What we've tried to do is make certain that they get off to a good start in their first semester, taking at least three, and sometimes four electives and gradually easing into their major course of concentration."

"That's all fine, Mr. McHale, but my job is to professionalize the academic counseling for athletes. While I have no doubt that your methods have been effective, I have a Ph.D. and I intend to use my expertise."

McHale could feel himself seethe, but maintained his composure. "Doctor Kirkwood, I'm in no way questioning your professionalism. What I'm saying is that our track record for graduation will stack up with any Division I basketball program in the country and that we've recruited three quality student athletes. Your input will be important, but so will mine. I've had extensive experience at this institution and have proven myself." McHale did not raise his voice but he looked at her squarely in the eye. When he wanted to, he could be a very forceful figure.

The Coordinator sensed this and decided that she better not tread too heavily. "All right, Coach McHale, send the three students in. I'll make some recommendations and then check back with you."

As McHale hoped, the Coordinator had simply intended to get off to a positive start. In all probability, he would establish a good working relationship with her. However, he wanted to make it clear that he was not exactly a country bumpkin when it came to advising athletes on courses. Her subsequent advice to McDonough, Lewis and Powers reflected her understanding of McHale's success.

The Coordinator suggested three electives, two of which would be considered "gut courses." In addition, each recruit would be given the introductory level course in the major he intended to pursue. The players and McHale were satisfied.

Brian McCray was in charge of the academic program for the Basketball Office. He took his job seriously. Since McHale's early years as a coach, the program had required that all freshmen attend nightly monitored study halls, which began around 7:15 p.m., immediately after dinner, and concluded at 9:30 p.m. All freshmen as well as any upperclassmen whose grade point average fell below 2.2 had to participate in these study halls. The study halls were monitored by McCray and sometimes by Lambert or McHale. In addition, McCray arranged for tutors to be available on each study hall night.

Another of McHale's policies, which had worked in spite of some grumbling from the players, was that freshmen were not allowed to go home for the first four weeks of the semester, with three hour study halls taking place both on Saturday and Sunday. Upperclassmen who fell below the 2.2 mark were under the same constraints. John Thompson of Georgetown had gotten considerable attention for his strict academic program. McHale, an admirer of Thompson, nonetheless knew that much of what Thompson had done had been implemented by McHale several years earlier. While the results were the same—a high graduation rate—McHale never received the same publicity as Thompson. Then again, McHale's teams had not been among the top ten in the country.

While freshmen and upperclassmen were being welcomed on campus and put through the rigid orientation process that McHale and his staff had developed, recruiting still continued by telephone during the first two weeks of class. Both McCray and Lambert had already lined up their home visits for the fall; McHale had warned them that the presence of this year's blue chip recruiting class could not diminish next year's efforts.

It pleased the coaching staff that their outstanding recruiting crop made it easier for them to get into the homes of the four and five star players. It looked like 1989-1990 would be a good recruiting year.

Once the upperclassmen had returned to campus, McCray's weight program and the well known afternoon runs were in full force. While the staff were not allowed to do any coaching before October 15, the NCAA allowed them to peek in on the full-court games that took place in the gymnasium every day at 4 p.m. While watching the games, the three coaches could hardly contain their enthusiasm. It was apparent that the heralded freshmen already were the three best players in the school.

Lewis, now a full-bloom 6'10", dominated the backboards. McDonough was the best pure shooter on the floor and ran the court like a deer. Powers, three inches taller and ten pounds heavier, was going to be even better than the scouting services had predicted.

Jack McHale knew that this team had great potential. It was now a matter of waiting for October 15 to get things in full gear.

Chapter 34

They had to be certain, for they had invested much in time and money. The time had been spent in the form of Hondo following Ted Patterson over a two-week period and observing his every movement, the money in the form of a tap on Patterson's home and business phones. Tapping Patterson's phones was not that difficult. Slater had used it as a common business practice. It helped him keep a leg up.

Their information culled, they felt all the more certain that Patterson was their man. He was desperate and therefore vulnerable. Despite this, they saw that he was still a man of pride, and that their initial approach would be crucial; they could not afford to alarm him.

"Ted, there's a Mr. Beame on the phone," said his wife. "Says he's an old friend from Central Connecticut State." Ted Patterson did not remember the name but, given his state of mind, this did not surprise him. The last six months had been the most painful of his life. Each night he went to bed wondering how he would get through the next day. Each morning, he woke up afraid. He had to push himself out of bed and into the office, knowing that the stream of unfriendly calls would be waiting.

His accountant had helped him secure a second mortgage on his home and sell virtually all his worldly possessions. After this was done, the accountant told Patterson that his debt was still in the vicinity of $125,000 and that he had no alternative but to declare bankruptcy. Patterson had resisted. The thought of bankruptcy was impossible to accept.

Patterson found that he could no longer make clear decisions. To make matters worse, his relationship with his wife had deteriorated to the point that they were barely on speaking terms. His life had become one large nightmare.

"This is Ted Patterson speaking," he said to the so-called Mr. Beame.

"Mr. Patterson, I know about your financial difficulties," replied Hondo in a calm but forceful manner. "I may have a way to help, but it's important that our discussion remain confidential. Not even your wife can know."

A thousand thoughts went through Ted Patterson's mind. Who is this guy? What is he proposing? Is it illegal? Patterson had been hoping for a miracle. The thought even crossed his mind that maybe this was it, but deep down, he knew it was not. He also knew that should someone come along and tempt him with a means of alleviating his financial ruin, he would be almost sure to succumb.

"Simply come and listen, Mr. Patterson. If you like it, we'll talk more. If you don't, leave the meeting and you've lost nothing more than an hour's time." Hondo recited his lines to perfection. His experience in the area of persuasion was telling.

They agreed to meet the next morning at 315 Front Street, in an office on the third floor. Questions continued to race through Patterson's mind. What is it? A drug deal? Some type of scam? Maybe, just maybe, it was something legitimate; something that would not lower his self-esteem any further.

Patterson's ritual continued. He went to bed wondering how he would get through the next day, yet felt comforted by the knowledge that there might be something or someone to help him. He arose the next morning, as always, afraid. He got dressed, left the house without saying good-bye to his wife and headed for 315 Front Street.

The building was a four-story office complex in a reasonably safe section of New Haven. The occupants included an insurance firm and several law offices. Nothing seemed out of the ordinary. Patterson took the elevator to the third floor. He exited and turned right, as "Beame" had instructed. He went to the end of the hall to an office marked BEAME. The door was locked, so he rang the buzzer and heard a voice come over an intercom adjacent to the doorway.

"Who is it?" Patterson recognized the voice as Beame's.

"It's Ted Patterson." The buzzer immediately went off, unlocking the door and allowing Patterson to enter. As he entered the room, the light blinded him to such an extent that he stepped backwards and threw his arms in front of his eyes.

"Don't be alarmed, Mr. Patterson," said Hondo.

"You've seen the *Thomas Crown Affair?*...one of my favorites," he continued, referring to the Steve McQueen movie of the late sixties. Patterson had seen the movie and recalled the actor Jack Weston entering a similar room and being blinded by the light so as not to see McQueen sitting at the other end of the room. "Look, if we're going to have any relationship, you can't see me...ever. I'm sorry about the lights, but that's the way it's got to be."

"What the hell is this?" asked Patterson, in a combination of fear and anger.

"You're right. I'm getting ahead of myself. Sit down and let me explain why I've invited you here." At no time did Hondo ever raise his voice, always remaining calm but persuasive. "Mr. Patterson, there's a way that, using your skills, we can both make a lot of money." Patterson could not help but laugh.

"What skills do you mean? If you've invited me here, you obviously know that my business skills aren't in much demand."

"No, no, it's not your business skills I'm talking about."

Hondo explained what he had in mind in great detail, with every word producing greater pain in Patterson's stomach. "The plan would start in December. We'd do only two games in December; neither of them would be televised and neither would involve much betting." He continued on with the plan through January, February, the NCAAs in March and concluded, "Mr. Patterson, how much debt are you in?"

"You know damn well how much debt I'm in, or I wouldn't be here."

"If you do your job right, I'll pay you $125,000 over the period of four months. In other words, five grand a game."

"Go to hell," said Patterson.

"I expected that to be your first reaction. As I said on the phone, if you don't want to do it, you're free to walk. You haven't seen my face. There'll be no questions asked. But you're desperate, friend. What I'm proposing isn't as bad as you think and won't be as tough as you might imagine. For probably half the games you won't even have to make a bad call. The team that we want to win often does so by the number of points needed. In maybe one or two other games, your partners will do all the work for you. Hey, every ref has a bad night. You're a good enough official in those remaining games to control things the way we want. Think it over. I'll call you at 9:45 sharp tomorrow morning at your office. I'll expect your answer then."

As Patterson got up to leave the room, he knew what his answer would be.

Chapter 35

"**K**ill the story? Like hell you're going to kill the story," John Massey shouted into the phone.

"Look, the decision came down just now that we're not going to run it, John," replied Ken Lindsey. Lindsey was the Sports Editor and he had always gotten along well with Massey.

"Ken, in my eleven years with this paper, this is the first time anything like this ever happened to me and I want to know why."

"The decision came from upstairs. That's all I know."

"Well, that's just not good enough, and I'm going to do something about it," said Massey.

What Massey did not know then, but would find out later, was that the corporate wheels at Gunderson Brewery had been turning ever since word escaped that Massey had overheard the argument between William Riley and Robert Steincross and was writing a page one story.

When word reached the top echelon at Gunderson that a potentially embarrassing piece was going to be written about their sponsorship of the multipurpose sports facility, the Brewery knew that the repercussions could prove harmful. Gunderson was in a business that necessitated major steps to avoid any type of embarrassment, especially when it involved a top-ranking official.

The public relations firm that handled the Gunderson account took the first step. This company's President rarely became directly involved in such matters, generally relying on one of his underlings to handle such problems. However, this was something he had to attend to himself. He called the Associate Editor of the *Star*.

"Your newspaper is considering running a story about the Gunderson association with this new sports building. It could prove to be pretty embarrassing—we'd appreciate your rethinking the whole thing."

"We're in the business to sell newspapers," replied the Associate Editor. "The reporter has uncovered a number of things that need to be printed."

The Public Relations President could see he was getting nowhere, that this issue would have to go to an even higher level. The next call came from the Executive Vice President of Gunderson to the Vice President of the New York Star, Inc.; the matter was now out of the hands of the PR firm and into senior management at the brewery.

The Gunderson V.P. found his peer at the *Star* to be slightly more accommodating than the Public Relations President had found the Associate Editor. The *Star* Vice President had a much better handle on the business aspects of the operation. Star, Inc. owned and operated not only the *New York Star*, but also nine other major newspapers throughout the United States. Its number one advertiser happened to be Gunderson Brewery.

"We're very concerned about this story. We feel it certainly is not in the best interests of anyone that it be printed," said the Gunderson Vice President.

"If we kill the story, it'll be a highly unusual decision and one that would not be made by me. My recommendation is you should get Bradford Gunderson involved directly. Let me talk with the chief. Then I would suggest you have Gunderson call him."

Two days later, Gunderson phoned the *Star* CEO. The subject of Gunderson's $28.6 million advertising expenditure with the *Star* Corporation never directly came up. Neither did a land deal the two had done together some years back.

"Our company takes a lot of pride in supporting worthy projects," Gunderson began. "The sports center is important to a lot of people. Unfortunately, some people who were in on it in the beginning might not serve the best interests of the overall project. This is basically what the discussion your reporter overheard centered on. As you know, I've always had a great deal of respect for you and your company and I think it's been reflected in our business relationship."

"Brad, I've owned this company for seventeen years now. We've never done anything like this. Let me think it over."

The following morning Gunderson's secretary received a message from the *Star's* senior advisor to the CEO. It simply read, "Brad—The story will not run."

This development caused William Riley much discomfort. First of all, it would have put him, the leader of the company, in a position of embarrassment. He knew that no matter how strong his hold was on the position of President and CEO, a couple of experiences like this would loosen that grip. He was livid when he found out that Massey had overheard his spat with Steincross; so livid, in fact, that he scheduled an important meeting with his Director of Security, who had been with him for sixteen years.

"It was inexcusable for the guy to be in that room. We'll get you another job within the company, but you will not be heading our security operation anymore," he told him.

Riley had another reason for concern. Very quietly, he had planted a seed with certain key members of the Building Fund Board. The seed was actually placed by his closest ally on the Board, Joe Kett of Merrill Lynch. Kett, after a confidential discussion with Riley, had gone to other members and told them that he felt the building should be named in Bill Riley's honor. He claimed the idea as his own.

"In light of Bill's and Gunderson's commitment to this, it only seems appropriate. It's obvious the building should be named in someone's honor," stated Kett, pointing to the Brendan Byrne Arena (named after the former governor of New Jersey), Shea Stadium (named after the noted lawyer from New York) and other such buildings. "Who better than Bill Riley to receive this honor?" Kett asked. He had received no objections. Riley was delighted with the response.

* * * * * *

Sean Riley's senior year at Westchester Country Day had been one of tumult. He was an average student and, at best, an average athlete. His father was a continuing source of irritation. He constantly bragged about his son, placing him on a pedestal where he simply did not belong. But Sean Riley, very much intimidated by his father, could not tell him so directly. This had caused a major communication gap between father and son.

Like everything else in his world, Bill Riley had assumed that the things he wanted for his son could be attained by money, sheer willpower, or both. He desperately wanted his son to enjoy success—as a student, as an athlete, as a person. In the summer prior to Sean's senior season, Bill Riley not only sent his son to several top basketball camps, but also saw to it that a Gunderson Brewery subsidiary, Stellar Chips, became a sponsor of the camps. In August, he asked an executive of the Knicks to write letters to college coaches at schools in which Sean (or better said, Bill) had interest. Naturally, Gunderson was also a major sponsor of the New York Knicks.

Bill Riley dreamed that his son would play college basketball. But it became obvious in the early fall of his senior year that he would not receive any full scholarships. The next best thing, then, was to attend a school of high academic repute with a good basketball program. Thus, Riley focused on several Ivy League schools and placed particular emphasis on two members of the New England Small College Athletic Conference, Amherst and Bowdoin. Both coaches quickly found themselves recruited to recruit Sean Riley.

As Sean's senior year progressed, it became all the more obvious that it would be difficult to gain admission to either school. By mid-season, he was averaging 9.2 points a game as a point guard on a Westchester Country Day team whose record was 6-9. Still, when it came to his son, Bill Riley had blinders on. He continued to push and cajole, calling the Amherst and Bowdoin coaches at least once a week and sharing with them "Sean's latest accomplishments." Both coaches, however, learned from other sources that the boy was, at best, a substitute guard at the Division III college level.

During the month of February, Sean's SAT scores came back. His combined verbal and math was 960, his class rank 61st out of 96. Amherst had just been rated the number three school in the country in terms of difficulty of admission, while Bowdoin was rated number eighteen. In neither case did it seem feasible that the boy had a chance.

But Riley would hear none of that. He next contacted both schools and offered a "gift." When the heads of Development in both institutions discovered this, they were also apprised by the Admissions Office as to the father's interest in his son matriculating at the school. They quickly wrote Riley that they would be most interested in the gift but felt it would be best to wait until a decision was rendered on Sean's candidacy. This did not deter Bill Riley. He then called several Board members of both schools. He was determined that his son be admitted, if not to Amherst, then to Bowdoin.

Sean Riley's mother, Kara Riley, had long ago lost her love for her husband. But she recognized his great affection for their son. She had also grown accustomed to the type of lifestyle which Bill Riley was able to provide her and the children. These things made her stay, at least on the surface, by Bill's side. All of that started to crumble when she received a phone call from the Headmaster at Westchester County Day. She became frantic when she could not get her husband on the phone.

"I'm sorry, Mrs. Riley, he's in a very important meeting and left word not to be disturbed," his secretary said.

"Tell him it's an emergency and it involves his son."

Two minutes later Bill Riley came on the line. Kara Riley, her voice quivering with emotion, sobbed into the phone. What she told her husband would have implications not only for Sean's opportunity to attend Amherst or Bowdoin, but also for his own position at Gunderson.

"It's Sean. The Headmaster called." She could barely get the words out. "He's been arrested."

"Arrested? Arrested for what?" Riley yelled.

"Possession of cocaine with intent to sell."

Chapter 36

In many ways, it was the best time of the year, a time of great anticipation. There were no victories, yet no defeats. Everyone was starting at
the beginning.

As had been his tradition since becoming head coach in 1974, Jack McHale
called for the first pre-season practice at 12:01 a.m. on October 15. In the
glory days of the '70's, it was not uncommon for as many as a thousand
fans to turn out for this inaugural practice. This had not been the case
in recent years. So McHale was fittingly delighted when he walked out on
the court and saw a throng of eager State diehards, numbering 2,000.

The word had now spread far beyond the coaching fraternity. *Street and
Smith*, the premier magazine for basketball junkies, had called State's recruiting
year ". . .the best in the country. . ." and, along with several other magazines,
had placed State in its pre-season top 20. In the pre-practice "runs," the
three recruits had been spectacular. The gym rats, who lived for the opportunity to play with varsity players, had done so in September and early October. They were favorably impressed and their words of praise spread
throughout the campus.

When Jack McHale entered the stark and dingy gymnasium, he was greeted
with a loud roar. And when the three freshmen trotted out together two
minutes later, the roar increased. Fans came fortified with Coke or hot coffee, hoping the caffeine would see them through the pre-dawn workout.

Because of the State squad's youthfulness, and particularly that the three
freshmen would be in the starting five, practices initially lasted forty-five
minutes to one hour longer than in the past. McHale did not like to cut
down on work relating to the fundamentals. He recognized that this team
would need more time to learn State's system, which included a variety of
multiple defensive and offensive sets that could prove confusing, especially
for newcomers.

Among the traditions in McHale's pre-season plan was his daily 6 a.m.
run. While the players referred to a "run" as a five-on-five full-court, off-
season game, McHale's definition now called for the team to gather in front
of the gymnasium Monday through Friday, at 6 a.m., for a five-mile trek
through campus. He mandated this for several reasons. While understanding that straight distance running was not the optimal way to prepare a

team for the shorter sprint-like dash involved in basketball, McHale structured the run so that at various intervals, the team would sprint twenty to thirty feet. In addition, the daily early morning run would include some backward running and backward sprinting. He learned this from an old friend who had been a boxing manager.

There were also personal reasons for the morning run. McHale, now forty-one, had taken special pride in his own physical conditioning. When he instituted this program in 1976, he ran every yard of every mile with the team. Not only did it show the players that the old coach was still in shape, but it also brought the team closer together. It was tough to get up that early, and still tougher to run the distance, but McHale felt that if the players saw a guy twenty years their senior doing it, they would be suitably impressed. Another more practical reason existed. If there was one aspect of his job that he consistently disliked, it was having to cut players. The 6 a.m. run pretty much eliminated those who were not really serious about making the squad.

Pre-season was a time when McHale tried to delegate as much responsibility as possible to his assistants. For one thing, he knew the season was long and arduous, and that he had to conserve some of his own energy. In addition, he recognized that pre-season was their opportunity to do what they liked to do best—coach the team on the floor. McHale assigned Brian McCray to oversee the conditioning aspects and Mike Lambert to handle the fundamental drill portion of practice.

A number of trends had developed in the pre-season practice schedules of teams around the country. While McHale had been one of the first to get his squad up early for a run, at no time did this ritual include any actual practice sessions. Such was not the case with a number of other teams. At some schools, the coach held practice before breakfast with a meeting during the lunch hour. In the afternoons, players who were not attending classes were asked to report to the gym for "individual" work. Afternoon practice would then start at 4:00 and run until 6:45. Dinner at the training table followed.

Although McHale favored a regimented pre-season program, he felt this was a bit excessive, not only in the overall educational scheme, but also because it might cause fatigue toward the end of the season. His own routine called for the early morning run, group breakfast, and a late afternoon gathering which included practice strategy, blackboard work and review of practice films. At 4:15 sharp, the team would be on the floor and would practice until 6:30, followed by the training table and mandatory study hall.

As the season progressed, the practices became shorter, but the intensity always remained high pitched. On weekends in pre-season, the team generally practiced twice on Saturday and once on Sunday. Staying with tradition, McHale chose mid-November to give the team its first weekend off. They would practice Friday afternoon and conclude at 5 p.m. McHale would allow them to go home, or wherever they wished, and report back to campus on Sunday night. Even in assessing his team's poor records in recent years, he did not feel that his pre-season approach needed an overhaul.

One of the most enjoyable days of the pre-season for McHale was Homecoming. On Homecoming morning, the team would have its "Jack McHale Invitational," a five mile run in which McHale made sure to participate. Even in the down years, the run received much attention from the alums and student body. McHale structured the run to finish adjacent to the football field where alums, parents and students would be tailgating. The rules of the race were simple—anyone finishing ahead of Jack McHale got Monday off from practice. Anyone finishing behind him was in for a tough Monday practice. In the early years, McHale had finished in the top two or three. This year he finished sixth; not bad, he felt, for an old geezer. Billy Powers, 6'2" and with a build reminiscent of Ron Delaney or Sebastian Coe, covered the five mile course in 25:02 to win by eight seconds over a senior back-up guard.

McHale took special care to observe the NCAA rules. While he did not agree with the NCAA on all issues, he viewed this body as a necessity and felt that it was his role to abide by the rules they set forth—with one exception. As an independent, McHale knew his chances to get to the NCAA post-season tournament were totally dependent on State's number of victories. This was not always the case with conference schools. Indeed, a team having a mediocre season in a conference always had a second chance in the form of the post-season conference tournament. No such second chance existed for McHale and other independents. For this reason, McHale had dropped his pre-season scrimmage with Rutgers in 1979, a scrimmage which counted toward the NCAA limit of twenty-seven contests. Instead, he scheduled a *secret* scrimmage with a traditional Division II power. He had been friendly with the coach of the school for years. They both knew and trusted each other. While such a secret scrimmage represented a clear NCAA violation, they both knew that many other schools did it.

McHale and other coaches also felt that teams playing against no one else but themselves for an intense three-week period grew stale. So, on the first Sunday night in November, with the campus at its quietest, and only one janitor (a friend of McHale's) on duty, the Parsons Tigers would arrive behind the arena in a van, enter through the rear door and play three twenty-minute periods. Assistant coaches would referee. Both teams were instructed not to utter a word about the scrimmage, not that it would cause either school the dreaded NCAA "death penalty"—a shut down of the program—or anything even close. Still, particularly in a situation like McHale's where the team had not been winning, any type of NCAA infraction could result in trouble for the coach.

The scrimmage against Parsons always proved revealing. While a team might look good playing against its own, new faces, new defenses and new offenses painted a more accurate picture for McHale and his staff. This particular scrimmage demonstrated many things, not the least of which was that State's talent stood levels higher than it had been in previous years.

While the scrimmage in general pleased McHale, he recognized that his team was young, inexperienced and still in need of much work. The first twenty-minute session pitted starters against starters. State fell behind 10-4 in the early going, struggled and sputtered, finally taking the lead with five minutes to go in the period. Then Cormack McDonough and Marvin Lewis took over, scoring six straight hoops between them. State won the period, 36-28.

The second period featured the subs. In general, the reserves of a Division I program were far better than those of a Division II team. In Parsons case, most of his subs were walk-ons. State won this one, 40-23. In the third period and with starters back in, State again showed inconsistency, but also flashes of brilliance. They trailed at the ten-minute mark, 19-17, and then ran off twelve straight points to win the period going away, 41-28.

"Jack, you've got a wagon," exclaimed the Parsons coach after the scrimmage.

"If we play like that at Virginia Tech," countered Mike Lambert quietly to McHale and McCray, "we'll get our doors blown off."

The coaches nodded their heads. While they were pleased with the display of individual talent, they realized that the team did not play consistent basketball as a unit. Against strong Division I opposition, they could not subsist on spurts of excellence.

The Monday following the scrimmage was a traditional day off for the team, while McHale and his staff pored over the films. They broke the films down into plus and minus situations, both offensively and defensively. They would show the strong and weak points of the films to the team on Tuesday and then destroy the evidence of the illegal workout.

The two weeks leading up to the opening game represented a time of anxiety. In a general sense, the period of October 15-November 1 was a time of great intensity in most college basketball programs. A lull would generally follow, leading to a period of increased intensity, finally culminating in a crescendo as the team put on the finishing touches in its preparation for the opening game.

McHale looked at his schedule and saw that December was a murderous month. He was not imperceptive. He knew that Ellovitch, despite his statements that he was "trying to help the team get ready for tournament time," had placed McHale in an extremely difficult position. State's schedule started with the season opener against Virginia Tech in Blacksburg, Virginia and included such dates as UMaine in Orono and a Friday/Saturday encounter on the road against Purdue and Loyola of Chicago. Only two of State's first ten games would be at home; both in Madison Square Garden, against Iona and Princeton. Because of Cormack McDonough's recruitment,

McHale, using his old contacts with the Irish Basketball Association, had agreed that on January 2, the team would spend a week in Ireland playing in the Cork City Invitational.

Another area in which McHale broke from tradition with most other coaches was that he never scheduled practice the day before, the day of, or the day after Thanksgiving. So he always tried to schedule his first game on the Tuesday after Thanksgiving. While this involved getting off to a later start than most other schools (as well as several battles with Ellovitch about scheduling procedure), he felt strongly that his players should be with their families at Thanksgiving. Because Cormack McDonough did not have that opportunity, young McDonough spent the holidays at McHale's home, where the two grew even closer. McHale had great affection for McDonough. Not only was he a great player; he was an extraordinary young man.

The team gathered back on campus on Saturday morning following Thanksgiving, in final preparation for the opener against Virginia Tech on Tuesday. It had been a difficult pre-season. The staff had worked long and hard in correcting some of the errors they had observed in the "secret" scrimmage. McHale decided that his offensive strategy would be to keep the reins on the team and gradually loosen them as the season progressed.

For Jack McHale, the week preceding his first game always proved to be one of the most anxious of the year. This year he had great talent, but his players were young, and the level of expectation they faced was probably far higher than it should be. He braced himself for the long ride.

Chapter 37

The sordid headlines about agent scandals and prominent Division I schools offering money to recruits had covered every sports page in the country and did nothing to alleviate Steve Ellovitch's anxiety. The NCAA, in existence since 1906, had now become a far more potent investigatory force. As recently as 1977, the NCAA, with more than 500 member institutions, had relied on four people to conduct all of its investigations—as futile as searching for the lost continent of Atlantis. In recent years, the investigation unit, armed with a larger budget and more backing from the member institutions, had grown to seventeen strong. The NCAA's investigating techniques were now up to contemporary standards.

Ellovitch kept a keen ear to the rumor mill, listening for whispers about Cormack McDonough and Marvin Lewis. He heard none. This was principally due to the fact that Jack McHale had a squeaky clean image, one which would not cause the NCAA to take undue notice of the recruiting coup. For his own part, Ellovitch felt that he had covered his tracks well. His meetings with Thomas Mahon and Michael McDonough were private. The payments were always made in cash, with Mahon's sent special delivery to a post office box in Worcester and Michael McDonough's sent Purolator Express to the post office in Killarney, Ireland. In both cases, Ellovitch used a New York City post office box as a return address.

The scheme he had devised to sift the money from the Athletic Department coffers, though simple, was effective. Ellovitch was becoming so confident that he felt tempted to pocket an additional $500 or $600 for himself. He had to watch this, because the Athletic Business Manager would get suspicious if too many liberties were taken. Thus, after removing a little extra on two occasions at the end of the 1987-88 basketball season, Ellovitch vowed never to do it again and stayed strictly with the amount needed to pay off the two fathers.

Ellovitch managed to find some satisfaction. Clearly, the two players far exceeded even his most optimistic expectations. Those two, along with Billy Powers, were capable of taking State to the Promised Land: the NCAA tournament.

After some initially tough sledding, Ellovitch found it easier to deal with Michael McDonough and Thomas Mahon. He sensed that neither parent would ask for more or cause any other problems.

Finally, the George DiOrgio deal was working. Ellovitch knew that someone had given DiOrgio those dates when State wished to play their home games in the Garden. His prime suspect was Mike Lambert. During the summer, as his suspicions grew, he devised a simple scheme. First, he checked into DiOrgio's background. Interestingly, Ellovitch found that DiOrgio and Lambert had been classmates at Rutgers. So he called DiOrgio's office.

"Is George there?" Ellovitch asked, trying his best to imitate Lambert's voice.

"No, he's not. May I ask who is calling?"

"Yes, this is Mike Lambert from State. I think we've talked on the phone before."

"Oh yes, Mike. No, George isn't in now. Can I take a message?

"No, I'll get back to him," said Ellovitch, deciding that at the right time he would repay Lambert for his indiscretion.

Still, Ellovitch was not all that displeased by his relationship with DiOrgio. The man had kept his word; DiOrgio had cut a better rental deal than Ellovitch could have. He had booked some great concert acts, including the Beach Boys and Neil Diamond. As an unexpected bonus, the National Association of College Athletic Directors, in its bi-yearly journal, published an article about "Steve Ellovitch's brilliant new marketing plan." The article detailed Ellovitch's rental of the Garden and booking of concerts. It barely mentioned DiOrgio's name, much to Ellovitch's delight. Even the Vice President for Business Affairs, in a memo to Ellovitch, noted that this marketing plan appeared to be a good one.

Despite all of this, Ellovitch still felt tense. He was forever looking at every angle to protect himself, wondering if he had slipped up somewhere, wondering if he would get caught, wondering if his career—so important to him and filled with such promise—would be destroyed by his under-the-table dealings.

Meanwhile, Athletic Business Manager John Connelly had readied the trap. His trained eye had told him that the paid attendance at the first home football game in no way corresponded with what he saw in the stands. He estimated from his frequent scan of the crowd that at least two hundred to three hundred tickets were unaccounted for, and that the culprit was still on campus, still stealing from the Athletic Department coffers.

Connelly considered the possible offenders. It could have been the Sports Information Director, who was young, married, a parent and certainly in need of extra cash. But Connelly just could not bring himself to believe the SID was the thief. It could also have been one of the student assistants. There were four of them, three of whom returned from the previous year. It was also possible that one of the secretaries could be involved. The most likely candidate of all, however, was Steve Ellovitch.

Connelly felt that Ellovitch had never treated him with the respect due him after twenty-six years of good service to State. No, Ellovitch could not hold a candle to his predecessor, Andy Farrell, when it came to human relations. But it was more than his dislike for Ellovitch that led Connelly to identify him as the most likely candidate. Ellovitch had the easiest access to the money and the ticket office, and the best understanding of how the records were kept.

Moreover, Ellovitch recently had balked at the idea of switching to a computerized ticket program. Virtually every major athletic institution in the United States now operated this way. The system not only allowed for better record-keeping and more efficient sale of tickets, but also offered more ticket-selling opportunities, including a direct linkage with such major chains as Ticketron. Despite Connelly's many pleas, Ellovitch seemed in no hurry to make this change. For this reason, as well as the fact that he simply did not trust Ellovitch, Connelly felt that his boss had to be the guilty party.

But why? Ellovitch was young, with no family to support, pulling down $75,000 a year and on his way to the top. Why would he do such a stupid thing? Connelly did not feel it necessary to determine a motive. He desperately wanted to catch the culprit. Deep down, he hoped that the person would be Steve Ellovitch.

Connelly knew that the money would have to be taken some time between the closing of the ticket windows at 3 p.m. on Saturday and 9 a.m. on Sunday. The accounting method had been one which Connelly implemented some twenty years earlier. On Sunday morning, all of the unsold tickets (or "dead wood") were gathered and counted. The sold tickets were then gathered and counted, and finally the cash.

The reason that Connelly had to wait until Sunday morning for the final accounting was that State had a number of ticket outlets around New York for its home football games. In many cases, the ticket returns were not brought in until late Saturday afternoon or sometimes in the evening. It was for this reason that all cash, sold tickets and "dead wood" were locked in the safe. Connelly would then come in each Sunday morning, as he had for the last twenty-six years, and with his staff of student assistants, repeat the process three times. He had never been off by more than $10 on his final accounting.

He devised a simple plan. He would not go home on Saturday night. He would stay in his office with the light out and the door cracked open, in full view of the vault. John Connelly knew that he lacked the physical presence needed to apprehend the thief. Instead, he would see who the perpetrator was, quietly take a picture with a camera borrowed from the Sports Information office, and present the picture and the coded tickets to the Campus Police on Monday morning.

Steve Ellovitch had not become an honors graduate of Brown and a college athletic director in his early thirties by chance. He had been obsessed with sniffing out any rumor, and stayed on constant guard for a vocal inflection, facial expression, or anything that might lead him to believe he was under suspicion. He neither liked nor respected John Connelly. He knew that if anyone could catch him sifting the money from the gate receipts, it would be Connelly. For this reason he had kept a wary eye on the veteran ticket manager. Perhaps he did this out of paranoia, but his sixth sense told him that Connelly had become suspicious. He detected a change in Connelly's attitude toward him. It was ever so slight, but enough to tip him off that Connelly was up to something.

The first game had gone according to plan. Ellovitch waited until Connelly's car had left the parking lot. He then slipped into the Athletic Business Office, opened the safe, placed three hundred additional tickets in the envelope marked "Unsold" and removed $3,000 from the strong box.

Ellovitch knew that if Connelly or anyone else were to catch him, it would most likely be while pilfering the safe. The following week, at the beginning of the Rutgers game, Ellovitch looked for Connelly's car. He found that it was not parked in Connelly's customary parking spot. This increased his suspicions. He then drove around the lot and found Connelly's car parked in the rear of the parking lot, behind the old gymnasium. After the game, Ellovitch once again drove to the rear of the parking lot and saw Connelly's car. He then went out to eat and returned at approximately 10 p.m. Connelly's car was still parked in the same spot.

John Connelly had been a bachelor for all of his fifty-six years. Ellovitch knew that he spent his Saturday evenings home alone, watching television; he knew this because he had overheard Connelly repeat it many times. So Ellovitch quietly slipped into his office and dialed Connelly's home number. It rang and rang, with no answer. Ellovitch then walked from his office to the rear hallway, put a glove on his right hand and with quiet force pulled the fire alarm. A shrill sound erupted throughout the whole building. Ellovitch's first thought was that anyone with a heart condition who heard that kind of jolting noise would probably go into cardiac arrest. He tiptoed down the hall, and from behind a trophy case, watched John Connelly's door. Ten seconds later, Connelly rushed from the door, through the corridor and outside into the cold autumn air.

On Monday morning at 9:30 a.m. Ellovitch summoned Connelly to his office. His curt words left Connelly stunned. "John, as you can probably tell from my recent written evaluations of you, I have not been overly pleased with your work. We're going to be making a change in assignments and move you over to the Bursar's office as an assistant."

Chapter 38

It was worse than a nightmare, much worse. Over and over again Sean Riley kept saying to himself, "If only I could change things." But he knew he could not.

What made the nightmare even more difficult to accept was that it had happened so fast. The whole awful experience, from the time Robby Nesbitt had first approached him to the time they were caught, had occurred in just fifteen days.

Robby was the kid every student at Westchester Country Day wanted to be like. He was smart, the best athlete, the best looking. He was the best everything. What Sean Riley envied most about Robby—and he found a great deal to envy—was that Robby had not been burdened by wealth or a father of influence.

Riley had first gotten to know Robby as First Formers at Westchester Country Day. While all the other kids in the First Form were driven to school in Mercedes, Sevilles, and even limousines, Robby took the bus from South White Plains through New Rochelle, where he got off and transferred to another bus, which took him to within one block of the school. From there, he walked. When Kara Riley drove Sean down North Avenue, he would often see Robby getting off the bus and walking. More than anything else, Sean wanted to walk with him.

Robby was fatherless. His mother, Katherine, worked as an executive secretary to the Chairman of the Board of a large manufacturing company. Her boss was also a member of the Westchester Country Day Board. Young Robby had taken a national examination as a sixth grader and scored in the ninety-ninth percentile. She knew her son possessed special skills, even from the time he was in kindergarten. When his teacher had called Katherine Nesbitt to tell her of the test scores, she also said, "This boy has potential far beyond what the public school system in White Plains can meet. Why don't you see if you can get him a scholarship to one of the prep schools?" At this point, Katherine talked with her boss. The rest seemed almost too easy. Westchester Country Day, the school in the suburbs which Katherine had never dreamed her son could attend, not only accepted Robby but gave him a full scholarship. Her boss beamed when he gave Katherine the news.

"What you have to understand is that Westchester Country Day and most prep schools of its type are delighted to get a boy like Robby, particularly at a young age. The Westchester endowment is over two million dollars per year. They have a healthy scholarship fund. While they don't advertise it, so as not to be overrun with scholarship applications, they want a boy or two like your son in every grade."

Robby did not disappoint his mother. As a First Former, he scored high honors and made the Second Form basketball team, the only seventh grader to do so. This set a pattern which he followed for the next six years, getting almost straight A's, becoming a leading scorer on the varsity basketball team as a Fourth Former and making friends, as many female as male.

While he kept it locked up well inside him, the hand-outs—which started in the form of the scholarship and extended to weekends at the lavish homes of friends, summer vacations on Fire Island and even a week-long trip to Bermuda with the Rileys—had become a heavy burden for young Nesbitt. He had grown tired of always saying thank you, always feeling that he owed and that he would some day be expected to pay back. But he never said no, for fear of rejection from a society that his mother seemed intent on his joining. Perhaps out of rebellion as much as the allure of money, he had recently gotten involved in selling marijuana on campus.

Robby Nesbitt became an ideal candidate. The New York dealer had done it so many times that he now knew exactly what to look for. With marijuana, speed, downers, uppers, poppers and cocaine, he took a number of things into account before making any decisions. For cocaine, it was a simple rule of thumb. You went where the money was. Going where the money was at first meant Wall Street, Park Avenue, the East Side. It then meant Vassar, Union, Hamilton, Bryn Mayr. Even more recently, it meant the wealthy prep schools.

He needed two people to do business at a prep school. In the leader, he wanted a kid who was on scholarship and who was not afraid to take a chance. There were good reasons for this. He knew from dealing with similar cases that scholarship kids in prep school usually needed money to keep up with their peers. Finding a scholarship kid, in this case Robby Nesbitt, was easy. It helped all the more that Nesbitt had already gotten into some low scale dealing.

He arranged a contact with Nesbitt and told him about a "business deal." They then agreed to meet at a back table of a local cafe. Talking Nesbitt into it was not easy, but the dealer could see from the outset that Nesbitt had the two traits necessary for this scheme. One, he wanted the money. Two, he was not afraid. At first, Robby deplored the idea, but the more the dealer talked, the more receptive Robby became.

"You'll need a partner," the dealer told him. "You'll need to make a list. Your list should include only the wealthiest kids at Westchester. Boys, girls, it doesn't matter, but someone you can trust. Remember, in making up your list we want to look at kids who have access to money. Once we get the operation rolling, that'll be important."

Young Nesbitt followed his orders. This was not difficult, as most every kid at Westchester had money. So he compiled a list of those whose family wealth appeared obvious. The ones whose families rode in limousines. The ones whose fathers appeared in the newspaper or on television because of their position.

The next week, he presented the dealer with the list. The dealer asked Robby questions about each person. The questions centered around how much access they had to money; to what degree could Robby trust them; and whether they had "guts." The dealer told Nesbitt he would need several days to check out each kid more thoroughly and left Nesbitt with this question: "Is there any kid on the list you would reject out of hand, and that includes asking him or her to do it with you?"

"No," replied Nesbitt.

Four days later the dealer told Nesbitt, "We'll go for the Riley kid." Nesbitt was mildly surprised, not having thought of Sean Riley as the top choice.

The dealer spoke with Nesbitt at length about what to say to Sean Riley. He went over every possible question Riley would raise and every answer Nesbitt should give. He repeated this process with Nesbitt over and over.

Sean was flattered that Robby Nesbitt had asked him to go into the city to "hang out." They met at the Bronxville Train Station and took the 1:05, which would get them into Manhattan a half hour later. Nesbitt said to Sean, "We'll spend the afternoon in town, just kind of hanging around."

Robby Nesbitt was everything Sean wanted to be, and Nesbitt knew this. So when it finally came time for him to broach the subject with Sean, he did so with confidence. At first Sean backed off—way off. But eventually, he was able to convince Sean.

"Sean," Robby said, remembering the exact instructions of the dealer, "the best thing is we try it just once. The first time will be easy. The guy assured me that he will put us in an absolutely no-risk situation. We'll take our $2,500 each. If we like it, we'll do it again. If not, we'll walk away."

Sean Riley, his sixth form year now a source of constant turmoil due in large part to his father, agreed. "Just once, Robby, then we'll have to see."

The sure thing, the deal that would be so easy, was set for the following Sunday. They would use Riley's car since Nesbitt did not own one. The dealer met with Nesbitt again on Wednesday, at the same local cafe, in the same back booth. He had instructed Nesbitt not to bring young Riley.

"You are the only one I'll meet with personally," he said for reasons Nesbitt would come to understand. His instructions were simple: "You'll go to the rear of the dump site in Bronxville. There will be two trash bins, one with white paint scrawled across the top. The coke will be in that bin. You pick it up and drive it to Trinity Pawling School, up in Pawling, off Route 287. It'll take you about thirty minutes. You should plan on arriving at Trinity Pawling no later than 2 p.m. You are to go right behind the gymnasium on campus. There will be two people there waiting for you in a blue 1978 Buick LeSabre. Under no circumstances are you to give them the cocaine until they give you the cash. You stay in the car and have Riley approach them. Riley is to pick up the cash and come back to the car, where you'll both count it. Once you're sure it's all there, you simply roll down the window, drop the cocaine on the ground and pull away. Make sure you pull away slowly, so as not to cause any undue attention. You got it?"

"I got it," replied Nesbitt.

Westchester Country Day played Rye Country Day on Saturday afternoon. Sean Riley, no ball of fire to begin with, played his worst game of the year. He was 0 for 7 from the floor, had five turnovers and was finally removed from the game in the third period. He had not slept in three nights. Robby Nesbitt scored twenty-two points, including six in the last three minutes to pull out a game that Westchester had expected to win with ease.

"Sean, you're sure you're up to this?" Nesbitt asked as they walked to the street after the game. "You looked awful out there today."

"I'm up to it," said young Riley, angered by Nesbitt's words and all too aware that he would have to listen to his father's game critique as soon as he got home.

Sunday morning Sean picked Robby up at 12:30 p.m. Both had told their parents that they were "going into the Knicks game." Riley was nervous; Nesbitt seemed calm. They drove the seven miles to the Bronxville dump and pulled in the back next to two trash bins. Sean lifted the package from the marked bin and jumped back into the car. He wheeled the car around and headed out of the parking lot.

"Stop!" The sound from the loud speaker system in the point cruiser echoed so loudly that when Sean Riley jammed on the brakes, Robby hit his head on the dashboard.

"Stop the car and get out. You are under arrest." Sean Riley's hands shook; his heart seemed to pound right through his chest. He was panic-stricken. Robby leaped from the car, ran five feet and stopped dead in his tracks, staring into a .357 Magnum held tautly by a sergeant of the New York State Police.

* * * * * *

John Massey was still seething. "We got bought off by that beer baron and you know damn well that that's what happened," he said to his editor.

"John, I'm just like you. I'm an employee."

For two months Massey had sizzled, trying to think of some way to get back at Gunderson Beer, to get back at his company owners, to get back at Bill Riley and every other corporate louse. It was his story. He had spent weeks on it. He had researched it, done all of his homework. It was a blockbuster story and they killed it.

"John, are you ready for this?" The smile on the desk reporter's face was ear to ear. "Riley's kid has just gotten busted for possession of cocaine and possession of fire arms." For Massey this seemed like a gift from above.

His story appeared on the front page of the *New York Star* the following day with a headline, "Beer Baron's Boy Busted." The subsequent stories would provide ample outlet for Massey's frustration.

* * * * * *

Sean Riley lived a lifetime in the twenty-four hours that followed his arrest. He had been handcuffed, manhandled and strip searched. He would soon be expelled from school. His father's hopes of Bowdoin and Amherst had disappeared. The turmoil he had experienced in the previous months now seemed trifling. He now understood real despair. The whole thing had been unbelievable—and the gun, the gun in the car. Where the hell did the gun come from? When he tried to tell his father about the whole affair, about all his feelings, his father would not listen—as always. His father simply raged.

Bill Riley's rage was not born merely out of anger toward his son. Neither was it born out of the huge despair his wife now experienced, nor out of the reality that his dreams for Sean were shattered. No, his rage had practical roots.

His position as President and CEO of Gunderson had gone unchallenged for eight years. He had led the company to record profits in each of these years. He was a dynamic and articulate spokesman for the company. For the first time in his eight years, the "killed newspaper story" had caused some slight erosion of his stature. For the first time in eight years, Bradford Gunderson, the man who had brought him to his current position, had questioned his judgment.

"Bill, they're your people," Gunderson had said. "There is no way they should have allowed that reporter in. This has caused us to pull in a chit that we never wanted to use."

The worst thing for a company such as Gunderson was to face scandal. The worst type of scandal, in light of already strained relations with the United States Congress over the Alcohol Advertising Act, was one that related to drugs or alcohol. *The Star*, the *Post* and even the *Times* had done a job on Riley, recounting every grim detail of the bust in the process. Massey had been particularly scathing, writing a three part series on Riley and making note, among other things, of a recent affair with a Gunderson secretary.

Bill Riley had been toughened to corporate power struggles. What worried him most was that for twelve straight days he heard nothing from Bradford Gunderson. When he finally did, it came in the form of a memo.

To: William Riley

From: Bradford Gunderson

The Board of Directors at Gunderson Brewery would like to meet with you at 8:30 a.m. on Monday in the Board Room.

Chapter 39

As Jack McHale applied the finishing touches in preparation for his team's opener, Ted Patterson readied himself for his fifteenth season as an official. The four months that had elapsed since agreeing to Hondo's plan had brought Patterson much anquish. He was unable to deal with the swarm of creditors who seemed to descend upon him every morning at the start of the day. Worse yet, he had committed to something that just months ago he would not have dreamed of, something he would have looked on with utter disgust. This realization brought whatever dignity he had preserved to a dispirited low. Still, he had decided to go forward. It was the only way out, not just for him, but for his family. The moral and philosophical issues would have to be dealt with later.

Contact with Hondo came every Tuesday, at the same time, 9:45 a.m. The phone conversation lasted no more than two to three minutes. Hondo insisted on this. "While I trust you, Ted, I can't risk any of my calls being traced," he would tell Patterson.

Their discussions centered on a game plan, which included several test runs in pre-season scrimmages. Scrimmages differed from the real thing in a number of ways. For starters, coaches generally did not question the calls of officials during these practice games. They were more in tune with their team's mistakes and not as prone to scrutinize the officials.

Patterson felt that the preparation had gone well. For each of the four scrimmages, Hondo and Patterson had agreed that in the late stages, Patterson would try to make two or three calls that would alter the outcome by two to four points.

The next phase would be the real thing, albeit a gradual easing into the process. Hondo arranged two December games for Patterson. Patterson would fix each game and point spread in favor of the home team. This was an easy decision to make.

"If we go in favor of the home team, there is little likelihood of any real controversy," said Hondo. "Sure, the coach and players on the other team may bitch. Better that than several thousand home town fans who may focus more attention on your calls than we want. A complaining coach is old hat."

Neither of the two December games would be televised. "We don't want a smart-ass former basketball official watching television and suspecting something fishy. Until you have a couple of fixes under your belt, we'll stay away from any televised games," Hondo said. "Lastly, we're not looking to make any significant money in the December games, only to get you some experience. We'll look for games where there is a minimal amount of betting. You need to get me your December schedule."

Referees generally received their season schedule in early September, giving them ample opportunity to make their travel arrangements and, most importantly, to make arrangements with their employers. Virtually every college basketball official was employed on a full-time basis in some other capacity. For many road games, it was not uncommon for the official to depart from work at lunch hour on game day. Very seldom would an official be late for work the following day, even if it involved driving most of the night.

Patterson, finding himself more and more protective, refused to send anything to Hondo in writing, including the schedule. "I'll read you the games over the phone and then we can talk about which two we'll choose."

After several discussions (which included the style of play of various teams, the likelihood of the losing coach raising a ruckus over some questionable last minute calls, the talent on both teams and the home crowd factor), Hondo decided that Patterson's first game, Colgate at Cornell, would also be his first fix.

"The Cornell team will be a slight favorite. Colgate is coming off four or five lousy seasons, so the game will draw very little attention. The Colgate coach is new and unlikely to say much," Hondo said.

Like most officials, Patterson had developed a routine on game day. He packed his bag first thing in the morning, always including an extra set of accessories and, most importantly, a second whistle. Why an extra whistle? Thirty-five years ago, Holy Cross was playing St. John's in the Garden. Holy Cross coach Buster Sheary, a real firebrand, had been harassing the officials from the opening tap. Late in the second half, the lead official was coming up the court and dropped his whistle. Sheary, taking two steps onto the court, picked up the whistle and threw it into the stands.

"Where's your auxiliary whistle?" Sheary snarled, knowing full well the referee did not have one. Neither did the other official, and none could be found in the building, forcing the red-faced official to go the last four minutes without a whistle. To make matters worse, on instructions from Sheary, the Holy Cross players became more aggressive, causing several turnovers, and went on to win the game by three points. Ever since then, it became an unwritten rule that officials carried an extra tooter.

Patterson also fell into a routine with regard to his meals and travel. He liked to eat light on game day, his last meal coming a minimum of four hours prior to tip off. He preferred to drive to the games whenever possible. Unlike many other officials, who would generally travel with a companion to break the monotony and tension (and to get some post-game feedback), he decided that he would travel alone, due to the circumstances surrounding this game and season.

Ithaca, New York was approximately a five hour drive from New Haven. Patterson always liked to arrive at the arena two hours before the game. This gave him ample time to ready himself both physically and mentally. His pre-game preparation was not at all dissimilar to that of the athletes, and included stretching exercises, some practice in throwing the ball up in the air and several wind sprints to break into a sweat. Early in his career, he had never worried much about his condition. In recent years, however, from September through the opening game, Patterson ran three miles a day and put himself through a series of calisthenics that would keep him physically fit for the rigors of a long season.

Along with becoming one of college basketball's top officials, Ted Patterson had become extremely adept in another area—keeping things to himself. While having difficulty sleeping, and dreading every day of work, Patterson felt that he had done a good job in avoiding any suspicion of wrongdoing from his wife. While he was a bit testy on opening game day, Joan felt that Ted's behavior was no different from that before any other opening game in his long career as an official.

On this opening night, he would be working with two upstate New York officials. One was a young referee in his third year at the college level. Patterson remembered working with him once in his first year and looked upon him as a real comer. The other, a guidance counselor at an Albany high school, had been in the game for thirteen years. While starting at about the same time as Patterson, he had not progressed nearly as well. He was an arrogant man, but unlikely to be suspicious of anything. He had enough difficulty with his own officiating to worry about anyone else's.

In the officials' locker room, which was always set well away from the team locker room for obvious reasons, the three referees went through their customary pre-game routine. This included deciding who would throw up the opening tap, which positions on the floor each official would cover, a brief discussion on the temperament of each coach and final review of new rule changes for the season. The discussion generally lasted about ten minutes. Officials were required to be on the floor thirty minutes prior to game time and before each team came out for warm-ups. This allowed them time to acquaint themselves with the lighting, the hoops, court, sidelines and game clock.

Perhaps because of the enormous pressure he had been under for the last year, as well as his extensive experience as an official, Patterson was surprised to find that he did not feel terribly nervous. In his discussions with Hondo, Patterson had been informed that Cornell was favored by three points. They agreed that should the game remain close in the first half, Patterson would do nothing. If the game continued to remain close until about the ten minute mark of the second half, Patterson had already determined there would be four safe calls which he could depend on if he needed to go to his whistle.

The most obvious of those calls would be the block-charge, long the most controversial call in basketball. Next would be the three-second call. Most college offenses had evolved into a power set, the basis of the offense being to get the ball inside. This made it relatively easy for an official to call three seconds. The last two calls would involve inside contact, one for inside screens and the other for boxing out on rebounds. While the block-charge might result in some complaining, none of the four calls would likely cause even the most astute observer to question the integrity of the official making the calls.

The arena at Cornell was fifty years old. It seated 5,300. Patterson estimated there were no more than five hundred fans in attendance. As was the case with most Ivy League crowds, they would not be terribly vocal. In fact, Patterson always got a kick out of working Ivy League games, looking up into the stands in a tight contest and seeing several students reading passages of Shakespeare. There were no pep bands, no cheerleaders, nothing that would cause the emotions of fans or coaches to run high. While standing at mid-court, waiting to toss up the opening ball, Patterson thought to himself that Hondo was right. This was a good choice.

The first half proved him correct. Cornell took an early lead with its methodical offense and pressure man-to-man defense. They maintained the lead and went off at half time ahead by seven. Patterson did not have to make any bum calls. He felt good as he ran off the court.

The second half proved more challenging. Cornell appeared tired at the start of the half. Colgate, with limited talent, came fighting back with aggressive trapping defenses. They cut the lead to two at the sixteen minute mark, tied it with 14:12 remaining and went ahead on a three-point play with 9:19 left. It was time for Patterson to go to work. As Cornell brought the ball up the court, a pass went inside to its center. He turned to face the hoop, faked and went to the basket. As the shot went up and with barely a touch by the Colgate defender, Patterson's whistle blew signaling the hoop good and a foul on Colgate. The Colgate coach jumped off the bench and screamed.

Patterson realized he had made a mistake. "Stay with the four basic calls," he said to himself. The Cornell player hit the foul shot to tie the game. While running down the court, Patterson got some more lip from the Colgate coach.

"Sit down, Coach," Patterson growled. The first-year coach, not highly skilled at baiting officials, returned to the bench.

Patterson's experience showed up in the next several minutes. He knew that a string of questionable calls might cause notice. Fortunately, Colgate missed its next three shots and Cornell scored two hoops to take the lead by four. The official from Albany, his reputation as one of the East's great "homers" shining through, then called a Colgate player for traveling. As the Colgate coach jumped off the bench, the official turned and hit him with a technical foul. Cornell made the two foul shots, scored off an out of bounds play and was now up by eight. Colgate made no threat from that point on, and Cornell eased to an eleven-point victory.

Patterson finished the game with only one "dump" call. He ran off the court feeling that the weight of the world had been removed from his shoulders. While not nervous prior to the game, he found that his tension level had risen significantly when Cornell lost its lead and he made his bad call. As he reached the locker room, Patterson actually experienced his first sense of relaxation in months. While he knew it would last only several hours, it was great to feel so good.

In section 102, a man looking to be in his late 40's, wearing a hat and glasses, quietly viewed the game. He had come in alone, and proceeded to the area where the largest number of fans sat. He had considerable experience blending into a crowd.

As he watched Patterson's adroit handling of calls at crunch time, Hondo felt certain that he had made the right choice.

Chapter 40

"**R**ubber Room Time." It was a phrase coined by former Celtics Coach Tom Heinsohn, and referred to the pressures of coaching in the NBA playoffs. The Hall of Famer likened it to "...being in a room all by yourself with nothing but a rubber hammer, and finding yourself going from wall to wall hammering away."

Jack McHale kept a clipping of Heinsohn's phrase in his top drawer. At the beginning of each season, he pulled it out and placed it in the middle of his desk. If nothing else, it served to remind McHale that all coaches experienced similar pressures.

In this, his fifteenth season as head coach of State University, McHale knew much of what to expect. For the next sixteen weeks, he would go through life feeling as if he had a piano on his back. He would experience sleepless nights, eat poorly, have periods of absolute and unadulterated euphoria after victories, low points after losses and, should two or three losses be strung together, he would border on out-and-out depression. He also knew that he could not reveal these moods to anyone. A coach, at least outwardly, had to appear above human emotions.

The attention focused on the team was unlike anything McHale had ever seen at State. Not even with his good teams, those of the '70's which won twenty games on a regular basis, was there nearly the amount of hype that surrounded this squad. Media day, for instance, was traditionally held the third Wednesday of November. In the past five years, State was lucky to get five or six sportswriters from the local papers. On a good day, perhaps someone from the *Post*, *News* or *Times* would show up. The best McHale could do was to curry favor with one or two of his old friends from one of the three major television stations.

But on November 17, 1988, one hundred and fifty reporters turned out for media day, including representatives from *Sports Illustrated*, *Sporting News*, and the major metropolitan newspapers from virtually every Eastern city. The SID at State had to hire three extra student assistants.

While McHale knew that every column written and every word uttered placed higher and higher expectations on his team's performance, he revelled in the fact that people were once again paying attention to his program.

The attention was so great that McHale had to do something in the last two weeks of practice that he had never done in all his years as a coach. He held closed practice sessions. While this met with some media grumbling, it was generally understood as a necessary decision.

"I approach my practices as any teacher would approach his classroom," McHale said to reporters. "I'm not trying to be difficult. We're a young team with much to learn. I simply have to structure the practices to limit distractions."

If there was one thing that McHale had become skilled at in his years of coaching, it was objectively analyzing his team. Without question in a year or two, with one more good recruiting class, this team could compete on a national scale. Such might not be the case this year. Yes, Marvin Lewis and Cormack McDonough had improved even beyond McHale's wildest hopes. And Billy Powers had gone from being a skinny 5'11" guard to a 6'2" bona fide Division I point guard, largely through the rigid weight program that Brian McCray had implemented, as well as some help from Mother Nature in the form of the three additional inches. The three were clearly blue chippers, but they were still freshmen. After them, the level of talent dropped appreciably.

"Right now, we're seven deep. Hopefully, by mid-season, we'll be eight or nine deep. We cannot afford injuries," said McHale on Media Day.

He was reluctant to say this too strongly. Both Lambert and McCray always cautioned McHale about being too honest regarding the limited abilities of the other subs. But he and everyone connected with State basketball knew that State's fortunes this season would rest primarily with the three freshmen. If any of the first seven went down to injury, little could be expected from the remaining five.

McHale's relationship with Steve Ellovitch had sunk to its lowest point. The more McHale looked at the '88-'89 schedule, the angrier he became. His anger was especially directed toward the early season games, particularly the opener at Virginia Tech. In addition, he was not pleased with Ellovitch's constant pronouncements to the media that "This will be our year." It did not take a genius to figure out Ellovitch's plans for Jack McHale.

Among the coaching fraternity, Virginia Tech was considered one of the teams "to stay away from." They were not a nationally recognized opponent, yet they were always tough, particularly at home. Should State go to Tech and win the game, it would be nothing more than what was expected. Should State lose, most people would not understand what it was like to play in Blacksburg, especially with three freshmen starting.

Brian McCray was in charge of scouting. The coaching staff knew full well the importance of jumping off to a good start, primarily because of the massive attention being paid the team. McCray thus spent even more time than usual in preparing for Virginia Tech. Since the December 2 game in Blacksburg would be the opener for both teams, McCray had to rely on films from previous years, as well as conversations with coaches familiar with Virginia Tech's personnel and style of play.

Coaching protocol called for coaches within a conference not to share information about fellow conference members. Virginia Tech was in the seven member Metro Conference, so their '87-'88 season included fifteen non-conference games. Because of this, McCray had little difficulty obtaining films and a good deal of written and verbal information on Virginia Tech.

The final practice before the season opener was always filled with anticipation. While McHale tried not to place too much emphasis on the opener, he found this an impossible task, not only due to the eagerness of the three freshmen but, moreover, the constant media blitz.

"Jack, Virginia Tech has credential requests from the *New York Times* and *Washington Post*," said State's SID. "In addition, the plane that the alumni office chartered is full."

The Virginia Tech game was to be played at 2 p.m. on Saturday, to accommodate Tech's cable television schedule. McHale had a policy of never missing more than one day of class for a trip. He scheduled the last practice at 3 p.m. on Friday. Much of the practice was spent reviewing Virginia Tech's personnel. As was his custom, the practice before game day was brief but intense.

The State team arrived in Blacksburg at 9:30 p.m. As they departed the plane, McHale likened their welcome to his old NCAA team days, with photographers and members of the print and television media awaiting the team. Fortunately, McHale knew what to expect and assigned the SID to inform the media that there would be no interviews from the players prior to the game. The Athletic Director of Virginia Tech was also at the airport.

"Glad you're here, Coach."

"I'm sure you are," said McHale, half in jest.

The players quickly boarded the team bus and headed off to the Marriott Hotel in Blacksburg. The team arrived at the Marriott at 10:15 p.m. The Team Manager, on whom McHale placed heavy reliance for all of the team's trips, had done his job well. The team had been pre-checked into the hotel. Thus, it was simply a matter of taking the bags off the bus and having the players go directly to their rooms, where a light snack consisting of salad and fruit awaited them. McHale instructed the players that as soon as they were done with the snack, they were to get to bed. Their wake-up call would be at 7:30 a.m.

McHale knew from experience that the worst thing a team could do, particularly when playing an afternoon game, would be to sleep late and arrive at the gymnasium logy. Because of this, he scheduled a light breakfast of fresh fruit and wheat toast for 8 a.m. sharp. They then went to the arena for thirty minutes of shooting, and back to the hotel to rest. The training table lunch was at 11:30 a.m.

McHale was often amused at how training tables had changed in the years since he was a player. "In the old days, we would have a steak, baked potato, and something to drink. Everybody thought that was the way to go. Now, the last thing they tell you to eat is steak. Now it's glycogen boosting," he laughed, along with his assistants.

State's training table consisted of a choice of pasta with tomato sauce or pancakes with fruit and hot tea. At 12:15, the players gathered in McHale's suite for fifteen minutes of discussion on Virginia Tech and then moved onto the arena.

Pre-game was a myriad of every quirk and nuance imaginable among the team members. One player had a ritual of performing twelve push-ups and a series of aerobics, thus breaking into a sweat despite the fact that his chance for playing time was less than remote. Another went into a corner and spent five or six minutes praying. The son of an Episcopalian minister, he often joked, "I don't know if it will help us win, but at least it makes me feel better." The three freshmen were noticeably nervous. Billy Powers took great pains not to show it, but his palms were sweating profusely.

McHale found the hour or two before the game to be the absolute worst. In order to alleviate the tension, he had taken up a new pre-game ritual of jogging. In 1986-87, under intense pressure from Ellovitch and the media, McHale decided he had to do something to clear his mind before each game. He had been an avid jogger in the summer and decided to give it a try before games. After considerable experimentation—in one case he ran six miles and was absolutely exhausted on the bench—McHale reached a comfort level of about two miles or approximately fourteen minutes of running. He did this faithfully before every game. Virginia Tech was no exception.

"It's a helluva' lot better than heaving in the bathroom," he told his assistant coaches.

At 1:25 sharp, his jog and shower completed, McHale walked into the locker room to address the team. While the days of Knute Rockne and pre-game firebrand talks had long since passed, McHale liked to have his squad up and hopping in the locker room.

Brian McCray, as the coach in charge of scouting, had spent approximately thirty minutes at the blackboard writing in the name of each Virginia Tech player. Included were each player's height, weight, and a "what to look for" synopsis, including strengths and weaknesses. In addition, McCray wrote what to expect from Virginia Tech on offense and defense. It was essentially the same information the team had received in a hand-out the previous day. While McHale sometimes thought that the staff might be guilty of overdoing it, the blackboard information was a habit he had developed from his days as an assistant under Red Mihalik. He found it hard to break.

As McHale entered the locker room, there was an aura of tension. While he had considerable strengths as a coach, he had never possessed the ability to loosen his team up with any degree of humor. After speaking for three or four minutes to the team about Virginia Tech, he turned it over to Lambert, who told one of his better stories. McHale was pleased to see the team, including the freshmen, laugh.

At this point, McHale took over again. "While this will not be the most important game of the season, it's certainly darn important. There are more people watching us than probably any team in the country," he overstated. He went on to describe State's tradition; how it had fallen off in recent years. "It's now time to bring it back. And you guys can do it," he implored. With that, he brought the team into the middle of the room where they all clasped hands and in their own way silently made whatever religious statement they wished.

"Let's go get 'em," said Lambert.

"It's gonna' be war," chimed in McCray.

State broke and ran out on the court.

For many weeks now, the staff had debated the style of play which they should adopt. McHale's great teams had been known for their thunderous pressure defense and controlled offense. While that same style had brought about mediocre records in recent years, in the minds of many astute observers, the results could have been disastrous had McHale employed any other brand of play. Perhaps out of habit as much as logic, McHale and the staff had decided to "go with what we know."

What they knew included a variety of switching defenses, all of which revolved around full-court pressure, both zone and man-to-man. Offensively, with Billy Powers at the point, the team would rely on a series of man-to-man and zone offensive sets, with the common purpose being that the ball go inside. Most importantly, McHale determined that in the early stages of the season he would hold tight reins and not allow much in the way of up-tempo, fast-break basketball.

"We'll loosen up as the season progresses," he promised the team at the last pre-season practice, "but for now we'll play percentage basketball."

At 1:58 p.m. the national anthem was played. The Virginia Tech field house was rocking. Tech was accustomed to drawing good crowds. For the State game, its 10,000 seat facility had been sold out for two weeks. Everyone wanted a first look at the heralded freshmen.

McHale stood for the anthem and as always, found himself swaying from his heels to his toes. It was a time when he generally experienced the most tension, often times dry heaving. Because of this, he always kept a towel draped over his shoulder.

Within two minutes after the opening tap, McHale realized that the reports about Virginia Tech were true. They were very athletic, very tough, very good. Tech jumped out to a 10-4 lead, with Billy Powers turning the ball over two of State's first five times down the court. As the game proceeded in the first half, State's pressure defense began to take its effect, causing Tech to abandon its offense, giving up the ball thirteen times in the process.

McHale had always liked pressure defense for a number of reasons, not the least of which was that when players were going all out the full ninety-four feet of the floor defensively, they tended to get untracked more quickly on offense. But this did not happen in Blacksburg. While State's defense was consistent throughout the first half, only the team's senior captain seemed at ease against the tenacious defense of Virginia Tech.

Both Cormack McDonough and Marvin Lewis provided testimony to the oft-repeated statement that the best thing about freshmen is that they become sophomores. Each youngster picked up two fouls in the first ten minutes. When McDonough picked up his third, with six minutes remaining in the first half, he went to the bench. Lewis picked up his third foul and went to the bench with three minutes left. At the end of the first half the score was Virginia Tech 38, State 27.

"We're lucky as hell it's that close," McHale said to McCray as they walked off the court, listening to the thunderous roar from the Tech fans.

By half-time, McHale generally found himself to be reasonably calm and in control, much like an athlete whose tension level rises to a crescendo just prior to the start of a contest, then levels off once the contest gets underway. But with all of the hype, and the realization that his job was clearly on the line, he found himself uptight at half-time. With fifteen minutes to regroup his team, he did as he always did, spending the first five or six minutes talking with his assistants, looking at the stats, discussing ways to improve performance.

"We absolutely stunk on both the offensive and defensive boards," Lambert said. "Look at these statistics."

The statistics were revealing. State had been out-rebounded 28-17. "And that seventeen includes one offensive rebound," said Lambert. "I think we have to emphasize the board play."

"I agree with Mike," McCray added, "but we also haven't gotten much out of Billy," referring to the freshman point guard who had shown his inexperience by committing six turnovers. "Six turnovers might not be a lot in a fast breaking game, Coach," said McCray, "but hell, we were walking the ball up every damn time."

As McHale entered the locker room, he found his left hand quivering and quickly put it into his pocket. He had decided that early in the season he would not lose his cool with the team, for fear of putting too much pressure on the freshmen. In addition, he recognized that McDonough and Lewis in particular were sensitive kids and that too much yelling might result in a number of things, not the least of which could be to compel them to look for greener pastures. Greener pastures for them meant different pastures for him.

Despite his good intentions, McHale found himself almost "losing it" in the first two or three minutes of his talk. "We have just played the worst twenty minutes of basketball in State's history," he screamed. He went on to use a string of profanities, but after noticing a pained expression on Cormack McDonough's face, he thought he had better slow down.

"All right, look, I've had my say. I don't mean to overreact, but goddammit guys, we're a better team than this." He proceeded to point out the errors the team had made and paid particular attention to Lambert's earlier point about rebounding. "Gentlemen, you will never win games by getting out-rebounded 28-17." He then asked McCray and Lambert for their comments.

Lambert blurted out more instructions on rebounding. McCray, continuing with his earlier theme, said, "Billy, just be calm, you're a good player. You have got to be under control, though."

McHale then brought the team together and said, "Look guys, we're a much better team than this, let's just go out and play loose."

When the team left the dressing room, he noticed a smirk on the team captain's face. It would have been hard for McHale to describe his emotions at this point, but it was clear to him that he might be losing some of the members of his team, particularly the upperclassmen. There was no worse feeling for a coach. As he walked out the door to the gym, he said to his two assistants, "Fellas, if we don't play better than this, they're going to ride my ass out on a rail."

The second half was more of the same. While State expended considerable effort, the home court advantage and the experience of Virginia Tech became more and more telling. Tech opened the lead to sixteen, with 15:30 left. State, with McDonough finally getting on track, cut it to eight at the ten minute mark. But Lewis and McDonough picked up their fourth fouls within sixty seconds of each other and had to sit out from the nine minute to the six minute mark. Tech upped the lead to fourteen during that crucial period and hung on for a 76-63 victory.

As McHale approached the Tech coach to shake hands, he heard amidst the throng of cheers, "Bye, Bye, Jack!" It came from some of the State grads who had flown down on the alumni charter and by now were well-oiled. As he walked into the locker room, what he saw did not please him. His captain was standing off to the side with his senior roommate, smiling.

"What the hell is so funny?" roared McHale.

"Coach, I'm just having a talk with Joe," said the captain.

"Like hell you're having a talk. Sit your ass down. If you think losing is funny, you'll not only be out of your captaincy, you'll be off this team," McHale bellowed, glaring at the captain. There was nothing like a defeat to bring out the best in people, he thought. He realized he was including himself in this group.

For the next five minutes, McHale, as calmly as he could, reviewed the mistakes of the team, trying to be as positive as possible. Despite the loss, he did see some good things and he pointed them out to the team.

"I honestly think if we had stayed out of foul trouble that we would have caught them and won the game. The big thing is we have to learn from our mistakes," he said.

The post-game press conference was more of the same. As McHale walked in, he was more than displeased to see Ellovitch sitting at the dais answering questions.

"I would hope we get better," said Ellovitch to one of the reporters. "We will have to get better."

For the first time since he had known Ellovitch, McHale found himself nearly losing control in his presence.

"Steve, I can take it from here," McHale said firmly to Ellovitch, in full view of the media. While he knew that this would probably add grist to the frequent rumor mill of the two not getting along, at this point he no longer cared. He sat down, faced the media squarely and handled the questions, the easy ones and the tough ones. One of the toughest came from a reporter who looked about seventeen years old: "Do you think if this team doesn't come around it will be your last year at State?"

McHale chose not to answer that one, but did respond to the others. As the press conference concluded, he walked around the corner and saw Ellovitch heading into the Tech Athletic Director's office. He instructed Lambert and McCray to go back in with the team and make sure they were ready to depart as soon as possible. As low as he felt, McHale was still a fighter, win or lose, and he felt the fires brimming from within.

"Could you excuse us for about two minutes?" McHale asked the Tech Athletic Director.

"Sure Coach," said the AD, who promptly left the room.

As soon as the door closed behind him, McHale wheeled. With his eyes flaming, he approached Ellovitch.

"If you ever go into a press conference and start answering questions after a game, I'll forget that you're a 5'8", 160 pound s.o.b." With that McHale departed the office.

Ellovitch visibly shaken, sat down. But after a few seconds, a smile returned to his face as the Tech Athletic Director came back into the room.

"What was that all about, Steve?" asked the Athletic Director.

"*That*," responded Ellovitch, "is why we may be looking for a new coach in March."

Chapter 41

Steve Ellovitch felt pleased. His plan to create an aura of excitement and anticipation while making new and important personal contacts was straight on course.

As an almost immediate reaction, the loss against Virginia Tech had brought out the bloodhounds. It relieved Ellovitch to see the bloodhounds chasing only Jack McHale. Any discussion of Ellovitch's role, written or otherwise, simply noted that Ellovitch was doing a good job in overseeing the program and that the weakness centered around McHale's coaching.

In addition to his master plan for basketball, Ellovitch also felt that his reassignment of the former Athletic Business Manager would keep John Connelly in tight check. At first, Ellovitch was concerned that Connelly might seek revenge by leaking his suspicions to his new superior. But Ellovitch heard nothing and anticipated no further problem. In fact, his sifting of cash, which had continued throughout the football season, did not raise as much as an eyebrow.

Finally, the payments to Michael McDonough and Thomas Mahon appeared to be going smoothly. Both were obviously in desperate need of the money. When it arrived, they seemed to be so gratified that they would not dare suggest to Ellovitch that the amount be increased. Ellovitch figured that his stern dealings with both, particularly Mahon, had headed off any future demands for an increase.

Indeed, for the first time in many months, Steve Ellovitch found that he was not constantly looking over his shoulder.

Another area which pleased him even more was his budding relationship with George DiOrgio, despite the fact Ellovitch was quite certain that DiOrgio had paid off Mike Lambert to get State's advance home schedule. He correctly assumed that DiOrgio had wanted to get into the sports promotion business, that he had utilized his contact with Lambert to find out the exact State schedule, and that he had been paying Lambert under the table for the information. Knowing Lambert, Ellovitch also assumed that DiOrgio was probably paying him a pittance in terms of what the deal had been worth. Despite this, he had developed a good relationship with DiOrgio and had now come to recognize him as the consummate professional, someone who could teach him many things that Ellovitch would put to good use in a later stage of his career.

The next step in the "marketing of State basketball," as DiOrgio liked to refer to it, was choosing concert acts that would follow the games. Of the twelve games State would play in the Garden, three could survive on their own and were in no need of the help of a concert to fill the extra seats. The remaining nine would need a boost. Once again, DiOrgio's expertise came into play.

"Steve, with a guarantee to the Garden of $65,000 and the $20,000 guarantee you're paying teams, plus our advertising and office costs and other expenses, we're up to $105,000 per game. We must average $20 per ticket. With all the hype surrounding the team, I think we can get away with what we refer to as medium level concerts for six of the nine games. The other three games will need some big hitters like the Beach Boys or Neil Diamond," DiOrgio explained.

"What kind of money are we talking about for these acts?" Ellovitch responded.

"Well, for the middle of the roaders, we're talking in the range of $40,000. This includes everything with the exception of air travel and hotel bills, so you can figure in another $8,000-$10,000. Any half-way decent act will only travel first class.

"For the bigger acts," DiOrgio continued, "the blue chippers, we're talking $80,000 to $100,000, so let's do some arithmetic. We're in agreement that our base cost is $105,000 a game. Let's say we bring in a Paul Anka for an additional $40,000 plus another $10,000 for his travel and hotel expenses. That totals $155,000. The beauty of having a flat rental, as opposed to the Garden taking a percentage of every ticket, is that we know exactly what we have to shoot for. By looking at the numbers and assuming a $20 average ticket price, all we have to do is sell roughly 8,000 tickets to make our nut."

"Let's take it a step further," he proceeded. "With all the hype the team is getting plus the fact that you'll be playing in the Garden, how many season tickets can we safely assume?"

"Well," Ellovitch answered, "last year with a lousy team we had 1,800. This year we are already up to 4,800. I would imagine we'll top out at about 6,000."

"OK," said DiOrgio. "So there's 6,000 toward our 8,000. How many fans will the opposing team bring?"

"We can figure an average of about 1,000," replied Ellovitch.

"We're up to 7,000," said DiOrgio. "Now, what about the students?"

"We're planning to run buses and it's only about a twenty minute ride from campus into the Garden. Our best guess is another 4,000, but remember, they pay only $5 a ticket."

"Bingo!" exclaimed DiOrgio. "That's our nut. Now, with our marketing plan, (he made particular use of the word "our") we should be able to add another 4,000 people for the medium games, adding another $80,000 to the gross. For some of the big games we could even bang out the Garden, which means 21,000 paid attendance. I'll have my bookkeeper do up some figures for you. I think you'll see we're all going to come out of this very well."

"By the way," DiOrgio added, "when you get the numbers you'll also notice that there is a lot of money involved for State, the Garden, the union, and George DiOrgio. I assume you'll want to be cut into the pie."

"What do you mean?" Ellovitch asked with some trepidation.

"You know exactly what I mean," said DiOrgio. "Do you want a slice or not?"

"Will it be traceable?" asked Ellovitch.

"Absolutely not," said DiOrgio.

"Then the answer is yes."

Two days later a Federal Express package arrived from DiOrgio's office, showing a detailed breakdown of the twelve home games. There would be a projected profit after all expenses of $1,540,000 before the "slicing."

"Good God!" exclaimed Ellovitch to himself.

Another pleasing aspect of their relationship was that DiOrgio, until this point, had no difficulty staying in the background. This left Ellovitch in the happy position of deriving all of the credit for the plan.

"Our theory is simple," Ellovitch stated in a story in the *New York Times*. "We're going to be renting the Garden anyway. To keep it open an extra two hours for a concert is a minimal additional cost, plus the Garden has probably the finest put-up and take-down crews in the country. They estimate that once the game ends, it'll be no more than twenty-five minutes to set up the stage and seats for the concert." As he spoke to the reporter, he followed very closely the notes he had taken from his conversation with DiOrgio.

"What you have to play up, Steve," DiOrgio had counseled, "is that the Garden knows what it's doing. They have huge egos over there and it's always good to stroke them in the paper. The same is true of the union. Make sure you say how efficient they are in the setting up and taking down of the floor. How this will allow the fans a chance to get up, have a beer and twenty or twenty-five minutes later come in, sit down and enjoy the concert."

DiOrgio, using his considerable negotiating skills, had impressed upon the union that this was a novel idea, but one that could work. "Look at the configuration of basketball. You guys have experience in taking the court down and getting ice hockey set up. What's the normal amount of time?"

"About forty minutes tops," said the head of Local 109.

"OK," responded DiOrgio. "In this case we're talking about going from basketball to a concert which does not involve any ice and should be an easier set up."

"That's true, George, but we've also got the stage consideration."

"I understand that," replied DiOrgio. "What we'll do is put the basic frame of the stage up before the game."

"You're talking about killing seats," said the union manager.

"I know that," replied DiOrgio, "but with the exception of two or three games, I don't see any way we'll sell anything out. What are we talking about in terms of killing of seats?"

"With the basic framework, we're talking about probably 500 to 600 seats."

"I'll take that any time."

As they continued the discussion, both men agreed that as long as the frame of the stage was erected prior to the game, it was very conceivable to have the concert in full swing within twenty-five minutes of the final buzzer.

Next came the marketing, with DiOrgio staying in the background but again assuming almost full control of the plan.

State's campaign included some deft thirty second spots on all three New York major television stations as well as the top four radio stations. In addition, DiOrgio was able to negotiate a corporate sponsorship arrangement with a soft drink company. The arrangement called for State to be allowed to "tag on" to all of the company's sixty-second commercials.

"We do this all the time, Steve," DiOrgio said. "What it means simply is that they become our corporate sponsor. Part of what they give us is the last ten seconds of a spot they run. This is a good deal for them, as they want very much to get into the college market. It's also a super deal for us. Their radio advertising budget in our market will be approximately $500,000 over the three months of our tag on."

What DiOrgio did not tell Ellovitch was that DiOrgio's in-house ad firm would place the ads, netting him the ten percent agency commission of $50,000!

"In addition to the tag ons, they'll provide us with $75,000 in cash, plus the printing of posters and other ad materials we can use in pubs, restaurants and grocery stores."

"Before we go any further, George, what do they get?" asked Ellovitch.

"They get to say in all ads, including the television ads that we're paying for, that its 'State vs. whoever, presented by them.'"

"That's it?" asked Ellovitch.

"That's it," said DiOrgio, "but don't kid yourself. It's a good deal for them."

DiOrgio, having shown Ellovitch his promotional wizardry, invited him to lunch at Toots Shors, directly across from the Garden.

"Steve, there's one other thing we haven't discussed that I'd like to bring up. It's the licensing."

Ellovitch knew that the licensing of a successful major college basketball team could mean big dollars. He also knew that his own staff was not capable of handling it, at least for the present.

"We can discuss it, but I want you to know I can't get into any long term deal," said Ellovitch.

"When you say long term, what are you talking about?" asked DiOrgio.

"I couldn't go beyond a three-year commitment."

Inwardly delighted (for he had hoped that he would get two years at the most), DiOrgio pressed on. "In all fairness, Steve, I think you realize what a good job we've done for you and that it's been mutually beneficial. Why don't we start with four years. I'm sure your Vice President can live with that."

An hour later a deal was struck allowing DiOrgio to serve as the exclusive licensee for all State University basketball products for a four-year period.

"Once again I'll have the bookkeeper get you some numbers, but if it goes the way I think, we could be talking about a net of $100,000 per year." DiOrgio's deal called for thirty-five percent of net profit.

"So, in other words, you'll end up with $35,000," laughed Ellovitch. "George, I sure as hell am in the wrong business."

While he said it kiddingly, there was an element of truth to Ellovitch's statement. He saw DiOrgio for what he was, as Machiavellian a businessman as anyone would ever find. But he was good, very good. And he had the advantage of dealing without the institutional constraints that Ellovitch faced. At the right time, Ellovitch thought, he would approach DiOrgio to see if they could team up in some joint ventures in other areas. He recognized that this was now premature. "Let's get a couple of dollars in DiOrgio's pocket and then we'll talk," he said to himself.

There was a lot that DiOrgio had not told Ellovitch about his various deals on behalf of State. Since becoming a highly successful promoter, DiOrgio had not paid for a restaurant tab, a clothier bill, a haircut or car in eight years. Ellovitch did not know about DiOrgio's arrangement with the Garden, which called for him to receive two hundred complimentary tickets to every State game, a value of $48,000 over the season. DiOrgio never sold complimentary tickets; he quietly made full use of them as bartering chips.

"Bill," DiOrgio would say to Bill George, owner of George's Cadillac, "I'll make certain that you get $12,000 worth of tickets to all my events; you make certain you keep me in a Cadillac." For Bill George, as well as for the others DiOrgio dealt with, it was always a good deal for both. No cash was exchanged. The IRS was never involved. In DiOrgio's mind, no one came out any worse.

Another area which DiOrgio used to considerable advantage was the rental of the twelve dates for State at $65,000 to achieve reductions in his overall rental deals. Certainly, the $65,000 was a good deal for State, but it was also a good deal for the Garden. Never one to be avaricious, he simply pointed out to the Garden, "I've negotiated a good deal for all sides. I would appreciate, when my concerts come in, a reduction of one percent on rental."

"Done," said the Garden representative.

DiOrgio likewise manipulated the unions. "You've got more basketball fans in your union than in any union in the country," DiOrgio told them. "I'll make certain that you get the best seats. Think about reducing your fees at my concerts, and I'd appreciate quality time."

"You've got it, George," was the predictable reply.

* * * * * *

DiOrgio's other "friend" in the State Athletic Department was not feeling much peace in his life. Mike Lambert could not get over the loss of the New Jersey State job. More importantly, the deal he had made with DiOrgio weighed on his mind. It was the first venture he had ever made outside of basketball and, surely, the first that could be construed as under the table. He found himself constantly worrying, constantly wondering, "When am I gonna' get caught?"

DiOrgio lived up to his end of the deal, which called for a check for $5,000 up-front money. In addition, DiOrgio promised that each check would arrive within twenty-four hours after each of the games. While Lambert looked forward to the money, it did not ease his troubled conscience. This uneasiness was not relieved when he received a phone call from DiOrgio.

"Mike, there's another project I want to talk to you about." Lambert sensed a sudden firmness in DiOrgio's voice that he had not heard before.

"What is it, George?"

"It's something we ought to talk about in private. It's a good deal, a safe deal," he stated, emphasizing the word "safe." "One where you can make a lot of money. Let's get together for lunch tomorrow."

Mike Lambert hung up the phone. He could not imagine what new deal DiOrgio would propose, but the tone of DiOrgio's voice suggested that it would not be to Lambert's liking. He also sensed that he would have no choice in the matter.

Chapter 42

William F. Riley, Jr. had not advanced to the position of President and CEO of Gunderson Brewery by a quirk of fate. From the very beginning, he had a plan, and as for any corporate head, the plan always demanded the unique ability to anticipate trouble and conquer it. When he received the memo from Bradford Gunderson requesting his appearance before the Board on Monday morning, he sensed trouble; perhaps that even his job was in jeopardy.

While Riley may have had certain flaws as a corporate leader, he did not lack the ability to think clearly under pressure. It was not that his on-the-job performance could be questioned; certainly the company had flourished under his direction. But Gunderson was image-conscious and the arrest of Sean Riley had brought an overwhelming amount of negative publicity to the company. Riley knew all too well that in other situations where a company's top man had been fired for the indiscretion of a subordinate, the operative term became, "It was your watch. Something went wrong, so you're out." Riley knew that the Board of Gunderson Brewery placed Sean Riley under his watch.

The weeks leading up to the Board meeting had been the most unpleasant of Riley's career. The papers, particularly the tabloids, had a field day. John Nesbitt of the *New York Star* had written a three-part series, one installment detailing Riley's affair with his former secretary. The latest article appeared on Wednesday under the headline, "Is Riley's Ship Sinking?" The *New York Times*, far more objective, also covered the story but had centered its attention on the problems of Sean Riley. The *Wall Street Journal* focused on Bill Riley's cut-throat business style that left behind a long list of enemies. The story suggested that Riley had burned many bridges in his illustrious and tempestuous career, but that in all likelihood a slap on the wrist was the most he would receive.

The whispers in the halls and cafeteria were hard to ignore. Riley's colleagues at the executive level had been cordial, but it was obvious from the tone of their comments that they were concerned about their own positions. Many of them reported to Riley and knew that a company shake-up might affect their own jobs as well.

Ominously silent in all of the proceedings, however, was Bradford Gunderson, the company's owner and chairman. Riley had developed a close relationship with Gunderson over his twenty-six years with the brewery. At no time could Riley recall such a long period of non-communication with Gunderson. This concerned him most.

Riley tried to examine the options the Board might exercise. First, he could be fired. He doubted this would happen. He was far too valuable to the company. A firing would produce an almost volcanic tremor at the brewery, something Riley doubted Bradford Gunderson would want. To expunge him completely from the employee rolls seemed excessive.

Another possibility was that he might be reassigned, given another title and stripped of much of his power. This appeared to be a feasible option, but one that Riley hoped would not be selected. Still another alternative was a light slap on the wrist that might come in the form of a public apology by the Riley family, as well as a personal apology to Gunderson employees; or it might be a more severe slap which could entail something as pronounced as removing Riley as chairman of the Building Fund. Since that had become his pet project, he hoped it would not be done. Of course, the Board might do nothing. Its members might simply say, "Bill, it's a personal matter. Let's get it cleaned up."

If nothing else, Riley was objective. After examining the various possibilities, he felt the Board would take the latter option. He knew that Gunderson, himself a strait-laced family man, would be bothered by the publicity surrounding Riley's affair. Yet, while one or two board members might express some disappointment, it was inconceivable to him that any definitive action could be taken which would remove him from office or decrease his power.

While struggling to stay afloat on the corporate side, things had gone from bad to worse at home. He simply could not forgive his son. After all his planning and prodding, how could the boy have failed him?

"You're taking it so personally, as if he did it to you," his wife charged. "Why don't you go in and talk to him? And rather than talking *to* him, talk *with* him. That's something you probably have never done since the day he was born."

Riley could not bring himself to do this. In fact, he had a difficult time even being in the same room with his son. While he would say nothing to Sean, his silence proved telling. He had created a schism which might never be repaired.

Sean Riley was expelled from Westchester Country Day School two weeks following his arrest. Other consequences were predictable, too, including rejections from both Amherst and Bowdoin and even his two back-up schools, Hobart and Dickinson. It was clear that no one wanted a druggie, especially one with a police record.

Riley knew that his marriage was over. He would ride it out until the Board had reached its decision. The marriage had been one of convenience for half of its twenty-three years; it seemed to serve no further purpose. His wife, as he had expected, sided completely with Sean.

William Riley tried to be honest with himself. His honesty told him that it was not concern for his family or the shattered dreams for his son that bothered him most. It was not even the potential loss of an enormous annual income, for he had become financially independent. No, it was the potential loss of power. The opening of doors when he arrived at work, limousines waiting for him, Gunderson employees doting on his every move, membership at all of the right social clubs, positions on Boards, almost complete control of the Athletic Building Fund. He knew that if all this were lost, even his portfolio, which included a net worth of roughly $7,000,000, would not be enough to save him from the hardest fall of his life. As others might do when confronted with such adversity, he found himself often drifting, looking back at his rise.

Riley had joined Gunderson at the age of twenty-two, after graduating with a C average from St. John's University. At a young age, he had discovered what most other successful corporate executives eventually learn: if you wish to ascend to the highest level of corporate power, you must either come from the family who owns the company or you must have a mentor. He had made good use of the mentor system in the person of John Spiro.

After Riley had been named Vice President in charge of Marketing, and at a time when Spiro was making his own move towards the Presidency of the Company, it was Riley, his ambition at full throttle, who challenged his former mentor. He had prevailed in a bloody executive battle. The lines had been drawn; people had taken sides and the wounds had still not healed. Because of Gunderson's enormous success, no one (including Spiro) ever brought those wounds out in the open. In the minds of all who were privy to the contest, however, it was not who won, but the manner in which Riley had trampled his way to victory. The payback might now be at hand.

The Board of Directors at Gunderson Brewery was comprised of twelve members, including Riley, and was chaired by Bradford Gunderson. Riley felt that in any decision about his fate, although Bradford Gunderson would listen to the Board, ultimately he would render a final judgment based on his own convictions. Riley was certain that even if the other ten registered disagreement with Gunderson's opinion, he would still do what he wanted. So it concerned Riley that he could not get in to see Gunderson, could not even reach him.

Riley felt that one thing counted in his favor and weighed more heavily with Bradford Gunderson than anything else: Riley had raised corporate profits from a level of $6,400,000 when he took over as President, to $43,000,000 in 1987. He was regarded by most as the premier corporate executive in the beer industry. For this reason alone, he predicted he would survive this ordeal.

At 7:30 a.m. on Monday morning, William Riley, as had been the case for the past eight years, was picked up promptly by his chauffeur, a native of Ireland who had become Riley's friend and confidant. He knew that Riley had been under tremendous strain.

"How are you this morning, Mr. Riley?" the chauffeur asked.

"I'll have a better idea how I am in a couple of hours," he answered.

Riley arrived at the Gunderson Tower, on Park Avenue in New York City at 7:45 a.m. The doorman issued his customary cheery greeting.

From there, he took the corporate elevator to the 48th floor where he was met by security. He immediately proceeded to his office. He had planned nothing from 7:45 a.m. to 8:30 a.m., when the meeting would start. He wanted to be alone, to gather his thoughts and prepare, if needed, a defense which would rest primarily on Gunderson's tremendous profitability under his regime. At 8:25 a.m. his buzzer rang. It was his secretary.

"Mr. Riley, Mr. Gunderson just called. He asked that you wait and he will call back in a few minutes to invite you in."

This concerned Riley. Why was he asked to wait? Had not the decision already been made? At 9:05 a.m., thirty-five excruciating minutes later, Riley was buzzed again.

"They are now ready for you, Mr. Riley."

William Riley walked down the hall and entered the Board Room of Gunderson Brewery. It was a long, rectangular room, 30' by 50', with twelve black leather chairs and an oak table featuring a marble top. The table was equipped with video cassettes at each chair, private telephones, headphones and television monitors to review new advertising programs. It had been a room to which Riley had grown accustomed, one in which some of the most important decisions in the beer-making industry had been made, so many of them under his direction.

"Good morning, Bill. Please come in," Bradford Gunderson said firmly as Riley entered. Riley eased into his chair. Although his stomach was tied in knots, he felt prepared for any possible inquisition. As he adjusted his seating and straightened in his chair, Gunderson looked him squarely in the eyes.

"Bill, I'm going directly to the point. As you know, the past several weeks have been difficult ones for Gunderson Brewery. Never, as long as our family has owned the Brewery, have we experienced such bad publicity. It has been reflected in the value of our stock and, in my best judgment, in the morale of the employees. There is probably nothing worse for a beer company to face, given the volatile political climate governing our industry, than any hint of a drug scandal. In terms of the values we try to foster among our employees, extramarital affairs don't bode well either. You have been..."

Riley tensed, knowing exactly where Gunderson was heading.

"You have been an effective and loyal employee," Gunderson continued. "Profits of our company have soared under your leadership. You have been a team player, a man who has given nothing less than one hundred percent. But, Bill, this is a business. Sometimes, however difficult, we have to make decisions in the best interests of the business and in the best interests of the many thousands of families whose livelihood depends on the good name of Gunderson Brewery. It is for this reason that the Board is asking you to resign, effective immediately."

The worst of William Riley's fears had been realized. He sat numbed, almost dazed. He had always prided himself on his reaction to adversity, but as he looked at his hands, he suddenly realized they were trembling. A thousand thoughts raced through his mind. Curiously, the one that seemed to stick out was that he would no longer be in charge of the Building Fund. That project alone had promised to immortalize him—to etch his name permanently in concrete.

"Bill, I know this is difficult for you to accept. But as I said, you've always been a team player. I have set up a meeting with John Spiro for 9:30 a.m. At that time, you are requested to issue a statement. The statement, naturally, shall have my approval, and should essentially affirm that you accept full responsibility for the difficult situation that Gunderson has been placed in and that your concern, as always, is first and foremost for the company.

"You must," Gunderson emphasized, his voice rising slightly, "go out in style. I'll get together with you late this week, and we'll arrange a fair and equitable financial settlement. As you know, you won't need a lawyer. We'll take very good care of you and your family. But this was the decision that had to be made."

"Is there anything anyone would like to add?" Gunderson asked the Board. The silence was deafening.

As Riley rose to depart, he found himself heading straight for the lavatory, where he spent the next ten minutes. He had not wept since his father had passed away when Riley was thirteen years old. He suddenly found tears streaming down his face.

"Pull yourself together," he said to himself. Moments later, he walked back to his office, where he found his former mentor, John Spiro, sitting behind his desk.

"This is the statement the company would like you to sign, Bill," Spiro said. Riley looked at it slowly.

Spiro, who had done so much for Riley, had grown to loathe him. Riley signed the document, handed it to Spiro and said, "All right, John, you can leave now."

Spiro stood up, looked Riley straight in the eye and said, "So can you, Bill."

Chapter 43

"**W**hen your team is in trouble, the best cure—in fact the only cure— is to work them out of it. That goes for coaches as well as players." It was a tenet that Jack McHale had heard Red Mihalik repeat time after time.

Since the opening loss to Virginia Tech, State had experienced considerable trouble and Jack McHale had spent endless hours trying to work the team out of it. The first "Ellovitch Extravaganza," as the coaching staff snidely referred to the Garden promotion, had been a success. More than 17,000 people turned out to see State manage a 75-69 win over Iona and then listen to Smokey Robinson rekindle Motown memories. Ellovitch, pleased with the turnout as well as the financial success for State, even shook hands with McHale after the victory. It was but a momentary truce.

Four consecutive road games followed the State victory over Iona. The first, at Purdue, had seen State perform reasonably well initially, only to lose 86-82. The next stop was Chicago, where State found itself in one of the great pits in the United States, against Loyola of Chicago. Loyola's team was in no way reminiscent of the '63 NCAA championship club which had been paced by Jerry Harkness. The Loyola coach now put together a rag-tag group of primarily inner-city kids from the Windy City. While Loyola had gained little notoriety outside of the Midwest, McHale and his staff knew they could play. Loyola took a twenty-two point lead at half-time and went on to blow State out 99-68.

McHale returned to campus with a 1-3 record and a team that was supposedly going to finish in the Top Twenty. While road losses were generally more acceptable to fans, the expectations had been so high that the vultures were already starting to circle. McHale trudged wearily to his office at 1:30 in the morning, the trip back from Chicago having been fraught with plane delays due to a Midwest blizzard. He found taped to his office door a story which had appeared in the student newspaper with the headline, "Jack Can't Do It."

McHale had learned from hard experience that there were no more dangerous critics than those writing for the student newspapers. He and his contemporaries often discussed how to handle these immature dilettantes, who were only eighteen or nineteen, but blessed with their first taste of the power of the pen.

McHale was anticipating problems with the student Sports Editor, a senior who had befriended the upperclassmen on the team. His article focused on how McHale had "forgotten" the juniors and seniors in his anxiety to please the three freshmen.

"It is obviously not working," noted the expert. "More time must be given to the experienced players, or the season will end up being another McHale disaster."

What troubled McHale was not so much the content, but the fact that much of the impetus for the story had obviously been provided by his upperclassmen, particularly his captain and clubhouse lawyer.

The next trip on Ellovitch's killer mission was to Orono, Maine. In 1973, in a *Sports Illustrated* article, the gym at the University of Maine in Orono was listed as one of the ten most diffcult places to play in the country. McHale often wondered if Ellovitch had not saved a copy of that article while putting together the '88-'89 schedule. Maine was traditionally short on talent, but always capable of pulling off an upset, something the Black Bears had done at home in recent years against the likes of Michigan State and Marquette.

McHale had been around long enough to know that it was difficult to dig yourself out of a hole early in the season, especially with a young team. Upon arriving at his office and reading the student newspaper, he spent the next three hours drinking as much coffee as his body could take and looking at films of Maine with his two assistants.

"They're not very good," said Brian McCray, "but then again, we're not so good either."

McHale, whose affection for McCray was boundless, found himself slightly irritated at his young assistant.

"Brian, I'll tell you this; if we have that kind of an attitude, we sure as hell won't become good."

"Sorry, Coach. I shouldn't have said that."

The staff finally left McHale's office at 4:30 a.m. As had been the case since the Virginia Tech loss, McHale found it almost impossible to sleep. He tossed and turned and awoke at 9 a.m., getting to his office by 9:30. Knowing that his players would be tired, but believing in the Mihalik notion that "you have to work them out of it," McHale planned a brisk ninety-minute practice. This was met with some dissent from his two assistants.

"I know you guys have your own opinions, but it's been my experience that the worst thing you can do after a bad loss is give the kids a day off," McHale told them. "It gives them time to mope around the dorm and accomplish nothing other than feeling sorry for themselves. If we can get a good hour-and-a-half workout, have them break a sweat, point their thoughts towards Maine and try to forget the past ten days, we can leave for Orono with a positive attitude."

"You know best, Coach," said Mike Lambert.

That afternoon, after a very slow start, the team immersed itself in practice. The players finished with a fifteen minute scrimmage which saw Marvin Lewis and Cormack McDonough again demonstrate their potential, combining for twenty-six of the white team's thirty-two points, while dominating both backboards. Despite all the depression, this brought a smile to McHale's face. As was customary at the end of each practice, the team met at midcourt with their hands clasped. "If we keep doing what we did today, we're going to win a lot of games, guys," McHale told them.

The team left for Bangor, Maine in good spirits and McHale, for the first time since the Iona game, found his own mood to be at an even keel.

As Brian McCray had predicted, Maine was not very good, but what they lacked in talent they made up for in conditioning and execution. The game was a physical war. Maine played a tough man-to-man defense and banged away at both McDonough and Lewis whenever they got the ball inside. As had been the case in most of the earlier games, State experienced difficulty getting on track and went into the locker room trailing 31-29.

McHale, having tried the screaming routine at earlier half times, decided upon a teacher-like approach. This seemed to calm the players. While the second half was not, in Lambert's words, "a Picasso," State played well enough to pull out a 71-63 victory. A win, any win, always left McHale with a brief feeling of euphoria.

While his team was still beset by problems offensively, McHale found himself getting eight full hours of sleep for the first time in three weeks. However, no more than ten minutes after he awoke the next morning, he was thinking about the last leg of the road trip, against Northeastern in Boston. He found himself tensing up immediately.

After the Maine game, he had told his assistants to meet in his room at 10 a.m. the following morning. Lambert had brought along a VHS and films of Northeastern. Unlike Maine, Northeastern was a team with real talent and a track record to go along with it, having appeared in the NCAA tournament in five of the last seven years. For two hours, McHale and his staff reviewed the films before meeting the team for lunch and then heading to the Bangor Airport for the thirty-five minute flight to Boston.

Northeastern, with almost devastating quickness, took control early, led at half time by sixteen and went on to an 89-67 rout. Departing the arena, McHale heard loud and clear the now-familiar "Good-bye Jack." This time it came from more than just a few hecklers.

At no time in fifteen years as a head coach had Jack McHale felt any worse. His squad was simply not responding. He had to do something to turn the team around.

* * * * * *

While McHale found himself in a crisis situation only six games into the season, things had gone reasonably well for Ted Patterson. When matters had gotten close in his next "dump" game, he stayed with his basic four "safe" calls of block-charge, three seconds, foul off an inside screen and foul off a rebound. During the game, he had been aided by the other two officials, who blew several calls, making his job easier and achieving the margin Hondo had desired. He was two for two when he received a call from Hondo at a time previously not agreed upon. He felt his stomach sink as he picked up the phone.

"Ted, I have it on good authority that a top official has broken his ankle."

"That's true," said Patterson, who had just heard of a colleague breaking his ankle in a game the night before.

"He was supposed to work the Princeton-State game in the Garden," said Hondo. "You're free that night. What do you think the chances are of you replacing him?"

"I'd say they're pretty good," said Patterson, wondering how Hondo had gotten all of his information.

"When would you find out?" asked Hondo.

"Probably tomorrow. We have a conference call with the supervisor of officials to go over some assignment changes. If they're going to give me the game, they'd let me know then."

Ted Patterson had found his job of dumping games to be manageable. But the payment of several minor bills had not made him feel any better. In fact, it had made him feel worse. He was constantly depressed and even his wife, from whom he had been able to effectively hide his inner-most thoughts for years, was invariably asking him, "Teddy, what's the matter? You're not yourself and it seems more than just the business."

The following morning, Patterson and three other senior referees participated in a fifteen minute conference call with the supervisor of officials.

"Fellas', as you know, one of your colleagues has broken his ankle and we're going to have to do some reassigning. In looking at the schedule, I see that both Teddy Patterson and Guy Francoise are free on December 28. We need an experienced official to work the State-Princeton game in the Garden. What do you guys say?"

Patterson said nothing, hoping that Francoise would offer to take the game. He had known both Jack McHale and Princeton Coach Pete Carill for years. He knew that from the time the ball was thrown in the air until the final buzzer, both would be scrutinizing his every move.

"My son John is playing in a big high school game that night," said Francoise. "Teddy, I don't know if you have any previous plans, but I'd really appreciate it if you could take it."

"What do you say, Ted?"

"Well, ah . . . ," Patterson paused.

"Teddy, we have two relatively inexperienced guys working the game. We need a guy with experience or Carill and McHale will chew those two guys up."

"OK," Patterson reluctantly agreed.

At 11:15 a.m., Patterson's secretary buzzed him. "It's Mr. Beame on the line."

"Do you have the game, Ted?" asked Hondo.

"Yeah, I have it. What's up?"

"What's up is that the line calls for State and six points. People have won a good deal of money in the past betting Princeton against inexperienced teams with supposedly good talent. Carill's a master at keeping these games close. We want you to keep it close, Ted. It's OK for State to win, but they can't win by more than six points."

"I thought we weren't going to do anything like this until January," Patterson countered. "This is a big game. McHale is having a lot of trouble with his team."

"Precisely," Hondo interrupted. "And that's exactly why we're amazed that they're favored by six points. It's important that you do this, Ted. It's a game we feel we can win a lot of money on. Make sure you're at your best."

With that, Hondo hung up the phone, not allowing Patterson a chance to respond.

* * * * * *

McHale knew that losing games on the road had built up more and more pressure on him and his team. But losing against Princeton in the Garden could be disastrous. He had decided on the trip back from Northeastern that he was spending too much time thinking how Ellovitch had shafted him by scheduling State into an almost no-win situation. Princeton was an obvious case. There was probably no better coach in the country, in terms of getting the most out of mediocre talent, than Pete Carill. In earlier years his Princeton teams had been giant-killers. McHale had to put his feelings toward Ellovitch aside and concentrate solely on bringing his team out of this tailspin.

"We have to work our way out of it," he said to his two assistants, probably for the one hundredth time, as they gathered in his office to review the Princeton films. He went beyond that, however. For the first time in his tenure as head coach, he spoke in honest terms with McCray and Lambert about their plight.

"Fellas', we've never really had a heart to heart about our own situation. I think the time is now. We all know what Ellovitch has done in terms of the scheduling. We also know that our rear ends are now on the line. We're 2-4, and in the public's perception we've lost to teams that are mediocre at best. They'll be 21,000 people at the Princeton game on Tuesday night. If we don't turn it around, we may be receiving our pink slips."

McHale had played against Carill's teams a number of times. Looking at the films, he knew that with the exception of some new faces, this was almost a carbon copy of Princeton's past teams. There was, however, a slight difference in strategy. Carill, traditionally a man-to-man coach, had gone to a tight three-two zone, which his team executed to perfection. On offense, they were as methodical as water dripping slowly from a faucet. They had no fast break and relied totally on a half-court offense, generally using thirty to thirty-five seconds before taking a shot, but in almost all cases, taking a high-percentage shot.

"The one thing we've never had any luck with against Princeton was staying with one defense. We have to mix it up and try to prevent them from executing their game plan. They're a typical Princeton team. Excellent perimeter shooters and more talent than Pete will admit to," McHale smiled. "The big thing is this. While I don't want to open things up offensively, we have to get into our controlled running game and not let Princeton dictate the tempo."

Two nights later, as McHale walked on to the Garden court, it was *deja vu*. The scene brought him back to the Mihalik days of the '50's and '60's and to his own great teams of the mid-'70's. There was not an empty seat in the house. This was a different kind of a feeling, though. It was obvious that a vast majority of the fans were there not only to see the game but the post-game concert as well. It might have been different had State come into the game with a winning record. As he approached Carill's bench to offer his pre-game salutation, McHale looked up in the stands only to find a large sign with a phrase which was now becoming familiar: "Good-bye Jack."

Carill, a fierce competitor, but long on loyalty, said to McHale, "Don't let those s.o.b.'s get to you, Jack."

As he returned to the bench, Brian McCray said, "Teddy Patterson is taking the injured guy's place. That's good. Teddy will let us play."

McHale nodded. Patterson had worked probably forty of his games since McHale became head coach at State. He respected Patterson and knew he would get a fair shake. Patterson would not be intimidated by Carill or the fans.

McHale repeated to his players, "You cannot get behind Princeton early." He said it so much, in fact, that he proved a prophet. Princeton took the lead 8-2. In so doing, the Tigers were able to get into what Carill commonly referred to as their "rhythm." The more Princeton executed, the more frustrated State became and the more the full house in the Garden got into the game. Getting into the game meant getting behind Princeton. State left at half-time, trailing 21-16. "Sixteen points," McHale hissed to his assistants as they walked out amid an almost overwhelming chorus of boos.

McHale did his best during half time to rally his troops. He had tried yelling and screaming in the early season, and then he had tried patience. He realized that, in this case, neither approach was appropriate and so he tried a new "Rockne-like" performance directed at their pride and egos. He worked himself up to such a fever pitch that he found himself almost fainting during his emotional appeal. He wondered what his blood pressure was at that time. But it seemed to reach the players, particularly the freshmen.

"Coach, I don't know what will happen in the second half, but that was one hell of a performance," McCray said to McHale as they departed the locker room.

His performance worked. McHale had instructed his players at half-time to utilize pressure defense for the full ninety-four feet, from both man-to-man and zone alignments. Early in the second half, Princeton began to falter. State cut the lead to three, 35-32, at the fourteen minute mark. At the eleven minute mark, they took the lead on a twenty-five foot jump shot by Billy Powers, 42-41. Two minutes later, in spite of two Carill time outs, they were ahead 52-44 and rolling.

Patterson had approached the second half with his fear having turned into mild relief. At half time, the officials did something that they were not supposed to do but commonly did; they discussed the game.

"Princeton has State totally befuddled," said one of the two young officials working with Patterson. "I doubt there's any way State can come back."

In the normal course of events Patterson would have scolded his young contemporary. In this case, hoping his partner was right, he simply nodded.

The more State pressured Princeton in the second half, the more uptight Patterson became. When Powers had hit his jump shot to give State the lead, Patterson found himself doing something that an official was never supposed to do, something that would surely be noticed. Each time up the court, he looked at the clock and, more importantly, the score. With eight minutes to go and State leading by seven, Patterson found himself becoming disoriented. Hondo had placed strong emphasis on this game and there was much money riding on it. Patterson's two young contemporaries were excellent officials and unlikely to blow any calls.

From the 7:30 mark to the end of the game, Patterson, for the first time in his career as an official, choked. He choked badly. On three consecutive State offensive possessions, Patterson called violations on State. McHale, generally not given to intimidating officials, jumped off the bench in each case, and while not going so far as to get a technical, verbally abused Patterson. With 4:19 remaining, State was ahead by six. Patterson's calls had clearly shifted the momentum to Princeton, but Billy Powers stripped the Princeton guard at half court and began to solo.

Patterson had been the trail official at half court when Powers stole the ball. As he was running down the court he found himself once again looking up at the clock right in front of Jack McHale. If Powers made the lay-up, State's lead would increase to eight. Chasing Powers, the embarrassed Princeton guard did his best to catch up. Just as Powers began his ascent to the basket, the Princeton player crashed in from behind him, both players flying into the stanchion under the basket. Patterson made no call. Another Princeton player snatched the rebound and in uncharacteristic Princeton fashion, wheeled up the floor quickly and passed to one of his teammates, who hit a thirty-foot, three-point jump shot. The State lead was now down to three. McHale completely lost his composure. He stormed past the coach's box onto the floor and chased Patterson, a stream of four letter words gushing from his mouth.

Patterson turned, looked at McHale and then, to the utter shock of his two colleagues, did nothing. For a coach to leave the coaching box and chase an official was one thing, but to go on the floor and say what McHale had said went far beyond a mere technical. It was clearly grounds for ejection.

Patterson's young contemporary, a full thirty-five feet away, seeing that his fellow official was in trouble, ran across the court and hit McHale with a technical foul. The bench technical provided Princeton with two foul shots plus the ball. They made the two shots and thirty-five seconds later hit a fifteen foot jump shot to take the lead by one. Patterson, now white-faced and completely at a loss for reason, did not blow his whistle for the rest of the game, despite several obvious calls in front of him. He did not blow the whistle, he would later recount, because he had lost all track of the game and of reality. Princeton, with a one-point lead and State's inexperience once again showing, took control of the game in the last two minutes and went on to win 60-57.

McHale, forgetting to shake hands with his old friend Carill, charged after Patterson. He caught up to the referee in the hallway under the stands and grabbed him by the arm. "Teddy, you screwed us, you son of a bitch!"

When he finished his tirade, he met Patterson's eyes squarely. What he saw was a pathetic blank stare. He had known Patterson for fourteen years and thought him to be one of the toughest, most fiery officials in the business. Take one inch and Patterson would hit you with a technical. He was always in control of the game. But this time, as Patterson's eyes met McHale's, what McHale saw was a confused, broken man. Patterson's lips said nothing but those frightened eyes spoke volumes, as if to say ... "Please, Jack, please understand." McHale, ready to physically assault Patterson only a minute earlier, just stared at him, not knowing what to think. He turned and headed toward his locker room to meet with his players, and then the press.

Reporters abuzz with Patterson's non-calls, first explored the official's performance with McHale.

"I have no comment," said McHale. The media then went on to a more personal matter.

"Jack, despite the officiating, you lost. Your team is now 2-5. What kind of pressure do you feel?"

"I feel the same pressure I always feel coaching any team," McHale lied.

Thirty minutes later, he left the arena, his mind racing with thoughts of his team, of Patterson's eerie stare, and the reality that this could be his last year as head coach of State. His disorientation was so great that he asked Lambert and McCray to bus the team back without him.

"We'll be leaving for the Irish trip on Monday. We'll give the kids tomorrow off. We'll meet for practice at 10 a.m. on Monday. Tell everybody to make sure they're on time."

McHale headed home. He arrived, looking to his wife for the first time like a broken man. "Honey," he said softly, "I can't even talk about it, it hurts so much." He knew he would not sleep, so he went to his study, sat down, opened a can of beer and stared at the wall.

Jack McHale was forty-one years old. The goals, those lofty goals he had set some years back, seemed out of reach. He would not achieve the level of coaching stardom of a Dean Smith or a Bob Knight. He felt trapped in a profession in which longevity played no part in any plan.

He wistfully recalled a scenario involving his son. On a crisp morning in 1977, Jack McHale had proudly brought Jack, Jr., then age five, to the St. Rose Kindergarten two blocks from home. Nine years later almost to the day, McHale drove his same son, now fourteen years old, to his first day of high school at St. Agnes. In watching his son get out of the car to greet his friends, reality struck Jack McHale squarely in the face. He had missed his son's early youth. His dreams of coaching glory had resulted in a complete lack of the quality of life he knew his family deserved.

As he looked down at his desk, he saw the latest *National Association of Basketball Coaches* magazine lying there. He found his eyes fixing on a cover article, authored by the noted sports psychologist Dr. Lawrence Falk. The article was entitled, "Letting Your Team Go." McHale picked up the magazine and opened it to page thirty-six.

Chapter 44

Steve Ellovitch's career was cruising on the yellow brick road. The past six months had been a pocket full of victories which culminated in a Sunday *New York Times* feature story on his imaginative role in reversing State's athletic fortunes. The story, freely invoking reference to Ellovitch's "promotional genius," had brought his career path exactly where he wanted it. Yes, there had been some bumpy roads, but they were now all behind him.

The first two promotions at the Garden were even better than expected. The Iona game, accompanied by a Smokey Robinson concert, attracted 17,146 fans, netting State a $185,000 profit. The game against Princeton, accompanied by the Beach Boys concert, was even better. A standing room only crowd of 21,276 provided the State coffers with an additional $260,000. Even the Vice President of Financial Affairs was impressed, sending Ellovitch a complimentary memo on the marketing plan.

Finally, his relationship with George DiOrgio continued to grow. Ellovitch was particularly pleased that DiOrgio seemed content with taking a back seat, allowing him to take credit for DiOrgio's genius.

There was one subject in which Ellovitch needed no crash course: how to fire someone within a complicated university structure. His legal background, coupled with his experience as Athletic Director at State (which already had included firing seven employees), made him a bona fide expert. He would now put this expertise to full use in getting rid of Jack McHale.

Ellovitch's animosity toward McHale continued to grow. Even during turbulent times, when his own power might have been in question, Ellovitch was able to keep virtually every member of the athletic department under his thumb—every member with the exception of McHale. Ellovitch's resentment ran deep, of course, and reached back much further than his candidacy for the Athletic Director's job. To Ellovitch, McHale represented the prototype of the many kids in Ellovitch's paranoid youth who had treated him with disdain: the good athlete, the kid from the Irish Catholic family. Ellovitch's hatred for McHale was largely irrational, rooted in nothing more than old wounds for which McHale was not responsible. But it nevertheless existed. Ellovitch wanted him out. He knew the time was now.

The most important requirement for firing an employee at a public university was careful documentation. "You have to build the case," Ellovitch remembered a university attorney telling him. Building the case meant recording anything that might emphasize the targeted employee's inability to do his job. Ellovitch knew that even if a coach's wins exceeded his losses, there were many other ways to fire him within the context of intercollegiate athletics that would barely bring a whisper.

Ellovitch's "file" on McHale began in 1983. He was required to present biannual evaluation reports of every department member, McHale included. Reports had to be reviewed and signed by the employee. Ellovitch's evaluation of McHale had been consistent in that he constantly found fault with McHale's program. Even when McHale had signed the three blue chip prospects, Ellovitch's July 1988 evaluation made note of the "team effort" of the entire Athletic Department in the recruitment of the athletes and further focused on the fifth consecutive "mediocre" season State had experienced. McHale, no novice when it came to university policies, had signed each of the reports because he had no choice. For each of the last six reports, however, his signature was accompanied by a cover letter making note of the points with which he disagreed.

In addition to the biannual evaluations, Ellovitch had seized every opportunity to send McHale a memo, with a copy to the President, detailing any action by McHale's that could be cause for criticism. Over a five year period, the McHale file had grown thick. Based on the 2-5 record and with a team that many experts felt would be in the top twenty by season's end, Ellovitch decided to contact President Pendelton's personal secretary for an appointment with the President.

In setting the appointment, Ellovitch carefully planned his agenda. He knew that Pendelton had been badly shaken by the firing of William Riley and its impact on the Building Fund. Ellovitch viewed Pendelton as essentially a weak person, one whose convictions swayed with the winds. His plan was to discuss his dissatisfaction with McHale first, to lay the foundation for McHale's firing. Ellovitch would then discuss the possibility of a Board position on the building campaign. He also wanted to find out if Robert Steincross was back in the picture.

"It's good to see you, Dr. Pendelton," Ellovitch said, entering the President's office. As he sat down in the uncomfortable green leather chair, his eyes wandered over the endless mahogany bookshelves and framed diplomas. The office was staid and typically academic in comparison to some of the corporate offices Ellovitch had visited during his tenure at State.

"Steve, let me compliment you on the story in the *New York Times*," Pendelton began. "Several prominent alums have commented favorably on it. They are also wondering, I might add, what's the matter with our team?"

This was all Ellovitch needed. For the next twenty minutes he proceeded to review in detail with the President his concerns about McHale, producing at every appropriate interval written documentation of this dissatisfaction.

When he concluded, Pendelton said, "It seems as if you have some compelling concerns. What do you think we should do?"

"I think we should recognize that unless this team can turn its fortunes around completely, that we'll have to ask for McHale's resignation," Ellovitch replied.

"What do you see as the timing on this?"

"No later than mid-February," responded Ellovitch. "If the team hasn't done an about face by then, that will give us time to get his resignation in place, form a search committee and have a new coach hired by the middle of March.

"By doing it this way," Ellovitch continued, "we will have little negative impact on our recruiting."

"Do you see any other position for McHale within the Athletic Department?"

"Dr. Pendelton, our budget is tight as a drum as it is. I honestly don't think it would be appropriate to, in effect, create a position for McHale, despite his long association with the school."

Pendelton nodded in agreement.

Buoyed by the President's positive reaction to his well-planned execution of McHale, Ellovitch pressed on: "I was most disturbed to hear about Bill Riley..."

Without having to say anymore, Ellovitch allowed Pendelton to ramble on for several minutes. He could see that the President was visibly concerned, knowing full well that if the Building Fund Drive collapsed that his own position within the University would be severely, if not fatally, compromised.

"Do you feel the Gunderson commitment is still intact? After all, they did have the press conference. I can't see them backing out." Ellovitch wondered.

"I don't think they will either; but, as you know, this was Bill Riley's baby. I've been trying to reach the Senior Vice President of Marketing over there by phone for the last two weeks, with no success."

Ellovitch leaned forward, "What about Bob Steincross? What's his position?"

"Well, as you've read in the paper, there were some real problems there. Riley, at the time, convinced me that Steincross was not the man who should take the reins on this. I went along with it. I hope it wasn't a mistake. I don't see any way that Steincross could be brought back to a position of leadership after the way he was pushed out. Certainly, he can continue to have a background role, but in answer to your question, Mr. Steincross' part in this project will be minimal."

Ellovitch, his adrenaline now flowing freely, pressed on: "Dr. Pendelton, in my judgment, if Gunderson has not indicated that they are pulling back on the commitment, I think it's important that a State University presence be firmly established in this project. I certainly could understand your sound reasoning in initially making this a corporate program."

Pendelton, shaking his head, responded, "Steve, you have no idea how concerned I was about doing that."

"I understand, and as you know, I supported that direction. But I think it's important that someone from the University bring the committee together and keep the thing on track. I honestly think that I'm the man to do it."

The President paused, then said, "I couldn't agree with you more. What steps should we take?"

Ellovitch was elated and, as always, prepared. He proceeded to outline his plan to assure continuation of the funding and to rid the program of any potential scandal. Twenty minutes later, the two agreed that Pendelton would recommend that Ellovitch be named Chairman of the Athletic Building Fund.

As the meeting concluded, Pendelton said, "I'm sure we can get the Gunderson people to go along with this as well as the other Board members. In fact, they'll probably all breathe a sigh of relief."

Chapter 45

Bob Johnson was a giant in sports journalism. From his beginnings as a beat writer at the *Newark Star Ledger*, he had risen to the exalted position of syndicated sports columnist for the *New York Times*. Seventy-six newspapers throughout the United States and Canada carried his columns. He was the consummate professional and he set the standard to which every young sports journalist aspired. Over an honor-filled, thirty-six year career, Johnson had won three Pulitzer Prizes.

Milo Casey, while not in possession of Johnson's international reputation, was considered Ireland's foremost sports journalist. As the top sports columnist for the *Irish Times*, Casey's assignments included virtually every prestigious international sporting event. Through such events, Johnson and Casey had developed a close personal relationship, which even extended to their families. In subsequent years, Johnson would bring his family to the British Open and Casey would bring his family to the Kentucky Derby, always spending four or five days at the other's home. Johnson had last seen Casey at the 1988 British Open and was looking forward to their planned sojourn to the Derby in April. When Johnson's phone rang at 6:30 a.m. on Friday, December 20, he half expected to hear Casey's voice on the other end of the line because of the five-hour time difference from Dublin to Bedford, New York. Casey knew that Johnson was an early riser and that this would be the best time to reach him.

"If you think I'm calling to wish you a Merry Christmas you're dead wrong," chortled Casey.

Johnson, with a smile on his face, responded, "It was no surprise that Kerry beat the Dubliners again in the All Ireland. When are the people in your part of the country ever going to learn to play that crazy game?"

This good natured banter went back and forth for several more minutes, until Casey, turning serious, said, "Bob, did you know that this State University basketball team is coming across to play in a Cork Invitational Tournament."

"No, I didn't," Johnson responded.

"I half expected you didn't, but I'm calling for a reason. There's an old Gaelic term called *scean*. It means a story...a big story. Robert, I think you should make the trip."

Chapter 46

Robert Steincross never enjoyed the morning paper more than during the weeks of Bill Riley's fall from grace. Also, he eagerly awaited the next building fund meeting.

The fall had been swift and hard. Riley was asked to resign from virtually all of his prestigious charitable boards. While this was embarrassing, it paled in comparison to the treatment now accorded him at the Gunderson corporate headquarters. During his rise to power, Riley was not subtle in forming alliances with co-workers who he felt could facilitate his career, while slighting those who could not. It was now their turn.

Riley made one final pitch to save his job in a meeting with Bradford Gunderson. But his plea did little to rouse sentiment in Gunderson. The Chairman stayed true to his word to take care of Riley and his family from a financial standpoint: $1.5 million in severance pay and 100,000 shares of Gunderson stock at a PMV of $11.30 per share. In addition, Riley would be retained as a consultant for a five-year period at $50,000 per annum. His benefit and retirement package would remain intact. He would have use of the President's office, his full secretarial staff and his driver for three more months. At that point, he would be provided with a secretary and office space in another building in Manhattan. "I don't think you want to put yourself in a position of coming to the corporate headquarters everyday, Bill, at least for the time being," said Gunderson. It was the typical Gunderson way of handling a problem. Riley not only knew it well; he had exercised it himself.

While he was financially secure, it was power which mattered to him most, and which he knew had been wrested from him forever. No longer would he render decisions that could affect the lives of thousands by simply picking up the phone. No longer could he cull favors from the elite. No longer would he be in the inner circle of the country's decision makers. Another Riley hater summed it up succinctly to him as their paths crossed at the Sleepy Hollow Country Club.

"No longer will your phone calls be returned," he smiled sardonically.

Meanwhile, Riley's son Sean was having difficulty coping with his own quagmire. It was clear to Sean that whatever affection his parents might have held for each other had ended with his arrest. Sean overheard enough quarrels to know that his mother would be the only one he could count on as he faced, at best, a stiff fine and hours of community service, and, at worst, imprisonment for as long as ten years. Ironically, his friendship grew with Robby Nesbitt. Uniting the two was their commitment to find out who had set them up. . .and why.

* * * * * *

As the two young defendants began to map a strategy, the Gunderson hierarchy began to reassess the brewery's role in the State building project. A Board meeting was called to choose Riley's replacement as chairman.

On the following Wednesday, the Samuel Adams room of the Union League Club was replete with two bartenders and three waiters walking about with plates of hors d'oeuvres ranging from crab quiche to caviar. All twelve Board members had arrived, the last being Robert Steincross. Two new faces were present. One was the Senior Vice President of Gunderson Brewery, who Bradford Gunderson had assigned to the project. The other was Steve Ellovitch. After hors d'oeuvres and drinks, the group retired to the Hoover Room, where they sat down to filet mignon and glazed carrots.

At 8:15, fundraiser Robert O'Connell gently tapped his Waterford crystal glass with a spoon and began.

"Gentlemen, we appreciate everyone being here. As you know, we have had some rocky times in the past six months. I am going to begin the meeting by asking our colleague from Gunderson Brewery to report on the Gunderson position in light of Bill Riley's resignation."

The Gunderson Senior Vice President pointed out to the Board that the Gunderson commitment was still firm. Taking his cue from a private session he had with President Pendelton prior to the dinner meeting, he said, "We think, in light of what is going on, that there should be a stronger University presence. Our corporate interests will be protected. I think you'll agree, however, that it is the University that will be the principal beneficiary of this effort and I know Dr. Pendelton feels very comfortable with the recommendation he is about to make. But before he does that I'd like to go around the room and ask for a show of hands of those still committed."

To no one's surprise, every corporate hand was raised.

Pendelton took the floor. "Gentlemen, State has been blessed with some excellent leadership in our athletic department in Steve Ellovitch. Steve's visionary marketing program has been the subject of a number of outstanding articles, one of which I have taken the liberty of placing at each of your table settings. In discussing this with the people at Gunderson, we all feel that it's appropriate that Bill Riley's position as Chairman of the Committee be taken by a University official. With the full support of Gunderson Brewery, I am recommending Steve Ellovitch. I would be interested in your reactions."

"I think it's a good move, Dr. Pendelton," said Joe Kett of Merrill Lynch. "I'm all for it."

The others all nodded.

Ellovitch, adept at reading facial expressions and body language, was convinced that all but one of the members were supportive of the idea. The lone dissenter, he suspected, was Robert Steincross. Usually a dominant figure in any gathering, Steincross sat silently through the entire meeting. His only response had been an almost sarcastic smile during some of the comments by the marketing executive of Gunderson and by Pendelton.

As the meeting concluded, Steincross got up from his table, retrieved his coat and headed for the door.

"Thank you for coming, Bob," President Pendelton almost yelled as he proceeded across the room to shake Steincross' hand.

Steincross, smiling, turned and looked at the President and then at Ellovitch. He nodded and then left the room.

Chapter 47

"**O**nce they pay you, they own you."

These prophetic words of warning were spoken to Mike Lambert in his senior year of high school by a community recreation leader who had taken a keen interest in him. He knew that Lambert, then one of the most highly recruited players in the country, was easy prey for under-the-table payments which had become commonplace in college basketball even back in the early '70's. Those same words came back to haunt Lambert in the form of George DiOrgio.

DiOrgio had lived up to every promise. The money for providing the critical information about State's schedule was received regularly. Lambert knew though, that he was at the low end of the payoff totem pole. Indeed, State, DiOrgio, the unions and the Garden were taking the big slices of the pie.

The tone in DiOrgio's voice had troubled Lambert during their last phone call. It had been firm and demanding, Lambert wondered about the "project" DiOrgio had in mind. Thinking back to the community recreation leader's warning, Lambert realized that DiOrgio now owned him. It would be extremely difficult for Lambert to say no to anything. He had already accepted money from DiOrgio in a deal that, if made public, would end Lambert's coaching career.

Lambert's concern focused on one possibility which he dreaded: drugs. While Lambert had never been a user, he had been around enough people, particularly in athletics, to know that the users were many and the money big. He did not know DiOrgio to have any connection with drugs, but he knew that DiOrgio liked money and that drug dealing offered the opportunity for big money.

If drugs were the "project," Lambert could not determine what his role would be. Certainly, if State lived up to its pre-season expectations, became a Top Twenty team and gained selection to the NCAA tournament, there would be a tremendous amount of money around. But Lambert knew DiOrgio was astute enough to recognize that the squad was floundering and that 2-5 teams were not on schedule to receive NCAA bids.

It would have to be another approach that DiOrgio had plotted; perhaps using Lambert as his liaison for on-campus dealings. State, while not attracting students of affluence as did the Ivy League schools or the Little

Three, certainly had its share of wealthy kids. Maybe this was what DiOrgio had in mind.

DiOrgio suggested the two meet at the Randolph Club, a quiet, private conclave whose membership consisted primarily of people in the entertainment business. It was located on 21st Street in the Lower East Side. The fact that this represented the first time DiOrgio and Lambert would meet in a public forum was not lost on Lambert as he entered the foyer.

The Randolph Club was unlike the staid, conservative, private clubs that graced many parts of Manhattan. It was posh and glitzy, with mirrored walls, chrome and glass fixtures and mauve and black upholstered booths. The Club's manager, attired in a powder blue tuxedo, greeted Lambert. "Good afternoon, Sir. May I help you?"

"Yes, I'm having lunch with Mr. DiOrgio," responded Lambert.

"You must be Mr. Lambert. Mr. DiOrgio is waiting in the dining room." The manager ushered Lambert to the rear of the dining room, and a quiet table set apart from the rest of the dining area. DiOrgio greeted Lambert warmly.

"Mike, it's good to see you."

As he shook Lambert's hand, DiOrgio noticed that Lambert's palm was stone cold. The two sat down and exchanged small talk, mostly focused on the team. DiOrgio, in testing Lambert with his questions, tried to gauge Lambert's reaction as to why the team was faltering and, specifically, his reaction to Jack McHale's coaching. It would be an important series of questions. In reality, DiOrgio was probing Lambert's loyalty, which he found to be intact with regard to McHale.

"It's not the coach," said Lambert. "We've had a very difficult early season schedule, but the kids are getting better. I think we can turn it around."

While DiOrgio sensed a lack of conviction in Lambert's voice, Lambert's response still satisfied him. So he went straight to the first problem, Lambert's nervousness.

"Mike, you seem a bit uptight. Is there anything wrong?"

Lambert, surprising DiOrgio with his frankness, recounted the old warning he learned from the community recreation leader many years ago. He concluded by saying, "George, in effect you own me. I just hope what we're doing here today isn't going to do anything to ruin Mike Lambert or my pride."

DiOrgio sat back and smiled. "Mike, in many ways you're one of the most admirable people I've ever met. Let me assure you that what we're here to talk about today is certainly not illegal, at least as construed by our system of jurisprudence. I'm not going to tell you that the NCAA would be wild about it, and I'm also not saying that it's something you *have* to do. But before I get into what I want to talk to you about, let's discuss your own life and where I see you going in the next couple of years."

It was now Lambert's turn to be surprised as DiOrgio candidly discussed

Lambert's career and the realities of becoming a Division I head coach. "Mike, you had a good shot at the New Jersey State job. You didn't quite make it. You know as well as I that if State continues to lose, the staff, yourself included, will be fired. There is little doubt that you'll be able to hook on with another school as an assistant. You've proven yourself to be a good recruiter, and most importantly, you've proven yourself to be loyal, something that I'm told weighs heavily with most head coaches. But if the staff is fired, and even if you do hook on at another Division I school as an assistant, your head coaching career is set back at least four or five years. At another school you'll have to prove yourself all over again and then hope the team wins so that you'll be in a position to become a head coach. Is what I'm saying essentially correct?"

Lambert nodded. "George, for a guy in the rock business, you sure have learned the ropes of college basketball pretty quickly."

"I learned them because I always do my homework, Mike. And my homework on Mike Lambert would lead me to believe that when you came in today, your first thought was that George DiOrgio was going to propose a drug deal. Am I correct?"

"You're right on, George," an astonished Lambert answered.

"Well, I may like big money but I'm not dumb and, believe it or not, I do draw the line on certain things...things like drugs. Plus, for me to get into it would be stupid. Being in the profession I'm in, I would be a logical guy for the feds to keep a close eye on. We're not here to talk about drugs, Mike, and I can assure you in any deals that you and I do, drugs will never be a part of them." DiOrgio could sense Lambert breathing a heavy sigh of relief.

"Now that you know neither of us will be going to jail for twenty years, let me tell you why we are here. Sure, there's money in drugs, but there are a lot of other ways to make money and one of them is representing athletes...being an agent. I know myself, Mike. I like reading my name in the paper and I like being associated with athletes and entertainers. I love the glamour...the excitement. Your pal Ellovitch likes his name in the paper too, so I've purposely taken a back seat in that deal so he can feed his ego. But basically what I look for are projects that can make a lot of money and can put George DiOrgio's name on the front pages with the stars."

Lambert began to speak, but was interrupted by DiOrgio.

"This is where you come in. You have a good reputation; you know virtually every basketball coach in the country. I'm sure you have good access to the football people as well. You're in the network; I'm not. In order for me to sign players, I need someone to introduce me. Once that's done, I can take care of the rest. What I've learned is that the key to any business is getting in the door."

"One thing strikes me as being a problem right away, George," responded Lambert. "If I become affiliated with George DiOrgio, Ellovitch will figure out that it was me who provided you with the dates."

"Let me say this about Ellovitch," replied DiOrgio. "Number one, I'm certain he already knows you're the one and doesn't give a damn. In fact, he's probably glad because we've made State more money than he could have ever made on his own. Number two, for reasons we won't get into today, you don't ever have to worry about Steve Ellovitch doing anything to you based on your relationship with me."

Lambert once again felt uneasy. DiOrgio pressed on.

"The first area I considered, given the fact that I'm working with State in the promotion of these games, is whether I, according to NCAA rules, would be able to represent athletes. The answer is yes. The fact that I'm involved in a joint venture on the promotion of State's games does not give the NCAA any legal basis to prevent me or my company from representing athletes. So, let's go to the next step, which is your role. At first, your role would be simply to act as my introducer. At the Final Four, at coaches' meetings and other places—all you say is that 'George DiOrgio is a guy who is honest and a good businessman. He told me he'd like to meet you. I think you should sit down and hear what he has to say.' If anyone asks why you're doing this, you simply tell them that you're sick of seeing kids get screwed by unethical agents and that DiOrgio is a straight shooter."

"Would I be doing this with coaches?" asked Lambert.

"You'd be doing it with coaches and players. I'm sure that some of the kids you recruited for State that ended up at other schools will still know and like you. I'm looking to get in the door both with the coaches and the players. For this I'm willing to pay you."

"What are we talking about?" Lambert asked.

"We're talking about $1,000 a month for now. As you know, taking money is a flagrant violation of NCAA rules, but believe me it's done all the time. We'll be able to structure your payments so that nothing or no one can ever come back at you. In three or four months from now, you'll probably be taking a hard look at your career and where you want to go. If the staff gets fired, I'll be prepared to offer you a full time job doing this at a salary of $60,000 per year."

"Well, why can't we wait until then? What's the need for me to take money under the table now?"

"First of all, you don't have to take the money. You can do it for free. I'm simply offering the money. The rush is because in order for me to sign any players before the June draft, I have to begin to establish relationships now. The NCAA rules, as you know, prohibit me from talking to any player directly, but the rules don't prohibit me from talking with coaches, getting my name around and even talking with parents. This is why it's critical that we get going right away. I'm not demanding that you do this, and I'm not demanding that you take any money."

"George, if that's the case, then I'll do it. But I don't want any money, at least for now. What I do want is your assurance that if I get fired and I don't want to continue in coaching, the job you talked about will be there," Lambert insisted.

"You can bank on it," replied DiOrgio.

Chapter 48

It was 7:30 a.m. and Jack McHale had not slept. He had not anticipated the effect that Dr. Lawrence Falk's article would have on him. His first reading of "Letting Your Team Go," some six hours earlier, had told him that Falk was uncanny in his analysis of why teams do not win. McHale realized that much of what Falk was saying applied directly to his own team. He re-read the article four more times, each time picking up something new, each time getting more excited. He decided that he would wait until 8 a.m., the earliest hour that any form of protocol would allow him to call a person's home, especially a person he did not even know.

At 7:55 a.m. McHale picked up the phone and dialed Information for area code 804, Charlottesville, Virginia. His first concern was soon alleviated by the Virginia directory assistance operator, who quickly recited Dr. Falk's home phone number. McHale breathed a sigh of relief, saying to himself, "I'm glad it wasn't unlisted." After jotting down the number on a piece of note paper, he then paced the floor waiting until one minute after eight. McHale, in dialing the number, hoped that Falk was an early riser.

"Hullo," whispered the obviously just-awakened male voice.

"Is this Dr. Falk?"

"Yes it is," came the sleepy response.

"This is Jack McHale. I'm the head basketball coach at State University in New York."

"What the hell time is it, Coach?" Falk asked.

"I'm awfully sorry. It's 8:01 a.m., but about seven hours ago, after a loss that may be the beginning of the end of my coaching career, I happened to pick up your article in the recent NABC *Coaches' Journal*."

"I knew I shouldn't have sold them that article," an awakening Falk replied in jest.

"Dr. Falk, I don't know if you know anything about me or my team, but your article seems to be almost written with my team in mind. I'm wondering if I can meet with you?"

"First, Jack, understand that you're talking to one of the great basketball junkies in the United States. I know all about you and your team. While my article was not written specifically with your team in mind, I do make it a practice to track five or six teams that I find interesting, in terms of the uniqueness of personnel and unusual obstacles they might face. I chose yours as one for this season. I have been following your team closely. In fact, I called Sports Line at about midnight and found that you were beaten by Princeton. To be honest, I had half expected to hear from you, although not quite this early on a Sunday morning."

"Again, I'm sorry for getting you out of bed, but since you're a junkie you probably know where I'm coming from. I really would like to get together."

"Let me pull out my calendar. Can you hold a minute?"

"Dr. Falk, you're really going to think I'm off the wall, but I was talking about meeting with you today."

"I definitely should not have sold them that article!"

"I don't blame you if you think I'm a bit off base, but I'm willing to catch the first flight to Charlottesville. You see, my team leaves for Ireland tomorrow. We'll be gone for a week. I'd really like the chance to discuss the situation with you before we leave."

"Well, if you can get plane connections to Charlottesville, I'd be more than pleased to meet with you. The only carrier that comes in here on any kind of semi-regular basis is Piedmont. Why don't you check with them and get back to me."

Five minutes later, McHale called Falk back and told him he would arrive at the Charlottesville Airport at 1:50 that afternoon. "I'll have to catch a flight out at 7 p.m. in order to get back to meet with the team tomorrow," said McHale.

"I'll pick you up at the airport. My home is only five minutes away."

"One last question, Dr. Falk. What's your fee?"

"Normally, it's $1,500 a day, but since this is Sunday, I'll throw in lunch."

"You've got a deal," laughed McHale. As he hung up the phone he wondered how Steve Ellovitch would react to a $1,500 consultation fee for a team that was now 2-5. McHale decided that he would pay out of his own pocket if Ellovitch balked.

Sally McHale and the two children were still asleep, so McHale left his wife a note, saying only that he would be back by 9:30 that evening and not to worry. He had found that it was sometimes best not to tell his wife too much about his work as a coach. While Sally McHale had become used to the pressure of Division I basketball, Jack knew that she was still highly sensitive to the criticism leveled at her husband. He also decided that he would call his wife once he concluded his meeting with Falk to assure her again that everything was fine.

After he landed at the Charlottesville Airport and made his way to the arrivals terminal, he immediately spotted Falk, who was short in stature and slightly balding, but possessed a professorial aura. McHale had become familiar with his face from the picture of Falk that accompanied the article in the *NABC* Journal.

"Dr. Falk, I really appreciate you doing this."

"Jack, anybody crazy enough to fly to Charlottesville on a moment's notice is deserving of my time."

McHale immediately took a liking to Falk, a feeling that deepened as they made the brief drive through Charlottesville to Falk's home.

The house was as McHale had guessed. Built in 1830, it was a Georgian colonial. As they entered the foyer, Falk's wife greeted them and ushered the two into the living room. An oriental rug covered the oiled oak floor and McHale felt at ease surrounded by the antiques. Patricia Falk had prepared bran muffins and tea, which she brought in promptly. The three then sat down in front of the roaring fire.

"Jack, we've had a great many coaches and athletes in this living room. While I was kidding you a bit on the phone, I want you to know that I have paid particular attention to your team. In fact, I watched your first game on cable against Virginia Tech."

"Ugh," responded McHale.

Falk smiled. "In all seriousness, I wouldn't have allowed you to make the trip unless I thought I could help."

McHale, feeling even more comfortable with Falk, looked around at the beautiful surroundings and thought to himself, "What a nice life this must be."

"I'll let you and Jack do your business," said Patricia Falk as she departed.

The two men stood up and Falk led McHale to his office, located immediately adjacent to the living room. The office, like the house itself, met McHale's expectations for a person of Falk's reputation. The study was decorated with pictures, plaques and other memorabilia.

Falk pulled out a notebook and a pen from his drawer, looked at McHale and said, "OK, Jack, tell me everything you can about your team."

McHale spent the next thirty minutes providing Falk with every detail he could. At certain points, when McHale thought he had fully explained something about a player or another aspect of the team, Falk would gently prod him to provide even more information. Once McHale finished, Falk said, "That's good. I think I have the picture. Now, give me the same picture of Jack McHale."

While comfortable talking about his team, McHale felt a little reluctant to talk about himself. With subtle but firm persuasion, Falk got McHale to talk and talk and talk. Forty-five minutes later, McHale realized that he had revealed more of himself to Falk than anyone, with the exception of his wife.

"You certainly know how to get a guy talking," McHale laughed.

"It's what I get paid for," replied Falk. "Look, I appreciate your sharing all that information. Some of it I anticipated, having followed your team. But a lot of the additional information you just provided I really need if I'm to help you. Let's see what we can do."

"The first thing I'd like you to do is to feel free to ask a question," said Falk. "Or, if you disagree with something I say, don't hesitate at all to tell me, but wait on this until I finish my initial points. In my opinion, in order for your team to achieve the level of success you are hoping for and, as you said, unfortunately, a lot of other people are expecting, you will have to make some major changes in your coaching philosophy. But we'll come back to that. First, I want to talk with you about my philosophy of the game as it relates to coaching, and particularly, as it relates to your team, based on what I now know."

Falk went on to break the game down into three components—defense, rebounding and offense. "In my opinion, it's perfectly acceptable to coach your team as much as you want in the first two categories, defense and rebounding," he began. "You need not worry about over-coaching. Nor should you worry about providing them with too much structure. From what I've seen and from what you've told me, those are two areas that are progressing reasonably well. Correct?"

"Yes. It's our offense that's killing us."

"OK, let's talk about the offense because it's here that I'll probably say some things that you might not agree with initially. The first thing I'll point out is that probably for the first time in your coaching career, including your great teams in the late '70's, you are now coaching truly gifted athletes. The thing about coaching gifted athletes is this: while it's perfectly all right to harness them in the areas of defense and rebounding, it's absolutely devastating to harness them on offense."

"Well, I agree with that to a certain extent, Dr. Falk, but...."

"Jack, remember, you're paying $1,500 and spending a lot of your valuable time to come and listen to me. Please, for now at least, just listen."

McHale, fighting his competitive instincts, sat back.

"My first suggestion to you is that on offense you remove all parameters. Before I get too far into it, let me provide you with some examples. While I get paid as a sports psychologist, I also pride myself as being somewhat of a historian of sports and, particularly, basketball. If you follow the evolution of the game, there are several coaches who have played critical roles in changing the entire thought process of the game. The first and perhaps foremost of all is Red Auerbach. While most people think of Auerbach as a genius in terms of his player deals, what should never be forgotten about the guy was that he was a coaching genius as well. Do you know how many plays the Boston Celtics ran when they won all the world championships with Cousy, Russell and Heinsohn?"

"Any basketball coach worth his salt would know that. They ran just seven," said McHale.

"Precisely, seven plays. Auerbach's entire philosophy centered around tough, aggressive defense, an offense that was based on the fast break and something very important to our discussions today—giving every player on his team the green light to shoot. As you read in my article, Auerbach was a true example of letting his players go. But let's talk about some of your own colleagues at the college level. Dean Smith is one of my favorite coaches and favorite people. If I had a son, Dean would be the kind of guy I would want my son to play for. But Dean Smith, arguably, has had the best talent year-in and year-out in college basketball, yet he has only won one NCAA championship.

"Now I understand how you coaches all think," Falk laughed, since he could sense McHale becoming a bit uneasy. "You are loyal to each other and Dean Smith is one of your gurus. Please understand, I'm not criticizing Dean; I'm just stating what I believe to be the facts, and the facts are these. Dean's teams begin each season literally months ahead of the opposition. His system is such that if you're looking for a coach who will win you twenty games a year, every year, there are probably none better. But if you're looking for a coach whose teams will win an NCAA championship, Dean is simply not your man. In my opinion, his Carolina teams, while great in talent and superbly coached, simply get wound up too tight at tournament time. If you trace the Carolina defeats in NCAA tournaments, you'll generally find that they were beaten by teams who, on that particular night, did a better job of letting go offensively than Carolina did."

"I'm not sure I totally agree with you," replied McHale.

"And I'm not expecting you to, I'm just trying to give you my views. Let's take another one of your great coaches, Bobby Knight. Knight has won three NCAA championships, yet in other seasons his teams have not done nearly as well. To me, if you look at his three championship teams, and particularly the team in '81 with Isiah Thomas and the most recent championship team with Alford, Smart and Garrett, Knight's team is the exact prototype of what I'm talking about. They play tremendous fundamental defense, get excellent rebounding out of all five players and they let go offensively.

"If you think back to the Isiah Thomas team, that was hardly the type of club you would call well-disciplined on offense. The same was true, to a large extent, for the '87 team. While Alford was certainly a good example of a somewhat regimented player offensively and clearly played a vital role in that championship, it was the addition of Keith Smart, a guy who often played out of control, that made the difference in winning the title. If you go back to some of Knight's mediocre teams and watch them carefully, I think you'll see that they reverted back to an almost too disciplined style, a style where players were literally afraid to make mistakes for fear of being pulled out of the game.

"This is exactly the kind of thing that you, as a coach with gifted athletes, must get away from. I'll reiterate a point," Falk continued. "I'm talking about the gifted athlete and not the ordinary player. Let me name you a coach that I think might be the best example of what I'm talking about. I'd be willing to bet that if the National Association of Coaches were polled as to who the best coach in the country is, that most of you would respond either Dean Smith or Bobby Knight. Is that true?"

"I'd say that's very true," McHale agreed.

"Well, I bet if you posed the same question to sports psychologists who had a particular interest in basketball, they would come back with another name, Denny Crum."

McHale smiled.

"Crum is a guy," Falk said, "who, in my opinion, has the best chance year-in and year-out to win championships. Because Louisville plays a murderous schedule and Crum doesn't always have the talent of a Dean Smith or a Bobby Knight, he may not have the same type of records, but put Crum in a tournament and his teams are extremely tough to beat. I'm not saying you'll agree with this, but my opinion of Crum's success is that he's a guy who recognizes that when he has gifted athletes, he must let them go offensively. More importantly, he has enough courage as a coach to be willing to accept some criticism."

"How do you mean?" asked McHale.

"I've made it my business to study coaches and their personalities," Falk continued. "For most coaches, the worst thing you can say to them is that they don't have control of their players. This is something that is the driving force behind a Knight or a Smith. They'll accept a loss on some terms, but never do they want to hear that their players were out of control. With Crum, there have been times in his career when you might hear that. But I believe Crum has been able to make the critical distinction that wins championships. There's a difference between controlling your players and controlling the game.

"Crum consistently allows his players almost unlimited freedom on offense. Sure, on occasion Louisville might look a little bit ragged. But put them in a championship game, when the lights are bright and the pressure is at its greatest and they respond. Why do they respond? Because they're not afraid of failure. If they miss a shot, they know they aren't coming out. They know, because they are taught to know that basketball is a game of mistakes. I won't bore you with too many more of my feelings about the great coaches, but I think you can point to most championship coaches—John Wooden being another good example—and say that while they were highly regimented on defense and in the fundamentals of rebounding, they provided a great deal of latitude on offense.

"Jack, in watching your teams," Falk concluded, "you are not giving them any appreciable latitude. If you're going to win, you've got to change."

"You certainly know how to hurt a guy," said McHale.

"I'm not trying to," Falk replied. "I'm just trying to help, but in that vein, let's take a hard look at you and your team. Let me ask you a question. When have you watched McDonough and Lewis play their best basketball offensively?"

"That's easy," replied McHale. "In the gym during the September and early October runs."

"Exactly!" Falk said emphatically. "And it's no surprise why. When these kids were growing up, they always had the green light. In the pre-practice runs, they were also given the green light. They knew that if they missed a shot or made a mistake, that no one was going to yell at them or take them out of the game."

"I see where you're going, Dr. Falk, but I still have some reservations. Don't you think that you have to have some rules for a team on offense?"

"Some rules, yes. But in your situation, particularly given that the team is so uptight, the first thing you must do is remove all rules and then, as they begin to get their confidence back, maybe add a few basic rules. But for God's sake don't go overboard."

"OK, but how do I convey this to the team?"

"The first thing you're going to have to do is something that will be extremely difficult for someone as proud as you. You are going to have to go to the team tomorrow morning, sit them all down and say to them, whether you believe it or not, 'Guys, the reason we are playing poorly is totally due to me.'"

McHale sat back. "Are you kidding?"

"No, Jack, I'm not kidding. First of all, you've been around kids long enough to know that they're not going to take the blame and that someone has to. Secondly, the reality of the situation is that you *are* the head coach and the team is *not* performing well. It may be difficult, but you don't have any choice."

Falk continued: "I'm not asking you to tell them that you're a lousy coach; only that in breaking the game down, you feel you've coached well on defense, rebounding and fundamentals, but that you've constrained them too much offensively. That from this day forward, you are going to let them go. Believe me, when you tell this to your players, watch how the tension in the room completely abates.

"The next thing you have to do is give them a pep talk, Rockne-style if you like, on the fact that they are indeed good players, but they've been placed in an almost impossible situation."

"In what way?" McHale asked.

"The best way to win with your team now is to portray them as the underdogs. These kids have been put into an extremely difficult position. In reading between the lines, I would say that your A.D. has had a lot to do with this. As a predominantly freshman team, they've been rushed into a role of favorites. What you have to do, at least in their minds, and if possible, in the minds of the media and the fans, is put them into the role of underdogs. State as unequivocally as you can to the players, and anyone else who'll listen, that you have a tough schedule the rest of the way, that there is no pressure on them, that you will take any and all of the pressure on your own shoulders and that whatever they accomplish the rest of this year will be a plus."

"A lot of that is almost totally contrary to my whole approach as a coach," McHale reminded Falk.

"I know that, Jack, but you have an attitude problem now on your team that you must deal with. The best way to deal with it is to change your players' mindset from being the favorites who are failing to the underdogs who have a goal, and now have the tools to reach that goal."

"What else?" asked McHale.

"The next key in my mind is your point guard, Powers."

"What about him?"

"McDonough and Lewis will respond immediately and favorably if you tell them you are going to loosen up the offense and let them go. Powers will be a different story. Is it correct that his father was either a coach or a good player?"

"Yes, in fact his father was one of the best guards ever to come out of New York City," said McHale.

"What you have to do with Powers then is sit him down alone," said Falk. "The gist of the conversation has to be directed toward the fact that throughout his entire career he was told to take great pride in not making mistakes, to be under full control. What you have to convey to him is that it's OK for him to make a mistake. He has to become more of a risk-taker on offense. Most importantly, if he turns the ball over trying to do this, he must know his job is secure. In effect, Jack, you have to tell him that no matter what happens offensively, he is your point guard. You want him to take risks, and no matter what the result, he's your man.

"In other words, with Powers and every other player on your team, you have to remove the fear of failure. Give them that same feeling they have when they're playing in the summer or in the gym before the season starts. The great offensive teams and the great offensive players possessed great physical talent, but also, in many ways, they had sort of. . .let's call it an 'air-head' approach to offense. In other words, from Havlicek to Maravich to Earl Monroe to Rick Barry to Dr. J, the great offensive players had absolutely no fear of shooting. If you take it on a more intellectual level, think of it in these terms. You have been preaching the middle class work ethic to your team. The middle class work ethic will get you to the middle class. But it will not get you to the upper class. Jack, it's those wonderfully creative air-heads, be they Pete Maravich or Sigmund Freud, that have made the world change. You are fortunate to have several of them on your team. Let them play."

Three hours later (after the meal that was promised as part of the $1,500 fee), Falk drove McHale to the airport and shared several final points. "You know, Jack, in many ways I envy you. In my job at the University of Virginia,

I get to establish some close relationships with my students, but it's nothing like being a coach."

"What do you mean?" asked McHale.

"Well, I guess what I really mean is that a teacher gets to a student's mind. But you, and guys like you...you get to a player's soul."

Both sat silent for a moment, reflecting on Falk's statement. Several minutes later, as they reached the airport, Falk said to McHale, "Jack, at probably every summer camp lecture you give, you talk to the kids about resiliency, overcoming odds. Now it's your turn to get up off the deck. You can do it, but it will take some guts. You have to let yourself and your team go."

McHale smiled. As he turned and headed for the plane, he felt certain that he had some of the keys needed to turn his team around.

Yet he wondered, "Can I change?"

Chapter 49

The cornerstone of Steve Ellovitch's lofty personal agenda had been laid by President Pendelton at the recent meeting of the Building Fund Board of Directors. Ellovitch's appointment as Chairman would enable him to exert considerable influence over an extremely important project, not only for the University, but also for the entire state. In addition, it plugged him into a network that he had not been able to crack, one which he needed to join in order to achieve his spiring aspirations. While his reputation and power base as Athletic Director of State had increased significantly during the past twelve months (due to what many considered as his visionary marketing of the State basketball program), his sphere of influence still rested primarily in the area of sports. As Chairman of the Building Fund, this sphere would now be extended to the highest levels of the corporate sector.

By steering the Building Fund to its completion and guiding State's basketball fortunes to those of a nationally ranked program, Ellovitch would be considered one of the hottest properties in the sports industry. He knew that what might have appeared unthinkable one year ago could, in a short time, become reality.

Ellovitch was a realist. If not for the unusual circumstances surrounding Bill Riley's dismissal, and the fact that corporate America always took the safe course (in this case the appointment of a University employee as Chairman), he knew that Lady Luck would not have dealt him such favorable cards. But he also knew that if the remaining pieces of the puzzle evolved into a perfect fit, his name would be considered viable for virtually any position in sports.

Given the Knicks' constant state of flux, and his new contacts at Madison Square Garden, Ellovitch would certainly be considered for President or General Manager of the pro team. With all the in-fighting in the football Giants' organization, the same positions were attainable. If this step could be navigated, then the next could be a commissionership of a major sport. Why not? He would have all of the credentials. His legal background and his years as a successful administrator and leader in sports marketing would bring him where he knew he should go—where he belonged.

Ellovitch knew, however, that he must play his hand carefully. He would now be dealing with Gunderson Brewery, arguably the most powerful entity in sports, since no other company spent as much for the support and sponsorship of sports events. Such expenditure increased the enormous sphere of influence that the Brewery enjoyed. Ellovitch now had entry into this world and could use the relationship with Gunderson's chieftains to his own personal benefit.

The other members of the Building Fund Board would also be in positions to help the career of Steve Ellovitch. As crafted by Robert O'Connell, the Board touched all the bases, from Merrill Lynch to the top law firm in New York City. Ellovitch would now be in close quarters with the very power base of New York society.

While focusing on his own career, Ellovitch did not lose sight of firing Jack McHale. On Sunday morning, while McHale was en route to Charlottesville, Virginia to meet with Dr. Falk, Ellovitch was in his office dictating a memo to McHale. The memo, which Ellovitch wanted typed and on McHale's desk by 9 a.m. Monday morning, read:

> As per my meeting with President Pendelton, this is to inform you that a formal review process has been implemented regarding your position as Head Basketball Coach. I have informed the President that your job performance has been unsatisfactory, that your position is now under formal review, and that a decision will be forthcoming as to your contract here at State University within the next four weeks.

He had requested his secretary to report early on Monday morning so she could type the memo and place it on McHale's desk before his arrival. Ellovitch knew that despite McHale's outward calm, he would be devastated by the loss to Princeton. He hoped that the memo would feed on this sense of devastation and bring Jack McHale that much closer to resignation. This would spare Ellovitch the distasteful task of having to fire him outright. It would be distasteful not because of McHale, but because of his supporters, who would certainly come out of the woodwork to defend him regardless of his record. While Ellovitch was certain that the general public would agree with the firing, he also remembered that McHale retained some friends of influence. If he were able to force McHale's resignation, he might avoid making an enemy of someone who could be of assistance at a later date.

On Monday morning, with the memo typed and placed atop McHale's desk, Ellovitch departed for his first meeting with Gunderson Brewery in his role as Building Fund Chairman. The Executive Vice President of Gunderson, now assigned to represent the brewery on the project, would be present. So, too, would be several other Gunderson executives, all of whom were company officers, all of whom Ellovitch wanted to get to know better.

Ellovitch arrived promptly at 10:30 a.m. and was escorted to a conference room adjacent to the main foyer. The buffet table at the entrance was replete with flowers and a tray of fresh fruits and croissants. Off to the side was a pitcher of freshly squeezed orange juice and a Royal Doulton coffee and tea service with assorted herbal teas. Ellovitch thought to himself that this professional lifestyle was something to which he could easily become accustomed. It was clearly unlike the mundane accouterments accompanying a meeting at State University. Six Gunderson officers were present in the room when Ellovitch arrived. Each of them, bedecked with some type of Gunderson insignia, greeted Ellovitch warmly, offering congratulations on his appointment as Chairman of the Committee.

The Vice President began the meeting by stating that Gunderson would retain an exclusive on the naming of the building and exclusive rights in the selling of beer, through a joint venture arrangement with the Farragher Company.

"As you know, Steve," said the Vice President, "we've had some unfortunate things happen related to this project. The Brewery simply wants to make certain that from here on in we get nothing but good publicity."

When the meeting adjourned, the Vice President invited Ellovitch to his office. As they proceeded through the executive suites, Bill Riley was exiting his office. As he turned the corner, he and Ellovitch came face to face. The Vice President, at first startled by the chance meeting, quickly regained his composure. "Bill, I would like you to meet Steve Ellovitch, Athletic Director at State University." Ellovitch and Riley shook hands.

Ellovitch was startled by Riley's appearance. While he had never met Riley, he had seen his picture and frequently watched him interviewed on television. He had always been impressed with Riley. His demeanor seemed almost flawless. What he saw today was a William Riley far different from that person.

"It's good to meet you, Mr. Ellovitch," Riley said. Without even acknowledging the Vice President, he continued down the corridor.

As Ellovitch entered his office, the Vice President remarked, "there goes a broken man."

Indeed, Bill Riley was a broken man. Even those closest to him had been surprised, almost shocked, at how hard he had taken the news. Riley's life had fallen apart. He had moved from his house and had filed for divorce from his wife. He had cut himself off completely from his family and, particularly, his son Sean.

As Ellovitch returned from his meeting at Gunderson Brewery, feeling buoyed by the relationships he had established, he was met in his office by the Sports Information Director.

"Steve, Jack McHale contacted me this morning. He has asked me to schedule a major press conference at the Viscount Hotel out at JFK Airport, just prior to the team's departure to Ireland."

"For what?" asked Ellovitch, his blood rushing.

"He won't say, but he said to put it out to the locals as 'very important.'"

"I've done it," Ellovitch smiled to himself. "He's going to quit."

Chapter 50

Sean Riley's life was as much in a shambles as his father's. Only his friendship with Robby Nesbitt, now even stronger, gave him strength.

Robby and Sean had made it a point to get together on a daily basis. While thought of the trial and subsequent jail sentences loomed large in the minds of both young men, their conversations focused not so much on the trial but on how and why this lurid nightmare had occurred at all. At first, these discussions had centered on their own stupidity. Nesbitt, in particular, had been hard on himself, saying he had not only ruined his own life, but also had taken his good friend down with him.

"Robby, what I did was my own choice," was Sean's response.

"Sean, you know I don't have a dime to my name, and whether you agree with it or not, I'm the one that got you into this. If we're going to get to the bottom of this, I'll spend every minute of every day working on it, but I can't come up with any cash to support it. With your father out of the house, I'm not so sure you can either."

"Money, even with my father gone, has never been a problem," said Sean. "I'll go to my Mom. I'm sure she'll come through."

The next day Sean Riley summoned the grit to approach his mother. "Robby and I have talked this out for the last several weeks," he said. "I'm not saying we were blameless, but we're convinced that we were singled out for some reason." Riley went on to explain to his mother that at the advice of Nesbitt's attorney, they had been in contact with a private investigator named John McCollough. "He's agreed to come over and see us. We have no idea of what he'll charge, but we'd like you to be there. If you think it's worth it, we need your help financially in hiring this guy."

John McCollough had been a decorated war hero. A graduate of Fordham University, he spent three years in Vietnam and was awarded the Silver Star. Upon his return to the States in 1971, he joined the FBI and was soon considered the bureau's leading investigator. At the pinnacle of his career as a special agent, McCollough realized that his skills, which then called for an annual salary of $56,000, were of far greater value in the private sector. In 1982 he resigned and formed his own private investigation agency. To no one's surprise, his agency, with only three full time employees (including himself, a former FBI colleague and a secretary) was soon turning away cases for which similar agencies would literally beg—all within three years.

When McCollough arrived at the Riley home, he began by saying, "I'm familiar with the implications of the case, having followed Mr. Riley's dismissal in the papers. When reading about it I had a feeling that something wasn't quite right, that something or someone might be behind this whole thing. It's just an instinct, but my instincts have generally been correct."

The four of them—Mrs. Riley, Robby, Sean, and McCollough—went on to discuss the case in detail.

"Mrs. Riley," said McCollough, "if you and the boys wish, I'll take this on. But I want you to know my fees are double what you would normally pay. Then again, I think my results are double what you would normally get."

"What are we talking about?" asked Sean, surprising himself with his directness.

"We're talking about $25,000 at signing plus $6,000 a week and all expenses. If I'm correct, it will take me at least six weeks to track this thing down."

"Will you be able to track it down, Mr. McCollough?" Mrs. Riley pleaded.

"Yes," responded McCollough with startling self-assuredness.

Chapter 51

After Dr. Lawrence Falk dropped Jack McHale off at the Charlottesville airport, McHale went to a pay phone and called his wife.

"Where are you? I've been worried sick," asked a concerned Sally McHale.

"Everything is OK," responded McHale. "I had to go out of town for an important meeting but I've had a good day. I'll be home in a couple of hours." McHale often marveled at his relationship with his wife. In a few brief sentences they were able to communicate more than most spouses could in hours. She was, among many things, his best friend.

McHale used the trip back from Charlottesville to reflect on Falk's advice. His initial reaction had not been one of total acceptance. But Falk, skilled in dealing with such resistance, was able to stay with his point while not offending McHale, who found himself coming around more and more to Falk's way of thinking. Falk had been accurate in emphasizing that one of the major difficulties facing McHale would be his willingness to change the offensive dynamics to which he had long been committed.

Jack McHale had spoken at many clinics and had written a number of articles which appeared in national coaches' publications on offensive basketball. His comments always centered on the fact that basketball is "a game of percentages and offensive principles must be geared to producing high percentage shots, those closest to the basket." McHale had become widely known for his half-court offense and was not thought of as a wide-open, fast break coach. The notion of change, particularly at this point of the season—after having coached a certain way for so many years—brought him discomfort. As Falk had said, "The first thing that's going to have to happen is you must let *yourself* go." While he may not have been in total agreement, McHale was going to do exactly as Falk had urged.

When he arrived home, his wife immediately sensed a change. "You certainly seem much more at ease, Jack," she said.

McHale told Sally about the Falk meeting, beginning with his staying up all night Saturday to read the article, to the trip on Sunday. He then looked at his wife and said, "What do you think of the whole idea?"

"Honey," she responded, "I think you have no choice."

"That's funny," said McHale. "I was thinking the same thing."

McHale arrived in his office at 9:30 a.m. the next morning and found an envelope on his desk marked personal and confidential. He opened it and, for the next ten minutes, read and reread Steve Ellovitch's missive. When he finally put it down, he recognized the extent of Falk's impact. At other times, a similar situation would have caused Jack McHale's stomach to churn in a combination of fear and anger. Today his reaction was different. His stomach did not churn. In fact, to his surprise and pleasure, he found himself almost laughing about the memo. He simply did not give a damn, a clear victory over Ellovitch's hectoring tactics.

As McHale walked to the gym for the 10 a.m. team meeting, he mentally reworked the points Falk had made: "This meeting will be one of the most important of your coaching career...There will be an aura of tension in the room...But if you recite your lines properly there will be a whole new atmosphere by meeting's end." He repeated these words to himself, as if chanting a prayer.

As Falk predicted, there was considerable tension when McHale entered the locker room. His first concern was soon alleviated. Every player was present. In light of what he had to say, he did not want the situation complicated by having to deal with a tardy player violating team rules.

Looking around the room, he saw a variety of attitudes reflected among the players. Several showed out-and-out contempt for him. Freshmen faces wore the shock of losing for the first time. Finally, that most dangerous of reactions, one which generally accompanied a losing team, was shown by the others: the "I don't care" attitude. McHale knew he had his work cut out for him as he began to speak.

"Gentlemen, I'm going to talk for a few minutes. What I'm about to say I've never said to any team in all my years as a head coach. To be perfectly honest, some of the things I'm about to say are not very easy. Let me start with the first and most important point. The simple reason we are now 2-5 is that I've done a lousy job."

The players were startled by McHale's statement, their intermixture of expressions turning to one. Realizing that he had drawn their attention, McHale proceeded to do exactly as Falk had suggested. He did not apologize for his ability as a coach but told the players that he had inhibited their offensive abilities and that this was the central reason the team had not performed well. He went on to praise them, not only as players but as people.

With each player now attentive to his every word, he concluded by saying, "Fellas, we've been put in an almost impossible position. I can remember few teams coming off a sub-.500 season with such high expectations. From here on in, we're gonna play it one game at a time. I'll handle the media and what I'm essentially going to do with them is take the pressure off you guys and put it on me. All I'm asking is for you to do exactly what we say on defense, and let it go on offense."

While McHale had done some reading on group dynamics, he had never observed the full effect as vividly as he did during this meeting. A group of sulking, beaten players had, in all of ten minutes, turned into a room full of smiles, excitement and optimism. Knowing that players adept at putting a ball through a basket were not always as adept at articulating their feelings, McHale then opened it up to the team. "OK, any comments on what I've just said?"

As the players looked at each other, McDonough, beginning to take on more of a leadership role (and showing the endearing naiveté from his first eighteen years in Ireland) stuck out his jaw and said in his best Kerry accent, "Spot on, Coach." The room erupted in laughter. Jack McHale knew he had them back.

As McHale left the meeting, he could tell that rumors of the press conference had already filtered through the athletic department. When he walked into his office, his secretary said, "Jack, it's been absolutely frantic since you left. The phone hasn't stopped ringing. Steve Ellovitch has called twice saying it's urgent that you speak with him. I have a reporter from the *Daily News* on hold. What do I say to everyone?"

"Tell them I'll see them at 3 o'clock," said McHale.

"What do I tell Steve Ellovitch?"

"Tell him the same thing."

The media had no choice but to accept his explanation. Steve Ellovitch was a different matter. Twenty minutes after McHale had closed the door to his office, a loud knock came at the door. Before McHale had a chance to respond to the knock, the door opened. It was Ellovitch.

"Jack, do you mind telling me what's going on with this press conference?"

"As a matter of fact I do mind. I'm busy getting ready for this Irish trip."

"In case you don't remember, I *am* athletic director of this institution."

"Believe me, I've never forgotten that."

"What role do you expect me to play in this thing?"

"The only role I can suggest is simply that you show up. Steve, if you'll excuse me, I'm busy."

Two hours later, as the players gathered on the team bus, they were aware of the rumors now in wide circulation. Marvin Lewis got up the courage to ask McHale, "Coach, what's this press conference about?"

"Don't worry about it, Marvin. It's nothing too major." As the bus proceeded through Manhattan to the tollgate at the Whitestone Bridge, McHale looked down to see one of the afternoon newsboys in his customary position barking *"New York Post! New York Post!"* The headline, held high by the boy, read, "McHALE TO QUIT."

The bus pulled into the Viscount Hotel. McHale was surprised to see the large group of media present. State's Sports Information Director said to him on the way in, "Jack, I don't know what it is you're going to say, but we couldn't get another person in with a shoehorn."

McHale, proceeding to the dais, took the microphone. "Ladies and gentlemen, if you would all sit down, I have a few things I would like to say. As many of you know, I have never once called a press conference, but in light of all the attention we've been getting, and since our club will be over in Ireland for the next several days, I thought it might be a good idea to clear the air on a few things."

While known as a good speaker, McHale had never been considered as eloquent as some of his contemporaries, like Dale Brown or Jim Valvano. This, however, was soon lost on those in attendance, for in the next ten minutes Jack McHale gave a speech that captivated his audience. Again using Falk's recommendations, McHale began by saying that while he always thought of himself as a good coach, he had been guilty of inhibiting his players. Following the same course he had taken earlier in the day with the players, he went on to point out that the expectations for this team were simply unrealistic.

"I'm not blaming anyone. In fact, if anyone is to blame, it's me. But this is a young team and I think a lot of people have unintentionally done us a disservice by expecting the moon too early," he pointed out. His adrenaline now flowing, he continued in resounding style.

"The State basketball program reached its lowest point on Saturday night. Beginning at a 10 a.m. meeting with my players today, I want all of you to know that things are going to get better. . .and better. . .and better. You guys have been good to me in the past. I'm simply asking for the players' sake that you show a little patience. I'm also saying, in no uncertain terms, that this club will start to gel. And last but not least,"—a smile now creased McHale's face—"I'm saying to all of you that Jack McHale is not going to resign as head coach of State. When I go out, it'll be on my own terms."

When McHale finished his comments something truly extraordinary, particularly for the hard-boiled New York media, occurred. "Any questions?" he asked. There were none. Instead, the room erupted into applause.

Ellovitch had positioned himself in the back of the large hall. Amid the applause which ensued when McHale had finished, he stood in stunned silence. After McHale spent several minutes in one-on-ones with the media, he spotted Ellovitch. He immediately approached him, pulled out an envelope from his suit coat and handed it the Athletic Director. The envelope was marked personal and confidential. McHale, saying nothing to Ellovitch, continued out the door.

Ellovitch opened the envelope and found an invoice for $1,500 payable to Dr. Lawrence Falk with a note from McHale: "Steve, please pay this promptly."

Chapter 52

He was in demand. Armed with impeccable credentials both as a Vietnam hero and special agent for the FBI, John McCollough had garnered a reputation as a leader in his field. As McCollough knew, and would admit only to those closest to him, his reputation had as much to do with his ability to select the "right" cases as it did with his considerable skill.

As his career and reputation developed, McCollough set certain criteria for the acceptance of a case: Was it an intellectual challenge? Did his clients have the ability to pay? Would the case produce significant publicity?

Having grown up in the mill section of Waterbury, Connecticut, and having been further hardened by his war experiences, McCollough was finally tasting the fruits of money.

McCollough knew that in most important cases requiring the services of a private investigator, his agency would be contacted. So he and his small staff spent considerable time reviewing media accounts of potential cases. This is how McCollough learned about Sean Riley's arrest. When the Public Defender for Robby Nesbitt called, McCollough was not surprised to hear from his old friend. He had been a classmate of McCollough's at Fordham.

The Public Defender was a person for whom McCollough had much admiration. Easily one of the best criminal attorneys in New York, he had sacrificed the riches and numerous offers from high-powered law firms to remain a "people's attorney."

"John, no doubt you've been reading about the Riley family in the newspapers. What you may not know is that I've been assigned to represent the other boy in the case, Robby Nesbitt."

"I must admit it's piqued my interest," said McCollough.

The Public Defender related the details of the case, adding that he believed that the two boys had been set up: "I don't know the reason, but if you put all the facts together, it clearly points in this direction." He then mentioned how much he had gotten to like the Nesbitt boy, and in their brief meetings, the Riley boy as well. "They are two good kids. It's really a tragedy what's happened. I want to do all I can to see that their lives aren't ruined from what appears to be one stupid mistake."

McCollough wanted the case. Something indeed seemed amiss, something the newspapers had failed to investigate.

While making it a practice never to get too close to his clients, McCollough was almost immediately struck by the accuracy of the Public Defender's words regarding young Riley and Nesbitt. Nesbitt, although devastated by the entire process, had retained his sense of self-esteem. McCollough liked him immediately. He also liked Sean Riley, but for different reasons. The sadness in young Riley's eyes and his reticent demeanor made it clear to McCollough that the boy's burden went far beyond the last four weeks. He was not unlike the sons and daughters of other rich and famous people who McCollough had encountered in the past seven years.

McCollough knew that Robby Nesbitt held the key to finding out who, if anyone, had set the two up and what the motivation had been. He asked Nesbitt to be in his office at 9 a.m. the next morning. "Robby, we're going to spend several hours going over every single detail of this case, from the time you met the dealer to the time you were arrested," he said. McCollough felt certain that the boys had been set up. But by whom? And why? To be sure, there were several people at Gunderson Brewery who appeared to be prime candidates.

The following morning Robby Nesbitt, attired in sneakers, blue jeans and a New York Knicks t-shirt, appeared at McCollough's office in White Plains, New York. The office, while functional, was by no means elaborate. It was decorated with pictures and clippings of some of McCollough's more famous cases, as well as a picture of McCollough sitting shirtless in front of a hut in Vietnam with an M-16 resting on his shoulder. As Nesbitt was seated, McCollough moved directly to the point.

"Robby, I want to start with step one. What was your first contact with the dealer?"

Nesbitt said that he was hitchhiking home.

"Do you hitchhike every day?"

"Yes," replied Nesbitt.

"From the same place?"

"Yes."

"Same time?"

"Yes."

"Go on, please."

Nesbitt explained that while he was hitchhiking the dealer had picked him up.

"What type of car was he driving?"

"A Cadillac Seville."

"What color?"

"Gray with a black vinyl roof." As McCollough asked the questions, his secretary sat by with a tape recorder and note pad, scrupulously writing down everything Nesbitt said.

"Did you notice anything unusual about the car?"

"Well, it was a beautiful car, polished to perfection on the outside and clean as a whistle on the inside."

"Let's talk about the inside of the car. What type of upholstery? What color? What kind of radio?"

Nesbitt went on to answer all of McCollough's questions. When he did not provide enough detail, McCollough pressed him.

"Robby, you're doing fine, but I'm sure there must be something else you're forgetting. Is there anything else about the car that you found unusual or special?"

"Well, now that I think of it, even though it was an '85, it smelled brand new."

McCollough looking up from his note pad, glanced first at Nesbitt and then at his secretary.

McCollough said, "OK, we're done with the description of the car. Now let's talk about what was said when you were in the car."

"Just friendly small talk, nothing important," Nesbitt replied.

"Let us decide that, Robby. Be very specific. What was said?"

"Well, the guy began by asking me where I went to school. When I told him Westchester Country Day, he mentioned how he had also gone to prep school."

"What else did he say?"

"He said though he went to prep school and had gotten a good education, he had hated it because he was on scholarship and always felt below the other kids. He asked me what I thought about prep school and I told him I was on scholarship, too, and that I had pretty much the same feelings."

McCollough smiled. "Robby, let's get one thing straight right now. You said that the early portion of the conversation was merely small talk and not important. I can already see it was important. I want to point out to you that anything that this guy said was important. It's absolutely imperative that you tell me everything you remember."

Nesbitt, for the first time, sensed an assertiveness in McCollough that had not yet been exhibited. While not intimidated, McCollough certainly had captured his attention. "I see what you're saying," he said to the investigator.

Nesbitt went on to tell McCollough that he told the dealer why he shared his feelings about being subservient to his fellow prep schoolers: "It seems like I'm always getting a free hand out. It gets to you after awhile."

"Keep going, Robby. You're doing fine," McCollough encouraged him.

"Well, at this point is when he started to bring up this 'business opportunity.' He said he sympathized with a guy in my position and he might know of a way I could make some extra money, 'to pay my own way,' were his words. Just as I started to ask him about it, I realized that I was coming to the place where I was supposed to get out."

"So what happened?"

"He said he didn't have time to tell me about it then, but if I was interested in hearing more, he'd be happy to meet me after school the next day at Green's Bar and Grill on South Street. I had been by there a few times. It's a crummy looking place. I told him that I'd meet him."

"Why did you do that, Robby?"

"Well, he seemed like a nice guy, genuinely concerned about my situation and I admit I was pretty impressed with his Cadillac."

"OK," said McCollough, "we're going to get to the meeting the next day in a little while, but before we do that, I'm going to bring in our resident artist." With that McCollough said to secretary, "Ask Fred to come in."

Nesbitt judged the artist to be in his early thirties. He looked like an artist—bearded, gaunt in feature and build, wearing a turtleneck jersey, khaki pants and Nike jogging shoes. As he walked into the room, Nesbitt immediately noticed that he was carrying both a sketch board and what looked to be a brief case. McCollough introduced the two and as the artist sat down, McCollough said, "OK, Robby, I'm going to turn it over to Fred for now. He's going to ask you a series of questions about what this guy looked like. Within an hour or so, you'll be looking at the guy's face." Sure enough, less than sixty minutes later, the artist had produced a sketch that looked exactly like the person who had caused Robby Nesbitt and Sean Riley so much pain.

"That's the guy!" exclaimed Nesbitt.

"OK," said McCollough. "It's noon and we've been at this for three hours. We're going to have lunch."

"I thought you said we were going to go through this for the whole day without taking a break?"

"I did say that Robby." McCollough was getting to like young Nesbitt more and more. "What I didn't say was that we're having lunch at Green's Bar and Grill."

Forty-five minutes later, McCollough and Nesbitt arrived at Green's. As they walked in, McCollough first told Nesbitt that he wanted him to speak softly, "I don't want anyone overhearing our conversation." He then asked, "Exactly where did you meet with the guy?" Nesbitt motioned to the rear of the room. The two proceeded to a back booth. "I want you to sit exactly where you sat when you met the guy. I'll play the role of the guy. Where did he sit?" Nesbitt gestured to the opposite side of the booth. "Was he waiting for you when you got here?"

"Yes," Nesbitt replied.

"So you come in, he motions you over, you sit down. What happens?"

"Well," said Nesbitt, "once again he started with some small talk." Nesbitt, realizing his mistake, laughed, "OK, OK. The small talk was him asking me how things had gone in school that day, how I got down here, if I had walked, taken a bus, hitchhiked. He then started talking about the prep school situation again, how tough it must be for me. He asked me questions about my background. I told him about my Mom, how my father had died when I was three and how she had brought me up."

"Did you notice anything about his reaction?"

"As a matter of fact I did," said Nesbitt. "It was something—call it a sixth sense—but it almost seemed as if he knew the answers before he asked the questions."

McCollough smiled. "Go on."

"After we talked more about the prep school situation he then sat back, rested his arm across the back of the booth and looked me right in the eye. 'Robby,' he said, 'how would you like to make some real money?' Just the way he said it, I knew that it was not the kind of money I would want to tell my Mom about."

"What was your reaction, Robby?"

"My reaction, and I swear to God on this, John, was that I told him 'no'; in fact I told him 'no' four or five times."

"What was his reaction?"

"His reaction was to be very calm each time I said 'no'. In fact, I remember how impressed I was with the guy's cool attitude."

"Keep going, Robby."

"As we continued to talk and as I continued to say no, he pulled a roll of bills out of his pocket and said, 'Look, Robby, here are five one hundred dollar bills. I'm going to give them to you with no strings attached. This is a $500 consulting fee. All I'm asking is that you think over what we've talked about for the next twenty-four hours. I'll be here tomorrow at 4:30. Sleep on it. If you don't show up tomorrow at 4:30, I'll assume that you've chosen not to get involved. If you do, we can make a deal. It'll bring you a lot of money and involves virtually no risk.' "

Nesbitt went on to tell McCollough how he had grappled with the decision the entire evening. He deplored the idea of hard drugs and knew it could bring him big trouble. But the man's calm, his smooth approach, his self-assuredness and the fact that Robby Nesbitt had never had $500 in his possession at any time in his life, persuaded him. "It was just too much of a temptation, so the next day I went back," he explained.

"So tell me about this meeting," said McCollough.

"Well, we met at Green's again and talked about how the deal would be done. He said I would need a partner. He said there were two important things about the partner. First, the partner had to be someone I could trust and secondly, he had to be someone with access to money, a rich kid."

"What reasons did he give you for the kid being rich?"

"Well, he said that as we get into it, we might need some extra money to finance some deals. He asked me to put together a list of the most likely partners. We agreed to get together the following Saturday morning. I brought along the list. He looked it over and asked me a bunch of questions about each person."

"What were the questions?"

"The same for each person—how well did I know them, how much money did I think they had, could they be trusted, did they have guts? Those were the four questions he asked about each person."

"OK, so what did he do?"

"He said that he would review the list and that we should meet Tuesday after practice. When I showed up, he was sitting here in the same booth. It was a very brief meeting. He said that he had looked over the list and he had chosen Sean Riley."

"Did you ask him for his reasons?"

"No. He seemed sure that Sean was the right one, but he did ask me what I thought."

"And what did you say?"

"I told him I might have chosen someone else, but I thought that Sean would be fine."

Nesbitt went on to relate to McCollough how he had approached Riley, how Riley was at first reluctant, and then went along with it. "I had left it with the dealer that I would see him the following Monday, after spending Sunday with Sean in New York talking to him about it. It was then that the dealer gave me the instructions. That was the last time I saw him."

"OK," said McCollough, "one last question, Robby. Other than the time you met him in his car, did every other meeting take place here?"

"Yes," said Nesbitt.

"And at every meeting he sat in the same place?"

"That's right," said Nesbitt.

"You also mentioned that at one point in your conversation he leaned back and put his arm across the back of the booth."

That's right," said Nesbitt, surprised that McCollough would remember.

"Do you remember what he did with his hand?"

"With his hand?" asked Nesbitt.

"Yes, where did he put his hand?" said McCollough.

"He put his hand right against the wall," said Nesbitt.

Twelve days later, at 8 a.m., the phone rang in the Riley home. Kara Riley, still half asleep, wondered who would be calling this early on a Sunday morning.

"Mrs. Riley, this is John McCollough."

"Oh yes, Mr. McCollough," she answered, immediately sitting up in her bed.

"I think we need to meet," he said.

Chapter 53

Finbar McKeon had been in the employ of Aer Lingus for nineteen years. Starting out as a mechanic's assistant at Shannon Airport, McKeon had risen to the position of Chief Ticket Agent for Aer Lingus at JFK. His duties included personal greetings to VIP customers. In his five years as Chief Ticket Agent, he had met them all—powerful politicians, corporate heads, movie actors. He always did his homework. When a VIP exited a limousine in front of the Aer Lingus check-in, McKeon was ready, not merely with a hello, but also a comment or two about the person's business, personal interests or, in many cases, special affection for Ireland.

When word reached McKeon that the State University basketball team would be travelling to Shannon on January 2, he quickly dispatched his assistant to do a "quick bit of checkin'" on the principals. The assistant reported back that the two people in the group to whom McKeon should accord special attention were Jack McHale and Cormack McDonough.

True to form, McKeon, through a friend at the *New York Daily News*, got last minute word of the McHale news conference. He sent an aide to the conference to get the details. "If Mr. McHale is resigning, I best know it in order to provide a proper greeting," he instructed.

When the State bus arrived in front of the Aer Lingus terminal, McKeon was prepared. As Jack McHale exited the bus, McKeon immediately approached him. "Mr. McHale, it is a pleasure and let me say how pleased I am to learn that you intend to be coaching the State team for some time to come."

A stunned McHale smiled. "I know Aer Lingus prides itself on good service, but I didn't realize your sources are so good. I just left the Viscount not twenty minutes ago," he laughed.

"Not to worry, Mr. McHale. I like to tell my staff that we're open twenty-four hours a day."

McKeon extended similar greetings to Cormack McDonough. It seemed to McKeon that just yesterday he was cheering Kerry and Michael McDonough in the All Ireland finals against Mayo. McKeon spent several minutes telling McDonough about the exploits of his father. McKeon passed off the boy's indifference as probably something he had heard all too often in the past.

As the team entered the terminal, McKeon had another staff assistant ready with pre-boarding passes for the State players. McKeon then approached McHale and his two assistants. "Lads, we've some good news for you. The bossman has consented to let me upgrade the coaching staff to first class. Right this way, if you please."

McHale was at first perplexed. He had always made it a practice to travel with the team whenever possible, including air trips. While the State Booster Club would have been more than willing to pay for first class tickets for the staff, McHale felt that it was not appropriate to put himself on any contrived pedestal, thus distancing himself from his players. Despite this, he recognized that McKeon had probably gone to a great deal of trouble and would no doubt be offended if McHale refused. He decided to accept, but made certain to spend time during the flight in the other section with the players.

McKeon ushered McHale and his two assistants to a private elevator, where he inserted a key which allowed the four to ascend to the fourth floor. As the elevator opened, McKeon led them into the plush first class lounge replete with fresh-smoked salmon, a variety of cheese and meats, and as Brian McCray pointed out, "enough booze to sink a ship."

The three sat in the lounge for twenty minutes, enjoying the surroundings and plentiful refreshments. Mike Lambert, looking around the room, said to his two fellow coaches, "You can just feel a sense of importance in here," as he motioned to the other ten or twelve first class flyers. "I once read a story about a guy who said that he always flies first class because in his words, 'You'll never get to meet anyone important in coach.' I guess we'll all find out tonight if he was right."

As the coaches finished their third serving of smoked salmon, a senior stewardess entered the room and graciously said, "Ladies and gentlemen, we will be departing in fifteen minutes. If you will be so kind as to follow me." Just as the group was heading out the door, the phone rang in the lounge.

"Mr. McHale, yes, I believe he's here." McHale, hearing the bartender, immediately turned. "Mr. McHale, it's security. There's seems to be a problem. If you could go back down the elevator, they'll be waiting to explain it." A number of thoughts crossed McHale's mind. Had one of his players done something so foolish as to bring drugs through a security check? As he descended to the first floor and the elevator doors opened, two uniformed security men stood in the hall waiting for him.

"Coach McHale, we had a problem at the check in with two of your players."

"What is it?" asked McHale, his heart pounding.

"The security area is well marked with signs indicating that jokes are taken quite seriously. As two of your players went through the security check, both made a joke to one of our agents about the contents of their bags and if she wasn't careful they would blow up. I'm afraid we're gonna have to detain them overnight." This was just what McHale needed.

"Look, I know you're doing your jobs and I'm in no way trying to defend the two players, but as you may know, we're going over to Ireland for a tournament. The next Aer Lingus flight is not until Wednesday, which means they'll miss the first game, which also means that this is sure to be picked up by the local tabloids. I don't know if you two guys are basketball fans, but we've been struggling a bit and I think we're starting to turn things around. I wish there was some way you'd reconsider."

"We have our rules, Coach."

"I'm not questioning that," McHale responded in polite but firm tones. "I'm just asking in this one case if you could reconsider. This will reflect on the team and the university as well as the two players."

The two looked at each other, then looked at McHale. Finally, one spoke. "OK, Coach, we'll go along with it, but I'd strongly suggest you give them a very strong talking to," he said.

"Believe me, I will," McHale responded, his entire body feeling a sense of relief.

Before boarding the plane, McHale found the two players, both upperclassmen, at the security desk . He took them into a private room marked "Security - No Entrance," which the supervisor had agreed to let McHale use.

"What the hell are you guys thinking of?" McHale yelled. "You are supposed to be upperclassmen. Do you realize how much time and effort has gone into this trip and how you guys nearly screwed the whole thing up?" Both players, almost to McHale's surprise, appeared genuinely contrite.

"Coach, we just got carried away. We're really sorry. Are they going to keep us overnight?"

"They damn well should, but no they aren't. Let's get on the plane. We'll talk about this more when we get to Ireland."

McHale joined McCray and Lambert in the first class section, told them of the incident and said, "I can't let this slide. Why don't you guys give it some thought? The thing that ticks me off is that if this blew up, no one would blame the two kids. It would be the coaching staff who can't control the players." Both Lambert and McCray nodded.

The three then went to the rear of the plane and McHale said to the group, "I know you guys are excited, but let's remember that we're flying overnight. You won't be getting any sleep for another twenty-four hours except for what you can get on the plane. Let's avoid the movie and try to get as many hours shut-eye as possible." As he looked around, he saw several grim faces. Most of the players had spent the three dollars on the earphones. McHale said to his two assistants as they proceeded back to first class, "They'll probably be so tired in an hour or so that they'd fall asleep during the movie anyway."

Aer Lingus Flight #104 touched down at Shannon Airport at 7:15 a.m. Irish time, or 2:15 a.m., U.S. time. The Chief Stewardess provided last minute instructions on customs regulations and then, at touch down, recited what must have seemed like the ten-thousandth time, "Ladies and Gentlemen, welcome to Ireland." Fifteen groggy players and coaches departed the airline and trekked like zombies downstairs with their landing cards and passports ready.

As the team reached the customs area at Shannon Airport, there was an almost comedic confusion. Rain had fallen for the last twelve hours, something quite common in Ireland. What was uncommon, however, was that the temperature had dropped to 19°F and the Irish roads, comparable to United States roads of fifty years ago, had frozen. As a result, the customs officials, with but one exception, had not yet arrived. The one who did had been a member of the Customs Bureau for all of six months and was ill-prepared for a solo. Within five minutes, the overwhelmed customs officer gave up, allowing the group of one hundred and seventeen passengers, including the fifteen from State, to pass through the initial clearance unchecked.

The group then went to the baggage claim area adjacent to the customs tables. More chaos ensued. Not only were the customs officials late in arriving but so, too, was the baggage crew. As a result, the flight crew, stewardesses and pilots alike, ended up working with several of the mechanics who had been called off their duty to come and help with the disbursement of baggage. Forty-five minutes later, with tempers now flaring, the bags finally reached the terminal. An elderly man, on his seventeenth trip to Ireland, leaned over to McHale and said with a half smile, "This is the only place in the world this could happen."

With baggage finally in hand, the team headed to the waiting area. Cormack McDonough had expected family members to greet him. When none appeared, he passed it off to the bad weather which would have made the two hour trip from Killarney next to impossible. There to provide welcome however, were the co-chairmen of the Cork Invitational Tournament. "Coach McHale and team members, it is a pleasure to welcome you," said Niall Crowley, bespectacled and standing an erect 5'4. "We have several members of the media here. Would you all be so kind as to accompany us to the far end of the terminal for some photos."

By this time moods were sour, but McHale, sensing the importance of the request, turned to his team and said, "OK, fellas, let's do as Mr. Crowley requests." Five minutes later, pictures taken, Crowley provided what McHale and the team would find to be an almost routine part of their trip, a speech. Reading from notes with only the team, coaching staff and his co-chairman as his audience, Crowley delivered a seemingly endless five-minute soliloquy, freely invoking reference to the strong relations between the United States and Ireland through basketball, and noting the historical significance of the State trip.

"For the past five years, we have been fortunate to have literally hundreds of coaches and players com across, but you are the first true Division I team to land on our island. We are delighted to have you." His Cork dialect allowed each listener to capture half his message at best, but McHale sensed how truly meaningful the trip was, if not to his own players, then to the Irish.

When Crowley finally concluded, his co-chairman beckoned the team and coaching staff to the exit door. "Lads, we have a coach here waiting—"

As the group rushed to get on the bus, Crowley approached McHale. "Jack, the two of us have driven up. It would be an honor if you would accompany us in our car. Besides, we'll get there 'a speck quicker.' "

When McHale agreed to do it, little did he realize what "a speck quicker" meant. The trip from Shannon to Cork was normally three hours by car. With the roads now free of the early morning frost, the three arrived at Jury's Hotel on Ashford Street two hours and fifteen minutes later, after a view of Ireland replete with hairpin turns and the running of several red lights.

"What I didn't tell you, Coach, was that my idol is your famous Mario Andretti," Crowley smiled.

"I sort of got that feeling about midway through the trip," McHale deadpanned.

Jury's Hotel of Cork was one of three of the Jury's chain in Ireland. The hotel was typically European in style and design. Crowley, with pride, pointed out to McHale that "this is indeed the finest hotel in all of Cork City." The three proceeded into the main foyer where they were greeted by the Hotel Manager who, for a full four minutes, again welcomed McHale to Ireland, to Cork County, to the City of Cork and to Jury's Hotel.

His speech concluded, the Manager ushered the three into the restaurant, where tea and hot buttered scones were waiting. Forty-five minutes later, the bus pulled in and fourteen haggard players and coaches descended into the main lobby. For many of the employees at Jury's, it was the first time they had ever seen people of such size. In addition, it was the first time they had seen any large, black males. "Stop the gawkin'," the Manager bellowed to his employees. Then, smiling at McHale, he stated in full voice to be heard by all (including the black players of State), "It's the darkies they've never seen."

McHale, shook his head and said to himself, "This should be quite an experience."

Despite the Manager's risible welcome, Jury's was well-prepared for the team's arrival. The Manager knew from long experience that travellers from the States arrived tired. The State players, all of whom had been pre-registered, were quickly ushered into their rooms with instructions from McHale to return to the lobby within fifteen minutes. McHale then had the team gather for breakfast and insisted, contrary to his normal approach to nutrition, that each player get an infusion of coffee or tea to keep him awake. As the players wolfed down their breakfasts, Crowley took the floor again, passing out typewritten itineraries to each member of the group.

While the State players and coaching staff pored through the four page itinerary, two thousand miles away, British Air Flight #116 prepared its departure for Dublin via London. Seated in the coach class was sports writer Bob Johnson. He had deliberately avoided the more direct Aer Lingus flight from JFK, knowing that he would be sure to meet up with the State team and coaching staff, thus raising questions about his journey. Johnson wanted to be by himself, to gather his thoughts and prepare his own investigation.

Chapter 54

The two had grown close. To be sure, their friendship was rooted more in mutual need than in genuine fondness. So when Steve Ellovitch invited George DiOrgio to lunch at the 21 Club, it was not merely to toast the success of their joint venture, but to discuss the future—their goals and how, perhaps, those goals might be interwoven for the common good of both.

"Before we start talking about the future," said Ellovitch, "I want to say how happy I am about the way things have gone with the concert tie-in. I was talking with our Vice President of Finance. If our projections are correct, and even if the team doesn't turn things around, the school stands to make a profit of $1,000,000." Whenever addressing DiOrgio, Ellovitch did so in a deferential tone, one which spoke to Ellovitch's awareness of DiOrgio's superior knowledge in anything related to marketing and promotion.

DiOrgio smiled. "As I told you from the beginning, Steve, it takes many people in a successful project like this. You've done your job and I'm glad you're happy. I know we are."

Ellovitch then turned serious. "George, it seems we have similar goals. I think we make a pretty good team. One of my reasons in asking you to lunch is to talk about the future and how we might get together on some other projects. Do you see any possibilities?"

DiOrgio paused, then told Ellovitch of his preliminary investigation into the player agent business, not mentioning any names. "It's an area that I'm excited about and one where I think you could be a big help," he said.

The "fee" that DiOrgio paid Ellovitch in cash had been off limits in their other discussions. With some trepidation, DiOrgio broached the subject. "I think you can see that I'm a man of my word in terms of our other arrangement. One of the things that's apparent is that if I'm going to get into the agent business, I'll need people in high places in college athletics to open the right doors. The way your career is going, I couldn't think of a better person."

Ellovitch asked him to elaborate.

"You know virtually every athletic director in the United States. We want to get into the network. I've already discussed this with some people in coaching whose names I can't reveal, but it's clear to us that if we're going to do this right, we have to gain credibility with the AD's. That's where you'll come in."

"Go on," said Ellovitch.

"Well, we've gotten some numbers from some of the other large agencies like IMG and ProServ. With the percentage they receive for negotiating contracts, plus handling the investments, as well as advertising and corporate sponsorship deals, it's a very high profit business."

"How high?" Ellovitch pressed.

"We estimate that the really good agents, the elite, all make in excess of a million dollars a year."

"Where do you see me coming in?" asked Ellovitch.

"Although we've never discussed it, it wouldn't surprise me if you've set your goals for professional sports," DiOrgio answered. "Right now, you can be a big help by introducing us to the right athletic directors. We're targeting the Athletic Directors convention in June. We intend to rent a suite and host several receptions. You can be our middle man. Then, if you're heading where I think you're heading, you can continue to be of service to us. A general manager or president of a professional team can have a big impact on steering players in a particular direction. To answer your most important question before you even ask it, we're talking about a sizeable fee for doing this."

"How much?" Ellovitch queried.

"In our initial phase we'd be prepared to pay you $25,000 cash per year to introduce us to the right people. We're going to give the project three years. The quicker we sign up athletes, the quicker we bring in revenue. As we go from a minus to a plus cash flow, we'll increase your payment. To what degree, I can't tell you. It'll be dependent on who you lead us to and how successful we are, but as I think you can see from the $25,000 retainer, we're serious in our intentions.

"Steve, there's another area about this that interests me," DiOrgio continued. "Up until now—with my blessing—you've received a lion's share of the credit for the Garden program. I view this player agent business as a way to get my name in headlines. Eventually, I want to own a professional sports team. I want my name in the papers."

"At least you're honest about it," Ellovitch laughed.

"What about you? Am I correct in my predictions about Steve Ellovitch?"

"You are. I've developed in my own mind a twenty-four month plan which will hopefully get me to the presidency of a major sports team. I think I can be a big help with the athletic directors and, if my own goals are met, an even bigger help once I get to the professional level."

"Where do you hope to end up?"

"As commissioner of one of the major sports leagues."

The conversation, no more than fifteen minutes in length, had brought the two to a frank expression of their goals. They finally glanced at their menu as the waiter approached. Ellovitch ordered oysters rockefeller and a bottle of Dom Perignon, and DiOrgio chose lobster salad. Several minutes later, as the waiter popped the cork from the bottle and gently poured the champagne into each glass, DiOrgio hoisted his glass, looked at Ellovitch and said, "To the future."

Thousands of miles away, Milo Casey was awaiting Bob Johnson's arrival in Dublin. It was 6:30 p.m., Irish time. Casey calculated they would reach Killarney no later then half past eleven.

Chapter 55

"**D**on't let the lads drop into dreamland the first day," was the sage advice given to Jack McHale by Cork Tournament Director Colm Murphy. On a European trip, with an overnight flight and a five-hour time change, Murphy advised McHale of the importance of the players getting through the first day without sleep. "It'll help lads get a good rest the first night and become quickly acclimated to the European time zone. If they go to bed during the first day, their inner clocks will be out of kilter for the entire tournament," said Murphy.

The warnings had been strong enough to make McHale dispatch his team manager to accompany the players to their rooms and make certain they unpacked their clothes and immediately returned to the lobby of Jury's Hotel. They then reviewed the itinerary which covered the entire visit and began, in Murphy's words, with a "half eleven press conference at the Lord Mayor's office."

Upon arriving at City Hall, a magnificent structure built in 1928, the team was greeted by the press secretary of the Lord Mayor. "You are all welcome," said the press secretary, attired in a flannel suit which had not been ironed for some time. Present at the press reception on this first day were the other three teams in the tournament: the Irish National Team, Murray's Metal of Scotland, and Team Audi from England, State's first round opponent.

While McHale and the players knew little of what to expect, it was clear that much preparation had gone into the tournament and the accompanying activities. For the hosts, it was a major sporting event, one upon which the eyes of Irish basketball were firmly affixed. Several minutes after their arrival, the players smilingly refused the Deputy Mayor's offer of Guinness Stout in favor of ginger ale and cola. "It's nice to see you lads are in trainin'," he commented. The festivities then began with Tournament Director Murphy taking the podium.

Murphy, a member of the Irish National Team fifteen years prior (when Irish basketball was in its infancy), spoke of the significance of the tournament, and particularly of how proud Ireland was to have its first Division I United States player returning home in Cormack McDonough. Two other city officials then provided none-too-brief messages of support.

At the conclusion of the reception, the players were ushered up one more flight of stairs to a grand style dining room. The table settings included Cork City-engraved sterling silver dinnerware, Waterford crystal goblets and a gift (a Waterford dinner bell) to each participant. The meal, a four-course extravaganza which included smoked salmon, prawn soup, roast rack of lamb and sherry trifle for dessert, proved every bit as enticing as the surrounding ornamentation.

After the meal, the team returned to its bus to travel to the north side of Cork and Parochial Hall, where they would run through a brief workout. Jack McHale, in his previous trip to Ireland in 1980, had become familiar with the country's lack of sporting facilities. The players, other than Cormack McDonough, had no such preparation. As they entered Parochial Hall, built in 1921 as a dance hall, Marvin Lewis said to McDonough, "Man, you call this a gym?" The hall was dark and dingy and had but one shower stall in each of the two team dressing rooms. The heat, when working, provided only a mild reprieve from the harsh climate.

As the players threw their well-intentioned barbs at McDonough, it became apparent to each what it must have been like for him to hone his skills in a country that, even in the 1980's, lacked a gymnasium comparable to a United States junior high facility.

McHale, recognizing that his troops were weary, made the session brief. He suggested at the conclusion of practice that the team hold off on a shower until they returned to the hotel, a recommendation the players welcomed with enthusiasm. As the squad packed their bags and prepared for their trip back to Jury's, Colm Murphy regaled McHale with more stories of the history of Irish basketball.

"When I was playing, Jack, there was a referee named Tahse Bruton. He would be referred to in your terms as a homer. In fact, there were those who would say he invented the term. Back in those days, there was no such thing as an electric clock. Tahse would keep time by the old village clock." As Murphy told the story, he ushered McHale to the front of Old Parochial Hall, opened the doors and pointed to the clock below in the valley some two-and-a-half miles away.

"As you might suspect, it gets very foggy here in Ireland. Many a time Tahse would quickly run out, open the door, come back in and say the fog was too thick to tell how much time was left, but he estimated at least four minutes more. Depending on the score, four minutes could end up being seven or eight, just long enough for the Cork team to make our comeback and go on to victory."

When the players returned to Jury's, tea and toasted brown bread with butter were awaiting them. After the snack and shower, McHale insisted that the team take a walk, despite the drizzly weather. It was now 4 p.m. If he could get them through the next several hours, the advice given by Colm Murphy and others would be followed. Three hours later, after another hearty Irish meal, the players were ushered back onto the bus for a quick tour of Cork. After looking at the Bells of Shandon and the Blarney Castle, the team returned to their rooms, barely able to keep their eyes open. As Colm Murphy had predicted, every member of the group got as good a night's sleep as they could remember, and awakened the following morning rested and ready.

State's first round opponent, Team Audi of London, featured, as was the case with most European teams, two Americans. Both were paid in the vicinity of $35,000, yet because of the strange International Basketball rules, both retained their amateur status. The rest of the team was comprised of English players who, in most cases, would have been solid Division II players in the United States, with some able to play at the lower Division I level. The team was coached by an American who was now in his tenth season of coaching in various European countries. Jack McHale had remembered him as a successful coach at a Division III school in the South, who had been forced to resign due to drinking problems. While McHale did not know him personally, he had appreciated the coach's warm greeting at the reception at the Lord Mayor's office the day before.

"It's always great to see an American coach over here, Jack. I've been here for ten years now and out of touch with the basketball world. One of the nicest presents I can get is the chance to sit down and talk about the game with an American." He was like a soldier of fortune with a clipboard. McHale had run into others like him, all with common traits. They possessed a high level of skill as coaches; otherwise, they would have been fired years earlier because of the cut-throat European way of doing things in their Division I leagues. However, they lacked the personal discipline required of a successful Division I coach in the United States.

Early the afternoon of game day, the State players gathered in McHale's suite to go through different bits of information the staff was able to gather about Team Audi. "Both Americans were outstanding Division I players in the States. They've got a number of other good kids. The big concern we have is the international rules," he said. McHale once again went on to discuss the rule changes and wider foul lanes.

"Gentlemen, this is an important game for us," said McHale. "It'll be an opportunity for all of us to see if I am right about you guys and, particularly, your potential on offense. As I said last week, we're going to stay pretty much the same on defense, but it's all yours offensively. I want you to really let it go tonight."

Let it go they did. In front of a packed house of 2,900 people, (McHale guessed that American fire laws would have allowed a maximum of 1,800), State vanquished their English counterparts. At the end of the first half, in an offensive display that even had McHale in mild shock, State walked off the court with a 78-38 lead.

The second half, as the three State coaches had expected, was not as devastating as the first. State, freely substituting, retained its lead of forty for much of the half. Team Audi made a minor spurt at the end against the State substitutes. The final score was 120-86. As the Audi coach went over to congratulate McHale, he said, "Jack, I'd made a couple of calls to the States about your team. Whatever I was told was way off. You guys can really score."

The excitement of the victory caused McHale to have difficulty sleeping. The restless night allowed time for reflection. In spite of the fact that Team Audi was in no way comparable to the American opponents State would face, their offensive display in the first half was probably the best he had ever coached. Thanks to Falk's counsel, he thought that the team could now break out of its doldrums. Still, he fretted over the one player who did not seem to be himself: Cormack McDonough. McHale figured that it was probably due to the enormous pressure the boy faced in his first trip home.

The following day was devoted to sight-seeing. The team took a five-and-a-half hour bus trip from Cork around the Ring of Kerry and back into Killarney for dinner. McHale normally would have insisted on a brief practice, but his boys had played well and the finals were two nights off. He knew he would be able to put them through a good workout the following day and felt certain that they would be ready to play against the Irish Nationals, who, the night before, had upset Murray's Metal of Scotland in overtime.

The trip around the Ring of Kerry was breathtaking even to the most disinterested members of the team. As they travelled up through Kenmore and Waterville, beholding the ragged mountains embracing the raucous sea, each player recognized that this was truly a special trip, one which would never be forgotten. On three separate occasions the bus driver had pulled over to allow the players to take pictures of Glen, Derryman and Ballaghoisean. At half past six, the Ring of Kerry now behind them, the team bus pulled into Killarney, where Colm Murphy had made arrangements for the team to dine at Dingle's Restaurant, one of Ireland's finest—and not three blocks from where Cormack McDonough had grown up. The dinner included king prawn grilled in garlic, followed by filet steak that cut like butter. The dessert was a speciality of the restaurant, a hot cherry tart with homemade cream.

Three tournament officials had travelled the ninety miles from Cork to Killarney to join the team for dinner. The Dingle's proprietor had brought in an Irish flutist to play several songs and a shanahy who regaled the team with stories. After the songs and storytelling, McHale become involved in a discussion that went far beyond what he originally would have thought.

One of the tournament officials, having downed a goodly portion of Guinness Stout, began to talk about Irish-American relations.

"The problem with you Americans is that you seldom get to see the real

Irish. You will come and visit and get a brief glimpse of us. In that glimpse, we will only reveal what we care to reveal. You will go home and assume we are a happy lot. Believe me, Coach McHale, there is a far darker side, one steeped in history and reeking of cynicism. If you look around our country you will see a political system strangling itself in bureaucracy, massive unemployment and yet a country teeming with people of high intellect. Higher, in fact, than most you will find elsewhere. Why are we in such a state of chaos? It goes deep, far deeper than you and I will be able to discuss this evening. But don't be fooled by our smiles and laughter. There is a sadness here Mr. McHale, one that goes to the very root of our existence."

The official had gone further than he should, and in the process had embarrassed his counterparts, one of whom said, "Perhaps we could move to a more productive center of conversation...like basketball."

McHale felt relieved by those words, for he did not wish to get into a deep and dark discussion of the Irish mindset.

The dinner concluded with Colm Murphy rising and saying to the team, "We matched you against the Brits because we knew you could beat them. As you may know, that is something we like to see here in Ireland." The historical implications passed over the heads of most of the State players. "Just take it easy on our Irish team on Friday night."

While Murphy's words were said in earnest, they did little to affect the State team. Their performance two nights later was equally devastating, as they ran roughshod over the outmanned Irish Nationals in front of another packed house at the Old Parochial Hall. The score at half time was 65-32. McHale, doing all he could to hold the margin down, substituted freely throughout the second half. State went on to a 126-79 victory, much to the delight of the Irish fans, who, despite their loyalty to the National team, enjoyed good basketball.

At the conclusion of the game, after a lengthy award ceremony typical of any Irish sporting event, the team returned to Jury's for another evening of socializing. The Americans now fully realized how important the social aspects of sport were to their hosts. McHale, while insisting that his players stay within the confines of the hotel, decided to loosen up training regulations and allowed his players to consume some of the famous Irish brew. At 11:30 p.m., the official closing time for Irish pubs and bars, the party moved upstairs to the "Residents Lounge."

"You see, Coach, they have this silly rule of closing the pubs here at 11:30," explained the porter. "We in the hotel industry, however, have the fortunate provision of a Residents Lounge." With over two hundred people jammed into the lounge, McHale suspected that the hotel keys were not checked with the greatest of care. The party went well into the night. McHale finally retired at 2:30 a.m. and instructed his assistants to stay at the party and keep an eye on the players.

As McHale reached his room he thought about the events of the last several days. Dr. Falk's advice had proven accurate, at least in terms of this tournament. The team performed brilliantly. Even the defense seemed to be more aggressive, due to the loose and free-flowing offense. McHale had installed several basic offensive rules, but he essentially allowed the team, including its poorest shooters, free license. The plan was working, even beyond McHale's wildest dreams.

Lying in bed, McHale thought that this edition of State basketball now had the capacity to win every game it played the rest of the season. He had not felt that way since his last twenty-win team.

Just as he was about to fall off to sleep, there was a loud knock at the door. McHale got up, looked through the peep hole and saw Cormack McDonough, obviously in distress. He opened the door and the gangly, 6'7" eighteen-year-old walked into McHale's suite. In the next five minutes, McDonough made McHale realize that his thoughts about the pressure on Cormack stemming from the boy's homecoming had been off the mark.

Seeing tears well up in the boy's eyes, McHale gently prodded. "Cormack, it's obvious that there's a problem. I want you to know that whatever it is, we'll be able to help, but you have to tell me."

At that point, McDonough burst into sobs. Through the tears, McHale was able to extract from McDonough that in the weeks preceding McDonough's departure to the United States, his girlfriend, Breda Caffrey had become pregnant and that she had told Cormack of her condition only days ago. "You see, Coach, here in Ireland it's a lot different from the States. In Ireland this will be treated as a scandal of the worst kind. It will be a great embarrassment to my family and to Breda's family. She'll never be able to live it down."

McHale went to McDonough, put his arms around him in a comforting embrace. "We'll work this out," he promised.

Many thoughts rushed through McHale's mind: his affection for the Irish lad who had given so much of himself to the State team, the realization of the pain young McDonough was feeling, and the fact that he had been slapped in the face with another challenge.

To lose McDonough would not only be a death blow for the team, but would surely reflect on McHale's leadership. He sensed that McDonough wanted to come back to State. McHale also realized that there were some financial implications. Should the girl come back, how would she and the baby be supported? Would State be able to bring her to America? Abortion was obviously out of the question, with Cormack's Catholic upbringing, and indeed McHale's, not making it a matter for consideration. McHale knew that the NCAA, archaic in some of its views, would not look favorably on any type of financial support for McDonough and his girl. Yet it was clearly in the boy's best interests to come back to State. His brilliant career would never get off the mark if he remained in Ireland.

"Cormack, I want you to go back to your room and get a good night's sleep. You and I will have to stay in Ireland for an extra couple of days. Don't tell anyone of this. I'll have Brian and Mike return with the team. We'll just say we have some personal business and leave it at that. Keep your chin up," said McHale.

Just as the door closed, McHale went back to his bed with a renewed sense of stress that had left him after the two big victories. The phone rang. It was Sally McHale.

"Jack, we just heard that you won. I'm so glad." While it was great to hear Sally's voice, it was something in her tone that caused Jack concern.

"Sally, is anything wrong?"

"It's Ted Patterson. He's committed suicide."

Chapter 56

"Welcome to sun-drenched Dublin," Milo Casey said with a wry smile. Casey and Bob Johnson had first met in 1974 at the "Thrilla in Manila," where Muhammad Ali defeated Joe Frazier in fourteen grueling rounds. A professional courtesy triggered their first encounter. Casey, intent on seeing the inside of each tavern in Manila, had overslept the fight's weigh-in and was stuck for a byline. As he half staggered into the press room several hours later, Johnson, who knew of the "Casey legend," could see that his colleague was in distress. He approached the Irish scribe and needled him for not having attended the weigh-in. While often railing against the generalizations placed upon sports writers about alcohol, Johnson, a teetotaler, grudgingly acknowledged that his profession did seem to have an unusually high percentage of arm-benders. Casey's reputation was that of the league leader.

It was common in sports journalism that when one writer's activities the previous night precluded the wherewithal to meet a deadline, another colleague would lend a helping hand. Such was the case on this day in Manila. After supplying the blurry-eyed Irishman with a much-needed cup of hot coffee, Johnson returned twenty minutes later with a fresh story: "Frazier Predicts Early Knockout at Weigh-in," by Milo Casey. They had become fast friends ever since, seeing each other at two or three major sporting events each year. Now they were coming together on a bigger saga.

After the usual welcoming remarks and customary good natured ribs, the two departed Dublin Airport and headed for Casey's 1976 Volkswagen, which looked as if it had been recently taken apart and put back together by a rival auto manufacturer.

"Since Killarney is a good five hour drive, I thought we should at least ride in comfort and style," said Casey as Johnson smilingly moved considerable debris from the front seat into the back so as to squeeze in for the long trip. "I didn't think we would see each other until the 19th hole at Augusta, but knowing how fanatical you Americans are about your game of rounders—or is it basketball?—I thought this trip might prove worthwhile."

Johnson was considered to be the preeminent sports writer in the United States. He could be, and often was, as tough as nails, frequently venting his wrath on the biggest of sports luminaries, including George Steinbrenner, Al Davis, Don King and anyone else whose actions were not, according to Johnson's judgment, in the best interest of sport. More than anything else, however, Johnson was a professional, one who took great pride not only in his considerable writing skills, but also in getting his facts straight.

When Milo Casey had first called Bob Johnson to tell him about the activities of Michael McDonough, Johnson's first reaction was one of sadness. While he did not know Jack McHale personally, Johnson made it his business to "know about" virtually everyone connected with sport, both on a domestic and international scale. Despite not knowing McHale, he had always had positive feelings toward the State coach, looking upon him as one who went by the book. Like many others, Johnson had been mildly surprised by the recruiting coup of State but, despite his normally cynical outlook on such an unlikely occurrence, he had not imagined McHale as a cheater.

Casey's first inkling that something was awry came during the semi-finals of the All-Ireland, when Kerry played Mayo at the Killarney Stadium on the outskirts of town. Like any other Irishman who ever read a sports page, Casey had grown up with the name of Michael McDonough, looking upon him in the same light that Americans would view a Mickey Mantle or a Jim Brown. Casey, like most sports fans in Ireland, knew that McDonough had succumbed to "the drink," and that hard financial times had befallen the former Gaelic football idol. Because of this, it appeared strange to Casey to see McDonough arriving at the stadium in a brand new Volvo.

At first, Casey thought little of it, but a post-game trip to the lounge at the Great Southern in Killarney increased his suspicions. After the game, which Kerry had won 15-12, McDonough appeared at the lounge, obviously in the early stages of intoxication. He bought drinks for everyone in the bar. Surely, the "Mickey Mac" Casey knew about could hardly afford a brand new luxury car and drinks for the house at the finest bar in Killarney. His quizzical mind now racing, Casey wondered how McDonough had acquired such good fortune. For an experienced journalist, the answer was not difficult to find.

Being the top sports journalist in Ireland reaped its dividends, as it did in most other sports-minded countries. The possessor had, among other indulgences, access to tickets for all major sporting events. Whenever a source needed to be tapped, the tickets proved very useful. With Kerry in the All-Ireland Finals a week hence at the Stadium in Dublin, Casey spent the next twenty-four hours in Killarney waving two choice seats in front of anyone he queried regarding the sudden fortune of Mickey Mac. The more tickets he gave away, the more obvious it became that Cormack McDonough's matriculation to State University had brought with it considerable financial reward to his father.

Casey recognized that he had the potential for a major story, not only in Ireland but in the United States as well. When he called Johnson, it was with a view toward a joint byline, to be released in Dublin and New

York on the same day.

"Robert, you have a much greater sense of what this kind of story means on the American university scene," he said. "Let's have at it together."

That had been all Johnson needed to make his reservations with British Airways. The five-hour trip to Killarney gave Johnson the opportunity to quiz his friend about every detail Casey had uncovered. As Johnson had suspected, Casey had done his homework, even to the point of knowing where and when McDonough picked up his "retainer."

"From what you've told me, Milo, the one thing we don't know is exactly who is sending the money," Johnson pointed out.

"That's correct. I have a pretty fair guess as to the amount, simply because as soon as McDonough gets it and converts it into Irish pounds, it seems to burn a hole in his pocket. We tracked him for a week after he received his last payment. He spent well over 1100 Irish pounds in seven days, which would be the equivalent of roughly $1,800 in American dollars."

The two arrived in Killarney at 11:30 p.m. and checked into the Great Southern Hotel. "The bar will be closed, but we can dash up to the Resident's Lounge for a quick jar, which I know in your case means a glass of ginger ale," said Casey. After the two had checked their baggage into the room and nestled into the comfortable chairs in the Resident's Lounge, Casey looked at Johnson. "What are the missing links before we can break this?" he asked.

"Well," replied Johnson, "we need to find out what, if any, money has gone to the boy and exactly who is involved and who is not. Before we go to Michael McDonough, we must confront Mrs. McDonough. Tell me what you know about her?"

This request brought a detailed summary of the life and times of Rose McDonough. "It's said that she was once the prettiest girl in all of Ireland," said Casey. "She grew up on a farm in a little town just outside of Killarney. When she was sixteen she was crowned Queen of the Puck Fair, which is a famous festival run each summer in County Kerry. At seventeen, she was the Rose of Tralee. As part of her duties as the Rose, she met Mickey Mac, fell in love with him, and, like so many girls of her time, was married by the age of eighteen."

Casey went on to explain Michael's fall from grace and the impact it had on his once beautiful wife. "I would say she is probably forty-two years of age and looks at least fifty. She had eight children in her first eight years of marriage, the second youngest being Cormack. Since the time they were married, Michael has literally dragged her through life."

"How much do you think she knows?" asked Johnson.

"I imagine she knows something. I would further imagine that if we approach her correctly, and as long as it does not hurt her beloved son, she would be ready to tell what she knows. You see, in this country, divorce is more than frowned on. Instead, couples just drift apart. In this particular drifting, there has been extreme bitterness—talk, in fact, of physical abuse. We'll have to approach her in a delicate manner."

With that the two agreed to retire for a good night's sleep, intending to knock at 21 Kilcaven Row, the home of the McDonoughs, the following day.

At breakfast the next morning, Casey outlined Michael's daily pattern which called for him generally to sleep late ("He needs maximum wear-off time!") and then hit one of the local pubs.

"I think we should wait until he leaves for his pub call," said Johnson. "We can then speak with Mrs. McDonough alone, at least at first."

At 1 p.m. the two drove to within one-hundred yards of the McDonough home. As Casey had predicted, at 1:15 p.m. the front door opened and Michael McDonough exited his home and headed west down Roanmore Street to his first stop of the day. The two waited ten minutes to make certain that he had not forgotten anything, principally his pub money. They then got out of the car and walked to the McDonough home.

The home was typical of many in Killarney. It was a two bedroom flat with a stucco exterior attached to two other flats. The two other flats had a much different appearance. The outside of each was freshly painted, with flowers and small but immaculate front lawns. The McDonough home had no flowers; the paint had been chipped on the stucco exterior and the lawn was in need of a fresh cut. The two approached the front door and rang the bell. When no one answered, Casey said, "In all likelihood, the bell doesn't work." Johnson issued a loud rap with his hand. Within moments, Rose McDonough opened the door.

As the door opened, Casey's words from the night prior were given new meaning. While her once great beauty was unquestionable, the two reporters looked at a woman who had grown old before her time; one whose eyes betrayed an almost pathetic sadness. "Mrs. McDonough, I'm Bob Johnson of the *New York Times* and this is Milo Casey of the *Irish Press*. We're here to talk with you about your husband and son. May we come in?"

Without uttering a word, she ushered the two men into the small, untidy dining room, adorned with pictures of Michael McDonough, replete with his All-Ireland trophies. "Please sit down, gentlemen," she said quietly.

"Mrs. McDonough, I'm afraid we're here to ask some very difficult questions of you," said Johnson. "Please understand, this is our job." Johnson then explained the circumstances surrounding his trip.

As he spoke, tears welled in her eyes. When he finished, she looked up and said. "What will happen to my son?"

"I can't answer that," said Johnson. "My understanding of our college rules would lead me to believe that it depends solely on whether he himself took any money."

"Mr. Johnson, I am certain that my son has done nothing wrong."

"Mrs. McDonough, I hope more than anything that you're right. Let's talk about your husband."

Thirty minutes later, Rose had confirmed virtually all of Casey's research. "What you should also know," she concluded, "is that whatever money he's taken has benefited him only, just like anything else he's done in his life. As you can see, none has gone to our home, to me, to our children."

Just as she finished her sentence, the front door opened. In walked Michael McDonough. Johnson's first reaction was unrelated to his reason for being there. Looking at McDonough, Johnson's thoughts briefly turned back twenty-five years and in a fleeting moment he thought, "What an attractive couple they must have been." Michael McDonough was still a broad-shouldered 6' 4", but with a paunch that reflected years of excessive imbibing. He walked into the dining room, eyed the two journalists and demanded, "Who the hell are ye?"

Before the two could answer, Rose stood from her chair. In twenty-seven years of what could only be loosely described as a marriage, Rose, like so many of her maternal counterparts in Ireland, had repressed her deepest feelings toward her husband. With Bob Johnson's comments fresh in her mind and with a fury held inside for all too long, she glared at Mickey Mac and said, "This is the last time in your life that you will ever mistreat me, our children, my friends, or in this case, our two house guests."

For the next several minutes, with Johnson and Casey fastened to their chairs, Rose McDonough unleashed a verbal assault on her husband, knowing with every word that their so-called marriage would end, and not caring. With whatever dignity she had preserved, she told him in no uncertain terms how his selfishness had ruined his own life and the lives of others, how her own dreams had long since perished because of him, and that his greed and stupidity would now make their son suffer.

Michael McDonough, already the recipient of several pints of Guinness stout, was not accustomed to such obloquy and embarrassment from his wife. He retaliated by raising his right hand. Casey, all 5'5" of him, sprang from the chair and threw himself at McDonough. Johnson, not as quick, but with similar intentions, bolted across the room and helped restrain the once powerful All-Ireland footballer.

While the two wrestled McDonough to the ground, Rose, her eyes now red with fire, said, "As God is my judge, you will pay for this." As her words cascaded through the small flat, Jack McHale and Cormack McDonough pulled up in front of the McDonough home.

Chapter 57

The investigation had taken only three weeks. Even for John McCollough, it was extraordinarily swift. There were two reasons. First, Robby Nesbitt had proven to be an extremely accurate source of information. Second, those behind the scheme had performed their functions with a sloppiness rooted in arrogance. It was this apparent arrogance that concerned McCollough.

The investigation had begun with McCollough's interrogation of Robby and Sean Riley. As always in the McCollough agency, everything had been taped. While McCollough's trained ear was generally able to ferret out anything that might hint of a clue, the recording provided him with time for a more thorough analysis of the statements.

McCollough insisted that his two assistants listen to the tapes separately and follow the normal agency procedure, which called for each staff member to prepare a "key points" report. The key points were simply anything said on the tape that might produce a lead. It was no surprise to McCollough that his two assistants focused on the same points Robby had provided: the new smell of the car, the facial description of the dealer and an unexpected bonus in the form of fingerprints.

When Robby pointed out the exact place where he had met the dealer and, more specifically, observed that the dealer had rested his palm on the wall, McCollough quickly dispatched an aide to the restaurant.

Getting the fingerprints would not be easy. McCollough assumed that it was not by mere happenstance that the dealer had chosen to meet at this particular restaurant. He was reasonably certain (a hunch later confirmed) that a relationship existed between the dealer and the restaurant's owner. When the aide went to the restaurant, he had to exercise caution, both in determining if any prints were left on the wall and then in removing them.

Since John McCollough had become a member of the FBI in 1971, crime prevention techniques had taken quantum leaps in many areas, the securing of fingerprints among them. Up until the late '60's, it would have been unthinkable to extract a fingerprint from a wall that had been left seven weeks earlier. Times had changed, and McCollough liked to relate the story of one of his most famous cases as testimony.

In his last year as head of the Criminal Division for the FBI, he was assigned to track down former Nazi war criminals. He located one such criminal living in a small village on the sea in Piran, Yugoslavia. McCollough's primary piece of identification was a letter, written in the suspect's hand some forty years earlier, which McCollough tracked down to an obscure museum in Yugoslavia. No other sample of the suspect's handwriting could be found. After months of East-West diplomatic maneuvering, McCollough was able to get the museum to send to him the original copy of the letter. Using laser technology, he extracted a fingerprint and brought the suspect to trial.

McCollough's aide spent a week sitting at the bar, drinking at several booths and in general making the owner feel that he was now a regular. This done, he was able to discreetly slip to the back booth, perform the necessary preparation and, on his second visit to the booth twenty-four hours later, take away a fingerprint.

While a trained staff and state of the art technology were important factors in McCollough's success, another strength was his ability to make use of his considerable contacts with the FBI and local authorities. It was not merely McCollough's former position as Chief of Law Enforcement for the FBI that allowed him such freedom. He had developed a system of perks (with the advice of legal counsel) which kept his sources happy. While perhaps having the semblance of unethical behavior, his system could never be construed as illegal. The perks McCollough offered to his "friends" included frequent tickets to major sporting events, always "comped" by the ticket agency which McCollough paid under the table. The "comping," should any investigation ensue, would show that no actual dollar value accompanied the tickets. In addition, McCollough made certain that other safe gifts were provided on a frequent basis. No money was ever exchanged and McCollough gained almost unlimited access to the files of the FBI and local law enforcement agencies.

John McCollough was tough and hardened. From his time spent in Vietnam to his dealings with major criminals as an FBI agent and private investigator, he had confronted situations which even the most experienced law enforcement agents would look upon with trepidation. But now, for the first time, McCollough was fearful. Fearful not so much for himself, but for his clients.

He called Kara Riley and asked that a meeting be arranged at the Riley home and that Robby and Sean Riley be present. The meeting was set for 8:30 p.m. the following evening. As always, McCollough arrived on time. Kara Riley opened the door and greeted him warmly. She had grown to like and admire McCollough, and in the deep recesses of her mind, had even thought of him as a partner. It was not merely his good looks, but his quiet confidence that attracted her.

When Kara opened the door, she saw that this confidence had been replaced by something else, something she could not quite determine. She ushered McCollough into the family room. The Riley family maid had prepared hot coffee and pumpkin tea bread. As he sat down, without looking at the coffee, he glanced at the two boys, both eagerly awaiting his report. He then looked into Kara's eyes.

"We are close to completing our investigation," he said carefully. "But before I get into any of the details, I want all of you to know something, something very important. If we pursue this any further, all of us in this room may be placed in a life-threatening situation."

Chapter 58

George DiOrgio's passion to become a leading player agent entailed more than his meetings with Steve Ellovitch and Mike Lambert. As was typical of any DiOrgio enterprise, he had spent considerable time researching the project, looking before he leaped.

He identified two points as being most crucial in the development of his new venture. The first was that for every true professional agent, there were literally a hundred who were motivated by nothing more than a desire to rub elbows with sports personalities or, to make a fast buck. The second finding: for those at the upper echelon of the business, there was an extremely high profit margin.

DiOrgio believed there was still room at the top for his agency. His research pointed to four key areas which would ultimately form the divisions of his company.

The first would be the legal division. DiOrgio was prepared to hire a full-time attorney to head it. The legal division would negotiate all player contracts and review contracts relating to any business venture, endorsement or other project involving a client.

The second would be the investment division. It was here that DiOrgio knew he must make the right choice. Agent misrepresentation had long been a part of the business. In recent years, the likes of Kareem Abdul-Jabbar and Ralph Sampson had lost millions, owing in some part to agent neglect. The NCAA, the professional leagues and the various players' associations were all seeking strict registration procedures for agents. DiOrgio knew that this was a consequence of increased publicity attached to client rip-offs.

The investment division would oversee the portfolio of each client. Included in the service would be the payment of bills, bookkeeping, filing of income taxes and, of course, the investment of money. It would also be the division of highest profit potential. It was no secret that even banks were spending considerable revenue to become specialists in money management of athletes and that their profit could be as high as fifty percent. DiOrgio wanted to make certain that his agency tapped these profits.

The third division would be the packaging division. All research indicated that proper packaging of athletes required significant expertise. For every Michael Jordan and Sugar Ray Leonard, there were hundreds of athletes whose representation either did not include consideration of packaging, or, if considered, resulted in poor advice. DiOrgio's packaging department would include specialists in speech and diction, as well as an in-house public relations firm whose sole role would be to develop the image of each client.

DiOrgio also determined that the number of clients would be kept to a minimum, and that certain criteria would be set for accepting clients. If an athlete was not a first-round draft choice, an all-league performer or a potential champion of an individual sport, the DiOrgio agency would have no interest. From a financial standpoint, it made no sense to represent any athlete below that level. Also, DiOrgio knew that third-round draft choices did not make for headlines.

Next, DiOrgio would put together a company Board of Directors. As with all of his ventures, he would spare no expense. Prospective Board members, all of whom would be former professional athletes whose images were untarnished, would be offered between twenty-five and fifty thousand dollars per annum. In return for the stipend, DiOrgio would require that Board members participate in the fourth and most important of all divisions, the recruiting division. He knew that former star athletes, now successful in other fields, could be major assets in the recruitment of potential clients. His Board would be comprised of both male and female, black and white—a cross section which would appeal to the entire client base.

In three short months, DiOrgio turned his theories into reality; he put the company together. Division heads and other staff were set, the Board was formed, offices were leased, glitzy brochures were prepared, and a major press conference was planned. DiOrgio's accountant authored a company prospectus which projected profit at the end of year two and seven figure profits by year four.

In addition to the Board, Steve Ellovitch and Mike Lambert, in their part time capacities, would also assist. DiOrgio saw Ellovitch as a key operative—for the short-term. If Ellovitch reached his goal of presidency or general managership of a professional team, he would be of significant value on the other side of the table.

It had occurred to DiOrgio in his growing relationship with Ellovitch that the two blue-chippers, Cormack McDonough and Marvin Lewis, had not just happened on the front steps of State University. While trying to suppress his knowledge of the situation, Ellovitch, due to his affinity for braggadocio, had tipped his hand several times.

In his office, DiOrgio affixed to the wall a giant blackboard with the heading, "Get List." The list included target clients ranging from individual to team sports, college and pro. For a variety of reasons, Steve Ellovitch would have difficulty saying no to any request from George DiOrgio. Because of this, DiOrgio had listed under "College Basketball—Hardship" two names at the very top: Cormack McDonough and Marvin Lewis.

Chapter 59

After his wrenching confrontation with Jack McHale, Ted Patterson walked into the officials' room, which in Madison Square Garden measured 12' x 14'. In the days of two college basketball officials per game, it was cramped. With the advent of three officials, there was barely enough room to move. As Patterson entered the room, his two fellow officials abruptly ended their quiet conversation. They both turned, stared at Patterson and then looked down at the floor.

Patterson's earlier state of frenzy had dissipated. He was now lucid and fully understood the consequences of his actions. Ted Patterson knew that he had just completed the worst game of his career. He knew his performance had been seen by more than 20,000 people live and countless thousands more on television. While it was unlikely that he would be pulled from any of his regular season games, any thought of NCAA tournament work was crushed. A mediocre or bad game would be tolerated. What would not be tolerated was the type of performance Ted Patterson had displayed.

His career as an official was irreparably damaged and so was his career as a fixer. He did not care. Without showering or uttering a word to his colleagues, Patterson changed into his street clothes and walked with a blank expression to the rear exit of the Garden and out to 34th Street. He had parked where he always parked for Garden games, on the corner of 37th and Broadway. The air was crisp. There were snow flurries. The shock of the cold brought him back even further to reality. Walking briskly down Broadway, he arrived several minutes later at the parking lot. Patterson produced his parking ticket and the attendant, with dispatch, stamped it. "That'll be $17, sir." Patterson handed over a $20 bill and said absently, "Keep the change."

He opened the door of his car and hunched into the front seat. He pulled the keys from his pocket, put them in the ignition and began to adjust the rear view mirror. There, sitting in the back seat and looking straight at him through the mirror, was a man whose face was covered with a woolen mask.

"Ted, we need to talk."

Patterson, startled by Hondo's presence, found his hands trembling. He said nothing. "It's obvious your effectiveness as an official will now be questioned. Our plan included three games in January. We're putting a hold on the three until we're certain that you're back in form. Despite your performance, you will not be pulled from any of the remaining regular season games. We'll look at February and the game between Rutgers and St. Joseph's as our next fix. Are you listening to me, Ted?"

As Hondo spoke, Patterson's fear had slowly turned to rage. He now realized that he could have dealt with whatever financial losses he had suffered. What he could not deal with was his complete loss of self-respect. For this he blamed Hondo. So he wheeled, lunged over the seat and grabbed his antagonist by the lapels.

"It's over you bastard. I will not dump another game as long as I live." His rage now almost out of control, Patterson found tears streaming down his cheeks. As he finished his sentence, he felt cold metal pressing against his skull.

"Ted, you'll do exactly what I tell you to do or there will not be a rest of your life."

Patterson slumped back on the front seat. Hondo, now pointing the gun squarely at Patterson's head, said, "You're not in the frame of mind to talk about this now. I'll call you at your office at 1:30 sharp tomorrow. Make sure you're there." With that, Hondo opened the back door and, never taking his eyes off Patterson, slowly walked to the rear of the parking lot and out onto Broadway.

During the ninety minute drive to New Haven came the realization that there was no hope. Ted Patterson was cornered, a trapped animal with nowhere to go.

When he arrived at his home well past midnight, the lights were on. His wife, despite their strained relationship, had been waiting up. As he entered through the back door, she stood there looking at him. There were tears in her eyes. She came to embrace him and said, "Teddy, it will all get better."

After the two went to bed, Patterson remained awake, thinking. His wife's parents, while not wealthy, were reasonably well off. The debt accrued over the past three years was in the company's name. Although his wife had been his working partner, Ted was the sole stockholder in the corporation. The more he thought, the more at ease he felt.

He arose the next day, Sunday morning. The Pattersons always ate breakfast together that day. Patterson looked at his two children and his wife. He loved them and knew what he was going to do would be best for all. After breakfast, he went to his room to think his plan through in more detail. Two hours later he returned to the kitchen and said to his wife, "I need to make a trip today. I won't be home this evening."

His wife's look was one of fear. "Teddy, where are you going?"

"Don't worry, honey, everything will be all right."

The holiday season had always been his favorite time. As he walked into the parlor and saw the Christmas tree adorned with lights and decorations the Pattersons had gathered over the years, he felt a rush of melancholy which he quickly banished from his mind. He kissed his wife and children and picked up the car keys. He drove the two-and-a-half miles to his office, arriving thirty minutes before the expected call from Hondo. At long last he felt a sense of relief. No more suffering, no more indignity. The cruel world would hurt him no more. At 1:30 p.m. sharp, the phone rang. Patterson picked it up.

"Ted. . ."

Before Hondo could go any further, Patterson immediately interrupted him. "What you didn't realize in your grand plan was that I took some precautions to protect myself and my family. There will be no more dumped games. Since our second phone conversation I've taped every one of our discussions. Those tapes are being sent to a friend of mine who, if anything ever happens to my wife or children, will bring them immediately to the FBI. You may have heard of voice prints. They are every bit as effective as finger-prints. That's all I have to say to you."

With that Patterson hung up the phone. He went downstairs and back out into the blustery winter day. The mail box was at the corner. He inserted the package, which was addressed to his old mentor, Billy Esposito, and then returned to his office. Five minutes later, Ted Patterson hanged himself.

Chapter 60

A s Jack McHale and Cormack McDonough approached the doorway of the McDonough home on Kilcaven Row, young McDonough sensed that something was wrong behind the oak door of that drab flat. Throughout his youth he had grown accustomed to such sensations, which almost always portended his father's mistreatment of his mother. As they slammed the claddagh knocker, Cormack silently hoped that his father would be sober and not harassing his mother. He hoped most of all that he would not be embarrassed in front of his coach.

Suddenly, McHale and Cormack heard shouts from inside. When no one responded to the knock, Cormack pushed open the door. His worst fears were affirmed. Lying on the floor, gasping for breath and being held down by Bob Johnson and Milo Casey, was his father. His mother stood off in the corner, tears streaming down her face. Her look quickly changed from anger to horror as she saw her young son enter the parlor.

A thousand thoughts rushed through McHale's mind. There on the floor, obviously being restrained, was the father of his prized recruit. One of the men restraining him was a familiar face, known to McHale only through the picture which accompanied his column in the *New York Times*.

"What's going on here?" he asked incredulously.

"I'll tell you what the hell is going on," blubbered Michael McDonough. "These two aegid's come into my house uninvited. . . ."

"Stop!" screeched Rose McDonough. "No more of your lies!" Both Johnson and Casey released their hold and McDonough struggled to his feet.

"I'll listen to no more of this bull dust!" he bellowed. Pushing his son aside, he staggered out the front door.

For what seemed to be an eternity, the five stood in the room looking at each other, not knowing what to say. Finally, Cormack went to comfort his mother. McHale motioned Johnson and Casey to the kitchen.

Still confused, McHale looked at Johnson. "What *are* you doing here?"

"It's a long story," replied Johnson. "We need to ask you a lot of questions, but it would seem best that you first take care of the boy and his mother. This was an ugly scene."

"Where are you staying?" McHale asked.

"At the Great Southern," responded Casey.

"Give me an hour or so and I'll meet you."

As Johnson and Casey departed, McHale reentered the den. By now, Rose McDonough and her son Cormack were sitting on two chairs adjacent to the fireplace, the warmth of the burning peat embracing the room.

"Mrs. McDonough, Cormack and I have come to talk to you about something very important. Obviously, something else quite important has taken place here today. Perhaps we should start with that."

"Mr. McHale, I don't know if my son should remain and listen."

"Your son is fast becoming an adult, Mrs. McDonough; I think he should stay."

With that Rose, regaining her composure, told both McHale and young Cormack all she had learned from Bob Johnson and Milo Casey. As each word sprang from her mouth, McHale felt his heart sink further into his stomach. "How many setbacks can I handle?" he wondered to himself. Thoughts raced through his mind: "Who did it? Did the boy receive any money? What will happen to my program?" As she finished, McHale looked at his young star.

"Cormack, it's difficult for me to ask this, but I have to know before we go any further. Did you know about this? Did you take any money yourself?"

"Not a thing and not a shilling," responded Cormack.

A relieved McHale continued.

"Mrs. McDonough, I hate to heap problem on problem, but we came here to tell you of a situation that must be dealt with. Cormack, I think you should explain to your mother what's happened."

Cormack McDonough had always harbored enormous affection for his mother. He knew of her awful mistreatment by his father, how she had done all she could for him and his seven brothers and sisters. He knew he was about to hurt her. . .a great deal. Summoning his courage, he began his tale. When he concluded several minutes later, Rose, with tears welling once again in her eyes, got up from her chair and embraced her youngest boy.

"Cormack, my son, there are many things that you don't know about your father and me. Many things that you never needed to know, many things that I never told you to protect you. Twenty-seven years ago your father and I were married. I was four months pregnant at the time. I was not ashamed. I loved your father. But there were many, many people in this town who looked at me as dirt. Many people who I know, to this day, still make their snide remarks behind my back. I do not want you and Breda to go through what I went through. Mr. McHale, something must be done to bring Breda across to America. They must be married there and live there, at least for the time being. You see, while our town and our lakes are quite beautiful, a vile undercurrent still exists that would plague my son and his wife for the rest of their lives."

"I think we'll be able to make the necessary arrangements for Breda to come to the States. Now, I'll leave you and your son alone. I have some other business to attend to," said McHale.

As Jack McHale left the McDonough home, he walked toward the Great Southern. He was now confronted with a situation that involved payment from someone connected with State to the father of one his prized recruits. The leading sports journalist in the United States had traveled to Ireland to uncover the scandal. Doubtless, his story would appear at the top of every sports page in America. In addition, he faced the problem of a young boy and girl who somehow had to be supported. The NCAA would take nothing more than a head-in-the-sand approach to Cormack's personal dilemma. In seventeen years, Jack McHale had never broken even the most minor and silly rules set forth by the NCAA, save for his pre-season scrimmage. Now, he would have to provide money and housing to support the young couple if, in fact, his whole program did not come tumbling down as a result of the impending scandal. He wondered if he could survive it all...or if it was worth trying.

McHale entered the lobby of the Great Southern Hotel where Johnson and Casey awaited him. The three ordered tea and brown bread, and Johnson began.

"Jack, although we've never met, I certainly know you by reputation. Let me tell you exactly what I know." With that, he recounted the entire scenario, from the phone call he had received from Casey several weeks earlier, to the explosive scene at the McDonough home.

When he finished, McHale glanced first at Casey and then Johnson. "What you have just told me is probably the worst news I've ever received in my entire career as a coach. I'm sure there is a major question on your mind. Let me answer it before you even ask. Until I walked in to the McDonough home today, I knew absolutely nothing about any financial gain for the father. In addition, I'm as certain as I can be that the boy took nothing and knew nothing of the situation as well."

Johnson, while respectful of McHale, followed his journalistic instincts. "I'm not suggesting that I don't believe you, but how could you not have known?"

"It may seem odd, but it's the truth." The force of McHale's statement made Johnson sit back in his chair.

"OK, then we have to find out who does know. I'm sure you're aware that I'm going to have to write about it." The three then conversed about all possible sources of the money. McHale could see why Johnson had such a fine reputation as a journalist. While unearthing the facts, he was interested in doing so fairly, so as not to indict anyone nor ruin careers or lives. After discussing a bevy of possibilities, McHale felt he knew the identity of the guilty party.

"Gentleman, with your permission, I think I should make a call to the States to prepare people in my department for what I'm sure will be a series of questions you'll want answered. For what it's worth, Bob, I appreciate the way that you've handled this."

"Likewise," replied Johnson.

After the normal difficulties in placing an international call from Ireland to the United States, McHale finally made contact with the Dublin operator, who put his call through to Steve Ellovitch's office.

"Steve said to tell you that he's on his way out to an important meeting and will have to get back to you," said Ellovitch's secretary.

"You tell him that what I have to say is a hell of a lot more important than any meeting."

Seconds later, Ellovitch picked up the phone and in an irritable voice said to McHale, "What is it Jack?"

Chapter 61

J ack McHale believed that loyalty was the primary job qualification for an assistant coach. In the early years, there had been several bad experiences caused by a lack of this quality, one of which forced McHale to let an assistant go. In Mike Lambert and Brian McCray, he knew he had two aides in whom he could place complete trust. He told them of Cormack's predicament and of the scandal State faced, but warned that under no circumstances could they reveal either problem to anyone, including the players—just yet.

McHale planned to remain in Ireland for two or three days to help Cormack McDonough and his girl, Breda, arrange to move to America. State's next scheduled game was January 12 against Seton Hall. McHale would return the day before the game. The three coaches then discussed the practice sessions and what should be accomplished. McHale looked upon his two assistants as equals, and his assignments in preparation for Seton Hall reflected this.

The next step was to meet with the players. The coaching staff had predetermined that the explanation would be brief. McHale began the meeting by praising the players for their great performance in Ireland, emphasizing that the team was ready to "explode."

"A situation has come up," McHale continued, "involving Cormack McDonough. I'm going to be staying on with Cormack for a couple of days in Ireland. We'll be back in time for Seton Hall. Until then, coaches McCray and Lambert will accompany you home and run practice. Gentlemen, we've come a long way in a very short time. Let's make damn certain that we continue in the right direction, which includes best behavior for the remainder of the trip and good practices until I get back."

On Tuesday morning the team departed Jury's. The Hotel Manager had arranged a gala send-off. Two of the female desk clerks were teary-eyed, having established close "relationships" with two State players. Before arriving at the airport, the team bussed through the Cliffs of Moher where they were treated to the breathtaking view of the famous cliffs majestically overlooking the Atlantic Ocean. At 1:15 p.m., the bus rolled into Shannon and an hour later the team was airborne.

After boarding the plane, it was apparent to Brian McCray and Mike

Lambert that the team psyche, so devastated ten days earlier after the loss to Princeton, was exactly where it should be.

"I don't know much about this guy Falk," said Lambert, "but he certainly has done wonders."

The six-and-a-half hour return flight provided players and coaches alike an opportunity for reflection. Marvin Lewis had been satisfied with his progress as a freshman. Despite the early losses, Jack McHale had lived up to all of his recruiting promises, including Marvin's starting position. He had grown to like McHale, the assistants and most of his teammates. The others whom he did not care for were primarily seniors who, at least until the Irish trip, seemed threatened by Lewis' presence. He was pleased that their attitudes were beginning to change.

Marvin found himself thinking about two concerns, neither of which related to basketball. Since Thomas Mahon moved to Worcester, Marvin had grown close to his father, particularly during Marvin's recruitment. After Marvin committed to State, and particularly in the last several months, he had noticed a disturbing change in his father. It was not anything that Thomas had said, just an attitude which Marvin sensed but had difficulty identifying. It was almost as if his father had lost interest in him, as if after signing with State, he had become less important to his father. This troubled Marvin Lewis deeply. He did not know quite how to handle it.

The other concern was far different. Improving his basketball skills and expending total effort to become a better student had consumed virtually all of Marvin's time. Up until his senior year in high school, he had never dated. He never had, or took, the time for any female relationships. He was still shy and retiring when it came to young ladies.

In an early season road game Marvin had noticed a girl, one of the most beautiful girls he had ever seen, sitting in the bleachers. That was not so surprising. What was surprising was that she seemed to be watching only him. Others would tell him that he had become an attractive young man. Despite this, he had never pursued female companionship, nor was he accustomed to any advances.

When Marvin first noticed this girl staring at him, he passed it off as his imagination. At the Iona game, he noticed her again. Again he passed it off. But at the Princeton game, as State left the floor after its crushing defeat, the girl was standing at the exit ramp. As Marvin, despondent in defeat, walked through the ramp, she leaned down and gently said to him, "You played a great game, Marvin." Stunned, he managed to look up and mutter, "Thank you."

* * * * * *

After dinner on the flight home, the players put on their headphones, sat back and viewed the movie *Crocodile Dundee*. Brian McCray and Mike

Lambert each drifted into their own thoughts.

Lambert pondered the future, about his meeting with George DiOrgio, about whether the team would survive the impending turmoil and, if it did, what coaching opportunities would be in store for him. Even before the Irish trip, he had decided to hold off any decision until the end of the season. The team's performance in Ireland made him realize again what he always knew deep down. He wanted to stay in basketball; he wanted to be a head coach.

McCray loved his job. He had grown even closer to McHale during the difficult times since his appointment in 1981. He had also grown close to Mike Lambert, yet it was Lambert who caused him concern. McCray knew there were only a few head coaching jobs available to assistants. Should the staff survive the season, any head coaching opportunities would first be pursued by Lambert as the assistant with the most seniority. McCray was twenty-nine with a wife and two children. He knew that coaching was a young man's profession. As he dozed off to sleep he wondered, "Will I get my chance?"

Aer Lingus Flight 303 touched down at JFK at 3:25 p.m. Thirty minutes later, the team exited through customs and out into the cold New York air. A bus was waiting, and it quickly sped down the Cross Island Expressway over the Triborough Bridge and back to campus. It was now 6:30 p.m., but to the players it seemed much later. Their days in Ireland had accustomed them to the five-hour time difference. The team manager instructed the players to leave their game bags in the bus. "I'll bring the bags back and unpack them," he said, showing again why Jack McHale had chosen him as manager in return for a full scholarship.

The players went to their rooms, most deciding to get right to sleep. As Marvin Lewis entered his dorm and trudged upstairs, he was met on the stairway by a dormmate and basketball fanatic who had befriended him on the first day of classes.

"Marvin, you know that beautiful blonde who spoke to you after the Princeton game? Well, she was here this morning and taped a note to your door."

Chapter 62

Jack McHale's words during the long distance phone call cut into Steve Ellovitch's stomach. He felt ill. His brain was numb. The message McHale had related brought the worst possible news.

What was odd was that Ellovitch had not been worried of late. In fact, he had been able to put the entire matter virtually out of his mind. Things seemed to be going so smoothly.

McHale was brief and to the point. For several chilling minutes he related to Ellovitch not only the findings of Bob Johnson and Milo Casey, but also the implications. "The results of this will be devastating for the guilty and the innocent," was McHale's concluding remark as he abruptly hung up the phone.

Ellovitch knew that he and other members of the Athletic Department would be hearing from Johnson and Casey within hours. The two journalists would soon pinpoint who was behind the pay-offs.

Trying to regain some semblance of composure, Ellovitch pressed the intercom, his hands shaking.

"Call the people at Gunderson. Tell them the meeting is off."

"But Mr. Ellovitch, didn't you say that this is a very...."

"Call the goddamn people and tell them the meeting is off!"

The longer he sat in his chair, the more disoriented he became. Bob Johnson was perhaps the most respected sports writer in the United States. The story would make national headlines. His future... his plans... it was over... devastatingly over.

Ellovitch sat in his chair, one emotion colliding with another. Finally, he broke down and wept. In his career—his ruthless quest—he had established no friendships. There was no one he could reach out to, no one he could confide in. Suicide? He considered it for a fleeting moment, but he was too much a coward for that. As a boy growing up on the East Side, he would run away when other kids ridiculed him. He would always run, always take the path of least resistance.

He pulled a pad from his drawer. To write the eleven words took virtually all of what remained of his self-control: "I hereby resign as Athletic Director of State University, effective immediately." He summoned his secretary. She took the handwritten note and typed it on State University stationery. He signed his name and walked out of the office. He would never return.

Chapter 63

After his laconic conversation with Steve Ellovitch, Jack McHale returned to the lobby of the Great Southern and spoke briefly with Bob Johnson and Milo Casey. "I've just gotten off the phone with our Athletic Director. I let him know that both of you would be calling State today."

"What was his reaction?" asked Johnson.

"Bob, I think it best that you determine that for yourself." Johnson nodded, as McHale continued. "Based on the situation, I've decided to fly back tomorrow."

"Jack, before you leave, there are two other important points I need to raise," said Johnson. His questions centered on the other two prize recruits, Marvin Lewis and Billy Powers. "Do you have any knowledge of the two players or their parents receiving any money?"

"No," responded McHale.

"Do you feel it's a possibility?"

McHale hesitated. He recognized that it was important to be truthful with Johnson. "I'm as sure as I can be that Bobby Powers took no money. He's an old friend of mine. He's done quite well financially. He's just not the type."

"What about Lewis' father?"

"Strictly off the record, that might be a different matter," said McHale. "I guess if I were sitting in your seat, it would be something I'd look into."

After McHale left Johnson and Casey, he went back to Cormack McDonough's home. By then, Cormack and his mother had talked things out and a more halcyon atmosphere had set in. Rose McDonough explained to McHale that, should he be able to assist with funding, a decision had been made: Breda would move to the United States, marry immediately and have the child. She also said it was unlikely that Michael would show up at the house for another two or three days.

"Mrs. McDonough, I've now decided that I better go back tomorrow. I think it best that Cormack and Breda follow a day later. That will give me twenty-four hours to begin to make arrangements for Breda. You said that Michael will not return for several days. What will happen when he comes back?"

"How do you mean?" Mrs. McDonough responded.

"Well, about you. What will happen to you?"

"The most important thing now is my son. I'll worry about myself when the time comes."

The plane trip home allowed McHale the opportunity to gather his thoughts. While he had not told Johnson the details of his conversation with Ellovitch, McHale was convinced that his Athletic Director was involved in the payoff. Although Ellovitch was generally adept at hiding his feelings, such had not been the case on the call. McHale wondered who, if anyone, was involved with Ellovitch.

Also, what about the larger implications? Clearly, NCAA rules had been violated by the highest-level member of the department. There would be sanctions. The sanctions would not be forthcoming for a year or so, as it generally took the NCAA many months to determine the extent of the punishment. The sanctions were likely to be severe, probably costing State a year or two in the NCAA tournament. He doubted that Cormack would be punished at all. The boy had taken no money; he was an innocent victim.

Moreover, McHale now felt that he would not be forced to break any NCAA rules in arranging to bring Breda to the States. He was acquainted with a number of Irish-Americans of wealth and influence, one of whom headed the Friendly Sons of St. Patrick in New York. The Friendly Sons underwrote a home for pregnant teenagers. McHale was certain he could get the Friendly Sons to make some type of contribution, perhaps in the form of housing for Breda until the child's birth. This was well within NCAA regulations and would allow McHale time to develop a long term plan.

He thought more of Steve Ellovitch, and what he would do. In the eight years the two had worked together, McHale had never gotten to *really* know Ellovitch. The shield Ellovitch placed in front of personal relationships prevented McHale from having any idea of Ellovitch's reaction to what surely would be a career-ending crisis.

What of himself? In the coming weeks, he would have to be exceedingly strong to survive. Although he had done nothing wrong, his own job would be in serious jeopardy. The innocent might fall with the guilty. And, he wondered what effect all of this would have on his players, who several days earlier had seemed on the verge of jelling into a team capable of winning every remaining game.

McHale, not having slept for a day, finally drifted off. As the flight approached the landing area at JFK, he awoke to the harsh sound of the plane's paging system. "Would Mr. Jack McHale kindly meet the Aer Lingus representative at the exit door in the front of the plane."

As he exited the plane, he saw the Aer Lingus representative with a copy of the *New York Times*. The front page headline read, "Pay-Offs in State Athletic Program—Athletic Director Resigns." The Aer Lingus representative added, "Your Sports Information Director is in the Press Room waiting for you. He has scheduled a press conference."

As McHale neared the Press Room, the SID approached him. "Jack, I tried to reach you in Ireland but you'd already gotten on the plane. I had to set this up." As McHale began to respond, three reporters came around the corner.

"Jack, Jack, can we get some questions?"

McHale looked at the SID. "I'd better go in and meet these people."

The questions posed to McHale were tougher than any he had confronted in his entire career. Even his friends in the press corps, those who had defended him in the down years, showed traces of doubt in their voices as they fired away.

As had happened so many times before in his life, McHale found that while he experienced great tension before moments of confrontation, he could respond logically once in front of his adversaries. He had many reasons for this, but chief among them was McHale's belief in his father's advice of long ago—"Jackie, if you haven't done anything wrong, you have nothing to worry about." So McHale met every question head on. He stated that he had no personal knowledge of the violations, nor did any of his assistants; that to his knowledge, none of his players had taken any money and, at present, only one parent of one player was involved.

"What about Ellovitch's resignation?"

"I have no comment on that," said McHale. "I was not aware of it until I walked off the plane ten minutes ago."

The press, hostile at the beginning of the conference, warmed as they sensed that McHale was telling the truth. Twenty minutes later, as their questions came to an end, several reporters shook McHale's hand, one of them saying, "Jack, I hope this turns out all right for you. It seems as if you've been caught in the middle of something you had nothing to do with."

As he walked out of the Press Room, McHale saw a face he had been hoping to see, particularly in the last twenty-four hours. It was Sally McHale. "Let me drive you to the office. We'll have some time to talk," she said. The thirty-five minute drive was good tonic for McHale. As always, his wife listened to the entire situation, assessed it realistically and offered sound advice. "Jackie, I think you should use the one step at a time approach. Go into your office with a clear head, meet with the right people, have a good practice and then come home and get some rest."

McHale entered his office and immediately met with his two assistants.

"How are the players taking all of this?" he queried.

"They seem pretty dazed," said Brian McCray.

"What about the administration?"

"Well," said McCray, "Tom Reynolds has been appointed interim AD. This all happened in the last two or three hours. The President has not issued a statement. I hear he's pretty shaken up. The word around campus is he'll probably have to resign."

"Where does that leave all of us?" asked McHale rhetorically.

McHale next met with Reynolds, who had been at State for twenty-one years. His first year as an Assistant SID had coincided with McHale's junior year. He and McHale were close.

"Tom, I want you to know that I had nothing to do with this."

"Jack, it never even entered my mind."

The two discussed the situation, then focused on the upcoming game with Seton Hall.

"It looks like we'll have a sell-out, particularly after all the controversy," said Reynolds.

"Leave all of the administrative details to me, Jack. You concentrate on the team."

McHale next met with the SID. "Keep the players completely off limits to the media. I'll deal with them personally, but I don't want the kids involved."

With practice beginning in thirty-five minutes, McHale picked up the phone, hoping there would be an answer at the other end.

"Lawrence Falk speaking."

"Am I glad to hear your voice," McHale sighed. The two discussed the awful chain of events that had occurred, with McHale first assuring Falk that he had nothing to do with what had happened. "Your counsel was sensational, Dr. Falk. The team could not have played better. I know the competition wasn't that good, but I swear to God we're ready to win. Now all of this happens. What can I do?" For the next several minutes Falk, in great detail, advised McHale.

"Jack, you must make the kids believe that you are all now on an even bigger mission...a crusade. It's you and the team against the world. You have to convey to them that no one, absolutely no one within the basketball program has done anything wrong. Make them aware that they will be confronted with some severe obstacles in the coming weeks and that now more than ever the team has to come together. It can be done, but you're going to have to do one hell of a sales job."

As McHale hung up, there was a knock on the door. Before the coach had a chance to answer, in walked Marvin Lewis. The 6'10" center sat down and immediately broke into tears. "He did it, Coach. I just know he did it. It hasn't been the same since I signed." As with Cormack McDonough, McHale felt great affection for young Lewis. There was a mutual trust and respect between player and coach.

"Marvin, just tell me all you know and we'll get through this. First, I have to ask you the same question I asked Cormack. Did you at any time take any money?"

"No, Coach; never."

McHale, greatly relieved, listened to the eighteen-year-old freshman explain why he suspected his father.

"He's been throwing money around like water," said Lewis. "He told me he had won some money in the lottery back in Alabama and I believed him. I believed everything he said to me in the last two years." The youngster again started to sob.

McHale put his arm around Lewis and said, "Marvin, everything will work out. The next couple of days will be tough. We've got to stick together."

Ten minutes later, McHale walked out on the court and blew his whistle with force. It seemed to wake up the silent players, who seemed in a trance, tentatively shooting baskets at the various hoops around the gym. Quickly, they jogged to center court. "Gentlemen, let's go into the Team Room. We need to talk."

McHale was in his best form. "First, I've told the SID that none of you are to discuss with the media the situation here at State. I'll handle it. Now, let's talk about our team and what we're going to accomplish in the next two months."

With that, McHale, using Falk's advice of thirty minutes earlier, gave a rousing talk, almost as if the team were getting ready to run on the court to play a game. "Gentlemen, we are going to face some real adversity in the coming weeks. There's one thing we have going for us—no one in this room has taken a dishonest dollar; no one in this room has done anything wrong. It's us against the world, fellas', and dammit, we're going to show what we're made of!" His team then had as good a practice as Jack McHale could remember.

The following night, Madison Square Garden was packed to the rafters. There were signs throughout the Garden, all referring to the pay-off, some suggesting that McHale resign. As the team ran onto the court, the Seton Hall fans sitting under the west-end basket pulled out dollar bills and waved them derisively. In the pre-game huddle, McHale reiterated his pep talk from the previous day.

"You see all those people out here," he screamed, trying to raise his voice above the noise level in the Garden. "Well, they've all convicted us without a goddamn trial. That's not the way things are supposed to go. Let's go out and show them how the hell innocent we are." The score at half-time: State 47, Seton Hall 29. The second half was twenty minutes of the same. As McHale said to the media afterward, "I don't recall a team of mine playing better basketball over a forty minute period."

This brief euphoria that accompanied the win had worn off by early the following morning. It was 6:30 a.m. and the sun was just coming up. When McHale saw the neighborhood paperboy dropping the *Times* off on his steps, he went to the door, expecting the worst. He picked up the *Times* and opened it to Bob Johnson's column. What he read brought tears to his eyes.

In his compelling style, Johnson made note of the terrible wrong that had been committed. He then went on to Jack McHale. In his final three sentences, Johnson provided as ringing a defense for a coach as McHale had ever read: "Fire Jack McHale? When you find a man in college athletics who confronts adversity with the integrity and directness that McHale has exhibited in the last several days, you don't fire him. You give him a long term contract."

Chapter 64

" **P**endelton Resigns in Wake of Sports Scandal." The headline roared across the front page of every New York newspaper a few days later. Edward Pendelton's future had been in a tenuous state since the doomed referendum fiasco which preceded the fund raising efforts for the new facility.

Despite his lack of involvement in the scandal, and the fact that he had inherited Steve Ellovitch as his Athletic Director, Pendelton rightly feared that Ellovitch's resignation would not be enough to placate the irate State Board members, many of whom were scurrying about trying to protect their own positions. A major head had to roll. Pendelton knew that it would be his. Three days after the scandal broke, he was forced to resign immediately.

The Michael McDonough story, broken in a joint byline by Bob Johnson and Milo Casey, was headlined in every major newspaper in the country. *Sports Illustrated* devoted eight full pages to the scandal. The ABC *Nightly News* ran a 45-second clip, interviewing Pendelton as he left his office. One week later, Johnson reported that Thomas Mahon had also taken under-the-table payments from Ellovitch. The news cycle repeated itself, although not with quite the same initial force.

Johnson had done preliminary research on Mahon prior to his trip overseas and had checked his facts thoroughly. Six days after his return from Ireland, he was certain. When he finally reached Thomas Mahon by phone, Mahon, in an advanced state of inebriation, blurted out, "I took the money. I wish to hell I'd taken more."

One of those not surprised by the scandal was George DiOrgio. He had viewed Ellovitch as one whose ambition could take him to the top but would possibly destroy him. Fortunately, one of DiOrgio's strengths was his ability to adjust to ever-changing circumstances. Without missing a beat, DiOrgio immediately turned his attention to others within the field who could fill Ellovitch's role in soliciting athletes to represent.

Ironically, the scandal offered DiOrgio a new and potentially exciting possibility. While the NCAA was not likely to penalize Lewis or McDonough, it could punish State's program. This might push Lewis and McDonough to declare hardship and turn professional. "Let's get Mike Lambert over for lunch and make certain we stay on top of this," he said to an assistant.

For Jack McHale and his team, it was an ongoing emotional crisis. Both

McDonough and Lewis were devastated upon hearing that their fathers had, as one tabloid described, "sold their two kids out." Young McDonough's other problem—his girl friend, now five months pregnant—was quietly being remedied by McHale. Due in part to the enormous pressure brought on by the scandal, McHale had contacted the NCAA, told them of the McDonough case and got clearance for assistance through the Friendly Sons of St. Patrick. "As long as the money goes directly to the girl and is used for her trip, housing, food and care of the baby, we have no problem with it," he was told by an NCAA investigations officer.

McHale wished the other problems could be dealt with as easily. He had assigned Lambert and McCray to spend virtually all of their spare time with the two wounded freshmen. For his own part, McHale found himself relying more and more on the counsel of Lawrence Falk who urged him, "Stay with the 'It's us against the world' notion and spend as much time as possible with those two kids. This is a time of crisis. They need a father figure. That father figure has to be you."

At Falk's suggestion, McHale invited the team to dinner at his home. After feasting on lasagna and homemade apple pie, the team adjourned to the living room where McHale reassured them that no one directly involved with State's basketball program had committed any wrongdoing but that the team might still be hit with shrapnel from the crossfire.

"Gentlemen, we have to circle the wagons. We've done nothing wrong and now more than ever, we must stick together," he sermonized.

To McHale's delight, the team responded. Two seniors, heretofore phlegmatic in their commitment to the program, drafted a written statement signed by each team member and released it to the media. The statement stressed that "We intend to stick together and, most importantly, stick with our outstanding coaching staff through this." Another formerly disenchanted senior was quoted in the *New York Post* saying, "There's not a better coach or a better person than Coach McHale."

As deeply as he had been touched by Johnson's column several days earlier, the quote by the senior and the statement by the team meant even more to McHale. He continued with the "one day at a time" approach. While McHale was walking on egg shells, none had broken yet.

Chapter 65

Steve Ellovitch had not been seen since departing his office a week earlier. Frequent calls to his home were met with a computerized response from AT&T: "We are sorry, this line has been temporarily disconnected." His whereabouts were unknown to all and quite worrisome to some. Among those concerned was fundraiser Robert O'Connell.

Since being approached by Robert Steincross nine months earlier, O'Connell had put considerable time into serving as chief consultant for the Building Fund campaign. He had steered the campaign ship through turbulent waters, managing the considerable egos involved with quiet aplomb. When William Riley had wrested control of the project from Robert Steincross, O'Connell was able, through deft maneuvering, to ingratiate himself to Riley without alienating Steincross. Since Steincross and Riley would not communicate directly, this allowed O'Connell to "confide" in the two. He played one against the other in the minds of both, all the while staying in their good graces.

O'Connell had sought out Steve Ellovitch after learning of the scandal. He wanted to meet with Ellovitch to ferret out as much information as possible. Ellovitch, as chairman of the Building Fund, might hold details crucial to the continuation of the project. When O'Connell could not find him, he had to implement his new plan.

The campaign seemed snake-bit to O'Connell. However, he had continued to work on it, turning away contracts for other projects in the process. He wanted to see it through. Most importantly, he wanted to be paid his remaining fee, which he knew was unlikely if the campaign ended because of the scandal.

With Ellovitch and Edward Pendelton out of the picture, and with William Riley out of a job at Gunderson, O'Connell looked at several candidates to take the lead. One was Joe Kett of Merrill Lynch, a friend of Riley's. Another was Steincross. While clearly estranged from a number of the other Board members, O'Connell knew that Steincross was a man of enormous ego, a man whose pride had no doubt been devastated since being steamrolled by the Gunderson Express. He guessed that Steincross might be plotting a takeover of the project, perhaps even bringing in new committee members over whom he could exert full control. O'Connell also guessed that while Gunderson's financial commitment would remain intact, the company would probably choose to distance itself from the project and might pose no objections to Steincross' resumption of control.

With this in mind, O'Connell phoned Steincross to arrange a meeting.

The receptionist at Steincross Industries hesitated. "Umm, ah, Mr. O'Connell, I think I better put you on with Mr. Steincross' personal assistant."

The assistant then came on the line. "Mr. O'Connell, this is Mr. Steincross' assistant." Her voice was close to cracking from emotion. "You evidently have not heard the news. Mr. Steincross and a friend were killed in a plane crash early this morning."

Chapter 66

" **M**arvin, I hope the trip to Ireland went well. Please call me—754-5321. Cecelia." The note, sealed in an envelope, was tacked to Marvin Lewis' door.

Since enrolling at State, Marvin had noticed a change in the demeanor of some females toward him. They seemed more friendly, more anxious to get to know him. All those who exhibited this behavior had one thing in common: they had all been black. Marvin knew only two things about this mysterious Cecelia who had written him the note: she was extraordinarily beautiful...and she was white.

The victory over Seton Hall had done little to allay the shock of his father's treachery. Finally, his friend, the diminutive dormmate who had told him of the note, approached Marvin and said, "Look, I know you're going through hell. Why don't you phone the girl? I mean it's not everyday somebody that beautiful *asks* to be called. Maybe it'll take your mind off things."

Marvin, confused and nervous, dialed from the public dorm phone.

"Hello?"

While only one word, it was said with such clarity, such self-assuredness and in such a feminine tone that Marvin Lewis was immediately taken aback. He looked at his friend who was standing beside the dormitory phone booth and implored his assistance. The friend quickly motioned to Marvin, mouthing quietly, "Say something."

"This is Marvin Lewis."

It was all that was needed. She took it from there.

"Marvin, I'm so glad you called."

After several minutes of conversation, the two agreed to meet that evening at a quiet restaurant about a mile from campus.

Marvin Lewis did not have a car, so at 7:45 p.m., his friend drove him to the restaurant.

"Marvin, when meeting a girl, you always want to be the first one there, especially when you're meeting someone like this girl. Relax, everything'll be fine," the dormmate advised.

Marvin Lewis felt comfortable walking on a basketball court in front of 17,000 people. This was not the case with meeting Cecelia. As he left the car, he found his hands were trembling.

"How will I get home?" Marvin asked.

"That's your problem," smiled his friend.

The restaurant was small and nicely decorated, and only half full. It specialized in Italian/American food and was quite popular with the students. Though he had heard of it through some of his teammates, it was Marvin's first visit to the Aldila.

After being seated, the young freshman immediately moved from one side of the table to the other, trying to keep his eye on the door so as not be startled by her sudden appearance. At 8:10 p.m., there was no sign of her. Marvin was certain she would not show up. He considered calling his friend to ask that he come and pick him up. At 8:25 p.m., convinced he had been stood up, he began to rise from the table to go to the phone booth. Just as he did, the door at the front of the restaurant opened.

There are few times in life when a person's entrance into a room provokes a cessation of all other activity. In most cases, it usually is an important person, a political figure, a head of a company, someone whose appearance is the reason for the people in the room to be present. Another case, such as what occurred in the Aldila Restaurant that night, might be the appearance of someone totally unexpected, someone whose sheer beauty makes everyone stop, turn and simply look.

Within seconds after Cecelia entered the restaurant, every eye was focused on her, including Lewis'. He was still standing in his now-aborted attempt to reach his friend by phone.

As she approached the table smiling, Marvin was overwhelmed. Her long blond hair draped well below her shoulders. She wore a black crepe cocktail dress, cut slightly above the knee. Her smoky blue eyes sensuously contrasted with her delicate features. She was a harmony of form, a contemporary Grace Kelly.

Not only was it Marvin's first meeting with anyone of such beauty, it was the first time in his life he had actually conversed with a girl not of his own race. Up until this point, he had always looked upon white females as forbidden territory. He recalled, somewhat bitterly, his one foiled attempt to enter such a relationship. It was his junior year in high school. He had mentioned in passing to some of his friends, most of them white, that he was contemplating asking one of the cheerleaders, also white, to the Junior Prom. The reaction by all, particularly his white "friends," was stone cold silence. The following day, the Assistant Principal called Marvin to his office, and spoke to him about a "rumor" he had heard, advising Marvin that it was best that he stick to meeting girls of, "your own color."

When the two sat down, Marvin was ill at ease, having no idea what to say. Within minutes, this all changed. Cecelia spoke in soft, caring tones, saying how much she enjoyed watching him play, how happy she was the team did so well in Ireland. No woman had ever spoken to him this way. As the conversation continued, he felt as if he had known her for years.

After the two placed their orders, Cecelia gently slid her hand across the table, placed it atop Marvin's and said, "I want to be your friend."

After they had finished their meal, the waiter brought the dessert menu. Cecelia looked at Marvin and said with quiet confidence, "Marvin, I picked up some things at the bakery this afternoon. Perhaps we could have dessert at my apartment."

Chapter 67

On Thursday morning, forty-eight hours prior to the Nevada-Las Vegas game, the NBC trucks rolled up in front of Jack McHale's office. Since the scandal had broken three weeks earlier, the State team had come together in resounding style. Even McHale, in his most intense reverie, had not imagined the superior play of his troops. Everything Lawrence Falk had suggested seemed to work. The team was now 12-6, winning its last seven games by an average margin of seventeen points per game. They were on a roll. McHale knew that if State could defeat Nevada-Las Vegas on national television, it would be a major step in its quest for an NCAA bid. The NCAA tournament committee placed heavy reliance on a team's improvement over the course of a season. Beating the Runnin' Rebels would provide ample testimony to State's progress.

Two NBC employees entered McHale's office.

"Coach, as you know, the situation surrounding McDonough and Lewis is on the tip of every college basketball fan's tongue. Al McGuire has decided he would like to center his half-time show around the two kids and how they're dealing with the problem. He would like to interview you, the two kids and several other team members. He'll be flying in this afternoon to do it right after practice."

McHale stiffened and said, "Under no circumstances will we do it after practice or, for that matter, will we do it at all. You know damned well that our SID contacted you a week ago, when the request came in, with a flat 'no.' The players have been through hell, particularly those two young kids. They will do no such interviews."

Very seldom had McHale reacted to people, particularly media members, in such a coarse manner. The team, however, was finally playing well. After an excruciating several weeks, the players were beginning to get their minds off the scandal. He wanted the matter over, at least as far as his players were concerned.

The game had been a major scheduling coup for State. Nevada-Las Vegas was a name team. In agreeing to come East, they had provided Steve Ellovitch with enough ammunition to approach NBC for a national television spot nine months earlier. The network's initial reaction had been lukewarm. Ellovitch's constant pleadings were aided considerably by a call from a

Gunderson vice president placed to NBC's advertising director. "We spend a great deal of money with you folks. This is a game we'd like you to consider." Forty-eight hours later, the contracts were signed.

As practice concluded Thursday afternoon, McHale headed back to the film room to review game tapes of Nevada-Las Vegas with his two assistants. As he exited the gym, he could see a familiar face. Al McGuire had always been one of his favorites. As they approached each other and shook hands, McGuire said to McHale, "Jack, I'd like to talk with you."

McHale motioned to his two assistants to begin watching the tape and proceeded to his office with McGuire. As he expected, McGuire was there to persuade McHale to change his previous and firm denial of NBC's request. As he also suspected, McGuire was a good deal more convincing than the two production assistants.

"Jack," said McGuire. "I want to do the take, but I guarantee you I'll do it so that it will do nothing to hurt your team or your players. I know you've been through hell. This is a story that needs to be told and I can assure you there's no one better to tell it than me."

"You hit it on the head when you said we've all been through hell," responded McHale. "I want your word that you won't do anything to take away from my team's progress."

"You got it," said Al.

Tip off was Saturday at 2:03 p.m. Knowing that Madison Square Garden would be packed and that there would be traffic jams, McHale made arrangements to have the team spend Friday night at the Penta Hotel, just across the street from the Garden. Normally, he preferred that the players sleep in their own beds. But this time he wanted to be certain that the team had a good breakfast and an opportunity for a brief workout at the Garden. As his team went through the lobby of the Penta en route to their shoot-around, Nevada-Las Vegas was just returning from the Garden. At the end of the pack walked their coach, Jerry Tarkanian.

Tarkanian, probably more than any other coach in NCAA history, had been the subject of repeated NCAA investigations. While McHale had no particular ax to grind with the NCAA, he did consider its treatment of Tarkanian excessive. He had talked with Tarkanian several times at NCAA coaching conventions. While he had little doubt that "Tark the Shark" may have shaded the rules, as most others did in the profession, McHale recognized that the Vegas coach had given many street kids the opportunity to improve their lot in life. He respected Tarkanian. When the two met in the lobby, they greeted each other warmly. "You've hung in real tough, Jack," Tark said. "I admire you for it. It should be a hell of a game today."

Tarkanian proved to be a prophet. From the tip off until the final buzzer, 20,216 people at the Garden were treated to a dazzling display of high-octane basketball. Thanks to Lawrence Falk's counsel, McHale had shaped his team into one which played intense full-court pressure on defense while "letting go" on offense. The Nevada-Las Vegas style was similar and made for an enormously exciting game. At half time, the two teams walked off the court to a thunderous ovation. The score was State 52, Nevada-Las Vegas 48.

McGuire's half-time show, taped the day before, went just as he had predicted. Using his considerable skill in communicating with young people, he put both Cormack McDonough and Marvin Lewis at ease. He spoke with them about the devastating impact the whole scandal had on their lives, and in soothing terms encouraged them to get on with their careers, that things would get better. Similar interviews took place with three State seniors and with McHale. With several million fans watching, the clip clearly showed that all those directly connected with the team had nothing to do with the scandal.

While McHale's speech at half-time was sprinkled with a good deal of praise, he also reminded the team that despite their great play in the last month, they still had six losses and could ill afford another if they wished to get into the NCAA's:

"Guys, we need this game. It's on national television and we're four points up. Let's do the same things we did in the first half and we can grab this damn thing."

Two minutes into the second half, Marvin Lewis picked up his fourth foul. At the ten minute mark, the team hit a dry spell, missing seven straight shots. At the final buzzer, Nevada-Las Vegas had won 106-98. It was a definite step back for State. Though they had played well for most of the game, they suffered from the foul trouble of Lewis. McHale admitted to the media at the post-game press conference, "We now have seven losses. We probably have to win the rest of our games to get into the NCAA's."

In another part of town, many blocks from the Garden, a person once closely allied with State's athletic program watched the game. The shades were drawn and the apartment littered. He had not shaved for weeks and had eaten very little. As he contemplated packing his bags, Steve Ellovitch hoped that he would be able to muster the energy to make his three hundred mile trip to the north.

Chapter 68

Robert O'Connell's initial reaction was one of disbelief, although not over the death of Robert Steincross and his assistant. Indeed, crashes of small aircraft were quite common, particularly in light of the circumstances surrounding this one. It turned out that the two had been flying in Steincross' small plane to Lake Melville in Newfoundland on a fishing trip. It was a foggy day with severe head winds. About one hundred and fifty miles north of the Newfoundland Airport, the air control tower received a distress signal. Several minutes later the plane went down; the bodies of Robert Steincross and his assistant scattered across the wilderness.

The deaths produced an eerie feeling in O'Connell. The building fund project had been going so well, almost too well, when a series of events, culminating in the death of Steincross, altered not only the course of the campaign, but also of many lives. O'Connell initially decided to contact each of the Board members and recommend that the campaign cease.

O'Connell, however, was not one given to reaction based on impulse. For several days following Steincross' death he mulled the matter over. In the end, he felt that the best course, at least for Robert O'Connell, was to continue. He had done his job and the commitments were in place. Most importantly, he was still owed $250,000.

In the normal course of events, any meeting of a campaign Board would be called by its chairperson. In this case, with no such person and the committee members all waiting for someone else to make the first move, O'Connell finally took it upon himself to contact them.

He arranged for a 6 p.m. meeting at the Downtown Athletic Club in New York City on February 24. Several days prior to the meeting, he sent telegrams to each of the Board members, reaffirming the date, time and place and briefly stating, "The only item on the agenda will be to determine the direction of the State University Building Campaign."

Every member of the Board entered the Fordham Room of the Downtown Athletic Club, and each demonstrated that he was not interested in socializing. Robert O'Connell had been in difficult situations in his lengthy career as a professional fund-raiser, but none which approached the uncomfortable atmosphere as the members of the Board sat down. It was obvious that no one in the room was willing to take any initiative. They were all looking to O'Connell for direction. With this in mind, he began.

"Gentlemen, I need not go into the unfortunate events which have damaged this campaign. We are here to determine our options which, as I see it, are two. The first is that we end the campaign this evening. Frankly, if I were in your chairs, I would not blame any of you for walking away. As you well know, there are some additional financial commitments still remaining which we can get into this evening should you choose this course.

"The second option is that we move forward," he continued. "It is one which I hope you will adopt tonight. Despite the difficulties we have, to my knowledge, the commitments made are still intact. While there may be some minor fallout, at this time I have not been informed of any. If we choose to go on, I believe the first thing we must do is elect a new chairperson. The floor is now open."

For the next several minutes, each committee member posed questions to O'Connell, most of which related to the exact financial position of the campaign as of that evening. O'Connell produced a balance sheet which showed that the Building Campaign had collected $900,000—$500,000 from Gunderson Brewery and $400,000 from the additional ten Board members. This money had been placed in an escrow account at the Bank of New York, in return for their pledge, secured months earlier by O'Connell and William Riley. From the $900,000, the Board had approved a $150,000 payment to O'Connell toward his $400,000 contract, the balance of scheduled payments due over the next nine months. In addition, $100,000 had been paid to the architect for the preliminary schematic drawings of the $18 million building. Lastly, $25,000 had been paid to the campaign law firm (hired by Gunderson to displace Richard Shoppels) for its preparation of various legal documents.

O'Connell pressed on: "In addition to the amount collected and as you all know, we have secured in writing, pledges for the remaining $23.2 million. First payments are due on March 15, with the remaining amounts due in six month installments over the next three years. All pledges received are from triple A-rated companies. All are bankable from a standpoint of borrowing."

As O'Connell concluded, there was silence. Finally, Joe Kett of Merrill Lynch broke the ice. "Bob, I think we have some business to conduct among the Committee members. Would you mind adjourning to the other room? We'll be out to get you in a short time."

Fifteen minutes later, O'Connell was asked to return. "Bob," began Kett, "let me get right to the point. We're all in agreement that at this time we do not choose to go forward with this project. The campaign is tainted and we simply cannot affix our companies' names to it. We recognize, however, that there are still some outstanding obligations. Contractually, there is little question but that we owe you $250,000. As you know, however, the contract was made in good faith and never assumed the terrible circumstances surrounding this campaign. I don't know if this is fair to you or not, but the Committee would like to know what you feel is an appropriate settlement, one that you will be happy with and that can put this whole project to bed?"

O'Connell had analyzed his options since Robert Steincross' death. He knew that his contract was iron-clad. Should he choose to play hardball, he would be able to collect the balance of $250,000. There were other considerations, however. In the room that evening were some of the most powerful men in New York. Perhaps as much as any business, fund-raising proved the axiom that "it is indeed a very small world." O'Connell knew that in taking the $250,000 he could well risk future business. So he put the ball back in their court.

"I appreciate your concern," he said. "As I believe you know, I have spent a considerable amount of time on this project and believe that my efforts have been productive." He paused, hoping for some show of reaction, which he received in the form of several affirmative nods. "I also recognize that it would not be fair of me to expect my full compensation since the building will not now be constructed. I believe you are all fair men and I suspect you have a figure in mind which you deem as fair. May I ask what it is?"

"We were thinking in terms of an additional $125,000, bringing your fee up to $275,000. That, plus what we intend to pay the architect and attorney, will be shared equitably among all of us in this room, with Gunderson agreeing to take the bulk of the loss due to their early commitment," said Kett.

When Robert O'Connell entered the room that evening, he had hoped to come away with another $75,000, should the campaign end. He was now $50,000 ahead of the game. "Gentlemen, if you feel that is fair, then I accept your decision. And in using the term acceptance, I am also stating that I feel that you have treated me fairly."

Two weeks later, O'Connell received a check for $125,000, with a note from Kett of Merrill Lynch. "Bob, I have been asked by my alma mater to chair their capital fund drive. Kindly make an appointment to see me about serving as chief consultant to the campaign."

Chapter 69

As Jack McHale left the press room in Madison Square Garden, he decided to do something that in past years would have been unthinkable. The nationally televised game against Nevada-Las Vegas had been played at 2 p.m. It was now 4:45 p.m. There were at least three games that evening within a one-hundred mile radius involving teams that State still had to play. They were games that McHale could easily get to. He decided against it. He would spend Saturday night with his family.

During the drive home, McHale found his thoughts centering once again on his own future at State. The scandal and surrounding circumstances had an almost deflective impact on him. Prior to the scandal, the focus on State's basketball team rested solely on wins and losses. Now, the woeful details surrounding the payoffs, coupled with favorable articles about McHale, had brought about a different perspective, one which called attention to the positive points of McHale and his program. For the first time in almost two years, McHale did not consider his job to be in imminent danger.

Despite this, he still felt the empty sense of defeat as he wheeled his car into his driveway. It was a hollow feeling, one which he wondered if those in other professions ever experienced, at least to the same degree. He turned off the ignition and thought for a moment. In the early years, Jack McHale had coached to win. In more recent times, with the enormous pressure heaped upon him, his approach—Lawrence Falk notwithstanding—had changed. He was coaching to keep from losing, as if a fear of failure had enveloped his thought process.

As he walked into his home, he was greeted affectionately by his wife and two children. Some things never change, even the good things, he thought. As he proceeded into the family room and instructed his oldest son Jackie to get the fire going, the phone rang, much to McHale's annoyance.

Several years earlier, the McHales had decided not to list their number in the public directory, primarily because of the crank calls. McHale suspected that the call was probably from a media member, who had been apprised of McHale's unlisted number, or from a personal friend.

"Your team was sensational," exclaimed the now familiar voice at the other end of the line. It was Dr. Falk.

"Are you calling because you really think so, or to give me a shot of adrenaline?" joked McHale.

"Seriously Jack, you played brilliant ball."

"Perhaps we did," said McHale, "but the reality is we now have seven losses, which doesn't bode well for an NCAA bid."

For the next several minutes Falk, who now felt a real kinship to McHale, spoke in friendly but forceful terms to the coach.

"Jack, your team is like night and day from two months ago. I know your goal is the NCAA's and, personally, I still think you can make it. But what's more important is that these kids are now performing at an extremely high level. I know this is difficult, but don't judge them merely by the final score. Judge them by their performance, which was terrific this afternoon."

McHale, as he generally did after speaking with Falk, felt better. He knew Falk was right again. Indeed, the team had played an excellent game against Nevada-Las Vegas. The fact remained, however, that it would be difficult to get an NCAA slot, even if the team won its remaining games and finished 20-7. Another loss might seal their fate. Two losses and a 18-9 record would mean, at best, an NIT berth. While meaningful in the '60's and even early '70's, the NIT was no longer of much interest to McHale.

The rest of the schedule, as crafted by Steve Ellovitch, was tough. The remaining games included road contests at Notre Dame and Michigan State and a season finale in Madison Square Garden against Big East power Villanova. While the axiom "We play them one at a time" had become an operative statement in athletics, McHale, like all of his contemporaries, knew that the statement had no real meaning. To win them all, State had to perform at an optimal level and, of equal importance, get through the rest of the season without injury. The next afternoon McHale, sticking to his post-loss theory of a good run to get the "mopes" out, put the team through a brisk ninety-minute practice.

Falk's words proved prophetic. State went on to rattle off four wins in a row, and in the process, became known in the college basketball world as a team "on the move." In their fifth game, at Notre Dame, a capacity crowd showed up one hour prior to tip-off to hear Digger Phelps, adorned in a blue and gold Notre Dame sweat shirt and with his fist clenched, bring the fans to fever pitch with a pre-game speech.

As the game began, State's offense sputtered. By the second half, the team once again faced foul trouble with both Cormack McDonough and Marvin Lewis going to the bench in the last four minutes. The final score was Notre Dame 88, State 81. State came back to win its next two games, one an impressive victory at Michigan State. Their record was now 18-8 with one game remaining, against the 1985 national champion Villanova at Madison Square Garden.

At this point of the season, speculation on NCAA bids was beyond the preliminary stages. Of the sixty-four spots in post season NCAA competition, thirty would go to conference winners. This allowed a mere thirty-four at-large bids for conference runner-ups or independents such as State. Of the thirty-four spots left, it appeared that most were spoken for, because teams such as Notre Dame had deposited in the bank the all-important magic number—twenty victories. State, along with Miami, DePaul and some conference teams, were looked upon as the clubs who would compete for the remaining slots. In State's favor were a tough schedule and a late season run. Clearly, however, a victory over Villanova was a must.

Despite Steve Ellovitch's resignation, George DiOrgio, with a binding contract and a top-level performance on behalf of State, was now in complete control of State's Madison Square Garden promotional program. The Villanova game would be played on Friday night, March 2, followed by a Paul Anka concert. The game was a complete sellout. Whereas earlier in the season, most fans attended State's home games for the concert, on this night, 21,263 turned out primarily to see if State could beat their Philadelphia rivals and perhaps gain an NCAA berth. The bids would be determined the following weekend after the post-season conference tournaments.

The game was played at a level that basketball fans hope for but seldom see. The lead changed hands thirty-six times. At the end of regulation, the score was 71-71. Ten minutes and two overtimes later, State won 89-87 on a Billy Powers' fifteen-foot jump shot. The Garden was in a frenzy. With a record of 19-8, and two major victories in their final stretch, it was now a matter of State followers waiting the nine excruciating days for post-season conferences to end. Then, the NCAA selection committee would gather in Kansas City, Missouri to render its decisions.

Immediately after the game, George DiOrgio returned to his office to review the evening's balance sheet. While DiOrgio's promotional genius had brought State to a level of profitability that, prior to his involvement, would not have been dreamed of, he wanted more. The development of his player-agent business had moved swiftly. In his private office, the chart of prospects hung boldly on the wall. These were the players who could quickly take his business to great heights. At the top of the chart, two names had remained for the entire season. Both were underclassmen. Both were prospects who, because of the terrible events surrounding their fathers and the likely sanctions to State, would look seriously at the possibility of "coming out early," or declaring themselves eligible for the NBA draft.

As part of his recruiting team, DiOrgio had signed a young and affable assistant who had graduated from State two years earlier and whose surname was Irish. His job: to befriend Cormack McDonough and, at the right time, introduce him to his boss, George DiOrgio. The friendship had been spawned six weeks earlier, just after Cormack learned of his father's betrayal. It had blossomed. The meeting with DiOrgio was arranged for Saturday lunch, just fourteen hours after the victory over Villanova.

Chapter 70

A ll they could do was wait. The Villanova victory had placed State squarely in the thick of contention for an at-large bid to the NCAA tournament. By no means, however, was the bid assured, for in the week following their victory, conference post-season tournaments would take place. The outcome of these tournaments would be crucial to State's hopes.

What concerned Jack McHale most was a scenario in which a number of also-rans in the conferences—teams who, without winning the post-season tournament would have no chance at an NCAA bid—could suddenly catch fire, win their tournament, and receive the automatic bid given to conference tournament winners. This meant that the top regular season teams within those conferences would then be competing with State for at-large bids. If, on the other hand, these favorites won the post-season-conference tournaments, State's chances were far better.

With all this in mind, Jack McHale and his staff ran intense ninety minute workouts each day following the Villanova victory. His team had clearly peaked. If State were selected, the major concern was that they would face a two week layoff and, in all likelihood, play a hot team coming off a conference tournament victory.

There were two schools of thought on the importance of post-season conference tournaments. On the one hand, those in favor of such tournaments pointed out that they were tremendous revenue producers. Moreover, the participating teams would experience the type of intense competition they would have to face in the NCAA tournament. Those opposed pointed to the Atlantic Coast Conference, one of the first major conferences to hold a post-season tournament, but one whose teams consistently failed in later NCAA competition. The pundits viewed this as a matter of the ACC teams burning out. Whatever the case, McHale felt it imperative to keep his team as sharp as possible and his workouts reflected this aim.

While McHale and his team practiced, waited and worried, the selection wheels for the NCAA tournament had begun to turn weeks earlier. The NCAA basketball selection committee was comprised of commissioners and athletic directors chosen not only for their expertise in judging basketball teams, but also for their geographic distribution to ensure fairness. Comprised of nine representatives, it was one of the most prestigious of all NCAA committees. In addition, it had proven on many occasions to be one of the most thankless.

The committee's work actually began in late January, with a series of weekly conference calls to begin the review of teams for the prized post-season bids. By mid-February, the committee had whittled the teams down to a manageable number. It then became a matter of tracking those teams through the end of the season.

State's late-season run, as well as the attendant publicity of the scandal, had placed the team on the minds and lips of virtually every basketball fan in the country. When the committee gathered in Kansas City on Friday, March 9 to begin its marathon review, no member had any lack of information, or opinion, on State's basketball dossier.

The committee members, while considered among the elite in their field, were human. All took pride in the integrity of their profession. All had been stung badly by the actions of one of their colleagues, Steve Ellovitch. No more than thirty minutes after they gathered in the Presidential Suite at the Hyatt, the matter was brought up.

"This State situation really bothers me," said an athletic director from a traditional NCAA power. "Here are the best two players on the team enrolled there as a direct result of a buy-off to parents. I know the NCAA can't take any immediate action on this, but I want to say it burns my butt that one of our supposed colleagues was behind the whole thing. I don't know about you fellas', but I'm not so sure I want to see them in this tournament."

After others expressed agreement, the committee chairman took the floor. "Gentlemen, I don't blame any of you for your reaction, but let's remember a couple of things. First, it was the parents and not the athletes who took the money. Secondly, there is absolutely no question about the coaching staff being involved. Last but not least, the NCAA has not taken any action, nor will it until the Infractions Committee meets in late May. For a number of reasons, not the least of which is that we could all have our rear ends sued by State University if we keep them out before their hearing, we cannot let the impertinence of Steve Ellovitch and two parents enter into our decision in any way," he said.

"You're right," said another AD. "As much as it upsets me, particularly a guy in our own profession doing what he did, we have to treat State as if nothing had happened."

For the next forty-eight hours, the committee conducted a series of seven meetings, each scheduled when new information was made available. As the results of post-season conference play continued to flow in, the list narrowed. Finally, on Sunday at 3:30 p.m. CST, the committee gathered for its final review. The top seeds had been chosen some hours earlier and had been assigned to the four regions: the East, Southeast, Midwest and West. All but a few other slots were filled, those pending the outcome of several conference championships which were currently being played. The process would conclude within ninety minutes.

"As soon as the ACC and Big Eight games end, we can wrap this thing up," said the chairman. "I have to go on national TV at 5, so we'll have to move quickly."

Forty-five minutes later, both the ACC and Big Eight had determined their post-season champions. The committee met once more for approximately twenty minutes and reviewed the final contenders. At 5 p.m., the chairman of the NCAA Selection Committee entered the main Ball Room of the Hyatt, amid throngs of news reporters and television cameras. Five minutes later, Jack McHale and his players, all gathered at the McHale house for pizza, let out a roar that could be heard throughout the neighborhood. They had been selected for the West region, the fifteenth seed in a sixteen-seed team bracket. They would meet 1983 NCAA champion, North Carolina State, in the first round.

Chapter 71

Cormack McDonough had grown an inch-and-a-half since the season began and was now a lithe 6'9" shooting forward. NBA scouts called him, along with his teammate Marvin Lewis, a "sure-fire first round pick."

George DiOrgio had delayed any formal announcement and official incorporation of his new player rep company for good reason. The NCAA prohibited player agents from direct contact with underclassmen. Recognizing that such direct contact would be his best chance to land McDonough as a client, DiOrgio decided to wait for the incorporation of his company until he was certain of McDonough's intentions. Through a face-to-face meeting with young McDonough, DiOrgio would determine his plans. The meeting had to be handled with extreme caution.

One possibility DiOrgio had considered was an offer of under-the-table payments to McDonough. Although a practice of other agents with a number of college stars, he decided against this course. It was obvious that the boy was still reeling from his father's involvement in a similar scheme. Also, at this stage of his player agency business, it would be a foolish and unnecessary risk.

DiOrgio had instructed his young aide to take great pains in explaining to McDonough that DiOrgio wanted to meet him because of his involvement in the promotion of the State basketball games at the Garden. At no time was the aide to mention DiOrgio's budding player agency business. The luncheon would be purely exploratory, a feeling-out process.

The lunch was set at the 21 Club. The young aide, driving one of DiOrgio's three Mercedes, picked up McDonough, who seemed eager to meet DiOrgio.

George DiOrgio was particularly adept at befriending people from all walks of life. Indeed, this had played a significant role in his rise to the top of the rock promotion business. That skill again proved fortuitous, for within minutes after the young star had sat down, he and DiOrgio took a liking to one another.

As part of his preparation, DiOrgio had read up on Ireland and was able to converse with Cormack on topics ranging from the country's harsh history to its present-day woeful economy. Gradually, he turned the conversation toward Cormack's career. Within minutes, Cormack painted a vivid picture of his aspirations that left no doubt in DiOrgio's mind as to what approach to follow.

"Mr. DiOrgio, it's always been my mother's dream that one of her children graduate from a university. In Ireland, the furthest any McDonough ever advanced in school was when I received my leaving cert at the regional high school last year. As long as Breda and I can make it financially, I plan to realize my mother's dream."

"Cormack, I want you to know that all of us who follow State basketball are proud of your accomplishments. On a personal level, if there's ever anything I can do for you or your family, please let me know. I want to be counted on as a friend."

Cormack smiled, thanked DiOrgio profusely for lunch, and returned to campus for an afternoon practice Jack McHale had called. DiOrgio went back to his office. An hour later his young aide, having just dropped Cormack off, phoned him.

"George, it looks like we got nothing out of that luncheon."

"I'm gonna give you your first lesson," DiOrgio replied. "What we got out of that luncheon was a friendly relationship with the kid. From a business standpoint, it may or may not bear immediate fruit. But I'll guarantee you this, those kind of relationships never hurt you. It's a long dance."

Chapter 72

As the State team entered the locker room to begin preparation for North Carolina State, each player found a new set of practice clothing resting on his chair. Jack McHale was mindful of the "look factor" among young athletes. In anticipation of a victory over Villanova and subsequent NCAA bid, McHale had instructed Brian McCray to "buy the best looking practice uniforms, head to toe, and make certain they have '1989 NCAA' written all over them."

After the customary taping of ankles and brief talk from McHale in the locker room, the team entered the practice court. To their delight, an enormous roar erupted as they took the floor. "State fever" had become an epidemic. Over 2,500 fans had taken advantage of McHale's loosening of his closed practice mandate and showed up on Monday afternoon to greet their heroes.

North Carolina State had just come off a successful post-season Atlantic Coast conference appearance and was facing no lay-off, so McHale decided that he would allow the fans only one open practice. Until the team departed for Albuquerque, New Mexico on Wednesday evening, the remaining workouts would be closed.

Preparation for tournament play differed from the regular season in one respect. A loss meant there was no tomorrow. Everything was channeled into winning one game. Players suffering from minor injuries, who might miss a game or two in the regular season, would put aside whatever ailed them. The same theory applied from a coaching standpoint. If during the regular season McHale had used Cormack McDonough and Marvin Lewis for an average of thirty-five minutes per game, in NCAA competition they would stay on the floor from beginning to end, save for foul trouble.

North Carolina State was an imposing first-round foe. Seeded number two in the West, the team was 22-7 and ranked eleventh nationally. Their coach, Jim Valvano, had, in the words of the master himself, John Wooden, "done the best coaching job I have ever seen in an NCAA tournament" in 1983, when he led the Wolfpack to the NCAA championship in none other than Albuquerque. McHale recognized that he would have to contend with Valvano's post-season experience and an arena in which North Carolina State had won many friends six years earlier. "If there is ever an example of a team having a home court advantage 2,000 miles from their campus, it will be NC State," he said.

Practices went smoothly from Monday through Wednesday. At the conclusion of Wednesday's drill, the team, prior to departure for LaGuardia, was sent off with a pep rally. It was the first since the early '70's on the State campus. The rally featured the school's marching band and over 5,000 wildly enthusiastic fans. As McHale approached the bus, the SID said to him, "Jack, it looks like we'll have about 1,500 people traveling out with you. State fever is back!"

The plane trip was the first opportunity McHale had to reflect on recent events. In a period of two short months, he had gone from ne'er-do-well to hero. People who had snubbed him or, in more direct fashion, had expressed their dissatisfaction with his coaching, were now touting him as the savior. One booster, whose signature had been affixed to a letter to the president asking for McHale's resignation only two months earlier, cornered him after the open practice and said, "Jack, as far as I'm concerned, I hope they add the title of 'Athletic Director' to your head coaching position."

The scandal still remained an issue, but it no longer demeaned McHale or his team. Indeed, McHale was portrayed as the paragon of virtue, one who had no involvement and whose integrity had remained intact. As the plane approached the runway in Albuquerque, the coach realized that in the last eight weeks he had experienced a range of emotions few people would experience in an entire lifetime. He wondered about its significance.

Albuquerque was a college basketball town. Its team, the University of New Mexico, while having experienced a scandal of its own in 1980 under then-coach Norm Ellenberger, attracted some of the most rabid basketball fans in the country. "The Pit," the famous home court of New Mexico, seated 17,000, and the notion of an empty seat was foreign to the local fans. Albuquerque had hosted a number of NCAA tournament games in the past and was well suited to the task. From the opening reception at the airport to the expansive fruit baskets in every player's hotel room, the organizing committee did not miss a beat.

Fearing distractions, since he still looked upon State as young and inexperienced, McHale decided that his players would not stay in Albuquerque proper. Taking a page from the book of John Thompson and Georgetown, he booked the team into a hotel some twenty miles outside of town to avoid the revelry and prepare for the task at hand.

While it was difficult to assess the value of such a strategy, the following afternoon his team appeared not only rested and ready, but also in the words of ESPN commentator Dick Vitale, "a force to be reckoned with in this tournament." NC State had assumed an early lead when, at the ten-minute mark of the first half, Cormack McDonough and Marvin Lewis literally took over the game. State led at half time by eleven. The second half was much of the same. As Jim Valvano pointed out at the game's conclusion,

"The final score of 85-69 in no way reflects how much State dominated us today."

Vitale went even further. "This is the best fifteenth seed of any NCAA team I can remember in a long time," he enthused.

There were now thirty-two teams left. State had in its favor something that all teams hoped for at this stage of the season: they were just peaking. It all seemed to be going so well. As McHale departed the arena after the post-game press conference, two men in dark business suits approached him.

"Coach McHale, we'd like to speak with you for a moment. We're from the FBI."

Chapter 73

"You must never leave the wounded behind." The war-time saying was one which Rabbi David Katzman had applied to his own life in helping those in need.

When he read the story in the *New York Times*, he was saddened; not surprised, in fact, not at all surprised, but deeply saddened. It had been twenty-five years since he last saw Steve Ellovitch. Even then, knowing what he did about the boy, and particularly his family, he had feared something like this.

Rabbi Katzman had first met Ellovitch when the youngster was six years of age. From then until age thirteen, young Steven attended Hebrew School twice during the week as well as on Sunday. He was not merely smart, he was brilliant. But with his brilliance came what Rabbi Katzman knew then would be a terrible burden. The burden came in the form of Ellovitch's father, who had emigrated from Russia in the early '50's, just after the war.

His own hopes vanquished, Hyman Ellovitch had transferred his dreams to his son. In so doing, he had provided him with everything but that which was most essential, love. Each year of growth was accompanied by new and more imposing demands by Ellovitch's father. If young Ellovitch received an A- grade on a test, it was not enough. Moreover, the lessons of winning at all costs, of trusting no one, were repeated over and over again. It was a home full of tension.

Rabbi Katzman watched the personality of Ellovitch take a twisted shape, molded by his father's overwhelming pressure and his schoolmates' cruel taunts about his frail physique and bookworm-like demeanor. In all his years of service, the Rabbi could think of no young boy with greater gifts or greater burdens. It was because of this that he developed a special concern for Steven.

He finally went to the father. It was an unpleasant, ugly meeting. The Rabbi was told to stay out of the family's affairs. One week later, young Ellovitch was pulled from the Hebrew School. At thirteen, he had lost the one person in his life whose perspective offered compassion and understanding.

Rabbi Katzman retired in 1978, but through friends he kept abreast of Ellovitch's career and the fatalistic pursuit of his goals. In 1979, the Katzmans had moved from the lower east side of New York to Brunswick, Maine where the Rabbi had taken an adjunct professorship at Bowdoin College. He taught one course in Jewish studies while residing on Bailey's Island in a home built in 1810, with a panoramic view of Maine's rugged sea and coast line.

After reading the newspaper story, he decided that he must extend his hand to the boy he had lost twenty-five years earlier. He had gotten Ellovitch's address from State. The telegram was succinct.

> Steven, it has been many years. Would like to help you. Please call, 207-782-9146. With hopes of hearing from you.
>
> Rabbi David Katzman.

For a week, he heard nothing. Then one evening, well past 11 p.m., the phone rang. The brief conversation caused Rabbi Katzman even more concern. Steve Ellovitch's voice was devoid of any hope or feeling. The Rabbi gently convinced Ellovitch to travel to Brunswick.

"Steven, we will talk and talk and talk," he promised.

Two days later, when Ellovitch arrived, his appearance brought tears to the eyes of Rabbi Katzman. He had never seen a face so full of sadness and defeat. He went to Ellovitch, embraced him and said, "I will help you."

For the first few days, Ellovitch barely spoke, his state of depression as severe as any the Rabbi had ever observed. With the fire roaring and the spectacular view of the sea in the background, the two sat for hours in the living room, where the Rabbi read from the Talmud. From time to time, he would probe for a response, any response to the readings.

At last, after days of silence, Ellovitch spoke.

"I have violated every tenet you have read. I have no worth."

It was the step, the tiny crack that Rabbi Katzman needed to reach the next level, a dialogue between them. In the excruciating days to come, he would draw from Ellovitch his deepest feelings of guilt, frustration and failure. He would stay with him, work with him, comfort him, do whatever was necessary to reestablish a sense of worth, balance and perspective within Ellovitch, qualities all lost so many years ago.

Despite their prolonged separation, he knew Ellovitch. He knew that at his very core there was goodness, goodness that had been sapped at a young age by pressures few outsiders could ever understand.

Rabbi David Katzman, meanwhile, had been told that his cancer had spread to the lymphatic system, that he had only months to live. He would use those months in a task as compelling as any he had undertaken. He would not leave this wounded man behind.

Chapter 74

"Some guys get better by the game, he gets better by the bounce," said Coach Jim Valvano, after North Carolina State's opening round loss to State.

"He's the best freshman center prospect since Ewing. He's got the whole package," CBS commentator Billy Packer added. State's charge to the NCAA tournament had been accompanied by the coming of age of Marvin Lewis. Still two months shy of his nineteenth birthday, Lewis had grown to 6'11", 240 lbs.

The package included a deft shooting touch, passing ability reminiscent of Bill Walton, piranha-like instincts on both backboards and the ability to run the floor like a gazelle.

For Lewis, the past three months had been an emotional see-saw, the likes of which few eighteen-year-olds were ever forced to confront. The low point had been the discovery that his father, a person in whom he had placed his unconditional trust, had betrayed him.

Several things kept Marvin going: the love of his mother and the guidance and care shown him by the State coaching staff, particularly Jack McHale. More than anyone, though, it had been Cecelia. In the few weeks since they had met, she had become his friend, his confidant and his lover. At a time of crisis, she was there to pull him through. He inwardly felt that his enormous improvement had been based in large part on Cecelia's preventing him from succumbing to emotional chaos. She had been a stabilizing factor during the lowest point of his young life.

Meanwhile, McHale's conversation with the two FBI men had brought the euphoria of the victory over North Carolina State to a crashing halt. They were there to speak to McHale about Marvin Lewis.

"Our assignment is sports gambling," the senior agent began the conversation. "For the last several weeks, we've been tracking your team and specifically, Marvin Lewis."

McHale could not believe his ears. He was certain that his young center had committed no crime other than naiveté. But he knew that Lewis would likely be in for a harsh fall. So, too, would the team.

"As near as we can tell, about eight weeks ago, Lewis took up with a girl who calls herself Cecelia. Her real name is Jane Blackwell. She's an impor-

296

tant cog in one of the most sophisticated sports gambling syndicates in the country. Her role is simple. She establishes 'relationships' with athletes who are in a position to tell her things, important things, about their teams."

"How the hell can whatever Marvin Lewis tells this woman be so important?" McHale angrily asked, thrusting logic aside.

"Gambling on sports teams is a lot more sophisticated than most people realize," replied the senior agent. "The Blackwell woman is not only skilled in establishing relationships, but she knows exactly what information to extract. This information, when put in the hands of the professionals in her syndicate, is invaluable. As you know, games are bet based on point spreads. Inside knowledge of a slight injury, change of strategy, anything that might affect the chemistry of a team, can and does provide professionals with an edge that can mean millions of dollars.

"To give you an idea of how professional they are, they obviously realized that the Lewis kid would be depressed over his father's payoff and thus vulnerable. It was the optimal time to spring the Blackwell lady on him, knowing his vulnerability would lead to the information they would need about your team," the agent finished.

In defense of Lewis' innocence, McHale said, "This kid has been through hell, what with his father and all. I'll guaran-damn-tee you that he's done nothing intentionally wrong. How do you propose we handle this?"

"First, we can pretty much assure you that this will never get to the press," the senior agent began. "We're close to blowing the lid off this operation and we want to keep it air tight. But we're going to have to talk with Lewis."

McHale had heard of big time gambling in sports, but he never paid it much attention. Occasionally, his office would receive a phone call on game day from a "fan," asking questions about the team. His secretary would hang up.

The information just provided McHale was more than merely troubling. He had overheard Lewis talk of Cecelia in the locker room. It was common knowledge to State's coaching staff that Lewis took the relationship seriously. McHale feared the emotional crisis would probably be too much to handle when the eighteen-year-old discovered Cecelia's true identity.

"I understand you have a job to do; so do I," said McHale. "Marvin may have a physical presence of a grown man, but I can assure both of you that beneath it there's a highly sensitive kid who is likely to be devastated by this. Before you talk with him, I want to talk with him. And before I talk with him, I'd like your permission to talk with an expert."

"Coach, I'm not sure we can let you do that."

"Look," McHale fired back. "I know a little bit about the law. Isn't it true in this country that before being questioned, a person can speak with an attorney?"

"OK, OK," said the senior agent. "I guess I was reacting too harshly. But you have to understand that we've been on this case night and day for the last four months. You do your business. We'll meet you at the hotel later. We'll get together with him then."

"One more thing," said McHale. "When you're speaking with him, I want to be there."

The two agents looked at each other, then at McHale and nodded in agreement.

Immediately upon his return to his hotel suite, McHale picked up the phone and called Dr. Falk. For the next several minutes, he told Falk about the conversation with the two agents. "I don't know how an eighteen-year-old kid can possibly handle all of this," McHale concluded.

Falk said nothing for several moments, then advised: "Two crises like this are tough for any of us to handle, let alone an eighteen-year-old. Once again, the entire situation rests on your shoulders. All of us have been jilted at one time or another, although not in such a scurrilous manner. You must relate this fact to Marvin. You must do it in a compassionate way. Most importantly, let him have his emotional reaction. All too often, we preach the stiff upper lip theory. In this case, if the kid wants to have a good cry, express anger, frustration or whatever, you encourage him."

Thirty minutes later, Marvin Lewis entered McHale's suite beaming.

"Coach, we're gonna take it all the way."

Moments later, McHale quietly related the truth about "Cecelia" to young Lewis. Lewis was stunned. He could not think. He just sat.

"Marvin, two FBI agents are going to speak with you. They'll ask you a number of questions. I'll be in the room with you. Be as honest as you can and remember, this may take time but it will all work out," said McHale, trying to be convincing, but doubting his own words.

The two agents, skilled and firm in their questioning, grasped the difficulty Marvin Lewis had in comprehending how someone could so completely deceive him. The session lasted only fifteen minutes. As the two got up to leave the suite, one pulled McHale into the adjacent room.

"It's obvious he had no idea what was going on. I really hope he can get it together. He's a good kid."

McHale reentered the room. He looked at Lewis. The freshman's normal expression of hope and exuberance had been replaced by a blank, languid stare. "Getting it together" might prove a far greater challenge than the FBI agent recognized.

Chapter 75

Vanderbilt was a school not commonly associated with powerhouse basketball. However, it had a formidable program. A member of the Southeastern Conference, Vandy, like State, had caught fire over the last third of the season and went on to win the SEC post-season tournament. Vandy had beaten Illinois in the first round game and would now face State in the western regional quarter-finals.

After the alarming news concerning Marvin Lewis, Jack McHale found himself awake most of the night, thinking about the Lewis situation and its potential effect on the young man as well as on the team. The following morning he informed his two assistants of the matter, instructing them to keep it in the strictest confidence.

McHale then spent the day reviewing the films of Vanderbilt's victory over Illinois. He called coaches throughout the country for additional information, and read the written scouting reports State had secured prior to its arrival in Albuquerque. Such preparation was now commonplace in NCAA tournament play. When a team went into a region, it had to assume victory. That implied not only getting information on the first-round opponent, but potential opponents in the following rounds as well.

The preparation went beyond the game itself. Brian McCray, in overseeing the academic activities of the players, knew that should State defeat Vanderbilt on Sunday and advance to the "sweet sixteen round" the following week in Salt Lake City, it would be impractical for the team to fly back to New York for classes Monday and Tuesday, then turn around and return to Salt Lake. Instead, McCray had been busy lining up tutors as well as making arrangements for each player's class to be taped. Should State win, the class tapes would be Federal Expressed each day to McCray's hotel room. As part of their daily routine, the players would then be required to listen to each of their own classes and spend time with a tutor.

"It's the next best thing to being there," McCray joked to McHale.

McHale agreed. While he had a strict policy of players not missing classes, competing in the NCAA tournament required some leeway from his normal rules. In this case, with the blessing of the athletic department's academic counselor, the alternate plan would suffice.

Practice was scheduled for 6 p.m., allowing McHale and the team to watch

Saturday's western regional quarter-final games on television and, hopefully, preview the team they would be playing the following Thursday evening in Salt Lake City. The major question in McHale's mind for the entire day was Marvin Lewis. How would he react to the emotional bullet which had hit him squarely between the eyes, or more accurately, in the heart?

At 5 p.m., the other quarter-final games all but completed, McHale prepared to leave his suite and meet the team in the lobby. There was a knock at the door. It was Lewis.

"Coach, I wanted to speak with you before we leave for practice."

McHale's initial thought was that the youngster had come to tell him that he could go no further.

"I've been thinking about what happened to me yesterday and what happened with my father. It's made me grow up a lot more quickly than I guess I wanted to. It's also made me realize what's important to me. It's this team. Coach, when the bell rings tomorrow, I'll be ready."

At first McHale said nothing. Then, clapping the big center on the back, he responded in a fatherly tone, "Marvin, some things that look great, sometimes don't keep their promise."

At 2 p.m. the following afternoon, in front of a national television audience, State disposed of Vanderbilt 96-77. Marvin Lewis scored thirty-two points, secured a western regional record of twenty-six rebounds and played like a man possessed.

Two hours after the game, the team boarded a flight to Salt Lake City. Four nights later in Salt Lake City, State continued its march, thrashing Michigan 103-89 in a game that was never really close. They were in the final eight of the country, a finalist in the western region. The opponent on Saturday would be Georgetown.

The program that Georgetown coach John Thompson had developed was as good as any in Division I college basketball. When Thompson had been named head coach at Georgetown in 1972, he was one of the first black head coaches in the country. He had faced a number of obstacles because of the racial prejudice still spilling over from earlier decades. While McHale objected to the "Hoya Paranoia" of which he felt Thompson was rightfully accused, he knew that the Georgetown coach had beaten long odds in building his dynasty. He also knew that the loss in Seoul had cut deeply into Thompson's heart. He respected, and understood, John Thompson.

Georgetown, while lacking the force of a Patrick Ewing, was still one of the best in the country. It was a team with everything—quickness, strength and great shooting. It was also a team that would "meet you at the bus" with its relentless pressure defense. Georgetown would be State's most difficult challenge to date.

The game started in the Hoyas' favor, as their full-court trapping defenses forced early State turnovers and gave them a seven point lead at the ten-minute mark of the first half. As the half wound down, State, primarily due to Billy Powers' outside shooting, fought back and trailed at intermission, 49-48.

The second half brought much of the same ebb and flow. State caught Georgetown at the 9:20 mark. The lead then changed hands seven times. With four minutes and twenty seconds remaining and State leading by two, Powers went down with an ankle injury. As important as Lewis and McDonough were to the State team, Powers was the glue. McHale had to go to his bench and a little-used senior guard, who earlier in the season had given McHale much trouble with his attitude. By now, however, the guard was attuned to State's mission.

In the final four minutes, the back-up guard did not commit a turnover and got the ball where it had to go, into the hands of McDonough and Lewis. The two freshmen did the rest, scoring twelve points between them, the most crucial being a McDonough three-point jump shot with fourteen seconds remaining. The final score: State 93, Georgetown 92.

As the game ended, McHale immediately went to check on his freshman point guard.

"We'll have to send him for an X-ray," said the State team doctor. "We won't know anything until tomorrow."

McHale then entered the locker room, his body drenched with sweat, but in a state of euphoric relaxation. With the team howling and cheering, he could barely contain himself, coming perilously close to tears. As he looked at his players, their spirits soaring to new and uncharted heights, it all seemed so worthwhile.

The Final Four: a lifelong dream.

Chapter 76

The lobby: it had become as much part of the lore of the NCAA Final Four Championship as strawberries and cream at Wimbledon or the green jacket at Augusta. More than anything, it was a place for coaches to congregate, to share their victories and defeats of months past with contemporaries, to get news of recruiting. For those whose season had not fulfilled the promise of November, it was a place to pass along resumes in hopes of a new opportunity.

The lobby's quiet solitude would begin to dissipate on Wednesday of Final Four week. By Thursday, most of the coaches, media and fans had arrived, transforming the lobby into a large assembly hall. The numbers would get larger on Friday. By Saturday, semi-final day, the lobby would erupt like a volcano, a mass of human flesh, elbow to elbow, jockeying for a position to conduct discussions that all centered on the round ball which was at the crux of most of their lives.

In this case, the lobby happened to be in Seattle, Washington at the Sheraton Hotel. Seattle, for the second time in ten years, was the host of the NCAA Final Four. It was now Saturday, semi-final game day; an aura of anticipation vibrated through the hotel's walls.

Activity took place not only in the lobby, but also throughout the hotel, including the room which housed the NCAA Coaches' Convention. The convention represented a time of reprieve for those whose paycheck was based on twenty-six nights of combat. Each dues-paying coach would receive the fruits of membership: two tickets to the semi-final and final round of the NCAA Championship. The rules were strict and had to be adhered to; any coach picking up his tickets had to do so in person and present appropriate identification.

While the coaches' convention took place, other forms of activity went on throughout the hotel. Leading sporting goods manufacturers seemed omnipresent. With their suites and exhibition rooms stocked with food and libations, they spared no effort in luring coaches to their products, many offering free samples of their new lines.

In the main ballroom, an all-day coaches' clinic was in full swing, with association members hearing the top names in college basketball, save those four whose teams were competing for the grand prize.

In the Presidential Suite, the CBS crew was making last minute preparations for one of its true glamour events. The celebrities of the crew, Brent Musburger and Billy Packer, were seated at a table with thirteen other CBS employees. Plates of fresh shrimp with Cross and Blackwell gourmet sauce were devoured as a fifty-seven point checklist, ranging from camera positions to television time outs, was reviewed.

Off in another suite, two committees gathered, one representing the NCAA and another the City of Seattle, its membership comprised of the city's elite. At this point their work, which in the case of the local organizing committee had gone on for two years, was virtually over. It was now, save any last minute calamity, a matter of sitting back and watching the fruits of their labor come to bear.

As the morning rolled on, and with tip off time three hours away, the members of the media, many ensconced at the host hotel, were gathering their equipment in preparation for their trek to the Kingdome.

Then, of course, there were the fans. In three of the four cases, the fans were now veterans of Final Four activity. For the newcomers, the State fans, the entire experience brought a new and special anticipation.

Outside the hotel were the scalpers, their prior discretion replaced with frantic daring. Given the Kingdome's seating capacity of 40,000, their anticipated profits were slowly turning to rubble. Those who had invested considerable sums in anticipation of high return were now simply hoping to get rid of whatever tickets they had left at face value.

That evening, with some fans joyously looking forward to Monday night's showdown, and others grimly packing their bags, perhaps the only example of the Final Four caste system would occur. Those with the most influence would descend upon Ray's Boat House at Shilshoe Bay for poached salmon, or the Leschi Cafe overlooking Lake Washington for fresh cut sirloin. Yet those not dining at the most stylish of restaurants would not really care. Simply being there mattered most.

The NCAA Final Four was an athletic happening unlike any other. The diamonds and tuxedos that accompanied many other major sporting events were replaced by jogging suits, khaki pants and Nikes. It was a gathering, not of the rich and famous, but of the diehards. Celebrities were limited to those whose backgrounds were in the game. While the Super Bowl was steeped in glitz, the Final Four had soul. It was, as one scribe reported, "simply the most marvelous sporting event in existence."

Thirty miles away, Jack McHale sat alone in his room at the Tacoma Sheraton, peering out the window at Mount Rainier. He wanted to distance both himself and his team from the maddening crowds, in order to devote full attention to the next, possibly the last, game. Their only trip into Seattle had been the day prior to participate in the customary Final Four public practice. The practice was a traditional occasion for the fans to watch the four combatants each proceed through a one hour drill. For all other practices, McHale had utilized the gym at tiny Pacific Lutheran in Tacoma.

At his request, State had hired a local security company, whose primary role was to keep media and fans away from the hotel. The phones in players' rooms had been disconnected at 10 p.m. to avoid middle of the night crank calls. The team ate its meals in a private dining room.

Many thoughts passed through McHale's mind as he stared out his window. In three-and-a-half hours, the first of the two semi-final games would begin. The first game would pit two Big Ten rivals, Indiana and Iowa. After that, McHale and his team would take the floor to the thunderous roar of their own fans and all others in the building who liked to cheer for the underdog. At the other end of the floor, adorned in powder blue uniforms, would be the opposition, the North Carolina Tar Heels, who had been there many times before.

Jack McHale had many fond memories of Final Four activities in his long career as a coach. One, however, far outdistanced the others. It had happened in Atlanta in 1977, the year the Marquette Warriors defeated North Carolina and, in so doing, firmly placed their coach, Al McGuire, into eternal lore. The Coaches Convention that year included a special program called "The Legends." In the Hyatt Atlanta, more than 500 coaches quietly sat and listened to three of the game's greats share their views on coaching and life.

The first speaker had been Henry Iba of Oklahoma State, who sadly would be remembered by many as the coach of the 1972 U.S. Olympic team that lost a controversial 51-50 decision to the Soviet Union. The next speaker was the Wizard of Westwood, John Wooden. Last to the podium was a man whose presence dominated the entire room.

Adolph Rupp had been the head coach of Kentucky for thirty-four years. He had won more games than any coach in the history of NCAA basketball. Perhaps as much as any who had achieved such exalted status, he had fought and overcome periods of enormous adversity in his career.

Rupp was then seventy-seven years old and knew, as did most present, that his cancer-racked body would not see another Final Four. Freely quoting Parkingham Beatty and Rudyard Kipling, Rupp eloquently brought home to those fortunate to be present the true essence of coaching. As he concluded, McHale recalled looking around the room and seeing tears stream down the faces of a group whose existence was based, as much as anything else, on their competitive zeal.

Jack McHale had never been so affected by anyone's words; so overcome in fact, that he did something he never had done before. After the program broke up, he watched Rupp exit the room through a side door. McHale followed him out the door and onto an elevator. There were nine or ten other people present as the doors fastened shut. As the elevator ascended, the others began to get out at various floors. Finally, at the twenty-sixth and top floor, there were only Rupp and McHale. The aging Kentucky baron exited first and McHale followed. As Rupp approached his room, McHale, in passive pursuit, finally summoned his courage.

"Coach Rupp, I want you to know how much your speech meant to me." While obviously accustomed to such deference, particularly by those in his profession, the man, in his customary brown suit, was visibly moved by McHale's sincerity. He proceeded to ask the young coach a series of questions, with McHale responding eagerly to each one and marvelling at the attention being paid him.

When the conversation ended, Rupp took his key and placed it in the door. He then turned to McHale and said, "I'll be watching you, son."

Chapter 77

B rian McCray and Mike Lambert, briefcases packed, departed their suites and headed down the elevator to the main lobby of the Sheraton-Tacoma. There they were met by the limousine driver who would chauffeur them to the Seattle Kingdome. At a rear door marked "Press Entry," they would be met by security guards and taken to their front row seats at the scouting table. In tournament play a team always assumed the best possible scenario. The best in this case meant scouting Indiana and Iowa and hoping to meet either in the showdown on Monday evening.

Preparations did not stop with Lambert and McCray. Jack McHale had legions of friends in the coaching fraternity. Among those friends, six of the closest and most trusted had also been asked to scout Iowa-Indiana. Should State defeat North Carolina, the six would meet with the staff on Sunday to review their notes.

In addition, three VCR's—one in each of the coach's suites—were timed and set. If any of the three did not function, there would be backup. Moreover, the staff would get the benefit of both the game and Billy Packer's commentary—analysis for which McHale had great respect.

McHale was busy too, not only with preparations for the semifinals and possibly finals, but also an annoying fact of life—last minute ticket requests. While he was able to pass some off as not important, others were from old friends—those who had been loyal to him in the down years. Despite the Kingdome's seating capacity, the choice seats—the ones which McHale felt obligated to secure for his friends—were hard to come by. He would do his best and hope they would understand.

Based on Dr. Falk's advice, State's coaching staff tried to shelter the team as much as possible from the many distractions surrounding the Final Four appearance. This protection included arriving at the Kingdome approximately ninety minutes prior to tip-off. Once in the arena, they would be allowed to watch only small portions of the Iowa-Indiana game, the viewing confined to a television monitor in the locker room.

"For a team like Carolina, an appearance in such a major event may be old hat," Falk told McHale. "But for your kids, you want to be very careful not to allow the enormity of the event to devour them. The best way to do this is to keep them away from the lights until they go on the court twenty minutes before the game."

At the pre-game training meal, in a private room at the Sheraton-Tacoma, McHale sensed the tension building. In anticipation of this, Brian McCray, along with a graduate assistant, had spent many hours preparing a relaxant in the form of a ten-minute film on miscues by State players during the season. From double-dribbles to a Marvin Lewis tip-in in the wrong basket, the film, narrated by McCray, broke up the team. Several of McCray's splicings had included some jibes at his boss. Even McHale could not remember having more belly laughs. The strategy seemed to work, as the team appeared far more at ease.

"NCAA championships often come down to the team that's able to play a normal game," Falk had reminded McHale. "The looser the kids are, the better they'll perform."

The bus trip from Tacoma to Seattle took thirty minutes. The security company State had hired was now assisted by the Washington State Police, who escorted the bus all the way to the rear door of the Kingdome. As the team entered the arena, several Carolina fans shouted from a distance, "You're twelve-point underdogs, guys! Go back to the hotel and pack your bags!"

"We'll see laddies," responded Cormack McDonough, his retort bringing smiles to his teammates.

North Carolina had no apparent weaknesses. Of the twelve players on the team, eight had been first-string high school All-Americans. Their coach, Dean Smith, had been the subject of a number of good natured arguments between McHale and Falk. While Falk in no way questioned Smith's overall greatness as a coach, he continued to point out to McHale that North Carolina had frequently fallen below expectations in NCAA tournaments. But to Jack McHale, Smith was one of basketball's greatest coaches, a true innovator who had withstood the most arduous of all tests, that of time.

While the faces had changed, the current Carolina team was much akin to many of Smith's past clubs. They relied on a series of changing defenses with the common denominator being constant pressure on the ball. The Tar Heels ran a controlled fast break which, when not available as an option, turned into an almost devastating half-court offense.

It was often said that no Dean Smith team was ever beaten until five seconds after the final buzzer. In the past, his teams had pulled off some miraculous comebacks. When behind, he was a master of using the clock, substitutions and time-outs. When ahead, he could be equally adept, as his four-corner offense was still a major force in college basketball, even with the addition of the forty-five-second clock.

While Carolina was twelve men deep, State placed complete reliance on its first seven players. The ankle injury a week prior to Billy Powers made the freshman point guard a question mark. McHale could not remember any player whose sheer willpower had been such a factor in overcoming an injury. When Powers was not at practice, he spent virtually every waking minute in treatment with State's athletic trainer.

"Coach, I think he'll be ready. We'll know in the first couple of minutes," State's trainer said to McHale as the team entered the locker room for the pre-game talk.

The event itself would provide all the impetus needed for maximum effort. So McHale determined that his pre-game talk would be primarily strategical and that he would conclude not so much with fire and brimstone, but with words of calm encouragement and of the great affection he held for the team.

"Good luck, gang. There has never been a team that deserves it any more than you," he said quietly, as the squad exited the locker room.

When State ran on to the floor, the coaches and players felt a rush of adrenaline they had never before experienced. As underdogs, the crowd was clearly on their side, and the roar which accompanied their entry confirmed this. When McHale headed to the bench, the State fans were joined by thousands of others in a standing ovation. By now, every basketball fan knew of the adversity Jack McHale and State had confronted.

"He's as much admired as any coach I can remember," were Billy Packer's words.

Three minutes after tip-off, the worst of McHale's fears was confirmed. Carolina had taken a 13-0 lead. Two of Billy Powers' errant passes had been turned into breakaway lay-ups and they were accompanied by three consecutive three-point jump shots. As the team approached the bench for a time out, the Carolina fans were chanting in unison, "Blow out! Blow out!"

Many times in his coaching career, McHale had been confronted with this situation. The best strategy necessitated calming the players down and reminding them "to get it back one at a time." The goal at this stage was to chip away slowly at the lead, climb back into the game and hopefully exit at halftime with a manageable deficit. While it took two additional time-outs and as much bench jockeying as McHale could ever remember, State left the floor after twenty minutes, trailing 42-36.

Prior to the game, McHale and the staff had analyzed every possible scenario they might face at halftime. The coach was ready.

"I didn't want to tell you this before the game, but I knew damned well that we're a better basketball team than North Carolina. We've just played as poorly as we're capable of and they could not have played any better. The margin is only six points. We've showed our courage; now we're going to show our skill. Guys, we're going to win this thing."

Five minutes into the second half, State took the lead by one. Carolina scratched back to take a three point lead at the twelve-minute mark. From there the lead changed hands eleven times. Finally, with 4:30 remaining, the Tar Heels hit a three point shot and led by four. State called time out.

"You're doing just great fellas'. We've got them exactly where we want 'em," McHale shouted. "Now, after we score, Carolina will probably go to their four corners. As we've been saying at practice, we're not going to play 'em man-to-man. We'll go 1-3-1 half-court trap. Let's try to force the ball into the corner. Remember, when it's there, the three guys off the ball cover strong side high, strong side low and weak side. You two guys trapping, seal the passing lanes. We'll get the steal if we execute it properly."

What the players did not realize was that a similar strategy had been used by Al McGuire and his Marquette team in 1977, when the Warriors defeated North Carolina in the NCAA finals. During that season, the Carolina four-corner offense had bedeviled every team it confronted. McGuire's approach was not only to trap from a 1-3-1, rather than straight man-to-man, but also to prevent the notion of the four corners from intimidating his team.

"Their four corners is not very strong. All we've got to do is set the trap and force the ball to the corner," McHale yelled as the team walked back on the floor.

On the next possession, Billy Powers, his ankle swollen but his heart as big as the Kingdome, hit a fifteen-foot jump shot. As McHale had predicted, Carolina came down and went to its four corners. State extended its 1-3-1 to half court. They then forced the ball to the corner, where Cormack McDonough and Marvin Lewis set a vicious trap. The Carolina player, having difficulty seeing over the two freshmen, forced his pass into the hands of the waiting Powers. The freshmen guard pushed the ball down to the top of the key and then, with a between-the-legs dribble reminiscent of Jimmy Walker, wheeled to his left, laid the ball in and was fouled. He canned the foul shot and State was now up by one. Carolina called time out.

Up until this point in the game, State had relied on a series of changing defenses, but had not yet employed its full court 1-2-1-1 trap. "We're going to spring the *one* press on them," McHale exhorted to his players. "They won't be expecting it and I know damn well we'll come up with a steal."

Eight seconds later, Cormack McDonough pulled an errant Carolina pass from the air. Dribbling down the court with the flash of a 5'10" guard, he stopped just outside the top of the key and calmly drove home a twenty-five foot, three-point jump shot. State now led by four.

Carolina, their tradition once again coming to the fore, came down and hit a three-point shot. State stormed back. Powers missed an eighteen-foot jump shot but Marvin Lewis, in what would be his twenty-second and final rebound of the game, soared above the crowd, caught the errant Powers' shot coming off the rim and, to the delight of every State fan (and all those throughout the country who liked to root for the underdog), ripped the ball through the cords in a thunderous slam dunk. He was bumped on the play and converted the foul shot.

When Carolina missed its next shot, McDonough secured the rebound. The game was over: State 86, North Carolina 82. Monday would bring the NCAA finals and an engagement with the Hoosiers of Indiana, 76-75 winners over Iowa in the first game.

Chapter 78

Those who visited this island country called it the Garden of Eden. Set off the eastern coast of Africa on the Indian Ocean, the Seychelles Islands offered an exotic retreat for the wealthy. With its ninety-two widely separated islands and islets, it also offered something more. . .a hideaway. It was for this reason, as much for its spectacular scenery and beautiful beaches, that Slater had chosen it.

With his wealth and power had come an obsession. Whatever he had was never enough. As his car dealerships and building business had prospered, so, too, had his need for more. Gambling had become a by-product. With the gambling came new acquaintances, those whose existence and subsistence were based on the exploitation of others.

For the past ten years, Slater had developed a small but potent gambling syndicate. In developing it, he had also crafted a web to insulate himself. His only direct contact with the syndicate came through his long-time, trusted aide, Hondo.

The two had first met when Hondo became a car salesman in one of Slater's dealerships. His powers of persuasion soon made him the dealership's leading salesman. As Slater's ambition grew beyond automobiles and high-rise buildings, he suspected that Hondo's unique abilities could be of assistance in his new endeavors.

An almost inevitable occurrence accompanied their entry into big-time gambling. As the stakes grew higher, so, too, did the temptation to control the outcome. They had decided on basketball. Referee Ted Patterson had been the obvious choice. As their avarice grew, and in order to exert even greater control, Cecelia, the ravenous beauty so skilled in befriending players and extracting important bits of information, had been retained. Her entrance into this squalid world had been related to a dependence, not on gambling, but drugs. While a psychology major at Columbia University, she had joined one of New York's most prestigious modeling agencies. Her circle of friends soon changed from nineteen-year-old coeds in her dormitory, to those connected to the power base of New York society. New friendships brought new habits, drug habits. Soon, her dependency was one which could not be supported merely by fees paid her for modeling. She had been an easy prey. With proper training, she performed her duties to perfection.

Slater, *aka Robert Steincross*, was driven not only by his obsession with power and wealth. His hatred for William F. Riley had brought a new and equally powerful force, revenge. The gambling interests had led him to another source of even larger profit. His business relationships in the drug world had made the set-up of Sean Riley and the subsequent fall from grace of his father an easy task.

Steincross' quest was so obsessive that he had paid little notice to the increased attention of the FBI and other law enforcement agencies focused on drugs and illegal gambling. In the end, it was Hondo who made him realize that his web was unraveling. "I feel they're getting closer to us, Bob. The Feds are infiltrating our operation like rats. I'm nervous."

There was a chain, a link between those in crime and those whose lives were based on preventing it. Steincross had been informed of John McCollough's aggressive attempt to unravel the web. He used that link in getting the word out on the street.

"John, word has come down, in very strong fashion, about this investigation you're conducting for the Riley family. I've gotten firsthand that they want you to know that if you continue the investigation, four lives will be taken. Sean Riley, Robby Nesbitt, Mrs. Riley, and yours. I got this from sources who know, John. You may want to rethink your involvement."

Those words had been spoken by the head of the New York City narcotics division, an old friend of McCollough's. Several days later, Steincross received word that McCollough was indeed rethinking his position; that the warning had brought its desired effect.

"I heard he was so tough," laughed Steincross to himself. "He's just like most of the rest of them, a chicken-shit scumbag."

It had been only four months out of his forty-four years on earth, but it was an experience he vowed he would never repeat. At the age of fifteen, Robert Steincross had spent 120 days in reform school. He would never experience incarceration again, no matter how extreme the measures of self-preservation.

Third world banks had one thing in common. They welcomed deposits and generally asked few, if any, questions. Profits from Steincross' underworld activities were sitting quietly in a Swiss account. There was more than enough for ten lifetimes, let alone one. When he decided on the Seychelles, he had a Swiss banker open two new accounts, one in Mozambique, another in Kenya. The Swiss banker chose banks with a track record of dependability. Steincross' "legitimate estate" had dwindled, due in most part to the deft sifting of profits by his accountants and his gambling debts. But the estate was airtight, the will in place. Many charities would gratefully prosper from his death. There would be no questions asked.

The fishing trip to Newfoundland had become a yearly ritual. As he tried to do in any important endeavor, Steincross had planned the trip carefully. He had earned his pilot's license ten years prior. For the past several months, on any trip accompanied by Hondo, Steincross had told him of his new phobia.

"I have this great fear of something going wrong in flight. I've decided to wear a parachute. You're welcome to join me if you choose." Steincross knew that Hondo, because of his cavalier approach to life, would never wear a parachute.

The plane was a four-seater. Hondo, who was quite rotund, preferred to sit in the back seat where there was more room. The feigned engine trouble started to develop as the plane was passing over Limestock, several hundred miles from the nearest point of civilization.

"What the hell's the problem?" Hondo screamed. Steincross, glimpsing at the horror on Hondo's face, nimbly opened the pilot's door and leaped into midair. The parachute then took over. From his descending perch aloft, he watched the plane crash violently into the wilderness of Newfoundland.

In the coming months, he would take the necessary precautions, including plastic surgery. With time, he would reenter the world of business, with a new name, a new face and a new base of operation. For a wealthy American, constructing a new web would be a facile task, provided it was done with caution.

He now sat on the deck of his idyllic home on Silhouette Island, several hundred miles from the main island of Mahe. As he gazed out at the Indian Ocean, a new and almost foreign feeling came over him, one of contentment. There was no one of importance left behind; the future had promise. For now, he would rest.

Chapter 79

Sunday of Final Four Weekend was traditionally a far more placid day than the others that accompanied the event. Many of the fans of the two defeated semi-finalists were departing, their thoughts now turning to October 15 of the next year and the new recruiting class that could take them to the championship. For the winners, it was a day of regrouping, of preparation for the Main Event on Monday evening.

One of the major effects of Dr. Falk's advice was now being experienced. After Saturday's great victory over North Carolina, Jack McHale had not felt any real sense of euphoria. He had drilled it into his team and into himself that State University's mission would not be completed until the final buzzer on Monday evening—and only with a victory at that.

Other than the exhaustive preparations which would take place for the Indiana game, there were only two other important items on McHale's personal agenda for Sunday. One was to tape the Al McGuire show, by now a tradition in the NCAA Final Four. It featured fifteen minute interviews with the two coaches appearing in the championship.

The other item would occur that evening, when the National Association of Coaches staged its yearly dinner in the ballroom of the Sheraton Hotel. At the dais would be Jack McHale and Bob Knight, both of whom had been asked to make brief speeches regarding Monday evening's game. The highlight of the evening would then take place, the presentation of the Division I Coach of the Year trophy. Jack McHale had been informed on Sunday morning that he had been selected for the honor. While an unquestioned sense of accomplishment filled McHale, he had now disciplined himself to store the reaction in the recesses of his mind. Smelling the roses would come later. For now, there was a more important task at hand.

On Sunday morning at 11 a.m., six of McHale's closest friends in the coaching fraternity gathered in his suite. For the next ninety minutes, each coach offered McHale his observations of Indiana from the semifinal game. Upon conclusion of the meeting, McHale and his two assistants reviewed a tape of Indiana's game against Iowa.

"Packer's analysis is dead on," noted McHale. "Mike, have one of the graduate assistants stay in the locker room tomorrow and watch the telecast. Tell him to be aware of any strategical points Packer makes and get them to us on the bench. We'll need a phone set-up for this."

After reviewing the game, the staff then looked at three other films of prior Indiana games. Finally, at 2:30, they descended to the lobby where the team was waiting. McHale had prearranged the use of Pacific Lutheran gym from 3 to 4. He would put the team through a brisk sixty minute run, then unleash his secret weapon.

Lawrence Falk had been brought to Washington as the guest of the State University Athletic Department. McHale had arranged for a private suite at the Sheraton-Tacoma for use after practice. The players had not been told what would take place, only to, in Mike Lambert's words, "Be ready for a surprise." The team arrived at the suite several minutes before Falk. When the sports psychologist entered, the players recognized him immediately. His picture had been placed atop the bulletin board in the State locker room.

"Fellas', our guest needs no introduction. You guys all know how I feel about Dr. Falk and what he's done for this team," McHale stated. "I thought this would be a good time for you to meet him personally. He's got some things he'd like to talk over with you about tomorrow night's game."

Falk's reputation had preceded him. But it was not only that reputation which brought about the perfect fit between Falk and the players. While not a physically imposing man, his deep voice, resonant and clear, immediately captured the team's attention.

"Guys, before we talk about tomorrow night's game, let's have some fun. . . let's first become basketball historians. Then let's take a shot at becoming futurists. On this easel, I'm going to write my all-time starting five plus a sixth man.

"By the way," he kidded, "there's no way you'll be able to come up with a team that can beat my squad."

With that, Falk affixed the following names:

> Center - Bill Russell
> Forwards - Larry Bird, Julius Erving
> Guards - Magic Johnson, Bob Cousy
> Sixth Man - John Havlicek

The screeches, howls and laughter produced the exact effect that Falk had sought.

"What about Kareem over Russell?" yelled long-time Laker fan Billy Powers.

"Forget that," barked Marvin Lewis. "How about Isiah in for Cousy?"

Even the coaching staff got into the fray when Mike Lambert exclaimed, "There's no way Elgin doesn't belong on that starting five."

"OK, we'll agree to disagree," Falk interrupted. "Now let's talk about the future. Coach McHale, what do you see the game being like in the year 2020?"

McHale, at first stunned by the question, made several points which aroused equal passion among those in the room, as had the all-time team discussion. Falk, obviously having given the matter careful thought, then stated some of his own feelings. "First, the court will be too small to accommodate the size of the players. Also, there will have to be new leagues formed with consideration to height, like boxing does for weight." He continued on with several other wrinkles, all of which evoked various reactions.

Jack McHale sat back and marvelled at the rapport Falk was able to develop with his players, all within the space of forty-five minutes. He knew that Falk's primary purpose would now be easily accomplished.

"OK, guys," said Falk. "Enough of this stuff. Now we're going to do something crazy. I mean really weird."

With that, Mike Lambert turned off the lights and drew the shades.

"Wait a minute," yelled Marvin Lewis, as his teammates howled. "I don't know if I want to do whatever it is we're going to do!"

"OK, guys, if you'll bear with me for a couple of minutes, I'd like you to get serious," countered Falk. "I want you to all lie down on your backs. What we're going to do for the next fifteen or twenty minutes is play out in our minds tomorrow night's game. You're going to watch yourself become winners, national champions."

Falk asked each player to close his eyes, then took the team and coaching staff through an imaginary scenario which began with their departure from the hotel, included a number of foils and obstacles both before and during the game, and concluded with Marvin Lewis hoisting Billy Powers above his shoulders to cut down the net in victory. Twenty minutes later, the lights were turned back on and the players beamed as they left the room.

Lewis, seeking out Jack McHale, said, "I liked that Coach. I *really* liked that."

After the players departed, Falk called McHale to his side. "Jack, I'd like to speak with you for a few moments before you leave for the banquet."

Falk then began. "Very few people in your profession—or for that matter in any profession—ever get a shot at the gold. Of those few fortunate enough to get the shot, only a small percentage actually grab it. There are a number of reasons for this, but I'll give you an important one. If you look at the true greats in sports, be they Ted Williams, Jack Nicklaus, Sugar Ray Leonard, or—and I almost hate to say it—in your profession, Bobby Knight, they have one very important trait in common. In the big event, when the money's on the table and the lights are at their brightest, they all have the unique ability to block everything else out, to concentrate totally on the task at hand.

"Tomorrow night may be your one and only shot. From the time you enter the arena until the final buzzer, block out any and all extraneous factors that are not related to your job that evening. Don't worry about criticism, boos, second-guessing from fans, or anything else that might in any way impair your judgement. Jack, this is your moment in the sun and dammit, I know you can do it."

Chapter 80

As Jack McHale walked onto the court at the Seattle Kingdome, he fully grasped the enormity of the event for the first time. Glancing around the arena, everything he saw reflected the best: the referees, the television crew, even the security guards standing erect behind each team's bench. Each person who in any way was charged with a function, be it large or small, would reach down and pull from within his or her best effort.

For his own part, McHale hoped that his psyche would achieve the proper balance. For some the balance was tilted in the direction of nervous energy; others prospered when the balance swung toward inner confidence. McHale liked to feel a combination of both, one constantly replacing the other, until the amalgam of the two allowed for a flow of adrenaline necessary to coach the best game of his career.

He had set a series of goals for himself that evening, the first of which would be met at the exact time of the opening tap. He vowed that once the referee tossed the ball into mid air, he would, upon Falk's insistence, block out every extraneous factor. Jack McHale would coach with no interest in a moral victory. He wanted it all.

The day had brought with it the usual, excruciating feeling of helplessness which accompanied any wait for a big event. McHale had tried to create as much a sense of normalcy as possible for himself, his staff and his players. During the day, the players remained sequestered at the Sheraton-Tacoma, with the hired security staff instructed in no uncertain terms to keep all visitors away.

As the team had reached the locker room in the Kingdome, the team manager was filling the locker room bulletin boards with telegrams from fans throughout the world. While each player went through his personal pregame ritual, McHale tried his best to create a relaxed atmosphere. There was a humorous tale by Mike Lambert and some general needling of the players, including Cormack McDonough who had a fetish for peeling his own orange and neatly depositing the remains in the wastebasket.

Immediately after State's victory over North Carolina, the odds-makers had established Indiana a firm four-point favorite. Over the last twenty-four hours, however, a great deal of the "smart" money had come into Las Vegas and Atlantic City on State. One hour before tip-off, the contest was rated as a toss-up.

While McHale fidgeted on the sideline, he heard a huge roar from the other end of the arena. Since the Indiana team was already on the court warming up, he knew that the roar was accompanying the emergence of his rival that evening, Bobby Knight. While most controversial sports figures experienced receptions of cheers and boos mixed, the greeting of Knight seemed one-hundred percent positive. Even State fans expressed their respect for the Hoosier coach with a loud ovation.

To McHale, Knight was the best in the business. McHale did not condone some of Knight's profane activities, but he also knew of the other side of Knight: his integrity, his loyalty and the enormous number of good deeds he did for others without fanfare. If there were any one person McHale could choose to coach against for an NCAA championship, it would be Knight.

As the pregame clock ticked down, McHale felt the familiar feeling of self-doubt which generally accompanied the moments just prior to tip-off. His entire insides were taut as a drum. It was this particular time of the game and, in fact, his life that he disliked most.

Dr. Falk had presented McHale a sealed envelope in the locker room just before the game. "Jack, do me a favor and open this as the teams are walking on the floor for tip-off," he winked. As his starting five marched to center court, McHale, his palms wet with perspiration, did as Falk requested.

"Don't overcoach!" the note read.

A smile came across McHale's face. It was time to go to work.

Two things became immediately apparent in the very early going. State was tight and Indiana's defense seemed as impenetrable as Fort Knox. With the Hoosiers ahead 6-2 and after only 1:46 had expired on the clock, Jack McHale called time-out. As the players ran over to the sidelines, he knew that his own state of nerves had no doubt been transferred to his team. He had to exhibit a sense of confidence and relaxation.

"OK, guys, we've been up and down the floor several times. The only reason I called this time-out is to tell you that everything is going to be fine. . . .We can beat this team!"

For the remainder of the half, the two teams brought the game to a level seen only in a championship game. The energy expended on the hardwood floor could be fully appreciated only by those at courtside, those whose lives were entwined with the outcome.

"These two teams are ready to compete for a championship," said Billy Packer. "It's as good a match-up in a final game as I can remember." The half time score of 46-46 reflected those comments.

Before McHale went in to address his team at halftime, as always, he consulted with his two assistants.

"I think it's quite simple," said Lambert. "When we're in an up-tempo, open floor game, it's to our advantage. When we have to go to our half-court offense and try to penetrate their defense, five vs. five, it's to their advantage."

"That's exactly what Billy Packer just said," chimed in the graduate assistant, fulfilling his responsibility of staying in the locker room to listen to Packer's analysis.

The closeness of the game and the enormity of the event once again limited McHale to a strategic half-time approach. "If necessary, I can give the abbreviated Rockne speech in the second half during a time-out," he quipped to his assistants.

For the first five minutes of the second half, the contest remained on even ground. Then, with sudden swiftness, the balance of power shifted and, in so doing, brought with it Jack McHale's first major challenge of the evening. Cormack McDonough, on a State 3-on-2 fast break, had brought the ball right at the Indiana defender and was called for a charge, picking up his third personal foul. Both Lambert and McCray immediately said to McHale, "Coach, we better get him out."

McHale hesitated and seconds later his lapse proved costly. By not reacting to the dead ball and opportunity to bring in a substitute, he had allowed Indiana the opportunity to bring the ball up court where they immediately isolated McDonough's man down low. The Indiana player, guarded by McDonough, squared toward the hoop, pump-faked, got McDonough off his feet and went up for the shot, his body crashing into McDonough's, the whistle blowing at impact.

In virtually every game, particularly those that are close and fraught with meaning, the coach faces a series of highs and lows. A hoop in your favor, which brings about a change in momentum, also brings with it a brief rush of positive emotion. Other occurrences, such as the one involving McDonough, reflect on a coach's judgment and force him to acknowledge, "I have just made a major blunder."

Jack McHale's blunder, seen by more than forty million basketball fans throughout the world, would send many of them into a flurry of second-guessing. A Hoosier fan seated behind State's bench summed up best what others felt when he bellowed loud enough for McHale to hear, "The difference in this game is the coaching, McHale!"

As players were often called to summon from within their best effort in the face of adversity, so, too, was Jack McHale. After a period of fifteen to twenty seconds of silent reproach, he blocked the error out—completely.

With Cormack McDonough now sitting on the bench, Indiana ran the lead to seven points at the ten minute mark. McHale's strategy would be to keep the freshman star out of the game as long as there was ample time remaining, and as long as the lead did not approach a critical zone. In McHale's judgment, this would be eight or more points. When an Indiana guard stole a State pass and soloed for a lay up, bringing the Hoosier lead to nine, McHale called time-out.

"Cormack, you're back in," he yelled to the freshman.

McDonough's reentry allowed Marvin Lewis greater freedom inside, since

Indiana had to concentrate on stopping two stars instead of one. The freshman center responded, scoring three straight hoops, two off offensive rebounds. The lead was now down to three: Indiana 75, State 72.

Indiana scored on the next possession, bringing its lead to five. Billy Powers, his ankle still swollen but playing an almost flawless game, came down the floor and calmly lofted a long three-point jumper through the cords, to cut the Hoosier lead to two. State, now in a full court press, stole the inbound's pass and scored off the steal. With four minutes remaining, and with the game tied 77-77, Indiana called time-out.

"Great job," McHale screamed, his voice rising above the thunderous din. "Hey, these next four minutes'll show everyone what a great club we are."

After the time-out, the lead changed hands two more times. Then State, with a two-point lead and the clock winding down to below a minute, secured a rebound on a missed Indiana shot. The top of the mountain was now clearly in sight.

As Powers brought the ball down floor, State ran its version of keep-away, a triangular configuration with one player at the foul line and two others at half court. They executed the offense brilliantly, when, all of a sudden, an Indiana player left his man in an uncharacteristic gamble and stole a State pass. He wheeled up the floor, 6'10" and 250 lbs., with only Billy Powers to beat to the hoop. Powers, 6'2" and 175 lbs., had but one choice, and he made it, offering himself up in the process. As the Indiana player crashed into the freshman guard, the whistle blew. "Offensive foul on #40!" the ref whooped.

Seventeen seconds remaining and State's best foul shooter on the line for a one-and-one, Indiana time-out. . . .

"Fellas', we're seventeen seconds away from the greatest victory of any team in the history of this tournament. After Billy makes the two foul shots, play solid defense. Let them have anything, but under no circumstances do we foul," McHale instructed.

Powers then went to the line, and with a titanic burden on his shoulders, he coolly dropped in both shots: State 83, Indiana 79.

"It looks like State's got it," said Packer.

Indiana quickly brought the ball in with no time-outs remaining. Their point guard rushed frantically up court and passed to the Hoosier's best perimeter shooter, stationed thirty feet away from the basket. The shooter received the pass, took two dribbles and let fly a three-pointer. Just as the ball left his hands, Marvin Lewis, his freshman exuberance getting the best of him, bumped the shooter. The ball caught nothing but net. The Hoosier fans went wild. 83-82, four seconds remaining; Indiana with a foul shot.

McHale had two time-outs left. He would use them both to try to "ice" the player, giving up the opportunity for a time-out should the player hit his shot. During both time-outs, McHale made plans for a last-ditch shot should the free throw not fall. The shot went in; the game was tied. State missed a desperation half court attempt. Overtime.

There was no worse feeling than a championship within reach and a major error preventing the victory. At no time in Jack McHale's thirty year connection with basketball had he experienced such blighted hope. As the players jogged over to the bench, all of them, particularly Marvin Lewis, were in a trance. Twenty seconds earlier, it had seemed impossible that they could lose.

For a full ten seconds, McHale stood in stunned silence. Then, with the stubborn reserve still left inside, he said to himself, "Damn it, pull yourself together."

"Gentlemen, the bad news is we didn't win the game in regulation. The good news is we're gonna win it in overtime." For the next ninety seconds, with two of the game officials converging on McHale's bench and imploring him to "Get the team on the floor, Coach," McHale let fly with his best version of Knute Rockne; he wondered to himself how he was getting the words to spring from his mouth.

Indiana won the tap and came down and scored to open the overtime. "That's a big advantage for the Hoosiers," said Packer.

State came back up and scored, then stole the in-bounds pass. Cormack McDonough quickly lofted home a ten-foot jump shot. State up two.

As inexplicable as the mistake of Lewis had been in the closing seconds of regulation, his play, along with that of McDonough, was brilliant over the next several minutes. The freshman center blocked two shots and the young Irishman hit three consecutive jumpers. Thinking as lucidly as he could ever remember, McHale employed the appropriate substitution strategy as State slowly built its lead, putting his best ball handlers and foul shooters on the floor during each State possession, then replacing them with two strong defenders when the ball went into Indiana's hands.

The clock wound down, and with sixteen seconds to go and State ahead by seven, McHale knew that his team would not be denied.

In moments of great triumph, most people find themselves reflecting back to a time in their life that had direct impact on the numinous moment at hand. As Jack McHale sat on the bench, seconds away from a victory which months and even moments earlier seemed unimaginable, he found himself thinking about his times at St. John's Parish. A thousand thoughts raced through his mind, all centering around his basketball roots, his oldest and best friends, all of the good things about the game.

As the buzzer went off, Billy Packer summed it up best: "There are no losers tonight. It was perhaps the best championship game ever played."

Bobby Knight immediately approached McHale, put his arm around the State coach and said. "It was a great game. . .you guys deserve it."

As McHale exited the court to the idolatry of the State fans, he experienced a feeling unlike any other. It was a feeling of complete and utter contentment.

In the locker room, emotions flowed freely. Players were hugging each other and joyful tears were shed as an incredible feeling of togetherness enveloped the room. Those closest to McHale in his life all seemed present: his family, his new-found friend, Dr. Lawrence Falk, his players and assistants.

The State SID frantically tried to pull the coach from those he wanted to be with most. "The President wants to speak with you. I mean the President of the United States wants to speak with you."

Ten minutes later, Jack McHale, surrounded by security guards, wife and family, entered the Press Room. The media, to a person, stood in thunderous applause. The questions went on for several minutes when finally a young scribe said, "OK, what's next for Jack McHale?"

In his first return from ebullience to rationality, McHale responded, "A long vacation...and a long look at Jack McHale." He surprised even himself with the clarity of his thinking.

Chapter 81

When Air France Flight 106 neared touchdown, those seated by the window seats gazed out at turquoise water which embraced the dazzling white sands. Moments later, as the 707 conjoined the landing terminal, the vacationers began their exit from the jet. The temperature was a balmy 76°F. In the waiting area stood the cab and limousine drivers, preparing to bring the tourists to their places of respite in this garden paradise. One such limousine had been contracted some days earlier. The company had been told that the visitors were from the States and that VIP service was to be in full force.

Their bags secured with help from the driver and his aide, these visitors nestled into the stretch limo, which was a welcome reprieve from the long journey. The drive to the Coral Strand Hotel, situated on the white sands of Beau Dallon, was only three miles.

When the death threat came, it had caused John McCollough serious concern for the three people with whom he had grown close. Gradually, the fear had turned to the sullen anger that made McCollough so good at what he did.

In every crime there are links. The first of these links had involved Hondo. Billy Esposito, Ted Patterson's mentor and friend, had sought out McCollough with the package Patterson had sent him moments before his suicide. McCollough, through the fingerprints left at Green's Bar and Grill, as well as the lifelike rendering drawn by his agency's bearded artist, had already identified Hondo. The voice prints provided by Esposito were a bonus—another thread in the large web.

For several years, virtually every U.S. law enforcement agency had a system of taping all incoming calls. The New York State Police had received an anonymous tip, the day prior to the arrest of Sean Riley and Robby Nesbitt. The voice prints of that tape matched those on the tape supplied by Esposito.

A few days prior to McCollough's planned dragnet of Hondo, the airplane had crashed in Canada. When news of Steincross' death roared across the New York newspapers, McCollough had not been fooled. He knew by then that Steincross was the last link in the web. He had studied Steincross, knew of the syndicate he had set up to satiate his gambling needs, of his recent alliance with drug dealers, and of his obsessive hatred for William Riley.

Most importantly, he knew that Robert Steincross was still alive. Bringing him to justice was fastened to John McCollough's mind.

With the use of local guides, McCollough did what Canadian officials thought impossible. He found the wreckage and saw that there was but one body in the plane. He then went to the airport closest to the wreckage. Two employees at the airport recognized the picture of Steincross.

McCollough had learned to get inside the heads of those he stalked, to think like them. He also knew one irrefutable fact: the easiest way to find a wealthy criminal on the run was to find the trail of his money. McCollough obtained Steincross' telephone records and could see that a number of conversations had taken place between Steincross' office and a bank in Lucerne, Switzerland. With the help of Swiss authorities, he took the next step. While Swiss law allowed their banks the well-known indulgence of keeping confidential the names of their depositors, transfers of money from a Swiss bank to banks outside the country were a matter of public record. Two days of sleuthing uncovered large amounts of cash transferred from the Swiss bank to accounts in Kenya and Mozambique. McCollough was able to determine that both banks had branches on the Seychelles Islands and that substantial sums of money had been wired into the Seychelles accounts.

Of the items left on McCollough's case agenda, one struck a personal chord. It involved Sean Riley. The meeting took place in McCollough's office. It was, at first, heated. "There is no goddamn way I'll go to see him," raged Sean.

McCollough knew that the hectoring tactics he had used with criminals would not work with this distressed young man. So he reverted to an event in his own life that had caused him much pain. "Two days before I left for Vietnam, my father and I had an argument, a very violent argument. Seven months later, in a slimy foxhole very close to hell, I read a telegram that he had died. It's a wound that'll never heal. Look, I know everything there is to know about your father and about what he did to you and your family. I also know that the two of us have some big challenges in the days ahead. I'm gonna' take care of mine. You're gonna' have to take care of yours. Sean, your father needs you."

The following day brought another quandary for John McCollough.

"I want the collar on this case," McCollough had said to his former superior in Washington.

"John, that simply cannot be done; there's no precedent," responded the director.

"Screw the precedent," snapped McCollough. "I gave blood to this agency. I've never asked for anything like this before."

After twenty minutes of acrimonious give and take, the director relented. "You'll be retained as a consultant. We'll give you team 'Maximus.' Technically, one of our people will have to be the team head. John, I need not say that I'm sticking my neck out for you."

When the group members arrived at the Coral Strand Hotel, they went immediately to the Presidential Suite. The local authorities were waiting. They had done their jobs well, pinpointing Steincross' whereabouts to the picturesque home overlooking the bay on Silhouette Island.

"The first thing you have to know about Silhouette," began the senior officer from the Seychelles, "is that it's an island where no vehicles are allowed. We've stationed a fishing boat approximately two miles off the shore. For the past week, with the use of an EOS 650 camera, we've been able to get a precise idea of Steincross' daily activities. Each afternoon at 3, he naps for approximately an hour. Between 4 and 4:30 he rises from the nap and takes about a two-mile walk. It's at this time we should make our move."

At 3:30 p.m. the following afternoon, a separate chartered fishing craft dropped McCollough and seven team members of 'Maximus' off at the south lagoon, approximately one mile from Steincross' home. By 3:55 p.m., the eight were positioned in a cluster of bushes, five-hundred yards from the home, with a full view of the rear door from which Steincross would exit for his walk. At 4:15 p.m., the door opened and out walked Robert Steincross.

"We'll have to move quickly," McCollough whispered to his associates. Within ten minutes, each had taken his position.

At 4:55 p.m., Steincross walked back up the path leading to his regal hideaway. He opened the door which led directly to his favorite room, the study overlooking the Indian Ocean.

The moment he entered the study, he stopped in almost paralytic fear. There, sitting on the chair, with a revolver pointing squarely at Steincross' head, was John McCollough. Steincross was terrified. His first thought was escape, but McCollough's coldly spoken words froze him.

"There are seven armed men outside this home. Each of 'em will blow your goddamn brains out if they see your face."

His ruthless greed had shattered many lives. As he stood there, staring down the barrel of McCollough's gun, he clearly understood the consequences of his actions. Robert Steincross would now pay.

Chapter 82

After the parades and parties and seemingly endless series of interviews, which lasted for several days after the championship victory, Jack McHale was finally able to get away on a vacation with his wife and family. As the intoxication of a major championship abated, McHale began to look at himself and his life more clearly. With this examination came a decision. He would quit.

The sweet nectar of victory had brought with it many new options for McHale. CBS had called to confirm a spot as a color analyst for college games. The State Athletic Director's job was his for the asking. His speaking fees, even if he left coaching, would quadruple.

There were more important considerations, too. He knew that his family, relegated to second-class status in the pursuit of his dream, should now come first. His health had no doubt suffered. The stress of the past months had caused, among other things, a twenty-pound weight loss. His normally rugged features were now gaunt. He would go out on top, leave the game a winner. . .get off the roller coaster. When he told Sally McHale of his decision, her reaction was guarded.

"It's a big step, Jack. Let's make sure we think it through."

The vacation over, McHale called Dr. Falk to tell him of his plan. Falk raised no objections, but merely posed a series of questions.

"I'm not saying I agree or disagree, Jack. I'm just trying to help you explore all sides of the issue. Once you make this public, there'll be no turning back."

On the day he returned to his office, the players, knowing he was back on campus, all stopped by. A championship brings with it many rewards, but the one which far outweighs the others is the bond between coaches and players. It is one so strong as never to be broken.

The two blue chip freshmen, Cormack McDonough and Marvin Lewis, made it clear that they wanted to stay. They wanted to finish their degree work. Both were aware of the consequences of their fathers' actions. Despite their young age, each was in a position to gain a lucrative contract with an NBA team. In addition, both might face the effects of their parents' actions in the form of an NCAA sanction, one that perhaps might preclude State from defending its championship.

For days, McHale continued to reflect on his decision to quit. It was agony. He had grown to love his players. Also, recruits who previously would not look at State were now knocking at the door. But the other factors, those which brought to Jack McHale's life such excruciating disorder, would still exist if he did not change careers.

Of the thousands of letters that had poured into the office, one with a postmark of Brunswick, Maine, had been the most unexpected of all:

> I have learned more in the last several weeks about life, morals, and integrity than in my entire lifetime. I only wish I had learned it before. Please know that my new-found beliefs have brought with them tremendous admiration for you. You are someone who belongs working with young people.
>
> Very truly yours,
> Steve Ellovitch.

McHale knew that his decision would soon have to be revealed. To do anything else would be unfair to State, and hamper its recruiting and long-range planning. Yet he was experiencing second thoughts. The agony was even greater.

Once again, he sought his wife's advice.

"Jack, you've been a coach for all of our married life. I know your feelings of regret about the family, but you've been a good father, a good husband, and we've adjusted to the life. Listen, whatever decision you make, we'll stand by it, and be happy with it."

"Honey, I just don't know what to do," McHale shrugged.

He wanted to be by himself. As he got into his car and drove toward the city, he exited the Williamsburg Bridge and found himself driving slowly through his old neighborhood, past St. John's Parish Hall and the old tenement on 79th Street where he had grown up.

He slowly pulled his car two blocks farther and stopped beside his favorite refuge as a youngster, the Greylag Playground. As the car came to a halt by the curb, McHale looked out on the court. It was a chilly April day with a slight drizzle coming down. There on the court, alone, was a boy no more than twelve years old. As he lofted his push shot softly toward the basket, McHale could see that he was a boy with special grace, one who had already spent many hours on the asphalt court honing his skills.

As the ball gently embraced the nylon cords, the swish sound speaking back to this boy of promise, he suddenly looked up and saw McHale staring at him from the car. The boy stopped and gasped. He knew it was the State coach. While McHale did not much care for much of the homage paid him since the NCAA Championship, the reaction of the boy brought a feeling of quiet pride.

McHale opened the car door and walked out onto a place that felt immediately familiar.

"Would you like to shoot some, Coach?" asked the boy, his eyes widening.

McHale took the ball and sunk a twenty-footer, the feeling of excitement still there. He then walked over to the boy and could see on his face the same hope and exuberance McHale had felt on this same court more than thirty years ago.

"What's your name, son?"

"Matt Tyler," the boy replied.

"Matt, have you ever heard of Earl Monroe?"

"Yes, sir. He played for the New York Knicks when they won the championship in '73."

"But you weren't even born in 1973," said McHale.

"But I know all about the Knicks," said the boy softly.

"Well, Earl Monroe had a move that I'm going to show you. It's a move that helped him to score a great many baskets. It's called the spin dribble."

With that, McHale put the ball down and said to the boy. "The first thing we're going to learn is the proper footwork." For several minutes, with no ball, McHale gently walked the boy through the foot movements of the spin dribble. The boy, attentive to McHale's every word, learned quickly.

"OK, now we'll pick up the ball and bring all of the parts into a whole," said McHale.

McHale patiently took the boy through the proper sequence of the move. At first the boy faltered, but with McHale's gentle and skillful prodding, he got closer...and closer. Finally, thirty minutes later, the boy executed the move to perfection. As the ball dropped through the net, Jack McHale felt that unparalleled feeling which coaching sometimes brings. He had shared a special bit of knowledge that would link the two forever.

McHale approached the boy and gently stroked his hair, "I have to go now, Matt. It's been real nice meeting you."

He walked toward his car. As he pulled his keys from his pocket, he turned to wave to the boy who was still standing there, awestruck by his chance encounter with the famous coach. The boy's eyes showed that he wanted to say something, but didn't quite know how to start.

"Is everything all right?" asked McHale.

A smile slowly took root. The boy then said, with utter conviction, "Mr. McHale, in six years I'll be coming to State to play for you."

"I'll be waiting, Matt," the coach replied.

THE END

Want A Copy of This Book As A Gift For

Sports-Minded Friends, Business Associates, Loved Ones?

YES, I want _____copies of *Are You Watching, Adolph Rupp?* at $18.95 each. Please add $2.00 per book for postage and handling. Rhode Island residents include $1.15 per book for sales tax. (Canadian orders must be accompanied by a postal money order in U.S. funds.) Allow 30 days for delivery.

Name _____ Telephone (___) _____

Title _____

Address _____

City _____ State _____Zip _____

_____ My check/money order is enclosed.

Bill my ☐ VISA   ☐ MasterCard   Signature_____

Account # _____ Expires _____

Make check payable and mail to: Stadia Publishers, Box 1677, Kingston, RI 02881. For quantity discount prices or special UPS handling, please call (401) 792-5460.

ATTENTION COACHES, SCHOOLS, SPORTS ORGANIZATIONS:

QUANTITY DISCOUNTS AVAILABLE

329